Also by Yvonne Cassidy

The Other Boy
What Might Have Been Me

First U.S. Edition
First Printing, 2016

Originally published in 2014 by Hachette Ireland, Dublin, Ireland

Book design by Bob Gaul
Cover design by Ellen Lawson
Cover images by iStockphoto/34629616/©filo
             iStockphoto/5898935/©DNY59
             iStockphoto/11654280/©Pillon
             iStockphoto/20602903/©Pingebat
Interior images by iStockphoto/34629616/©filo
             iStockphoto/22035653/©FrankRamspott

Flux, an imprint of Llewellyn Worldwide Ltd.

Library of Congress Cataloging-in-Publication Data (Pending)
978-0-7387-4745-3

Flux
Llewellyn Worldwide Ltd.
2143 Wooddale Drive
Woodbury, MN 55125-2989
www.fluxnow.com

Printed in the United States of America

HOW MANY

Letters

ARE IN

Goodbye?

Yvonne Cassidy

flux
®
Woodbury, Minnesota

For Danielle, who helped me write my own next chapter.

Dear Mum,

It's a long time since I wrote to you—since I even wrote the word "Mum." Over here, everyone says "Mom" and I nearly wrote that by mistake, but when I used to write to you on those Friday nights with Dad, it was always "Dear Mum."

Do you know how long it's been since my last letter?

I hate Penn Station at night and I hate this café. I hate that when I was paying for my coffee, the guy who works here had a porno magazine open, right there on the counter.

I hate that Sergei is so late. He's never this late.

The last time I wrote to you was nearly eleven years ago. I remember that, because it was the summer Aunt Ruth came over, the summer before the accident. Before that, we used to write to you every Friday night, me and Dad, when we cleared up after tea. He'd sit in his seat near the back door and I'd bring my chair up next to his, so close that sometimes our elbows bumped. My letters were in crayon and I drew you pictures as well—I filled loads of pages. He took ages writing his, printing out the words in black ink, his face concentrating. His letters looked nothing like the way he talked—they didn't match him at all.

Sometimes, I read mine out to him, even though he said it was okay if I didn't want to because they were private. He never read his out to me. When we were finished, he'd seal them in a narrow blue airmail envelope and he let me write your name on the front, before he'd fold it in two and put it in his cardigan pocket and say that he'd make sure you got it. And even though afterwards I was allowed to have a Double Decker and a Coke when he had his bottle of Guinness, I always felt

1

sad seeing that, the bulge of letter against the wool, because there was a whole week to go before we could write again.

I'm seven the summer we stop writing and at first I think Dad's only messing. It's the Friday after Aunt Ruth leaves and I get the paper and the envelope from the sideboard in the back room like I always do, but when I come into the kitchen, Dad is sitting there with his Guinness already open. He shakes his head and says we're not doing that anymore, that it's a stupid thing to be doing, writing to someone who's dead. I think he'll change his mind and I get the paper and envelope the next Friday too, but he gets annoyed and says he was an eejit for ever starting it, and I hate Fridays after that.

The porno man is walking around now, straightening chairs and cleaning up coffee cups, and I'm glad there is a lid on my cup so he can't see it's empty. There's a glass cabinet up by the counter that has loads of cakes in it and I wish I had money to buy a muffin or a black and white cookie, but they're $2.95 and I can get two pizza slices for that. I've already spent $2.50 on this notepad, which was a total rip-off, and, anyway, Sergei will be here soon.

I always knew you were dead, by the way. I always knew Dad didn't post the letters. He'd already told me you were in Heaven, just like he told me that you were from America, from a place called New York, and that one day we'd go over and visit together and see all the places where you'd lived as a little girl. Before we stopped writing the letters, he used to say things like that all the time, he used to talk about you all the time. But once we stopped writing, he stopped talking too.

Before then, his favourite story was about the night you met, when he was playing in the Meeting Place. It was a Sunday night and he'd thought about not going because it was lashing and he'd nearly stayed on in the Drop Inn instead of going into town. The whole way through the first half of the session, all he could think about was his trousers sticking to him, still soaking from the rain, and that's what he was doing when you came over at the break—

2

lifting the damp material away from his skin. When he looked up, you were standing there saying something about a drum, and he couldn't follow what you were talking about at all, until he realised you meant his bodhrán.

He always tells the story the same way, about how you were smiling and talking the whole time and he felt like all he could do was listen, as if he was transfixed by you or something, and how, suddenly, it was time for the second half of the session and he hadn't been to the loo or to the bar to get a fresh pint or anything. He always laughs at that part when he remembers how he was bursting so hard for a piss, it was hard to concentrate on the music, and that between that and trying to spot you in the crowd to make sure you hadn't gone home, he missed his cue twice.

You hadn't gone home. You stayed till the end and afterwards you sat at the bar together and he bought you a fizzy orange and you talked for ages until your friend came over and said you had to go. You kissed him on the cheek when you said goodbye and it was only after you left that he thought that he should have asked you your last name or for your phone number or something. All he knew was that you were from New York and that you liked Irish music and that that was why you'd come to Ireland to study in Trinity for a year.

That's the part of the story where he always pauses—used to pause—to get a fresh Guinness maybe, or to light a cigarette. And then he tells me how he couldn't get you out of his head, that the whole next day he thought about the next Sunday and if you'd come again, even as he was telling himself a young one like you would never be interested in an auld fella like him.

But he didn't need to wait until the next Sunday, did he Mum? I'm getting to his favourite part of the story now, the Tuesday afternoon when he's wrapping up Mrs. Hannon's three quarters of round steak mince, when the bell tinkles and he looks up and you're standing there behind her, bold as brass, smiling that smile.

I used to love that story. I'd make him tell it over and over and the part after, about how he closed the shop early and took you for a walk on the beach and you got fish and chips from Joe's. I loved that the door in the shop was the same door you touched, that the tinkle of the bell sounded the same, even Mrs. Hannon with her mince was the same. But I was a kid then, and kids love stories. Now I'm seventeen—in two weeks and five days I'll be eighteen—and I'm old enough to know that stories are only stories and that happy beginnings don't mean happy endings and that when people are dead, they're just dead.

And I'm sure Sergei's fine. He's probably fine, there's no reason to think he's not fine. It's just that it's 4:42 a.m. and we were supposed to meet by 2:30 at the latest, and the bars close at four and he never, ever, goes home with any of them, that's his golden rule. And even if something has happened, it's not like writing to you is going to do anything about it, it's not going to change it, but maybe it makes me feel better to have something to do, maybe filling up this page with words makes it easier to ignore the porno man staring at me from behind the counter and the guy outside in the hallway talking to himself and beating the wall with one hand with a bandage around it and a stain that could be blood.

If you were here, what would you get from the cabinet? Would you choose a muffin or a piece of coffee cake or one of the cinnamon swirls? Or would you prefer a cookie? The cookies are huge, much bigger than in Ireland, and even bigger than they are in Florida. They'd probably take longer to eat than the muffin would. Would you get halfway through and push it away and say you were full? Or finish every last bit and lick the crumbs off your fingers, the way I always do? Did you miss New York food in Ireland the way I missed Irish food in Florida? Did you already know that Tuesday you walked into Dad's shop that you might stay? That you might marry him? That you'd never come back here again?

These are the small things and the big things that I want to know.

Rhea

4

Dear Mum,

I only noticed when I wrote the date on this letter that it's been over three weeks since the university results were all sent out. Three whole weeks. After all this waiting, it's fifty kinds of crazy that there could have been an envelope from Columbia University with my name on it on the hall table in Coral Springs for the past three weeks. I wonder if Aunt Ruth has opened it. I bet she has. She knows my future before I do—not that it's my future anymore anyway, so I suppose it doesn't matter.

Sergei finally showed up last night, by the way, with a roll of dollars he lifts out of his pocket like someone from a gangster movie. When I ask him where the hell he'd been and what he thought he was doing leaving me all on my own, he smiles his perfect smile and says he'd been "swept up by some yank" and that he'll buy me McDonald's.

I don't say much while we eat our Big Macs, so he knows I'm annoyed. To make it up to me, he pays for a room in some hotel on Eighth Avenue. It's a dump—the hotel—but they only charge us half price because it's nearly six o'clock by then, and I'm so tired I don't even care about the stain on the bedspread or the dip in the mattress that means we keep rolling into each other.

When the chambermaid shouts through the door at half eleven, it feels like the middle of the night and Sergei shouts back at her in Polish. She shouts something back in another language and Sergei starts cracking up and I do too. He's like Dad—when he's in a good mood, it's hard to stay mad with him for long.

We met at the Y, Sergei and me, not even three weeks ago but it feels like we've always known each other. And in case you're thinking he's my boyfriend or something, he's not. He's gay, you'd know as soon as you saw him. That's how we met, some big black guy

5

was giving him hassle outside the bathroom at the Y—he had him up against the wall, saying he wasn't going to share the shower with some faggot—and I went over and tapped the guy on the back.

It's not like I'm really brave or anything. Aunt Ruth is always telling me not to get involved in other people's business, but sometimes I can't help it. You should have seen his face, the black guy, when he turns around and sees it's only a girl—a short girl, with only one arm instead of two. He stares at the place my arm should be and I want to cup my stump, but I don't. Instead I stand up taller and tell him to get his hands off my friend. Sergei's not my friend yet, but the guy doesn't know that. He's not scared of me or anything, but he doesn't know what to do with a girl involved so he just laughs and gives Sergei a final shove before he walks away.

Sergei smiles and blows his hair out of his eyes and I see that they're dark brown—like your eyes—and they're shiny, like he might have been going to cry.

"Thank you," he goes, all formal, with a little bow.

"No problem."

"What happened to your arm?"

He asks straightaway. Most people don't ask. That's one of the things I like about Sergei, how he always says what's on his mind.

"I lost it in 'Nam," I go. "Dirty war."

He laughs and asks me if I want to go for a beer with him, so I do.

It's nice having someone to talk to, even though he does most of the talking, which is fine by me. That night he tells me that he's been in New York since January, that he came here from Warsaw. He says he's twenty-one, but I don't know if I believe him because the barman doesn't ID either of us. He tells me he can't get a proper job because he has no visa, but I don't know if I believe that either because a few days later, we're passing this restaurant near Grand Central and he says he had a job there waiting tables for a week before they fired him for being late two days in a row.

I hate that he tells me that, because then I know the visa thing is a lie, and because I'd love a job in a restaurant like that and if I got one I wouldn't be late, even by one minute. No one will give me a job because they don't think I'll be able to wait tables, to serve customers, to do anything with only a left arm. I've tried everywhere, every restaurant, every bar, even a butcher's I found on a scummy block on Ninth Avenue, but they all look at me like I'm fifty kinds of crazy that I think they might hire me. I tell them that I worked in Cooper's restaurant, but this is New York and they don't care about Florida and no one has ever heard of Coral Springs. No one listens long enough for me to tell them I was the quickest busser in the place, how I had tables cleared down and set up again while the other lazy asses were hanging out by the waitress station talking about what to spend their tips on before they'd even made any.

At times like that I wish I'd brought the stupid prosthetic with me, instead of leaving it on the floor of my room in some "up yours" gesture to Aunt Ruth and Cooper. Don't get me wrong, I don't miss all those stupid straps, and it would make working way harder, but maybe someone wouldn't notice until it was too late and they'd offer me a job.

It was Sergei's idea that we should move out and live on the street. What was it he said? "Pitch our wits against the city." Something like that. My money was running really low anyway, I wouldn't have been able to afford another week at the Y. And he made it sound like fun, like it was an adventure, a game that we could be in together—which we are most of the time, except when we're not.

We do our own thing during the day sometimes, even when he's not in the bars. We're not joined at the hip or anything. My favourite thing to do is to go on the subway. The first day I got the map, it was horrible because it wasn't the same as the one on my bedroom wall, the one that used to be yours. I wished I'd taken it with me, even though it was tearing really badly along the folds and the sun had faded the top half. Two of my favourite lines have changed—the AA is just the A and the RR is just the R—but I'm used to it now, the new map. It's not that different really.

I can spend hours on the subway, once I was on it nearly all day. Sergei came with me one time last week, but he was bored after twenty minutes so now I go on my own. I like it on my own.

These are the things I like about going on the subway:

1. For $1.50 you can ride it all day and go anywhere in New York.

2. You can sleep and no one cares. The E train is the best for sleeping and if you get one of the corner seats, like I did today, you can sleep for a couple of hours sometimes with no one bothering you.

3. One of my favourite things is when you see another train in the tunnel, a whole carriage of other people next to you, or sometimes the front of the train with the letter lit up— a big yellow Q floating out of the dark, like *Sesame Street*.

4. I like watching the people in the carriage—the books they're reading and what they wear. I imagine them getting up in their apartments all over New York, taking those clothes from hangers and drawers and putting them on, not knowing they would end up here with all these other people, just for a few minutes, a group that will never be the same again.

5. Most of all, the thing I like best about the subway is that I get to play my game in real life. I made up the game when I was ten, using your map. It's easy, you just have to choose two stops with your eyes closed, and when you roll the dice that's the most transfers you can make to get from the first stop to the second one. Lisa never liked playing, she said it was boring, and then when I changed it so you got more points for using more lines, she said that wasn't fair because you couldn't see half the stations anymore and I had an advantage because I remembered them all. After that we

didn't play much but I played on my own sometimes, at night when Dad was out, and sometimes I played it in bed, even when the lights were off, even when I could only see the map in my head. I bet if Lisa was here now, she'd get it, I bet she wouldn't think it was boring anymore.

Do you like making lists? I do. Lists are like the subway—you can't get lost in a list.

Today, I got out at 116th Street, on the 1 Line. You know where that goes. That's where I'm writing from—Columbia University. It's not my first time here—I came on Wednesday, but I couldn't come inside the gate. I don't know why—I got off the train, like normal, go up the steps with everyone else, just like normal, but when I get to the top, right outside the gate, I stop. I just stand there on the sidewalk, watching people go in and out the gate, down the main path or along the red-brick ones on either side, up the steps into buildings that I've read about in their brochure. I stand there and I try and move but it's like my body won't let me move any closer, so after twenty-five minutes I get back on the train to go and meet Sergei.

Today, I walked through the gate. I made a kind of run at it and walked really fast looking straight ahead so I wouldn't have to think about it. I walked past J-School and Hamilton Hall like they're any old buildings. And now I'm sitting on a bench outside the Butler Library where your book *Will You Please Be Quiet, Please?* is now twenty years, five months, and fifteen days overdue. Right now, it's in my backpack next to me, along with two pairs of jeans, my navy Champion hoody, three T-shirts, five pairs of knickers, four pairs of socks, one bra, and my sketchpad, which I haven't looked at since I left Florida. Fifty thousand times a day I kick myself for taking that and forgetting my Discman and my CDs.

The book is one of the only clues I have, along with the subway map and the two photos of you that Dad gave me. Not that it's much of a clue. There are no notes inside, no turned-down pages. Did you even read it? And if you did, which of the twenty-one stories was your favourite? Did you mean to steal it or did it come to Ireland with you by accident, hidden in your luggage? I've read them over and over, those stories, and I want to love them but I don't love them. If you want to know the truth, I don't even like them really. I don't get most of them—nothing happens, no beginning, no middle, no end. They're kind of like life, not like stories at all.

Do you want to know about the two photos I have?

1. The first one is of you taken here. I know it was taken here because it says "Columbia, 1978" on the back in loopy writing in blue pen that Dad says was your writing. The ink is faded now and I keep it in a Ziploc bag, inside the Raymond Carver book, so I won't wear away any more of it.

   If it wasn't for the writing, I wouldn't know where it was taken—it's just a close-up of your face, you can't see the background. You're very pretty, smiling and young-looking. I wish I knew when in 1978 it was taken. It looks like the autumn or winter. You were born on 23rd November 1959, so if it was before that you are eighteen and if it was after that you are nineteen. I think you are eighteen. I'm nearly eighteen but you look nothing like I look. Our hair is the same colour, but yours is straight and brown and clips your chin and mine is only stubble since Sergei shaved the rest of it off except for the long part at the front. And your eyes are brown, like Aunt Ruth's eyes, and mine are blue, like Dad's. You have this amazing smile, it's a really real smile, almost a laugh. Your mouth is a bit open. It's not a fake camera smile. You are wearing a polo neck in the photo and something with a cream collar. I decided that it's a trench coat, am I right? Did it have those funny things on the shoulders? Did it have a belt? Who took the photo? Who made you laugh?

2. I can never decide which photo I prefer. I love the Columbia one because you're happy in it. I like the second one because we're both in it, like it's proof that we were on the same planet together for a while, even though it wasn't all that long. But I wish it was taken somewhere else instead of on the beach in Rush. Dad probably took it and he must have had shaky hands because it's a bit blurry, but you can make us out, just about. You're wearing a black bikini and your skin looks really white. Your hair is longer than in the Columbia photo—down to the top of your bikini straps—and your sunglasses are huge, blocking most of your face. I've got a bucket in one hand, a spade in the other, and I'm wearing a huge red sunhat so you can't see my face properly either.

Did you have other photos that Dad got rid of afterwards? I think you must have had some of your family or friends or something, but the only other photo I have is part of a newspaper clipping of your dad and his business partner at that awards ceremony. Your dad doesn't look like you, at least not in this photo—he's not properly smiling, only a half-smile, and he looks very serious, standing there holding the plaque they won. At first, I thought it was weird that the other man was sitting down while your dad was standing up, until I noticed he was in a wheelchair. You'd only know it was a wheelchair because your dad's hand that's not holding the plaque is resting on the handle at the back. The wheelchair man has a bigger smile than your dad—it's a kind smile and he looks happy to have won the award. He must have been looking right into the camera because it's like his eyes can look out and see me, right from the photo. The caption says: "Commercial property partners Cal Owens and Jerry Davis are recognised for their role in redeveloping Upper Manhattan." Underneath, it talks all about these new buildings that are zoned and planned and it has a quotation from Mr. Owens but not from your dad. You must have been proud of your dad, for you to have kept that.

I thought there were more photos. I was sure I remembered a blue packet of them—square ones with white borders. I was sure I'd find them when I cleared out the top part of Dad's wardrobe, which is why I insisted on doing it, even though Aunt Ruth offered a million times. But I didn't find anything at all. Apart from his winter jumpers, there was only a Hendrix tape with a broken case, three plastic combs, and an out-of-date driving licence. I was throwing them all in a black plastic bag, along with his trousers and shoes and the Homer Simpson tie I got him one Christmas, when Aunt Ruth came in and asked me again if she could take over. When I said no, she sat on the bed and said she knew it was an upsetting thing to do, which just shows that she didn't know me at all, because I wasn't upset. I was fine.

It's funny how it seems like forever ago—clearing out the house in Rush, putting it up for sale—when it's not even two years yet. Would you think I was fifty kinds of crazy if I told you that sometimes I forget that Dad is dead? That sometimes I think he's still back there, in Rush, which I suppose he is, except he's in Whitestown Cemetery next to Nana and Granddad Farrell who I never met, and his little brother who died when he was only four.

Did you get the train to Rush that Tuesday or did you take the bus? I think you took the train. Sometimes I imagine you, Mum, walking down that road from the station, all the way into the town. It's a long walk. What kind of shoes had you on? Did your feet hurt? Were you nervous?

You would have walked past Whitestown and I wonder if you'd have stopped and looked at the gravestones and made up stories about the dead people's lives—but maybe it's only me who does things like that. If you'd been buried there too, if you had a dash in between 23rd November 1959 and some date in June 1984, I might have gone there to make up a story about your life too. It might have been nice, something to do after we stopped writing to you, but you didn't have a dash because you weren't buried there. You're not buried anywhere—because they never found your body.

This bench is cold, I can feel it through my jeans. And the lights just flicked on, which means it won't be long before the rats are out. This is the part I hate, when it's dark enough for them to come out and bright enough to see them. It was around this time last week in Central Park when this huge one ran out from under a bench, right in front of me, its long tail slinking across nearly the whole path.

I'm not going to call Aunt Ruth, I'm never going to call her, but seeing a rat like that would make you think about it, just for a second.

If I called now, Laurie might answer. She'd be home from soccer practice by now. That's if she's back at soccer, but why wouldn't she be? Cooper's hardly going to make her stay home from school and everything. He'll want life to get back to normal as soon as it can, like it was before I came.

I'm meeting Sergei at the pizza place at Port Authority. Slices are $1.50 everywhere but this is the best place because the slices are bigger and they give us pepperoni for the same price as plain. One time, this guy, some tourist, bought me and Sergei an extra slice each, and Sergei ate his in four seconds but I wanted to save mine. Sergei laughed at me smushing the pizza up into my pocket in a napkin, just like he laughed at me the time I suggested saving our money and going to a soup kitchen instead. But later, on my own in Penn Station, I was glad I had that pizza, smushed up or not.

I'll write more later. Or tomorrow. Maybe I will. The problem about writing is that I start to remember things I want to tell you. And sometimes the things I remember are the same as the things I want to forget.

Your daughter,
Rhea

Dear Mum,

We have an apartment! Me and Sergei! Well, it's not really our apartment, it belongs to Michael—this Wall Street guy Sergei was with
two nights ago. Last night, he asked Sergei to stay, and Sergei said
he'd only stay if I could stay, so we did. Michael lives somewhere else
on the weekends, and we were meant to leave this morning when
he was, only it's raining and Sergei starts bitching about having
nowhere to go, so, eventually, Michael takes a key off his key ring
and tosses it at him and says that everything had better be just like
he left it when he gets back.

We don't leave all day and it's brilliant—both of us on the black
leather couch, clicking through the channels, eating fried rice and
pork dumplings that Sergei ordered and blueberry Pop-Tarts we
found in the freezer as a kind of dessert. A *Law & Order* marathon
is on and Sergei loves it too, even though he's never seen it before.
Everything is perfect, until we hear the key in the door and then
Michael's standing there, with his hands in the back pockets of his
jeans, saying he's decided to stay in the city after all.

This couch is okay for a couch but shit for a bed and I don't have a
blanket or anything. *Law & Order* is still on, I've turned it up so I won't
hear Michael and Sergei in the bedroom, but it's one I've seen before
and I can't get into it. Olivia's comforting this woman whose daughter
was murdered and she's been crying in every scene in the episode.

Aunt Ruth was always on about crying, after Dad died. It seemed
like those first few weeks in Rush, she was always manipulating it
into the conversation—all this stuff about crying and grieving. She
tries to be subtle, as if it's general chitchat, as if I'm stupid and don't
know she's talking about me. I don't really say anything back and it's

a couple of days before we're due to leave when she finally comes out straight and says it. I'm on the floor in my room, sketching one of the stones I've picked up from the beach, when she comes up to my door and knocks on it, even though it's already open.

"Hey there," she goes. "What are you doing?"

It's pretty obvious what I'm doing, so I don't answer her, I don't look up even, just keep adding in shading on the underside of the stone.

"You want anything to eat?" she goes.

"No thanks."

"Cookies and milk? Some toast maybe?"

My eyes flick between the stone and my drawing. "I'm grand."

I hear her move and I think she's going to leave but when I glance up she's only rearranged herself against the door frame, her arms folded.

"How are you doing, Rhea? You know… about your dad? You've hardly said a word about what happened. I haven't seen you cry once."

There's a pause, no sound. My pencil moving on the paper, a dog barking outside.

"You know you can always talk to me about him… if you want to."

That's when I look up properly. One hand is still across her middle, the other is pulling down her fringe.

"Why would I want to talk to you about him? You two hated each other."

Her eyes go big. "Why would you say that? I didn't hate your father, honey. You know that's not true."

"Honey." It sounds so fake, just like those cards she used to send with the fakest messages inside. The messages that sounded hilarious when Dad put on his ridiculous American accent and read them out.

"Maybe you didn't hate him—but he hated you."

She makes that face then, you know the one with the twist in her mouth when she's trying not to cry? I feel guilty for a second, until she makes her face hard again and rolls her eyes.

"I don't know why I bother, Rhea, I really don't," she says, and shakes her head. I go back to my drawing and when I look up again, the doorway is empty and I can hear the sitting-room door slam.

Sometimes I wonder what would have happened if I hadn't said that, things like that, but I couldn't help it. Lisa said I was mean to her, but it was okay for Lisa. *Her* biggest problems were liver for dinner on a Monday night and how to sneak her sister's jeans into the wash without her noticing she'd worn them. She annoyed me then, Lisa, she was supposed to be my best friend but those few weeks she was always sucking up to Aunt Ruth—bringing her over a lemon for her tea and asking her to show her how the breakables should be wrapped for the shipping company. Not that much got shipped, most of it was sold or thrown away. It was funny how quickly the house changed. You think a house is permanent, a home, but it's not. It only takes a couple of weeks to clear it all out so there's only carpet and bare walls left and it's ready for someone else's life.

The couple next door are fighting now. Screaming.

She screams first: "You never loved me the way you loved her!"

Then him: "Fuck you!" Louder. "Fuck you!"

Something smashes.

Fighting or fucking, that's all people seem to do in New York. You hear them, all over the place, having rows on the subway and in the street and in McDonald's. They'll cry anywhere too, they don't care who sees. At least in Ireland we only have rows at home.

I didn't want to fight with Lisa on that last night. I'm not even sure why we were fighting, except that she kept going on about how her mum could drive me and Aunt Ruth to the airport instead of us getting a taxi. She went on about it for the whole walk down to the harbour and back around by the beach. She didn't get that I didn't want any more time to say goodbye, that I wanted to skip to the part where I was already gone.

On the plane, I'm really quiet. Aunt Ruth doesn't know I've never been on one before and I don't tell her. It's not as if I'm scared or anything, I always used to want to fly back to America with her when she visited, until I didn't anymore. As soon as we sit down, I put my headphones on and pretend to sleep and when I open my eyes she's sleeping too. She sleeps through the meal so I eat hers as well as my own and fall asleep properly then, so it's not until we get to Orlando and take the second flight to Fort Lauderdale that we have to talk at all. In the taxi to Coral Springs, she fills up the space by chatting a mile a minute about Cooper and Laurie and how they're dying to meet me, and how we're all going to go for lunch tomorrow to one of Cooper's restaurants. She talks so fast there is no room for me to say anything, so I just sit there as the taxi driver leaps from one lane to another, his driving as jerky as all her talking.

When we pull in through the gate, the house is just like I pictured —low and white with a semicircle driveway. The front door is open already and there's Laurie, standing on the porch steps in bare feet, one on top of the other. Cooper is behind her, both hands on her shoulders. The first thing I notice about him is his slicked-back hair. He's smiling, Laurie's not. Her blonde hair covers one of her eyes and she's sucking a strand of it in a way that makes her look really babyish, and I wonder then if I got her age wrong and she's not fifteen at all.

"Here we are, honey. Home sweet home," Ruth goes, her voice shrill. She brushes her fringe down before she opens the car door. I feel a blast of heat. "Coop! Laur! Look who's here!"

I reach over to open my door, get out. The sun reflects off everything, making me squint. It feels like it is seeping into my black Hendrix T-shirt, my Docs, like they have no place here. Like they will be the only black items in their white home.

Aunt Ruth is paying the taxi driver. Before I can get my backpack from the boot, Cooper is already there, still smiling.

"I got that," he says, lifting it from me easily with big hands. He gives me a quick half hug with the arm not holding the backpack. A strand of his slicked-back hair comes loose.

"Laurie!" he calls. "Laurie, come and meet your new sister!" He says that, actually says that, I swear I'm not making it up. At first I think it's a joke, that he's being ironic, but his smile hasn't changed, it's still the same, fixed. You can't smile for that long and have it be real. Laurie comes over slowly, her feet in flip-flops now that she slides across the grass. She's still chewing her hair, holding it with one hand, the other making a visor on her forehead. Even through the shadow on her face, I see her eyes are a piercing blue.

"Hi," she says in a flat tone, so I know she's bored with me already. She drops the hand holding her hair and reaches it out formally for me to shake. Too late, she realises her mistake and her expression changes—the two blue eyes widen, two white teeth press down on her lips.

I know what to do—I've been doing it all my life. I take it with my left and shake it, even though we're not really shaking, more like holding hands. Right before she lets go, I notice how cold her fingers are.

"I'm Rhea."

She nods.

"I guess you knew that," I say. "I suppose not too many Irish strangers show up at your house on a Saturday morning. And the ones that do probably have two arms."

As soon as I say it, I hate myself. She doesn't crack a smile and then I hate her more. I hate the way she looks at me for a second before she turns away. I hate her shoulders, bony through her white T-shirt. I hate the slap her feet make against her flip-flops as she slouches back towards the porch.

Cooper and Aunt Ruth are watching us from the doorway, the rest of the luggage stacked up on the porch next to them. The taxi drives towards the gate, indicates, slows. The back door is inches away from me. I could reach out, open it, throw myself in and lock it. But there is nowhere I can ask him to take me.

"Come on in out of the heat," Aunt Ruth calls, "Cooper's made brunch!"

If you'd asked me then, Mum, what I thought of Laurie, I'd have been definite. I'd have said I hated her. Maybe I was right to hate her. Maybe the first time you see a person is how they really are, and maybe everything afterwards is all just pretend.

That's the kind of thing I'd ask you about, if you were really here.

Rhea

18

Dear Mum,

Michael left this morning, early. He said his sister was having a christening party and he had to go. Sergei thought he was joking, that he was going to come back and surprise us with breakfast, but I didn't care when he didn't.

I'm just happy to have the bed for a while, even if I have to share it with Sergei.

Sergei's asleep again. It's funny how someone's face looks different when they're sleeping. His looks younger, like he could be seventeen or even sixteen, and he looks like a girl with his long eyelashes and the shape of his lips. There's no way he's twenty-one. I don't believe that any more than I believe his parents are going to come over and visit once he's settled in a place of his own.

We had our first fight earlier—nearly a fight—but I think it's okay now. I didn't want to snoop through Michael's drawers in the first place. Everything was so tidy—his shirts and T-shirts and boxer shorts—and Sergei wasn't putting things back properly, even though he thought he was.

We find the money in the middle drawer—a clip of it, folded tight, inside the hood of a grey sweatshirt that says "Florida State" on the front. I find it and Sergei snatches it from my hand.

He whistles, like someone in a film. "How much do you think is here?" he goes.

"I don't know."

"Come on, Irish bullhead—guess!"

He's been calling me that for a few days, since I wouldn't let him help me lace up my Docs.

"I've no idea. Five hundred dollars?"

He lays it out on the bed, like Monopoly, only real. There are eight hundreds, four fifties, nine twenties and one five. One thousand, one hundred and eighty-five dollars. Sergei whistles again. "What would you spend all that on?" he goes.

I've only ever seen that much money in Cooper's restaurant at night, when he's cashing out the till.

"I don't know."

"Come on, Rhea—a thousand dollars, you must have some idea? An airplane ticket to Ireland?"

"No!" I blurt that out and I sound really definite, more definite than I knew I was.

"Why not?"

There are loads of reasons why not. Fifty reasons, more than fifty. There is nothing here, but there is less there. Less than nothing. I shrug.

Sergei's not waiting for an answer anyway. He's lying back on the bed, staring at the ceiling. "I'd buy a skateboard—a Birdhouse. And a surfboard, I'd learn to surf. And a jet ski! I've always wanted to jet ski!"

That would all come to way more than one thousand one hundred and eighty-five dollars but he is rolling over now, on the bed on top of the money, and he looks so excited I don't want to be the one to stop him.

"I know," I go. "I'd get a new Discman. And CDs. All my Hendrix ones again, and Eminem. I'm going crazy without music."

"Come on, Rhea." He keeps rolling till he gets to the edge of the bed. One of the hundreds falls on the floor. "A thousand dollars' worth of CDs? You can do better than that! There's got to be something awesome—something you've always wanted."

Sergei sounds funny when he says American words like "awesome." My brain is thinking that but my mouth says something different.

"I'd pay for a private detective to find where my mother lived."

He stops mid-roll and pushes himself up on his elbows. I've never talked to him about you before. He claps his hands. "I knew it! I knew you had something. A secret!"

"Come on, let's put the money away."

I bend down to pick up the hundred, it's halfway under the bed but I can reach it.

"You never tell me anything about yourself, Irish bullhead. I didn't even know your mother was from New York."

I pick up the rest of the money, crumpled now from where he's rolled over it. My thumb and index finger hold the clip open, but then I mess up and the notes flutter to the floor. "Fuck!"

"I got it," he says, sliding off the bed and onto the floor. "I got it."

I hate that I can't manage the stupid clip, so I leave it on top of the dresser and I open the next drawer without really thinking about it. And that's when I see the photo frame, on top of a pink-and-white striped shirt, face down.

I'm going to shut the drawer, but Sergei has already seen it, and he puts the money next to the clip and reaches past me to pick up the frame. He turns it over so we can both see the perfect smiles. I notice Michael first, in the middle, next to a blonde woman holding a little girl, who she is making wave at the camera. There are two blond boys on either side of him, both wearing red T-shirts and blue shorts. He has his hand on the shoulder of the smaller one who comes up to his waist. The older boy is holding a skateboard. Sergei shoves the photo back so it catches the edge of the shirt and crumples it up. He doesn't fix it, only closes the drawer harder than he needs to. When he looks at me, that shine is in his eyes.

"We're taking the money," he says.

"Stop messing," I say, even though I don't think he's messing.

"That money's ours." He picks up the pile of money and starts to count it again. "Why not?"

"Because…" I want to say different words than the ones on their way but I can't find any. "Because it's not right."

He's shoving the notes in his jeans pockets too fast and one of them tears. "So, sleeping with these men to get us money is fine, but taking it—that's not right?"

"No, I didn't mean that—"

"That's exactly what you meant."

I've never seen his face sneering before. He looks different. Ugly.

"No, Serg, I—"

"You're a coward, Rhea. It's okay for me to do these things, but not you. You're afraid, a coward."

That's the word that does it. I hit his arm, hard, so his hand jerks and some of the notes fall to the floor. My fist hurts but I bet he hurts worse.

"Fuck you, calling me a coward, Sergei. Remember how we met? Remember? I saved you from that guy at the Y. Who was the coward then?"

"Fuck off!" He rubs his arm and gets down on his knees again to scramble for the notes.

My heart is going a hundred thousand beats a minute, that's what it feels like. And then I'm back on the beach in Rush, it's scorching and Susan Mulligan and her crowd are laughing at me because I can't get in and swim, because I don't even have togs. *Diarrhoea Farrell's a coward! Diarrhoea's too scared to learn to swim.*

"I'm not a fucking coward, Sergei. Don't say that again."

He's still on his knees, he has the money in his hands. When he looks up at me there are red spots on his cheeks.

"So, if it's not that you're afraid, why not? Why not just take it?"

"Because it'll be gone by the end of the week. We'll blow it all on some hotel room half the size of this apartment. A thousand dollars doesn't last long in New York City, dumbass."

Dumbass. Laurie used to call me that. I've never called anyone else it before. He stands up slowly, blows his fringe from his eyes. He's still angry but he's listening to me as well.

"If we play our cards right, we can stay here in this apartment every weekend, maybe even during the week too. That's worth way more than the money. You know that."

What I'm saying is true and Sergei hears it. I don't say anything about the photograph, I can't let him know I saw the shine in his eyes. He takes out two fifties from his back pocket, lines them up properly against each other.

"Maybe you're right, Irish bullhead," he says. "Maybe you have a point."

He puts all the notes back, one by one. Smoothes them, lines them up, and folds them inside the clip and puts the clip back inside the hood of the Florida State sweatshirt.

"You're the smart one, Irish bullhead. You're the brains, I'm only the pretty face."

He sticks his tongue out and I stick my tongue out and that means things are back to normal, nearly normal. We get into bed again, leave the last drawer unchecked. He rolls over so I can't see his face but I can hear what he says.

"You know I was only joking about you being a coward. You know I didn't mean it."

"I know. I'm sorry if I hurt your arm."

He fell asleep straightaway. Sergei can sleep anywhere, we joke that he can sleep standing up. But I lie here and I can't sleep. I'm back on the beach in Rush, the sand squishy cold under my toes at the edge of the water. It doesn't get deep for ages and I walk out really far before I have to stop because the bottom of my shorts gets wet. The others are way out. Susan Mulligan and Paula O'Brien are the furthest, specs above the sparkle on the waves. Lisa is closer in, with Aisling Begley and her sister, and their voices carry over the water, their laughter does.

I want to be with them, but I don't want to be with them. I know I can't. I don't know why except Dad always says it's the most important rule. And I know that the rule has something to do with you.

Rhea

23

Central Park, New York
26th April 1999
2:25 p.m.

Dear Mum,

When I was a little kid and New York came on the telly, I'd sit up extra close to the screen so I wouldn't miss anything. I wanted to see everything, to hear all the sounds. I wanted to climb inside the TV so I could smell it. Today, New York smells like sugar and grease and some kind of car-fumy smell all mixed up together. Sometimes Florida smelled like car fumes too, and parts of it smelled like the sea, but different from the sea in Rush.

Did you like it, living in Rush? If there was a scale and New York was at one end, Rush would be at the opposite one. You couldn't find places more different. I don't just mean because it's quiet and a village, it's the flatness too. Rush is as flat as New York is tall. Rush is the flattest place in the world compared to New York.

I bet you wouldn't have stayed if you hadn't got pregnant with me. I did the maths, Mum, you got married in November and I was born in May. Would you still have married Dad if it wasn't because of me?

Since I've been here, I can't stop thinking of all these questions I want to ask you—it feels like a million questions every hour, but that can't be true because I read somewhere that humans only have 70,000 thoughts a day and something like half of them are the same thought, over and over. But it feels like a million, all questions, questions I want to ask you.

What is it like to drown?

Shit.

The first Sunday in Coral Springs, me and Laurie are sitting watching *Baywatch*, waiting to go for lunch and I'm thinking that I've never once seen an episode where someone actually drowned. I'm about to say this to Laurie, but she speaks first.

24

"How do you say your name again?" She's on the cream couch, her bare feet pulled up under her. I'm on the brown leather chair, my feet are on the floor in my Docs. Aunt Ruth has already been going on about sandals. Laurie doesn't look at me, her blue eyes are still on the screen even though the ads are on now. If there'd been anyone else in the room, I'd think she must be talking to them, but there's only me.

"Rhea," I go. I say it again. "Rhea. When I was a kid I used to get slagged about it."

"Slagged?" Her eyes flick over.

"Take the piss—you know, make jokes." I pause. "They used to call me Diarrhoea."

She makes a face. "Gross."

I don't know why I tell her that, except that I wanted to say something, maybe I think she might even laugh, but she doesn't laugh. Maybe I want to say it first, before she can. I look down and I'm kneading my stump. I let go. Her eyes are back on the telly, I don't think she noticed.

"No one seems to know why my mum called me Rhea. It wasn't a name in the family or anything. She must have liked it, but I always wished she'd called me something else."

She pulls a strand of her hair, starts to chew it.

"So change it."

The show is back on. David Hasselhoff is grabbing that orange plastic thing and running towards the sea. I'm watching him but remembering being little, saying my prayers at night, praying I'd wake up with a new name like Sinead or Emma or Amy. But in the morning, I was always Rhea.

"What? Just change my name? Just like that?"

She shrugs. "A girl in my grade changed her name from Victoria to Tori."

"That's shortening a name—not changing it." I laugh a bit, so it doesn't sound like I'm disagreeing with her.

"Shortening it would be Vic or Vicki. Tori sounds different, it just uses some of the same letters."

"But I only have four letters in my name. There's not enough to shorten it, never mind make up a new name."

She doesn't answer and I think that's the end of the conversation. She adjusts her legs so she's sitting cross-legged, her feet turned upwards on the back of each thigh.

On TV, another lifeguard has joined David in the sea. A girl is screaming for help, going under the waves. As I watch her, I am scanning through possible variants of my name but none of them make any sense.

At the ad break, Laurie stands up. "I've seen this one before."

She throws the remote control at me without any warning so it bounces off my thigh and hits the cabinet next to me, making a crash before it falls on the floor.

"What about Rae?"

I've bent down to pick up the remote so I can't see her face as she says it. When I turn to look at her, she's already on her way out the door.

"Ray? That's a boy's name. Anyway, I don't have a 'y' in my name."

"R-a-e, dumbass. The girl's version."

She doesn't look back, so I can't see her face, but writing this now, I bet she was rolling her eyes.

I think about it all day, the new name, say it over and over in my head. Rae Farrell. Rae. It sounds kind of cool, different. Rae doesn't rhyme with diarrhoea. I like the short, crisp sound of one syllable. Rae. As we sit having lunch, I tune out of Cooper's story about the famous actor who came into the restaurant because I am imagining what Rae Farrell would order, what she would say. I never get to that part though because when I look up they're all looking at me, and I realise I forgot to laugh at Cooper's punchline.

Later, I want to ask Aunt Ruth what she thinks while she's emptying the dishwasher. I offer to help but she says no, even though I offer twice. I stand by the patio door looking at the garden, the darkness of the grass, the pool an oblong of blue light.

"Did you ever think about changing your name?"

Her back bends and straightens as she unloads, piling white plates on the black marble counter.

"No," she says, without skipping a beat. I wait for her to ask why I am asking, but she doesn't, she just carries on stacking plates into the open cupboard and then bends over again.

"A lot of people do."

"I wouldn't."

She wipes the inside of the casserole dish with a tea towel and bends down again for the knives and forks, looks up at me through her fringe. "Why?"

"Nothing," I go. "No reason."

The next day is the first day at school and I know what to do, have thought about little else all night. The school bus stops at the end of the road and two other girls get on ahead of me and Laurie. I let her go first and I keep my eyes on her ponytail swinging down her back, so I don't have to see everyone looking at me. Halfway down the bus, one guy says something to his friend and they both laugh. I've already passed them but I walk back to their seat, stare at them. The one who made the comment has fifty thousand freckles that leak into each other like a big tea stain. The other one is smaller, afraid looking. They snigger for a second, then stop. I want to get my stump and shove it in their faces. I want to ask them what their fucking problem is and if they've never seen someone with only one arm before—only they probably never have seen someone with only one arm before.

I assume that Laurie and me will sit together, but there is a girl with dark shiny hair under a white baseball cap who waves and slides her bag from the seat and Laurie sits down without a backward glance.

I walk on. I don't care. This shouldn't hurt more than the sniggers, but it does. What did I expect? It's not like she's my sister, and even if she was, we wouldn't sit together. Most sisters hated each other, didn't they? Lisa always said her sister was a moody cow. It wasn't a good time to start thinking about Lisa. Four rows behind Laurie, there is an empty seat next to a girl with long red curls. I sit down. She turns around and I wait for her to tell me it is taken, but instead she smiles to show a mouthful of braces.

"Hi, I'm Glenda," she says. "What's your name?"

"Rae," I say. "Rae Farrell."

And that's how it starts—how I start—in Florida. I'm Rae Farrell. No one cares, no one asks, no one knows any different. I'm embarrassed that night, saying it at home, in case Laurie thinks I changed it because of what she'd said, but she barely looks up from her meatloaf and Cooper smiles wide and says he thinks it sounds great. Only Aunt Ruth frowns and says she preferred it the old way, but after a while even she calls me Rae most of the time too.

So for nearly two years now, I've been Rae, Mum, but—and I don't know why—ever since I got to New York, I feel like I want to be Rhea again.

I told Sergei my name was Rhea, from the start, and that's how I've been signing these letters. For some reason I can't explain, I feel like maybe I made a mistake. That maybe I should have been Rhea all along.

Rhea

Dear Mum,

Even if I don't get the photos of you back, I can still see them. They live in my head, those photos, they are etched onto the backs of my eyelids. I can still see you in Columbia, smiling, on Rush beach in your sunglasses. I know every speck of those photographs from looking at them so much. I don't know why I spent so much time looking at them. It's not as if I don't know that photographs are lies most of the time, fake snapshots of a moment when everyone smiles and pretends they're happy before they go back to not smiling or not talking or snapping at each other, or whatever they were doing before.

That's what I said to Sergei over breakfast this morning, that's what starts everything.

"Photos are lies, most of the time. You know that, don't you?"

He's just taken a bite and he chews for a minute before he answers.

"What are you talking about?" he says. A bit of food lands on the table between us. It looks like egg.

He's in a bad mood—I can tell by the way he hacks his pancakes up into any old shape, instead of slicing them longways like he usually does. He didn't smile at the waitress or move his menu out of the way when she went to put down the water. Earlier when Michael offered him money for breakfast, he snatched it out of his hand and didn't even say thanks.

I know it's about the photograph, the one of Michael and his family. I think it is, but if I say that he'll get in a worse mood. I want to tell him that Michael sleeping with him means he's gay, no matter what the photo says. But I can't talk about the photo, so I talk about another one instead.

"I was just thinking about the day after I arrived in my aunt's house and we all went out for this stupid welcome lunch for me. It was so awkward, we had nothing to say to each other. And just at the end, Cooper got the waiter to take a photo of us. And we're all smiling like we're so happy, like we're not all dying for it to be over."

Sergei rips a bite from his bagel. "Who's Cooper?"

"My aunt's boyfriend."

"This was in Ireland?"

I shake my head. "Florida."

"Florida? When were you there?"

"I lived there, with my aunt. For two years nearly."

"I thought you came from Ireland."

"I do come from Ireland. I lived there my whole life before Florida."

I focus on my omelette, trying to swirl the runny cheese around my fork. Telling Sergei about the stupid photo makes me picture it—the frame on the low white sideboard in the living room, my stupid smile, my hair still long, my black-check shirt in between Laurie's yellow top and Ruth's pink dress. The photos around it were all of Laurie: Laurie in the pool in a rubber ring, waving at the camera; Laurie and Cooper and Minnie Mouse at Disney World. I didn't know anything about Laurie's mum then or why she wasn't in the photos. But even then, I knew I wanted to line up all the photos of Laurie and chart her childhood, to see when it was her hair changed from white to blonde, when her smile went from being her whole face, to only part of it.

Sergei is looking at me, chewing.

"We're supposed to be friends, Irish bullhead. We're supposed to be friends and you never tell me anything. I don't know anything about you."

He emphasises the "anything," twice he does. It's not a fight yet, but it's the cusp of one.

"Don't be stupid, Serg, you know all about me. What do you want to know?"

He shrugs. "I don't know. Anything. Everything. How did you get here?"

I cut up a bit of omelette and put it on my toast. "I got the bus. It took, like, twenty-four hours."

He shakes his head. "I don't mean that, not just that. I mean, what happened to you? What happened to your arm?"

He gestures across the table, nearly touches my stump. I twitch away from him, I can't help it. To cover up, I sit back like I'm about to tell him the story but I know he has seen it, the twitch.

"Okay then, if you must know, it was a shark attack—there's not too many of them in Dublin, but—"

He curses in Polish and smacks his hand off the table. The waitress has just filled up the coffees and some of his slops into the saucer.

"Sergei—"

"No! No, no." He holds up his palm. "Don't tell me anything else unless it's the truth. I'm sick of these bullshit stories. You think they're cute, but they're not. They're just bullshit. We're supposed to be friends, Rhea."

"We are."

"No." When he shakes his head the curl at the front bounces a bit; he needs a haircut. "Friends are honest with each other. The other day you tell me your mother was from here and you want a private eye to find her. Yesterday, I ask where she lives now and you clam up, won't say a single word—"

"Sergei, come on—"

"I don't even know if it's true that she's from here or where you're from—this Florida story, this Cooper—it could all be bullshit, like this shark story—"

I get mad then, Mum. I can't help it.

"Like you always tell the truth? You're really twenty-one, Serg? Your parents are really coming over to visit you? When are they coming over?"

"I go to touch your arm and you pull away, like I have a disease. We're supposed to be a team, remember?"

My legs are jiggling under the table and my heart is going really fast. Part of me wants to run out of the diner and down Seventh Avenue so I never have to see Sergei again, but there's all this food on the table and I'll be hungry again in an hour, and all my stuff is at Michael's house. I know I should shut up, stop, but somehow I can't.

"It doesn't feel like we're a team when I'm stuck in Penn Station and you're hours late, having fun with one of your guys in some bar—"

His face has a red spot on each cheek. "Take that back! You think I want to do it? You think I enjoy it? I do it for money, Rhea. For you, for us."

"Don't lay that on me, Serg—you could earn money in other ways. You told me you had a job before. You choose—"

He holds both his hands up now.

"No, no, no. I'm not listening to this."

"Why not? Because it's the truth? Isn't that what friends do? Tell each other the truth?"

I don't know when I started shouting but I know that I am by then because people are looking. Sergei shoves his plate across the table, so it bumps into mine and makes a kind of ringing sound.

"The truth? Ha! Rhea, you couldn't tell the truth if your life depended on it."

He's putting on his jacket, he's about to leave, but he's kind of delaying. If I stop, take back what I said, he'll stay. But I can't stop, not right then.

"Just because we're friends doesn't give you the right to know everything about me, Sergei."

"Fuck you!"

He pushes himself out of the booth. The waitress has already left the check and he pulls Michael's fifty out of his pocket, throws it on the table.

"Sergei, what about your change? Wait for your change."

"Keep it, you're going to need it."

They nearly come then, stupid tears, pinpricks behind my eyes. He's not going to see me cry.

"What? This is it? The end of everything, because I won't tell you what happened to my arm?"

He shakes his head. "It's not about your fucking arm. You're so fucking stupid sometimes. It's about letting someone get to know you. About trusting."

That's the last thing he says before he storms out the door of the diner. They're all looking at me, the waitress and the customers. They're looking at me like it's my fault and all I did was talk about the stupid photograph. He's the one that was in a bad mood before we even got here. He's the one that was probing and prying.

I wait to see him pass the window, but he must have gone the other way. My tummy feels all jangly, but I'm not wasting the food, so I cut up the rest of my omelette and put it on the toast and chew it and swallow it. And when I'm done, I eat the rest of his pancakes, his bacon. I even drink his coffee, which makes no sense because I can get a free refill on my own. That was hours ago, Mum. That was this morning and now it's 10:18 p.m. and I'm sitting opposite Michael's apartment, thinking Sergei's going to show up, only what if he doesn't? I haven't touched his $31 change, it's in the back pocket of my jeans and earlier when I bought a pizza slice I made sure to keep my own money separate.

My stuff is in there, Mum, I was so stupid. I left my backpack in there for the first time—the Carver book, your photos. Fuck Sergei, talking about trust—that was the first time I trusted we'd be going back there. All day the fight has been rolling around in my head, Mum. I don't know where I was right and where I was a bit wrong. Why does being friends with someone mean you have to tell them every single fucking thing about you? Why can't it be like with Lisa, when we were best friends because we were in the same class and she lived two doors down so I could call into her house whenever I wanted and eat the dinner her mum made? Tonight is Monday, they'll be having liver tonight and Lisa will be bitching and saying things like, "It's barbaric to make people eat things that make them want to be physically sick." I didn't like liver either, but with enough ketchup it wasn't too bad, so I'd eat it first to get it out of the way and then enjoy the peas and mashed potato. Tuesdays were my second favourite day because we had homemade burgers. Wednesdays were okay, with pork chops, but Thursday was my absolute favourite because on Thursdays her mum made lasagne and garlic bread. Lisa preferred Fridays, when they had chipper chips from Joe's, but Dad got chipper chips loads of days, so they'd stopped being a treat.

I should have written to Lisa more, Mum. Aunt Ruth kept saying I could use the phone whenever I wanted to call her, and I don't know why I didn't. She stopped writing to me after a bit. In her last letter, she said she didn't think I was missing her at all, that I must have forgotten about her with my new life in Florida, but that wasn't true, Mum. It doesn't make any sense but writing to her, ringing her, made me miss her more and if I didn't do that it was easier not to miss her at all.

Sergei doesn't know what it's like, Mum, having everyone look at you and want to know what happened. It was different in Rush, I didn't have to tell anyone because everyone already knew—everyone always knew everything about you. So it wasn't until Coral Springs, until that night when me and Laurie were hanging out in my room and she asked me, that I ever told anyone.

I remember her eyes wide, having her full attention in a way I'd never had her full attention before as I told her about that day, how I was messing around, showing off to Lisa. How Dad had always told me not to play with the machine, but that I did anyway, that day. I didn't tell her why.

She asked me loads of questions—if it hurt and if I was scared. She asked me if there was a moment, right before it happened, when I knew it was going to happen.

I told her the truth, that night, most of it, nearly all of it. I went through the memory, frame by frame. There was no moment before it happened, I didn't think there was—it wasn't happening and then it was happening. One second I was reaching into the machine and I could hear Lisa saying not to, and the next the sound was so loud, way louder than when Dad did it. A sound that filled the shop, filled my head. I don't remember pain, not really, more like a pulling, something heavy, heavy pulling, pulling, pulling, pulling. And my head against the cold metal of the machine and Lisa's mouth was open, like she was screaming, only I couldn't hear her. I couldn't hear anything until Dad was there and then everything stopped.

When I was telling Laurie, I forgot she was even there, it was like I was telling the story to myself. I could see it all again, feel Dad's arms under me, so strong, see his foot kick the door of the shop open, hear his voice shouting, feel myself bumping against his chest as he ran out onto the street, first towards the harbour, before he turned around and ran the other way again.

Why do I have to tell Sergei that, Mum? Why do I have to tell anyone? He says it's about trust but why should I trust him? You can't always know if you can trust people, can you? I mean look at what happened with Laurie.

In the end, there's only one person I know for sure I can trust, Mum, and it's not Sergei—it's me.

Rhea

King Street, New York
27th April 1999
12:35 a.m.

Dear Mum,

I need to pee again. Jesus. I just peed half an hour ago, I couldn't need to go again. The worst thing about being on the street isn't the hunger or the cold or even the boredom. It's never having a toilet around, having to pee outside sometimes. I did it in Rush before, with Lisa, down by the beach the night we'd been drinking some of Dad's beers, but it was funny that night. It's different here, on your own, in an alley where anyone could come in and when you know there's rats hiding behind the bins.

Thank God I got my period when I was in the Y, that will be a nightmare when it comes. I should have another two weeks before I need to worry about it, although you never know. You could time your watch by Lisa's period but mine's never been like that. Mine comes when it feels like it.

I'm going to hold my pee longer, until they come. I don't want to see those fucking rats again. I keep trying to remind myself that rats are only animals and I love animals, but it doesn't work. I still fucking hate them.

One time on the way home from school, around the time Lisa got her period, she starts this whole conversation, bitching about her mum and what a control freak she is and how nosy she is and what a bitch she is. And then she says something else: "I wish my mum was dead sometimes." She says that part all casual, scuffing her shoe along the side of the path, like she's just thought of it.

"Don't say that," I go.

"Why not?"

"You know why not, it's not true. You'd miss her."

She turns to me, her hands in her pockets. "You don't ever seem to miss yours, though. You've always just had your dad and that's that. And he doesn't nose around in your business."

She's right, but she's not right too. I shrug. "He can't cook, though."

"Mine can't either, but we could get chips. And pizza. Have sandwiches. It drives me mad, having those same dinners every night of the week. You and your dad get on just fine." My dad is way more fun than Lisa's dad, and we both know it. Lisa's been there when Dad puts on his Hendrix records, his "happy music." She's even seen the dance he does to "Stone Free." "Stone Free" is his favourite Hendrix song ever, the first song that he ever wrote. It was a B-side to a song called "Hey Joe" in 1966, but it was released as its own single in 1969. Dad tells me this every time he's taking the record out of its sleeve. I watch him carefully drop the needle onto just the right place and try and imagine 1966, 1969—Dad being my age.

When I look at Lisa, she has that face on, the one she always has before she wants to ask a question.

"If you had a choice, that you could have your mum back, but it meant your dad had to be dead, what would you choose?"

I laugh. "That's a stupid question."

"If I could only choose one of mine, I'd choose my dad, I totally would."

I don't like Lisa's question, but it's like a hook inside my head. It makes me think about the night me and Dad played "Stone Free" seventeen times in a row when the O'Loughlins were banging on the wall and Dad bangs back, in time with the music, and tells them to "go fuck themselves" and I'm scared but then I'm laughing too, and afterwards he finds some vanilla ice cream in the back of the freezer under all the ice and makes a Coke float for me and a Harp float for him.

When I think of happiness then, I think of that night, Dad's face streaming with sweat, his smile. But thinking about that night makes me think about the next morning, when I want to do it all over again, but he won't—he won't get up or open the curtains or do anything all day nearly, and I don't know what I've done to make him so sad.

Lisa nudges me with her elbow. "Come on, it's only hypothetical, it's not like it matters." We're almost at Billie's shop, where Aisling Begley and Alison Ryan are standing outside eating Mr. Freezes. She wants me to answer before I get there.

"It's a stupid question, Lisa. Of course I'd choose my dad." That's what I tell Lisa but, in my head, I say something else, Mum, something she doesn't hear, something no one does except maybe God, if there is a God.

If you want to know the truth, in my head I chose you, not Dad. Are you happy now? I made a big mistake and chose you. And I got what I deserved—fucking no one.

Rhea

Dear Mum,

How many letters can I write in one night? I'm sorry about earlier, that was stupid. I know Dad's car accident on the way home from the Drop Inn was nothing to do with that thought in my head and everything to do with the pints he had before turning on the ignition, but I feel like I'm going crazy sitting here, waiting outside this apartment. I thought maybe I missed them earlier, when I went to pee again or when I fell asleep for a second, but there are no lights on upstairs or anything, so I don't think they're back.

What if they never come back?

You know what I'm craving? Crisps. Hunky Dory's, the salt and vinegar ones in the blue packet. Over here the next best ones are Ruffles, but they're not as nice, even though they come in a bigger packet. I'm losing weight, I think I am—my belt is on the next buckle down. Aunt Ruth would be delighted, she was always going on about my weight. The first time she says it is when she walks into the kitchen and I'm making a crisp sandwich and she looks at the clock and says it's only an hour till dinner. Next thing you know, she's sitting down, talking about healthy eating and exercise, and how hard it can be to get rid of "puppy fat." My face burns when she says that. Mrs. McManus used those stupid words too, "puppy fat," when she kept me back after school in fifth class to say I should ask my dad to give me an apple or a banana for my lunch to go with the Skittles and crisps and Coke.

So the night Aunt Ruth brings up the prosthetic, I think it's going to be more of the same. We're in the kitchen again, clearing up after dinner this time, when she says she wants to talk to me, and Cooper goes, "Hey kiddo, let's watch TV" to Laurie and leaves me there with her. She leans against the counter and pulls down her fringe.

"I signed up for soccer trials," I say. "I'm going to practice on Thursday." The only time I've played before is with the boys on the road, but the other sports were swimming and tennis so I had no choice.

She looks confused for a second and then smiles. "Great. That's great. It'll be a great way to make new friends."

She's said "great" three times in one sentence, and I know then that's not what she wants to talk about, that there must be something else.

"Listen, Rhea, what I wanted to talk to you about—"

"Rae."

"Sorry, Rae. What I wanted to talk about, I mean what Cooper and I wanted to talk to you about, is the possibility of … of … getting a prosthetic." She is looking at the electric juicer, not at me. "You know, for your arm."

She gestures at her own arm, in case I don't know what a prosthetic is. More words gallop out. Now she's talking to the stainless steel spotlights over my head. "One of Cooper's friends is a surgeon and he was saying how much better they are these days, how much progress they've made in the past few years." She glances at me, catches my eye but I don't say anything. "They're expensive, of course, but Cooper and I, we don't mind … I mean, we can afford it."

"Save your money—I don't want one."

"But it would help you—you could do so much more—"

I look down at my stump. "I can do everything I want now."

"They have a brochure. In it, there's a boy riding a bike, tying his laces."

"I lace up my twelve-hole Docs. I rode my bike in Ireland."

"But that was Ireland, honey. Here, there's so much traffic."

"Exactly, no one rides bikes here. You'd probably die of heat stroke riding a bike here."

40

She brushes her fringe down again, trying not to frown. "This isn't just about riding a bike, let's not get hung up on riding a bike—"

"You're the one who brought up riding bikes. I don't want to ride a bike."

"The bike is just an example, Rhea. It would help you with other things you can't do."

I clench my toes inside my Docs. "I can do anything I want the way I am."

She shakes her head. "We both know that's not true, Rhea."

"Name one thing! Name one thing I can't do now!"

It comes out like a shout, when I say that. The kitchen door opens and Cooper comes in, fast, like he's been listening outside all along.

"Is everything okay?" he asks Aunt Ruth, even though he's looking at me.

"Fine." She smiles, tucking her hair behind her ear. "Just fine. Give us a few minutes, Coop."

He stays by the door, his big hand around its edge. "Okay. I'm just in here, if you need me."

He watches me as he closes the door, as if he's leaving her with a rabid Alsatian. I look back to Aunt Ruth. Her anger is in her face now, she's not trying to hide it like before. When she talks, her voice is nearly a whisper.

"Don't you ever shout at me like that again, Rhea. We don't talk to each other like that in this house."

"My name is Rae. How many times do I have to tell you? Do you use each other's names in this house?"

Her lips go white where she clamps them together. I can nearly see the anger ready to jump out, and I wish it would but instead she takes a deep breath.

"Cooper's doing a lot for you and I don't want him to think you're ungrateful."

I don't know how what I do with my arm relates to Cooper and her, but somehow it does, just like somehow what I eat does too.

"I won't be grateful or ungrateful, because I'm not getting one."

My stump is starting to hurt, the way it always used to, the way it hasn't for years.

"Well, you're a minor, Rae, so, for now, that's my decision."

A line comes into my head, a line that's been there all along waiting for an opportunity to be spoken.

"You're not my mother."

She blinks twice, folds her arms. "No, I'm not. And I don't want to be." The kitchen is silent. Outside there is the sound of the sprinkler on the grass. It sounds like this: ppppttt ppppttt. I count, it makes that noise every thirty seconds. She flicks her hair behind her ear.

"Rhea, I mean Rae, I'm sorry—"

"Don't be. It's the most honest thing you've said to me since I got here."

She starts to walk towards me but I walk around the breakfast bar so it's between us. "I didn't mean it. I just got angry. I can't understand why you don't want a prosthetic, that's all. I know you have trouble fitting in..."

I shake my head.

"I mean, this isn't just about you. There are other things to consider—how it looks to people, how it makes them feel. I'm sure you don't always want to be known as "the girl with one arm.""

She says that, Mum, actually says that. I nearly laugh, but I don't. "Why not, Aunt Ruth? It's who I am." We stand there, looking at each other for a few seconds and I think she's going to say something else, but she doesn't. She just turns around and goes out the door into the hall, leaving me on my own in their fancy clean kitchen with the sound of insects hitting the glass patio doors and the ppppttt ppppttt of the sprinkler, on and off and on again.

Every thirty seconds.

Rhea

42

Grand Central Station, New York
27th April 1999
7:14 p.m.

Dear Mum,

It was 4:23 a.m. when Sergei and Michael got home. I knew because I was looking at my G-Shock when the taxi turned the corner. It was good they came then because after that man walking the dog stopped to talk to me a second time, I'd decided I'd only give it until 4:30 before I headed to the diner.

They took ages to get out of the taxi and the funny thing was, after all the waiting, I nearly didn't want them to see me at all. And then the taxi drove away and I could see that Michael had Sergei's arm around his shoulder, that he was practically carrying him.

I don't know if Michael would have let me in if it wasn't for the fact that he couldn't hold Sergei up and open the door at the same time. When he sees me, he hands me the key and I get the outer door and open it for them. Sergei's head is kind of rolling back and there's sick all down his jeans. The smell is gross.

I lead the way up the stairs and, behind me, Michael is talking to Sergei in a whisper, telling him to lift his feet, that he has to learn when to stop. It sounds like he might be going to cry but I don't look around. I don't ask if he's okay with me staying, I just unlock the apartment door and help him get Sergei on the couch.

"He'll be okay," I go. "Get me a basin."

Michael looks at me for a second and then goes into the kitchen. I roll Sergei onto his side, pull the neck of his T-shirt looser. I take his runners off and his jeans. I leave his socks on. He's listing backwards, towards the back of the couch, and I tip him forward again, take the basin Michael's brought back and put it by his head.

Michael is standing with his hands on his hips, watching.

"You seem to know what you're doing," he says.

"You figure it out."

"You've seen him like this a lot?"

I shrug. I have, but that's not how I know how to do this. I feel like I've always known how to do this.

"I don't know what happened," Michael says, running his hands over his head. "We're having dinner and he says he's going to the bathroom and he never comes back. Just leaves me there, with both of our meals. I looked all over for him, for hours. All the bars. I found him in the park opposite Stonewall, like this."

Sergei rolls backwards on the couch and I make a line of cushions to keep him propped forward.

"We need to keep an eye on him," I go, "make sure he doesn't roll over onto his back."

"I'll do it, I don't care. I have to be out of here in less than three hours anyway." Michael sits down on the armchair, puts his head in his hands. "You have the bed."

"You sure?"

He looks up, nods. "Yeah."

I pick up my backpack, hold it in front of me. He's looking at me like he's not finished talking, like he still has something to say. He's a man in a suit, but his eyes are someone else's eyes—his eyes are a little kid's eyes.

"Anything could have happened to him," he says. "He has to get this under control. Talk to him, will you? He listens to you."

My backpack is heavy and my head feels heavy too. Michael wants an answer, thinks there is one. I don't think it's that easy, but I'm too tired to tell him and, anyway, sometimes I think you need to find out for yourself, so I say what he wants to hear. "I'll talk to him." That was last night. This morning, when I woke up, the radio alarm clock said it was 10:07 and I thought that Sergei would still be sleeping but when I go into the living room he's in his boxers with a blanket half over his knees, a glass of water on the coffee table in front of him. When he sees me, he half smiles.

"Hey," he says. "Irish bullhead."

We don't talk about the row, the diner, none of it. We don't talk about why he left Michael in the restaurant or what happened after or how he got home. Instead, we watch Ricki Lake and when it's over, we watch Montel Williams. I make us Pop-Tarts and when Sergei makes a gagging face, I eat his too. It's when Sally Jesse Raphael is on that Sergei gets up and starts to pace.

"I can't do this!" he goes.

"Do what?"

"I can't watch this. I can't watch any more of this shit. Doesn't it make you want to just kill yourself? Watching these shows?"

He's pacing around the tiny room, holding his head. I'd thought we were having fun, I thought everything was okay again, but it's not.

"What do you want to do?"

"Anything. Everything. We're in New York City, Rhea, we're in New York fucking City and we're watching shit TV that we could be watching anywhere in the world."

He stops in front of me. His eyes are excited, red rimmed. I know about eyes like that.

"Come on, Rhea, let's have an adventure. We need an adventure."

He grabs my hand and pulls me up off the floor. All of a sudden, the apartment seems tiny, claustrophobic, like the whole city outside is waiting. And that's when I come up with the idea.

"We could go look for my mother."

———

I want to make the letter pause there, Mum. If this was a film, there'd be a pause button I could push and then we'd cut to the next scene when we were on our way to Columbia and I'd leave out the boring parts about us getting ready and the row we nearly had about tidying up the apartment for Michael (I wanted to, he didn't) and how Sergei ate two Big Macs and I pretended I wasn't hungry, even though I'm always hungry, because I didn't want any more of his money and I didn't want to spend mine because pizza slices are cheaper than Big Macs and keep you full for longer. No, I'd leave out all that. We'd just be rattling along on the 1 train, trying not to laugh at the guy sitting opposite us with the big Afro and the red socks and black knee pads saying "testing, testing" into what looks like a radio alarm clock and then in the next scene we'd be walking through the gates of Columbia together.

In the admissions office, there's two people ahead of us waiting. It's really quiet and Sergei is driving me crazy, the way he keeps pumping his legs up and down.

"Stop doing that."

"What?"

"Jiggling your legs like that, you're making me nervous."

"Sorry." He stops for 0.2 of a second and starts again. He sees my look. "Sorry."

I'm nervous too. I think I am, I think that's why my heart is galloping as fast as Sergei's legs. It's all the questions he asked me on the way here—what you'd been studying, what year you'd started, if you'd ever graduated. Simple questions, but questions I don't know the answers to. How come I don't know the answers to simple questions like that? How come no one told me?

"Next."

The woman behind the counter doesn't look like how I thought people at Columbia would look when I was filling out the forms and writing my personal essay. If I'd had to guess how a woman at a desk in the admissions office would look, I'd have guessed she'd be Aunt Ruth's age, or older, with short black shiny hair and glasses, those horn-rimmed ones. But this woman is younger, this girl—she can't be much older than me—with her short spiky hair, and purple and green beads over a purple top. She's not even wearing glasses.

"How can I help you?"

She's not rude, but not friendly either. Sergei is next to me, leaning on the counter, and she looks from him to me.

"Hi," he says, and gives her his flirty smile. "We wanted to find out about someone who attended the university."

"This is the undergraduate admissions office, Columbia College. If you need information on the graduate school you need to—"

"No," I go. "That's right, Columbia College, she was an undergrad here."

She nods. "Okay, I'll look her up. But I might not be able to give you any information unless it's in the public domain already. Name?"

"Rhea Farrell," I go. She starts to type something into a computer, and I realise she didn't mean my name, she meant your name, and suddenly I'm terrified that she's going to see my own record, my own application and tell me if I'd got in. Or not. And I don't want to know that. More than anything, I don't want to know that.

"Sorry!" My hand shoots out, across the counter, towards her computer. "Sorry, that's my name. Not the person I'm looking for. The person I'm looking for is Allison Davis. With two *L*'s."

"Oh." She backs up on the delete key, starts typing again. She hadn't hit enter, she hadn't seen. My heart slows a bit. Sergei is looking at me. I don't know why I didn't want her to see so bad, why I don't want him to know I've applied here too.

"What year did she graduate?"

I knew that question was coming, and I answer another one. "She was here in 1978—I think she started in the autumn term of 1978."

"And the year of graduation?"

"I'm not sure."

I know you didn't graduate, I'm 99 percent sure you didn't, but there's something about this girl that makes me not want to tell her that, which is fifty kinds of crazy because it's the only way I know to find you. And all her questions make me think of my Columbia application form, the part where I'd had to fill in about you and Dad being deceased. There was a box that said "Date of death"—I'd never seen that written down before. I wrote Dad's date straightaway, like it was any old date, let the pen do its job. I didn't have a date for you, I didn't even know the date you went missing, not the exact one. Why couldn't you have had a date? A stone somewhere with two dates and a dash in between? Why couldn't something be definite with you? Something. Anything.

Couldn't you at least have given me that?

The girl is looking at me, kind of smiling, but she's getting impatient too, you can tell. Sergei is leaning across the counter, as if he might be trying to see the screen.

"You're not sure if she graduated or you're not sure of the year she graduated?"

I feel myself go red. "I don't think she graduated."

If you started in 1978, you'd have graduated in 1982, had a degree. But you didn't have a degree, did you? You had me instead. Me and Dad.

"I'm sorry," the girl goes, "there's no definitive record coming up. Even if I found her, I'm not able to release information to third parties."

"We're not a third party." Sergei smiles wider, tipping his head closer to her computer. "She was Rhea's mom—she passed away, she died. You can give information to family, no? To next of kin?"

I hadn't told him, yet, that you were dead. How did he know? The girl looks from Sergei to me.

"I'd need some proof of your relationship with her and that she's dead. But anyway, I can't find her."

"What if we give you her date of birth? Rhea, what was her date of birth?"

"23rd November 1959."

I must have said that, because I heard it, my voice. But somehow I don't remember saying it, making the decision to say it.

The girl is hesitating. Sergei is still smiling. "It would mean so much to us, any information at all."

She types the numbers in. Slowly. Each key sounds like a bullet. We wait. Sergei blows his curls out of his eyes. My Columbia application is in that computer too. That white plastic box has the power to ruin my life, change my life, make my life. Something happens on the screen. She shakes her head.

"What is it?" Sergei says.

"I'm sorry. There's nothing here that would help you."

"Anything at all would help us," Sergei says. "Rhea's mom is dead. She's come all the way to New York from Ireland to find out more about her."

The girl looks up.

"You're from Ireland?"

I nod. She's waiting for more. "I'm from Dublin." I make sure to speak with my normal voice, to keep the American sounds out of my words.

"My mom was from Ireland," she goes. "Meath." She says "Meath" so it rhymes with "teeth."

"Meath's nice." I say it the proper way. This is a lie. I don't know anything about Meath.

"It sounds like your mom told you about your heritage," Sergei goes, "but Rhea's mom never got the chance. Please, if you have anything there on your screen, anything at all, please tell us."

She glances over her shoulder, as if there might be someone there, but there is no one there. When she talks her voice is low, nearly a whisper. "All it says here is that she enrolled in 1977 and went on a student exchange programme in her sophomore year. It looks like she didn't come back. She never graduated, that's it. That's all there is."

She's talking about you. It's definitely you. 1977 you enrolled. I'd always thought it was 1978 but I was wrong. It was 1977.

"That's her!" Sergei goes. "She went to Ireland on her exchange. Do you have contact information? An address? Phone number?"

The girl clicks something else. "There's an address, but it's twenty years out of date. I'm sure whoever was there has moved by now."

"Can you tell us what it is, so we can check it against the one we have?"

Sergei has a pen and paper out—I don't know where he got it

from. The girl hesitates before quickly reading out an address on Park Avenue. You lived on Park Avenue.

"Thank you," Sergei says as he shoves the note in his back pocket. "Thank you, thank you, thank you." He drums his fingers on the counter, turns around to leave.

"When do you go back to Ireland?"

The question catches me, pulls me back. It's like a trick question.

"I don't know," I go. "I don't know if I'm going back."

"Oh."

She looks disappointed, like she wanted me to say something else, but it's the truth. Sergei is already holding the door open for me, so I pick up my backpack and thank her again. When we're outside, he puts his arm around me, spins me to face him.

"That was awesome, Rhea," he goes. "Awesome! What a team! With your sad Irish charm and my quick wit, we don't need a private eye."

He is too close, his face inches away from my face. I can smell the drink from last night. The light is bright, reflecting off the glass of one of the buildings, and I don't know if that's making me dizzy or if it was the way he spun me around or both. I take his hand off my shoulder, make a space between us. "Come on, let's not talk right outside, she's probably watching us."

He pulls the piece of paper from his pocket. "830 Park Avenue, Apartment 78A. That's the Upper East Side, Rhea! Park Avenue! You're rich, Irish bullhead!"

I need to breathe, find my voice. "Serg—"

"Let's walk over there now, check it out."

"Serg, it's all the way on the other side of the park. It's going to take us an hour to get there, more."

"Okay, so come on, let's go!" He's walking backwards, facing me, his arms outstretched. "The longer we hang around here, the longer it'll take."

My feet won't move. I want to get away from this building, from the girl and her computer, but it's like the day they wouldn't move to take me inside the gate—now they won't move to let me out.

50

"We don't have time," I go. "You've to meet Michael at six? Remember?"

Sergei frowns. "So, I'll be late. He'll wait."

I raise my eyebrows. "Serg, you told me he had somewhere specific he wanted to take you. He's already pissed off after last night."

He makes a face, blows his curls from his forehead. "So what?"

"So, Michael's is the only security we have right now. Don't blow it, Serg, please."

He kicks his runner out to swipe the edge of the grass border, his face a frown. I'm pretending this conversation is about Michael, but it's not, it's about something else. I just don't know what yet.

"Okay, then." Sergei sighs, folds his arms. "I'll be a good little boy and be on time for Michael. So we can sleep at the apartment tonight and go there tomorrow. Early, though, okay? I don't want to hang out for hours watching dumb American TV."

"Okay."

I smile, relief floods in. He gives me a high five and I high five him back. We'd started doing it the week we met, taking the piss out of some people we saw at the Y doing it for real, but now I think we both like it.

We take the subway back together. It's too crowded to talk, and I'm glad we don't have to. My stop is before his, 42nd Street.

"You going for pizza to the usual spot?" Serg goes.

I shake my head. "I'm going to change it up tonight. I'm going to Grand Central."

"See you back at Michael's, come over early. We won't be late tonight."

That's the last thing he says before the doors close and I wave at him through the glass even though he's already turned away. I let myself be carried by the flood of people over to the S line. I like the S, because it only has two stops and because there's always a train there and because it only takes a minute.

When I get to Grand Central, there are signs to the 4, 5, and 6

51

trains, the green ones that go up the east side of the park. I could take one of those trains—I'm in the station already, I wouldn't need another token. I'd get out at 68th or maybe 77th and I could walk over to Park Avenue and walk right up to number 830, the building where you used to live.

And after all this time, after all this waiting, I don't know why I don't. Except I want to stay here in the station and sit down, and eat a black and white cookie, one of the big ones, even though the prices are a rip-off, even though it won't fill me up like the pizza would. And after all this waiting, what does waiting another day matter anyway? I don't think it matters at all.

Rhea

Dear Mum,

These are the things I like about being in Grand Central Station:

1. You never have to queue too long for the toilet because there are loads of them.

2. It doesn't feel weird to have a backpack with me because everyone has backpacks and bags with them.

3. You can sleep and no one will bother you.

4. The ceiling.

5. The tables with the pretend tickets and maps on them.

The thing I don't like about Grand Central is that the only real place to sit—the place where the cool tables with the pretend tickets and maps are—is in the food court, so you have to deal with all the smells of Chinese food and chips and walk past loads of glass counters with cookies and shiny cakes and giant sandwiches, and they're all too expensive to buy.

I'm starving tonight. I'm craving everything, all of it, only it's my own fault for spending my dinner money on the stupid black and white cookie that didn't fill me up, just like I knew it wouldn't. I'm not spending any more money tonight. The guy and girl next to me are eating this giant piece of cheesecake and I'm watching them, each time they dig their forks in. I'm watching them chew and swallow, even though I don't even like cheesecake.

These are the names on the fake tickets on the table I'm sitting at:

1. South Norwalk

2. Harrison

3. Chappaqua

4. Hartsdale

5. Mount Vernon

The maps are of the Hudson Line and the Harlem Line. I want to go on both. I want to buy a ticket and get on a train and sit in a seat by the window and watch everything passing by outside until we leave the lights of New York behind and all I'll be able to see in the glass is the reflection of my face in the dark.

They didn't finish the cheesecake. They left a lot of it behind on the paper plate and if they hadn't thrown it in the bin, I might have finished it. I might have cut the parts off that their forks had touched and eaten the rest. I hope you don't think that's gross, Mum. I mean, they looked clean, and it's not any different really from eating from the plate of someone you know, is it? I don't think it is.

Laurie caught me one time, eating off one of the plates I'd just bussed at Cooper's restaurant and she was grossed out. You'd swear I'd been eating off the floor or something. It was only a mozzarella stick. It wasn't like they'd taken a bite out of it or anything.

I'm thinking a lot about Laurie tonight. I'm trying not to, but I can't help it. I'm wearing my baseball cap, the one that used to be hers, the Boston Red Sox one. The one I used to wear was a navy one with a white NY, a New York Yankees one, but Cooper took that away the night I sat down to dinner with it on. I'd got my head shaved that day, only the underneath part, so at school it looked like I had long hair but when I put my hair up under the cap, it looked like my head was shaved. Aunt Ruth didn't like it either, but she was ignoring it, pretending she hadn't noticed. When Cooper made me give him my cap, I thought she'd say something, but she didn't, she just kept on eating her salad. He said it was because it wasn't right to wear a hat at the dinner table but we all knew that wasn't the reason. Later when Laurie knocked on my bedroom door and handed me her Boston Red Sox one, she said she thought that Cooper was a control freak and that he'd had no right to tell me how to look or dress or anything else.

If I'm going to write to you about Laurie, then I need to write about the times she was nasty, the times she was horrible, not when she was nice. And I need to keep it in order. That was probably six months or so after I got there, the cap thing, but loads had already happened by then. Like the soccer tryouts. I haven't told you about the soccer tryouts.

Laurie makes it pretty obvious that she didn't want me on the team, even to try out. She ignores me in the changing room, gets dressed and out of there as soon as she can. I don't care. I'm only doing it to get Aunt Ruth off my back. I think my shite play will be enough to keep me off the team, but I didn't count on the whole team being shite.

The heat is a killer and I think my lungs are going to explode every time I chase the ball, but I keep chasing, keep tackling. At home, the boys on the road called anyone who couldn't tackle a chicken—just like you were a chicken if you couldn't do a wheelie or climb up the O'Neills' wall and jump from the end of it onto the roof of the McEvoys' shed. So what if you fell? Bruises, stitches, even the time I fractured my collarbone, all of that was better than being chicken.

So I tackle everyone that day, even the tall, fast ones with bouncing ponytails—especially them. I can't keep up with them, but I stand in their way. I kick for the ball and I don't care if I kick their legs, if we get tangled up together and we both fall. After Jane Friedman goes off with her knee bleeding, the coach calls me aside and says I need to tone it down, that sliding tackles aren't allowed. I tell her I don't know what a sliding tackle is, that I'm only playing the way I used to play back home. She hides her smile. She likes me, I can tell, and I know I'm going to make the team.

Afterwards, me and Laurie are the last ones waiting in the car park because Cooper's late.

"Dad, where are you?" she says for the billionth time. "God, I can't wait to get my driver's licence."

"We could walk," I say. "It's not that far."

"Walk?" She makes a face. "You're kidding, right?"

She sits down on the kerb, stretches her legs out in front of her. After a minute, I sit down next to her.

"Who are this team we're playing on Saturday?" I go. "Do we have a good chance?"

She pulls a strand of her hair into her mouth, sucks it. "You're not seriously going to play on the team, are you?"

At first I think she's joking, but there is no laugh, no smile. Before, I wasn't sure if I wanted to play. Now I am.

"Why wouldn't I play?"

She turns away to face the gate, rests her chin on her arms.

"Um, maybe because you can't run three feet without almost having a heart attack."

It makes it worse somehow, that all I can see is the back of her head when she says that, and it takes me a second to reply.

"It's fucking hot, Laurie! It takes a while to get used to the heat—"

She whips her head back around. She looks angry, she is angry.

"Does it take a while to get used to the altitude too? Is that why you kept falling over?"

"Just because I wasn't afraid to make tackles—"

"You call those tackles? You spent more time on the ground than on your feet! You've no technique, you—"

I pull my legs in to my chest, wrap my arm around my knees. "Technique? Like you'd know technique if it hit you in the face! I saw you out there—you're not exactly Ray Houghton yourself."

I know she doesn't know who Ray Houghton is and that she won't ask. She taps one runner off the other.

"You know Coach only put you on the team because she feels sorry for you?"

56

She's looking right at me to see my reaction. My insides react before my outsides. I feel something boiling, gushing up. I want to grab a fist of her hair, I want to smash her head against the concrete, over and over until there is blood. I shouldn't say that, I know I shouldn't think it, never mind write it down, but that's how I'm feeling when I see Cooper's car nosing through the gate.

She stands up, smiles at me.

I grab my bag. I can't pretend I didn't hear her, I can't say nothing. My heart is pounding and I hope she can't hear the echo of it in my voice.

"Why do you hate me so much, Laurie? What have I ever done to you?"

Cooper pulls up in front of us. Laurie's still smiling.

"I don't hate you, Rae—or Rhea or whatever you're calling yourself today. If you want to know the truth, I don't really think anything about you. I don't have an opinion at all."

She gets into the front seat, next to Cooper. He's too preoccupied with some late delivery at the restaurant to notice that we're fighting or that my cheeks are flaming red. But later, when Aunt Ruth comes in to tell me my music is too loud, I think she knows.

"Rae, can you lower that? We can't hear the TV."

I turn it down.

"Don't you have any other music? You must have played that song ten times in a row."

It's 4 Non Blondes' "What's Up." I've played it eight times.

"Sorry," I go.

She's nearly out of the room when she turns back. "Is everything okay?"

There's a second, a split second, where I could have told her. I think about telling her, but tell her what? Anyway, she doesn't want to know, not really. She wants to get back to watching her show.

"Everything's fine."

After that, I put on my headphones and play the song nine more times, seventeen altogether. But even after playing it over and over and over, I still can't figure it out: why Laurie having no opinion of me is worse than her hating me. Why her not even thinking about me is the worst, the absolute worst thing of all.

Your daughter,
Rhea

830 Park Avenue, New York
28th April 1999
9:12 a.m.

Dear Mum,

I got excited writing the address at the top of the letter because you'd have written letters with that address at the top too! Not that I'm inside, I'm at the corner writing this, sitting on a little railing, but I still have a great view of the entrance and of everyone coming up and down the road, so I can see Sergei when he comes. Although I don't know why I think he's going to come, since he never showed up at Michael's last night.

Your entrance is the nicest one on the block, I think it is, with the awning set back so much further than all the other awnings and the little trees in pots lined up at either side. I walked up as close to the door as I could, but there were two doormen on the other side of the glass and I turned back again as soon as I saw them. One of them has come out four times, to get taxis for people, and he has a fancy uniform with gold buttons. Seven other people have left the building, apart from the taxi people, but three of them had dogs with them and they went back in again.

I still can't believe Michael wouldn't let me in last night. I knew they were home, because the light was on, but no one answered until I held down the buzzer with my thumb for ages. When Michael finally picked up, he sounded like some whimpering kid, telling me to leave him alone and that Sergei wasn't there. He wouldn't pick up again, wouldn't tell me where Sergei was. It was raining and I got soaked through, sitting on that step across the road. He's an asshole, Michael. I'm still wet and my throat feels like I swallowed razor blades. Maybe Sergei was right, maybe we should have taken his money.

Twenty minutes ago, this old lady on a cane comes out of your building with the doorman and I imagine it's Nana Davis, let myself believe it's her. I only ever met her once, the time she came over with

Aunt Ruth and had the fight with Dad because he ruined the teddy bear she brought me by accidentally burning a hole in it with his cigarette. I can't remember what she looked like, all I can remember is the black charred circle in the teddy's ear and the smell of burning fur. This woman could be her, I'm able to pretend it's her until the doorman hails her a cab and says "Have a good day, Mrs. Silverman" as she gets into it. Then I can't pretend anymore.

Aunt Ruth has no photos of Nana Davis in her house, or of you, or of Granddad Davis. Is that weird? I think it's weird, especially with all those photos of Laurie, but maybe it's only because Cooper's the snap-happy one. She never talked about Nana Davis either, except when I asked her, and even then she hardly said anything, only that she was in a nursing home. That might have been a lie, about the nursing home. People tell lies more than they tell the truth. That's one of the things I've learned in my seventeen years and 351 days on this planet. If you were to ask me what it means to grow up, I'd say it was learning to spot the lies.

This is a list of things that people do when they are lying:

1. They buy themselves time before they answer the question you asked them.

2. They say too much or they say too little.

3. They laugh at things that aren't funny.

4. They don't look you in the eyes.

5. They change the subject really quickly to something else.

I don't know if this list should be longer, there might be other things, but these are the things I know so far. I also know that lies can be things you don't say, things that you leave out on purpose to make the person think something different. That's the way Aunt Ruth usually lies, but she tells real lies too, like the time she told me about your favourite ice cream flavour.

We're in Jaxson's after one of my prosthetic fittings. That's Aunt

Ruth's way of pretending me getting fitted for a prosthetic is fun, by letting me choose where we go for lunch afterwards. It drives her crazy that I always pick Jaxson's instead of some fancy restaurant along Las Olas. Every time she asks me, "Where would you like to go for lunch, Rae?" all smiley, I smile too and say "Jaxson's!" and she tries not to let her smile go wonky. I pick Jaxson's because I love the ice cream sundaes and the monkey outside and the piano that plays itself. I also pick it because she hates it.

This day isn't the first fitting but it's not the last either because I don't have the stupid hulk of plastic strapped to me yet. I order a cheeseburger and fries and a hot fudge sundae and a Coke just like I always do. Aunt Ruth always orders the Cobb salad and this day, just as the waitress walks away, Aunt Ruth calls her back and orders a waffle for after, with peanut butter ice cream and whipped cream.

"You never order dessert," I go.

She shrugs. "Sometimes I do."

"I don't think I've ever seen you eat peanut butter ice cream. I didn't think you knew peanut butter ice cream existed!"

She laughs, picks up a knife, cleans it with her napkin. "It used to be my favourite. Every summer on vacation, we used to go to this old-fashioned ice cream parlour called the Candy Kitchen. I'd always get peanut butter."

"Where?"

She puts her knife down, straightens it.

"Long Island."

The waitress brings my Coke and Aunt Ruth's seltzer with lime. I hold the straw in my hand and pull the paper off with my mouth, the way I always do.

"Where in Long Island?"

Aunt Ruth takes a second too long to answer. "Bridgehampton."

"Did you always go to the same place?"

She takes a sip of seltzer, squeezes the lime into it. "Yes, we stayed in a house there."

"Was it your mum and dad's?"

"No. We stayed with Daddy's boss and his wife. It was their house."

She stirs her seltzer with her straw, is about to say something else, but I talk next.

"Was that Cal Owens?"

She can't keep the shock out of her voice. "Who told you that?"

I think of the man with the smile in the wheelchair and I think about lying, but I don't. "My mum had a newspaper article about him and your dad in her things."

The waitress is at the table again. She places the burger down in front of me with a red basket of fries. Aunt Ruth's Cobb salad is giant.

"I'm looking forward to this," she says.

I've never heard her say she's looking forward to it, and it's something about her saying it that makes me ask what I ask next.

"Did they have kids?"

She's putting the dressing on the salad. She doesn't look up but her hand pauses.

"Who?"

"Cal Owens and his wife?"

She laughs, dumps on the rest of the dressing. She never uses all the dressing. "No. They didn't. This salad looks really great today."

"Did you like going on holidays with them?"

She puts down her knife, fixes her fringe. She smiles. "Yes, of course. Daddy always said Uncle Cal and Aunt Annabel were more like family than his boss and his wife. They lived in the apartment upstairs from us. The penthouse."

I don't know why she's lying, Mum, but I know she is. And then I ask something else, a question that needs a sudden and immediate answer.

"What ice cream did my mum get? In the ice cream parlour—what was her favourite?"

"Her favourite?"

She scrunches up her face like she's trying to remember, looking up at the glass lightshade as if it's written there. I hold my burger but I don't bite it yet. She looks back down into her salad, cuts it with a knife and fork.

"Strawberry," she says to the salad.

Strawberry is my favourite flavour, on its own I mean, not in a sundae. If I'm going to have a scoop of ice cream on a cone or in a cup, I'll always pick strawberry. Aunt Ruth knows it's my favourite, has started to stock the freezer with low-fat strawberry frozen yoghurt to stop me buying the proper ice cream at the mall. I want strawberry to be your favourite too, I really do, but I don't want it to be a lie.

So I decide to tell my own lie, just to check.

"That's funny. Dad always said chocolate was her favourite. He used to tell me that she always went for that, that she'd never get anything else."

She blinks, smiles, blinks again.

"You know what? Now that you mention it, I think he might have been right. I think she went through a phase of strawberry, but, yes, chocolate, chocolate was her thing. She always loved chocolate."

I take a bite of my burger. I chew it slowly. She cuts up her salad and starts to talk about the barbecue her work is planning and how she's hoping that Cooper can leave the restaurant early to be there and that Laurie and I don't have a soccer game.

I know she's lying about the ice cream, Mum, just like she was lying before. I know that she can't remember or she never knew or that maybe you never had a favourite flavour, but it's easier to say "strawberry" or "chocolate" than tell me any of those things because it's not like I'll ever know, will I? She probably thinks it's only a small thing, that it's only a white lie, that it doesn't matter.

She might think that, but it does matter.

It fucking well matters to me.

Writing all that down about Aunt Ruth makes me think about Sergei. He lied to me too, about how he'd be there last night, how he'd come with me this morning. He's just like Aunt Ruth with her lies. Why do people keep lying to me, Mum? Why do they think they can do that?

And what is wrong with me, that I keep on believing them?

Rhea

Dear Mum,

The truth is I lie too. The truth is I lied first. I should have told you that. I should have told you before but, fuck it, I'm telling you now. Does that change things? If you lie to someone is it okay for them to lie back? Does everything become lies then? If I hadn't started it by telling that lie, would things have been different? Would Aunt Ruth have told the truth all along?

I've been on this corner all day. All fucking day. I had to go all the way into Central Park to find a loo because there's nowhere around here and I'm starving because there's no pizza places or McDonald's or anything either. Where the fuck is Sergei? Fuck him. I know I could have missed him when I went to pee, but I was really quick, I didn't hang around to look for the bench with your name on it or anything, the one Dad said was there, unless he was lying too. I didn't tell Sergei about the bench. I haven't told him because I haven't been able to find it yet—but it's fun looking—and maybe because that's something I want to do on my own.

The lie I tell Aunt Ruth is the time she visits right after the accident. It's only a few months since her summer visit—usually I'm a different age every time she comes, but this time I'm still seven. No one tells me she's coming, or maybe they do and I forget because I'm in hospital and sleeping all the time. In the middle of one sleep, I open my eyes and she's there. I think it's a dream and I fall back asleep, but then I'm awake again and she's still there, next to the bed. I don't know how many times I fall asleep and wake up again until I'm awake enough to stay awake. I know it's her but because of all the drugs and everything, I make a mistake and I say, "Mum?"

I don't know if that's what makes her cry, or if she was crying already, but she sniffs to make herself stop and picks up a paper bag off the floor. There are furry ears sticking out, grey and white, and I know it's a bunny rabbit even before she lifts it out so I can see its face and its body and its white fluffy tail. I reach out to feel its fur before the machines and tubes yank me back and she turns away to look out the window, but really I know she's crying again.

Time is funny in the hospital. Sometimes when I wake up, Dad is there instead of Aunt Ruth, but it's mostly her and they're never there together. I don't know how long anyone stays or what day it is. After a few days, I'm allowed up and I walk down the corridor to the TV room. Two days after that, I'm allowed to go home. At first, I think it must be Sunday, because it's the afternoon and Dad is off work, but it turns out it's Wednesday, and that I've been in hospital for over two weeks and that the shop has been closed since the day of the accident.

Aunt Ruth stays with us, in Nana Farrell's old room, instead of a hotel the way I always wanted her to, only it's not like the time she came in the summer. In front of me, her and Dad smile at each other and say nice things, but whenever they think I'm asleep they're always fighting.

I know the shop is still closed because they argue about it, and I don't know where Dad goes during the day, but she's the one who's there. She's the one who cuts a line down my pyjama sleeve so it folds in two flaps and I can get it on over the bandage. She's the one reading me stories, holding my bandage outside the bath so it doesn't get wet. She's the one who practises cleaning her teeth with me, both of us using our left hands, turning it into a game. I don't remember my stump hurting but it must have been hurting because I remember her in my room at night with a facecloth, wiping my head.

It's not like Dad wasn't there at all, he's nearly always there at dinner time, but he hardly says anything. At the end, he stands up and brings his plate to the counter before kissing my hair and saying "I'll leave you two to it" and going out the back door. One night, he comes home from the Drop Inn early and he sees me drawing with my left hand, holding the page with my stump the way Aunt Ruth showed me, and he puts his head into the inside of his elbow and leaves again. That's the night she follows him out and they argue in the garden, but low, because they think I won't hear.

I want her to stay, that's what makes me tell the lie. I want her to stay and even though she stays for ages and ages, even after I go back to school, I know she won't be able to stay forever. She's on the phone more, nearly every night, whispering in the hall, waiting until she thinks I'm sleeping or watching telly and not listening, but I'm always listening.

That night, I'm going to the loo when I hear her.

"I know," she says. "It's been a month and a half. I've used up all my time. Steve put it to me straight—either get back or I'll have no job to get back to."

I make myself breathe the way a feather would breathe.

"She seems much better. They're so resilient, it's amazing. She's back in school already."

I peek over the banister. I can see the top of her hair. There's a row of silver in the brown I don't remember from before.

"He's not great." She pauses and looks out through the porch glass, as if she's checking to see if Dad is coming home, even though it's dark so you can only see black. "I've persuaded him to open the shop again, but he won't talk about what happened. I've tried, but he gets so defensive, runs out to the pub. The only thing he'll say is that he's sure the safety guard was on, that he always leaves it on."

I close my eyes.

"I know, that's what I keep asking myself too: how does a seven-year-old get a safety guard off a meat grinder?"

I make my steps tiny, squinchy little baby steps that take me back to my room. In bed, I remember I still need the toilet but I'm afraid to go out again. I can hear her voice but not the words anymore. The phone gives a little ring when she hangs up.

When I start to cry, I'm crying for real, not faking, only maybe making it a bit louder so I know she'll definitely hear. The floorboard on the landing squeaks and the door opens and she's there.

"Rhea, honey, what's the matter?"

She sits on the bed and I move my legs over.

"Was it another nightmare?"

I nod. Her fingers are cool on my forehead.

"It's okay, honey, those dreams aren't real. They're scary but they're not real."

She pulls a tissue from her sleeve and holds it for me. I blow my nose into it.

"Are you hungry?" she goes. "Would you like a treat?"

I'm not, but I say I am, because she buys fancy biscuits to make me feel better and she wants to give me a treat. When she comes back, she has a tray with a glass of lemonade and a plate with Viscounts and Jaffa Cakes. I take a Viscount but before I can unwrap the foil, I start to cry again.

"Honey," she goes, "what's wrong?"

The crying is worse than before—breath and snotty tears all caught up together. She puts her arms around me and I smell her perfume, and that makes me cry harder.

"Ssssh, it's okay. It's okay, baby." Her hands rub ovals on my back. I don't think she's ever done this before but it's like I remember her doing it, I remember someone doing it.

"What is it?" she goes. "You can tell me."

I cry. I hiccup. I cry more. She thinks I can tell her, but I can't. Not because I don't want to, but because it's all tangled up in my head and I don't know where the beginning is to start to unravel it. It might have been Dad not letting us write the letters or it might have been when he stopped listening to Hendrix or going on our Sunday walks. It might have been after her visit last summer. It's all knotted together, along with the safety guard on the meat mincer and the way I go to sleep every night pretending that I'm sleeping in her apartment in New York and not in my bed in Rush. I want to ask her to take me to America with her, or to stay in Nana Farrell's room forever, only I can't ask her because she might say no, and that'd be worse than never asking at all.

"Sorry," I go, when I stop crying enough to speak.

"Honey." She brushes my hair back from my face. "You've nothing to be sorry for. What are you sorry for?"

I can barely hear my own voice. "I didn't mean to make you and Daddy sad."

"Baby, Rhea." She holds me a little away from her so I can see her properly. "You didn't do anything wrong. What happened—it wasn't your fault. You know that? You shouldn't have been there on your own."

I shake my head. "Lisa was with me."

"But your Dad, Rhea, an adult—"

"Daddy was in the big fridge. The delivery came, it was only a few minutes—"

"Even for one minute, honey, you shouldn't have been alone." She looks close into my face. Her eyes are brown like yours in the pictures. "Can I ask you something, honey? The machine—can you remember if the safety guard was on? Had your daddy put it on the machine?"

There are webs of red across the white bits of her eyes. I don't want her to be annoyed with me, to hate me. I want her to stay. And that's when I think of the lie.

"No."

She's too quiet and I know I need to say something else to make her believe me.

"Before the delivery, Daddy was making Mrs. Sinnott's order. I wanted to help him and show Lisa that I knew how to do it."

That part is true, but I don't tell her the rest—how Dad put the safety guard on and I tell Lisa I know how to take it off, and that if I do the order right he's going to let me work in the shop every Saturday.

"You're sure, Rhea? You're sure the safety guard wasn't on?"

Aunt Ruth is holding my shoulders then, her fingers gripping me hard.

I nod. The lie comes out like normal words. "I'm sure."

We eat the biscuits between us and even though I don't want them, I keep eating anyway. There are crumbs on the blanket, six little balls of rolled-up tinfoil on the tray. Aunt Ruth looks like she's far away and, in my head, I can hear Lisa's voice over and over, so loud I think she might be able to hear it too. *Rhea, don't. Rhea, leave it. Rhea, stop.*

Later, I hear them fighting, Aunt Ruth and Dad. They're shouting in the hall until someone remembers me and they go into the sitting room. I can still hear bits of the fight through the door but I don't get up and listen. Instead I go to sleep, because I think the lie is working and that they're fighting because she wants to take me with her. And I think she's going to win.

The lie doesn't work, Mum. Maybe lies never work. She goes anyway. She goes the next weekend and, by then, it's way too late to take the lie back. And she never asks me again—ever—and Dad never does either. And now he's dead and I'll probably never see her again, so I wanted to tell you the truth. I wanted to tell someone.

Aunt Ruth cries at the airport when she's going, but I don't. It doesn't make sense, her saying it breaks her heart to leave me, because she's the one who's going, she's the one who won't stay. None of it makes sense and even as she kisses me and hugs me hard and says she'll phone all the time and come and visit, I'm deciding that I don't care and that she's never going to see me cry again.

She doesn't come that summer, because of work, and then at Christmas she has to cancel her flight because Nana Davis is sick and she sends me a letter with American money to pay for tickets for us to come to see her, but Dad says we can't go because Christmas is too busy in the shop. He says we'll go another time, but we never do and I don't know what happens to the money. The next time I see her is when she comes for my birthday, when I'm nine, and she brings me three books that are way too babyish and a Barbie, but I've never liked Barbies.

After that, she comes over three more times, between the birthday when I'm nine and when Dad dies. Three times in seven years and one of them is when she's on her way to London for work and she only stays for the weekend. The phone calls go from every week, to every month, to Christmas and birthdays to check her presents have arrived. By then, her presents are American money, and even though I like the green twenty-dollar bills, like something from the telly, it's a pain to get Dad to go to the bank to change them, and half the time he forgets.

I wish I had those twenty-dollar bills now.

I don't know what the connection is between my lie about the machine and the lies she told after that. Maybe there's no connection, maybe it's just a coincidence, maybe everyone lies. Maybe growing up isn't learning to spot the lies, maybe growing up is not expecting people to tell the truth.

I always knew Cooper was a liar, you could tell by his smarmy smile and his hair, but it turned out Laurie was a bigger liar than him—a better liar than him—because she'd hide the lie in part of the truth so it made it harder to spot.

But even though they were bad, Aunt Ruth was still the worst. I never heard a bigger lie than the one she told me the night I left. That was horrible, what she said about you that night. That was the absolute worst lie of all.

Don't worry though, Mum, it's not as if I believed her. I didn't believe her then and sitting here, outside the apartment where you lived, I don't believe her now.

I've never believed what she said, not even for one second.

Your loving daughter,
Rhea

Dear Mum,

There's something I have to tell you. I can't keep writing all about truth and lies without telling you something. Something big. It's not like I've been lying to you, everything I've told you is true. But like I said, lies can be the things you don't say and there's something I haven't said to you: I'm gay.

I just thought of something that made me laugh. You know that song "50 Ways to Leave Your Lover"? It was on one of Dad's records, a Paul Simon one he didn't listen to much but I always liked it. I'm making up a new song to the same tune: "Fifty Ways to Come Out to Your Mother." It goes like this:

> *Send her a letter, Esther,*
> *Give her a bell, Danielle,*
> *Drop her an email, Gayle,*
> *And set yourself free.*

4:05 a.m.

I'm not in Penn Station anymore, Mum, I'm here now, at Michael's! Can you believe it? I wasn't even thinking about Sergei when he came over. I was trying to make up the next line of that song and I only half register that someone else has come into the café and it takes me a few seconds to see that the person is Sergei and that he's crying. I've never seen him cry before, not like this, and before I decide I'm going to, I'm standing up and we're hugging each other, really tight. He has a cut down the side of his face and he jerks away when I go to touch it, so I don't ask what happened, just like I don't ask where he got the money from when he takes out a fifty to pay for the cab to Michael's.

The whole drive over, I'm afraid that Michael's not going to answer the buzzer, just like he didn't last night, but when we get here Sergei pulls out his keys and unlocks the door. It turns out that Sergei saw Michael earlier and they'd made up, and now Michael's upstate for the weekend but he said we could stay, like before.

Sergei explains it all quickly but he won't look at me, and I know that's because Michael must have been the one to give him the cut on his face, even though I can't imagine Michael doing something like that. Sergei's asleep now, snoring, and even though I was so tired that I couldn't stay awake in Penn Station, now that I have a place to sleep, I'm wide awake and I can't stop my mind thinking and thinking and thinking, so I want to finish this letter.

Tell her out straight, Kate.

Maybe, if I write it again it will help...
I'm gay, Mum.
Mum, I'm gay.
What would you say now, if you could talk back? If you weren't dead, I mean. Sometimes, when I was younger, I used to pretend that you weren't dead. There was no body, no proof. And no one ever drowned in Rush. Everyone said you were a really good swimmer and that the sea was as flat as a pancake that day. It didn't make any sense. Sometimes, I'd imagine that you swam away, up the coast as far as Drogheda or across the channel, even. Maybe you'd lost your memory and thought you were someone else? Or maybe you were still out there, still swimming? And one day you'd get tired, you wouldn't be able to swim anymore, and you'd wash up on the beach, your body would, or just a sandy shape of you like the swirls of sand the lugworms leave behind.

Since I'm making all this up, I'm going to make up that you're someone who would hug me straightaway and tell me that it's okay and that you still love me. You don't try and talk me out of it, you don't say it's a phase. You don't tell me that I'm disgusting, a pervert.

Shit. I'm sorry. I don't know how Cooper's words ended up in your mouth, Mum. You are nothing like Cooper, I know you're not. I don't know much, but I know that.

Even now, it's hard to write about this. Even after everything that has happened, I want to put the word "think" in there, to give myself a safety net, because thinking you're gay has got to be better than being gay, right? Anything's better than being absolutely sure.

I don't know if this is making sense, but the thing is when you want to be something else—someone else—so badly, it's easy to convince yourself that you are. It's easy to hide—not like my arm, I could never hide that—but this gay stuff, you can hide even from yourself, you know? Like you only see a sneak peek of it from the side of your eye and when you try and look at it head-on, it's gone into hiding again.

I need a list, Mum, a list will help this make sense. Here are reasons that made me worry that I was gay:

1. When Dad bought the *Sunday World* I used to like looking at the pictures of the girls with no tops on and tassels on their boobs.

2. In second year, I got an art book that had loads of pictures in it. Some of the pictures were of women in the nude, paintings I mean. I could tell you every page number those paintings were on.

3. Once, I had a dream that I was kissing Dr. Lewis from *ER* and I tried to make myself have the dream loads of times after that but it didn't work.

There was other evidence too, but it was what they'd call circumstantial evidence if it was an episode of *Law & Order*—I never liked dresses or high heels or makeup, but lots of girls were tomboys so maybe that didn't mean anything. One time in Billie's, when I was looking at the penny sweets, I heard Mrs. Mulcahy saying to Mrs. O'Loughlin that wasn't it terrible that I looked more like a little boy than a little girl, and Mrs. O'Loughlin said that with no mother and Dermot Farrell for a father, sure, it wasn't surprising. I walked out without buying anything that day, even though they'd just got a new batch of white chocolate fish and chips.

This is a list of reasons that made me think I wasn't gay:

1. I got off with loads of boys, nearly all the ones my age, in the estate. "Getting off with" is what you'd call "making out." Kissing. They were crap at it, most of them were, with tongues like washing machines or teeth that would take the mouth off you. I preferred playing football with them to getting off with them, but I did it anyway.

2. Here are the boys I got off with: Shane Kenny, Simon Gaffney, Richard O'Toole, Tony Donoghue, Alan Roche, Dominic Kelly, the McManus twins, and Tony Duggan. That's way more boys than loads of girls got off with. Lisa only got off with John O'Sullivan, Raymond Roche, Pat Cronin, and Dominic Kelly (after me).

3. I went out with Alan Roche for two weeks at the beginning of second year and Alan McManus for a month in the summer between second and third year and when we were getting off with each other in the tunnel down near the harbour I let him feel me up and I didn't mind it.

4. Once, when me and Lisa were watching *Police Academy*, there's this scene with girls all with their tops off, dancing around a campfire. I liked that scene but I didn't let on and Lisa was the one who rewound it so we could see it again, who paused it just at that part. I remember the look on her face as she did it, kind of mischievous and guilty at the same time. I remember the relief—I knew Lisa was normal, she wasn't a lezzer, which meant I mustn't be one either.

In primary school, it was the boys who called the girls lezzers and even though I didn't know what it meant, I knew it was bad. One time, Tony Donoghue said it about me and Lisa, and I chased him and gave him a dead leg, and he never said it again. In secondary school, the girls started saying it too but in a different way—speculating, investigating. One in ten people were. One in six, no, five. Did you think she was? Or what about her? Looking at someone the wrong way, standing too close, saying the wrong thing would get you labelled a lezzer. You had to be careful. So, there was no way you'd choose to be one. Especially when the evidence was fifty-fifty. But then, halfway through second year, Nicole Gleeson joined our school.

I'm nearly afraid to write about her, Mum, Nicole Gleeson, to bring all that up again, but I want to tell you the truth, and she's part of the truth. And I told Laurie before, so if I can tell her, I can tell you too.

Nicole's mum and dad had split up over Christmas. She was the only girl in the class who had parents who'd split up and I don't know how we all knew that about her from the start, but we did. We knew Nicole and her little brother and her mum had moved in with her granny, and that she had had to leave her posh school on the southside because it was too far away, although some people said it was because her dad wouldn't pay for it anymore. Some of the girls took the piss out of her accent but they were only jealous because you could tell straightaway that she was cool. Everything about her was cool—the silver ring she wore on a chain around her neck, her blonde highlights, the way she flicked her head to get her hair out of her face. It didn't take long for Nicole to find her place in Susan Mulligan's cool gang, but none of them did art, so she sat next to me. I usually sat next to Áine Geraghty, but she was in hospital then, getting her appendix out, and by the time she came back, me and Nicole sat next to each other every class. Wednesday mornings were the best part of the week, because we had double art. I hated Wednesday afternoons, double maths, and a whole other week to wait until double art again.

It might look obvious now, writing it down, but it wasn't then. Art was always my favourite class anyway and Nicole was just someone I thought was cool. A friend—only not really a friend because we were only friends in art, the rest of the time she hung around with her gang and I hung around with Lisa. But in art we talked about proper stuff. She told me about her mum and dad splitting up, about her little brother crying and wetting the bed every night, about how she hated Saturdays now, sitting in McDonald's with her dad, about how she missed her old friends. I don't remember telling her anything about me. I don't remember her ever asking.

It was when the summer came that I started to know—to know and not know. Every morning, when I woke up, she was there in my head, even if I was only getting up to go to the loo in the middle of the night, she was there. They lived over in Lusk, and whenever I needed anything from the shop, I'd go to the one over there instead of Billie's or even Leonard's. I was in that shop so much that the woman behind the counter asked me my name. At night, I'd get Lisa to go for a walk that took us in that direction, and it's on one of those walks that she tells me that Nicole's gone to Spain with her Dad for a month. She says it all casual, like it's any old thing she's saying, and even though we keep walking, I feel the breath all gone, like someone has kicked me in the stomach.

And that's when I start to know.

It's a Thursday evening, a few weeks after that, when Nicole shows up in the shop right before we're due to close. Dad's in the back. I hear the little jingle of the bell and, when I look up, she's there, with her face all tanned and her hair blonder than before. She buys a chicken and a pound of sausages and says she could have gone to a butcher nearer her granny's but she wanted to see me. She misses me, that's what she says, she misses our chats during art.

Dad says I can finish up early and we go and get Magnums that she pays for, and we sit on the wall by the harbour eating them. The stone is still hot from the sun. I ask her about Spain and she shrugs and says it was okay. She says she's going to a disco in town on Saturday in a hotel along the quays, and asks if I want to go. There's a square of chocolate from the Magnum stuck on her lip when she asks and when I say yes, she smiles and licks it away.

Lisa's not allowed to stay out past eleven but she stays in my house and pretends that we're watching a video. We're meeting Nicole at the bus stop and Lisa keeps going on about how it's a stupid place to meet because her mum could easily see her all dressed up, but I'm not really listening because I'm nervous too, because Nicole's late and I think she might have forgotten and gone with someone else. And then I see her in white jeans and a denim jacket, hurrying towards us.

I think that journey on the 33 into town is the happiest forty-five minutes of my whole life up to then. It's way better than art, sitting next to Nicole at the back of the bus, with her leg up against my leg and her hand on my arm every time she laughs at my jokes. Lisa's sitting opposite and she hardly says a word, but Nicole laughs at everything I say. When she tells me I should be a stand-up comedian, Lisa folds her arms and looks out the window.

Would it sound crazy, Mum, if I told you that one of the things I miss most about Ireland is the smell of the bus fumes? The bus fumes smell different over here. Irish bus fumes and Nicole's perfume all mixed together, that's the smell I miss—the smell of a secret dream starting to come through. A dream so secret, I didn't even know what it was.

Outside the disco, Nicole takes a naggin of vodka from her bag. Me and Lisa didn't really drink vodka but that night I drink it back fast, even though it's burny and horrible, and Lisa is looking at me funny. It feels right, the vodka, the summer evening. I can do anything now, I know I can. And inside when we meet some fifth years from school who are way cooler than me I don't care, because I'm with Nicole and I'm the one she missed. In the beginning, no one's dancing but then we're all dancing in a group, even Lisa's dancing, and it's fun, all of us laughing at the fellas standing along the sides like gobshites except for the ones who are really drunk and falling around. I'm in the toilet when the slow set starts, Sinead O'Connor, "Nothing Compares 2 U."

When I come out of the toilet, I see them straightaway—Nicole and Paul O'Riordan. I didn't even know he was there, hadn't seen him, but now I can't stop looking at him—the way he knows how to hold her, his hands on her hips. I know him from the shop, sometimes he picks up his mum's order on a Saturday: sausages, rashers, and a small housekeeper's cut. He's way older—he's just done the Leaving—but he's always friendly and that makes it worse somehow. It'd be better if it was some guy I didn't know, if he was from anywhere else in Dublin except Rush.

They're moving really slowly, kind of into each other, and he's not grabbing at her the way boys our age do, he's acting like he has all the time in the world. I can still picture them, as clearly as I can see Sergei sleeping next to me—the two of them, so close, the slow turns of the spots of light on the floor all around them, I can hear Sinead O'Connor counting out the days and the hours and the minutes. When he finally goes to kiss her, it takes forever. He touches her cheek and their kiss is in slow motion, gentle, like a kiss in a film, not anything like the fellas wearing the faces off the girls on either side of them.

In the toilets, there's a fat girl pretending to do her makeup and I know she won't say anything about seeing me crying. It's the drink that makes the tears come so fast, but even with the drink I hold most of it until I'm inside the cubicle. I don't know why I'm crying because if I feel anything, I feel angry, not sad. Not with Nicole, it's not her fault, I'm angry with myself. Because I don't know what I expected to happen. Because I don't know why I'm so sad. I'm angry because I don't want to know, because once I know, really know, then I can't unknow it.

It's not fair, Mum, you know? That's what I'm thinking that night in that cubicle. Sticks and stones can't hurt me, I know that I don't care what people say about my arm, what they say about you. But I don't want to be a lezzer. I can't be. Not a lezzer, not that as well.

Lisa's glad when I want to get the bus home early that night instead of waiting till the end, and when school starts again in September, I sit next to Áine Geraghty in art. Áine gives me the cold shoulder for a bit, but then she's fine and there's no seat next to me so Nicole sits beside Julie Kennedy. They're always laughing, her and Julie, and when Nicole looks over sometimes to catch my eye, I pretend not to see her. And after a while, it's as if nothing has happened. Because nothing did happen. I could make myself believe it. I could even make myself forget.

Until it happens again.

Rhea

Dear Mum,

Whenever Cooper had something to tell you, he'd always ask if you wanted the good news or the bad news first, he'd never just tell you what happened straight out. Laurie always wanted to know the bad news, but I'd always ask him for the good news first. Nine times out of ten, the bad news cancelled out the good news, so at least if you got the good news first, you could enjoy it, even just for a little while. This is my letter, so I get to decide what order to say things, and I'm deciding to tell you the good news first…

We found your mum! Nana Davis, we found her! I even spoke to her!

It's been such a long day and so much has happened, it's good to write that down, to know that it's real.

It starts at your apartment building. Sergei doesn't want me waiting on the corner with the bags and everything, says it'll look suspicious, so I have to go to the park while he talks to the doorman. He's wearing a shirt and tie of Michael's and a grey blazer over his jeans and even though it's a bit big for him, he looks good. Smart. He's even slicked his curls down a bit at the front. I told him how posh the building is and he's made an effort, he wants to make things up to me for the other day.

He's gone for ages and I wish I knew what was going on, that I'd been able to watch from across the street even, but he was right, with all those doorman buildings along the block, there was nowhere to watch from. I don't know why he insisted that we bring our bags anyway—he usually wants to leave them in Michael's—and I'm thinking that I must ask him about it but then I see him crossing at the lights. His hands are in his blazer pockets and his shoulders are hunched. He has bad news, I know it. I forget about the bags.

I wave at him, but he doesn't wave back and when he stops in front of me, he looks down at his shoes. One of his curls is sticking up.

"I'm sorry, Irish bullhead—"

"What happened?"

He shakes his head. "I'm really sorry."

"Serg? What happened? Tell me?"

His face is solemn when he looks up, but there's a twitch on the left side of his lip and there's something about his eyes that gives him away.

"Serg?"

His smile escapes, he can't hold it in any longer.

"Sergei? What the fuck? Tell me!"

He grabs my shoulders, starts jumping on the spot.

"I got it!"

His curls are coming loose, into his eyes, and he blows them away.

"Got what? Serg? What did you get?"

"Clover Hills Nursing Home. 67th Street. Between 1st and York."

Every bounce he makes drags me forward. I try and pull away, to stand still.

"Clover Hills Nursing Home?"

"That's where your grandmother is! We've found your grandmother, Irish bullhead!"

Aunt Ruth was telling the truth. That's my first thought, Mum, that she didn't lie to me.

"Oh my God. How did you find out? I mean, are you sure?"

He stops jumping but keeps grinning. "Oh, you know, Paul thought it was nice that her grand-nephew was coming to visit her, that she could probably use some visitors."

"Paul?"

Sergei picks up his bag from the bench. "Paul, the doorman. Nice guy. Keep up, Rhea!"

I'm still trying to digest what's happened but Sergei is already heading out of the park to find a payphone. He's got a plan figured out, he's explaining it to me too fast to make sense—how he's going to call Clover Hills, pretending to be from a funeral home with a bill for a Mr. Miller who died last week.

"What are you talking about, Serg? Who's Mr. Miller?"

He stops at the first payphone, checks that there's a dial tone.

"Do you have a quarter?"

"Serg, I don't get it. Who's Mr. Miller?"

"Hopefully no one. Do you have a quarter? Two, just in case."

I have sixty-five cents in change in my left pocket. I know exactly. I reach in and take out fifty cents, hand it to him. That's a toasted roll with butter I'm handing over for a phone call. A phone call that I still don't get why we're making.

"Why don't we just ask for Mrs. Davis? Catherine, her first name was Catherine."

I catch myself speaking about her in the past tense, as if she's dead, but she isn't dead, she's in a nursing home a few blocks away. He has the phone in his hand, about to put in the quarters.

"Maybe I'm wrong, Irish bullhead, but aren't there people related to this woman? People in Florida who might be looking for you?"

My face flushes. I can hear Laurie's voice: *Dumbass.*

"I guess."

"And you don't want to be found by these people?"

Sergei talks slowly, like he is explaining something to a five year old.

"No."

He slides in the quarters, starts to dial. "Then trust me."

His plan has two parts. It's a good plan, Mum. In the first part, he puts on an American accent that sounds oddly real. I'd never heard him sound American before. He says he's from a funeral home, Crosby and Golden. He has an invoice for the funeral of a Mr. Miller and he needs contact information for the Miller family. *There's no Mr. Miller?* Perhaps he has the name wrong, the handwriting is hard to read. He's only the administrative assistant. *Mullin maybe? Or Malone? Had anyone passed away recently with a name like that? A gentleman? Mr. Shapiro passed away last week? No, not Shapiro, definitely not. There must be some mistake.*

He gives me a thumbs-up when he says "Shapiro." When he hangs up the phone, his smile is wider than before. "Let's go find your Nana!"

On the way to the nursing home, he explains the second part of the plan. He's Mr. Shapiro's grandson who has just arrived from Poland, too late to pay his last respects but he very much wants to see his grandfather's final home.

"But what about my grandmother?" I ask when he stops talking long enough to let me speak. "How do we get to see her?"

He rubs his hands together. "That, Irish bullhead, is the best part. My dear old grandfather told me about his great friend, Mrs. Davis. Catherine. And my fiancée and I would really love to meet her!"

"Your fiancée?"

We look at each other for a second before we both burst out laughing at the idea of us being engaged, married. We're still laughing when we get to the corner of the block. He takes off my baseball cap, stuffs it in my backpack, brushes my fringe to the side, flattens down the collars of my jacket. He holds his head to one side, assesses me. "I wish your hair was longer."

"What's wrong, Serg? I'm not fiancée material?"

"Not for me, although if I ever do have a fiancé, I'd probably like him to have a shaved head."

We're both giggling again at the idea of that, or maybe because we're nervous, I'm not sure. I've been carrying his bag since the park and he takes it from my hand. "Let me take that. No groom would have his bride carry everything."

I'd forgotten about the bag. "I meant to ask you that. Why did you want to bring the bags today?"

He's slicking down his hair, pauses for just a second before he answers.

"We've just travelled from Poland to see my grandfather, Irish bullhead. Don't you think we'd have some luggage?"

I should have seen it then, Mum, the lie in the pause, but I'm excited, following Sergei through the revolving door into the lobby, feeling the soft carpet under my Docs. There's a dark wooden reception desk and wing chairs and lamps on little tables and a fish tank—it's more like a hotel than a nursing home. The only giveaway is that the heavy black woman behind the desk is dressed in white, some kind of nurses' uniform. Sergei winks at me, walks straight over.

"Hello there," he goes, "my name is Sergei Shapiro and I'd like to talk to someone about my grandfather. He was a resident here."

I notice he makes his accent thicker, he sounds more Polish, less likely to be confused with the man on the phone. But I don't think he needed to have worried because I don't think this nurse is who he spoke to on the phone. Whoever he spoke to on the phone seemed helpful, friendly. This nurse has a frown.

"You've come to see who?"

"Mr. Shapiro. I mean, not to see him, I know he passed on last week. I'm his grandson, Sergei. This is my fiancée, Natalie. Natalie Peterson."

I try and look like Natalie Peterson might look. I'm glad the counter is too high to shake hands. "Hello."

The nurse is standing, looking from Sergei to me. "And what was it you wanted?"

My heart is galloping. This isn't going to work. She isn't having any of it, she can see right through us, has probably pushed some button to call security even as we were speaking. If Sergei feels the same way, his voice doesn't betray him. It sounds casual, calm.

"Dziadzio wrote so much to me about this place. Didn't he, Natalie?"

I nod.

"And even though he's no longer with us, I was hoping we could see it—this place he spent his last days."

She's already shaking her head. "I'm sorry, Mr.—"

"Shapiro, like my grandfather. Back in Gdansk, where we're from, there's many of us Shapiros, but here—"

"Mr. Shapiro, I'm sorry for your loss, but this is a private facility and I can't just—"

Sergei moves closer to the counter, rests his elbow on it. "But Dziadzio always said we could visit him, anytime."

She's shaking her head, her frown deepening. "Our visitors policy applies to our residents who are living, Mr. Shapiro. Your grandfather is dead, so there's really nothing I can—"

It's right on the word "dead" that Sergei puts his hand over his face. His shoulders shudder. The nurse stops talking, so the only sounds in the lobby are his breathy sobs and the whirr of the fan.

I put my arm around his shoulder.

"I'm sorry, he's still very cut up," I go. "You see, we couldn't make the funeral."

Sergei's shoulders shake more.

I keep talking because if I don't keep talking we're going to have to leave. "We'd been planning this trip, saving up. We hoped we'd make it on time. When he passed away, we thought about cancelling, but Sergei wanted to come anyway, to say goodbye—"

Sergei's sobs are louder now, and I think he's overdoing it because the nurse's frown deepens more.

"I'm sorry, but I don't make the rules. I'm not even supposed to be on this desk, I'm only covering while the other person is on lunch. Usually we have two people, but—"

Sergei speaks in a strangled voice, interrupting her. "I just thought I could see his room, meet Nurse Small—"

"Meet who?"

"Nurse Small." Sergei still doesn't look up. "Dziadzio's favourite nurse. Do you know her?"

The nurse's hands are on her hips now. She points a pudgy finger at a black plastic badge with gold lettering: *F. Small.* "You're talking to her."

Sergei looks up, slowly. Somehow he looks like he's been crying too, only maybe his eyes are just bloodshot from last night. He looks from the nurse to me and back to her. "Natalie, this is Nurse Small. Remember all those things Dziadzio wrote about her?"

The nurse leans forward, so her huge breasts rest on the reception desk, her hands on either side.

"What things?"

Sergei spreads his fingers long on the counter top too, so they almost touch hers. "Your kindness, the way you took care of him so well."

There's something else in Nurse Small's face other than her frown—relief, maybe, or surprise. "He said that? He said I was kind?"

"He called you his gentle angel." Sergei beams and turns to me. "Didn't he, Natalie?"

I'm sure he's gone too far, blown it, laying it on so thick, but all I can do is smile too. "His gentle angel," I repeat.

"He said if it wasn't for you and Catherine, he wouldn't know how to keep going."

Nurse Small shakes her head. "I'm not sure what your granddaddy was telling you, but there's no nurse called Catherine here."

"Not a nurse, a patient. A resident. Catherine Davis."

She keeps shaking her head, her hands back on her hips. "He wrote all this? In his letters?"

She doesn't believe us. She has to believe us.

My hand is still on Sergei's shoulder and my fingers stroke the hair on his neck.

"Sergei only met his grandfather a few times, when he was a little boy, before he moved to New York. He wrote to him every week. Nothing would get in the way of him sending his weekly letters. They were the only connection they had." They're both looking at me. I'm shocked by how real the lie sounds. "We saved up for so long to come here—it broke his heart that we were too late. Please, Nurse Small, it would mean so much to him, to us."

Afterwards, Sergei tells me he's as shocked as I am when Nurse Small lifts the hinged part of the countertop to come over to our side.

"Two minutes, that's it. I'm not supposed to leave the desk unattended. And you won't be able to see his room because Mr. Stieber is in there now."

For a large woman, Nurse Small is fast on her feet. She pushes through a set of double doors to the left of the fish tank. After another set of doors, we're in a corridor with tiles instead of plush carpet and walls painted two shades of pink. It smells like a hospital and I don't know how they stop the smell leaking into the lobby. Most of the doors are open and even though we're whizzing by, I can see some of the people inside, in pink leather chairs or low beds nearly on the floor.

The televisions are really loud, competing with each other, but not loud enough to cover the sound of someone shouting. Here in this corridor is the truth—that this place is a nursing home, hidden behind a lie that it's a hotel.

At the end of the corridor, it gets nice again, or nicer at least, because there's floor to ceiling windows looking out onto a garden with a fountain in the middle. There's more of the comfy chairs like in the front, but some of the pink ones from the bedrooms too. A man in a wheelchair looks out through the glass, at the trees finding their way towards the sky in the little patch of green surrounded by buildings. Two women sit next to each other and I think they are having a conversation until I notice one is sleeping.

Nurse Small turns to Sergei. "This is the conservatory. Mr. Shapiro liked to spend time here."

Sergei looks around, taking it all in, and I suddenly realise that one of these old women, the one chatting or the one sleeping, could be Nana Davis. Would I recognise her? They both look kind of the same. And if it is her, what am I going to say to her? Sergei and I haven't talked about this part of the plan. How could we not have talked about this part of the plan?

"It's just like I pictured," Sergei says. "I could see him here with Catherine having their conversations."

"I don't know what he said in those letters, but the only time Mrs. Davis leaves her room is when we take her up and down the corridor to get some exercise," Nurse Small says.

"Catherine's sick?" Sergei goes.

"She's got severe dementia. Beats me how he was having any conversations with her. I've been here four years and I've never heard her say anything that makes any sense to anyone except herself."

"Is it possible to see her?" Sergei asks.

Nurse Small checks her watch. "Real quick, then I got to get back to work."

We're heading up another corridor, two shades of green now instead of pink. We're moving too quickly for my mind to digest what the nurse has just said. I need to stop, to stand still, but we're racing through more sets of double doors. It's as Sergei's holding one open for me that he whispers, "When we find her, say you need the bathroom." He walks ahead of me then and turns around, raises his eyebrows again to make sure I've got it.

Ahead, Nurse Small pushes open a door to the left and we follow her into a room that's surprisingly spacious. In the middle is a hospital bed, with rails down the side and a green bedspread. On the wall facing the bed there's a whiteboard, with the date and the weather written on it. Next to it, there's a printed sign with the name "Davis."

My eyes go back to the green bedspread, to the hands on top of it clutching at the covers. The woman in the bed is tiny. Her mouth is open and her eyes are closed. Her hair is long and wavy and white, spread out over the pillow.

"This is Mrs. Davis," Nurse Small says. "I've no idea how your grandfather even got to know her, or what they could have talked about. She's like this almost all the time now."

"She has dementia?" I go. She's already told us this, I know she has, but I want to make sure, I want to know Aunt Ruth was telling the truth.

"Alzheimer's. End stages. Although, physically, there's nothing wrong with her. No telling how long she'll stay like this."

Sergei keeps his voice low, respectful. "Dziadzio always said she was a good listener."

We stand there for a minute, all three of us. I'm trying to see something in her face, some of me, some of you from your photo, some of Aunt Ruth, but there is nothing recognisable there. Her thin white hair is like any old woman's white hair. Her face is more hollows and shadow than face. She is nothing to do with me, this old woman, this body. Nothing to do with you.

Nurse Small is turning to leave, and after all our efforts, all our work, this is it, this is all there is. I scan the room then for some other clue. The bedside locker is hospital furniture—no books, no photographs, only a green plastic jug of water and matching cup. There's a narrow wardrobe and on the wall next to it, there's a painting of a horse in a field looking towards a river. Nana Davis was an artist, she painted. I don't know how I know this, but suddenly I know it is true.

"Is that her painting?" I hear myself say. "Did she paint it?"

Nurse Small glances back to where I'm pointing at the wall. She shakes her head. "No, those paintings are in all the bedrooms."

She leads the way back into the two-tone green corridor and we're following her out as quickly as we followed her in and Sergei turns back and gives me a look, mouths something, and then I remember.

"Oh, I'm sorry, can I use your bathroom?"

I don't know what I would have done if she'd said there was a bathroom back at the lobby or that it was only for residents or if she'd wanted to escort me there herself. But that's not what happens. She points me back down the hall we'd come from, back towards Nana Davis' room, and tells me that when I'm finished, follow the hall straight back to reception.

I walk towards where she pointed, past the door to Nana Davis' room. I do actually need the loo, but I don't have time to do both. When I hear the double doors closing, I look over my shoulder and I see the hall is empty so I turn around, go back the way I came. I'm outside Nana Davis' room. My heart is beating a gazillion beats a minute. It's going to explode, that's what it feels like.

What if someone comes in? Another nurse? What if Aunt Ruth decides to visit today? What would I do if she walked in? I take a deep breath. There is no one, no one is coming.

Nana Davis is in the same position—mouth open, fingers clasped. She could be dead, she looks like she's dead. Only if you look at the sheet, the green blanket over it, you can see her chest is rising and falling. Just a fraction, but a fraction is enough.

I have no idea what I'm supposed to do.

"Nana Davis?" I go. Silence. "Nana Davis, it's me. Rhea, your granddaughter."

Nothing happens. I don't know what I think is going to happen. This isn't a movie, she's not going to hear my voice and wake up and suddenly be okay and conscious and able to have a conversation, and, even if she was, what do I think she might tell me? What do I want to know?

The double doors close again. Voices. It's Nurse Small, I know it is. I can't be in here. I look out the door but it's not her, it's another nurse who has gone into another room. This is my chance to get out of here and I'm just about to when the idea comes into my head. I know it's a bad idea, that I should ignore it and hurry up the hallway and back into the lobby, but my feet don't want to ignore it, and they take me across her room and to the locker, next to her bed.

I open the drawer first. I don't think I'm breathing then, I know I must have been but I don't know how I could be, with my hand rifling around to find something among the sleeve of plastic cups, two packs of tissues, a pair of glasses in a case. I close it, open the door part instead. There's a shelf that separates it into two: two rows of clothes. Nightdresses on the top, something silky, a blouse or a slip.

On the bottom part, there's proper clothes, winter clothes, jumpers. It's a long time since she's worn any of these. I'm about to close the door; I've done everything I can, there's nothing here. And then something makes me push my hand underneath the black cardigan with the gold buttons, something makes me push my fingers right to the back.

I feel cardboard and I pull it out—a cardboard wallet, blue with white writing on the front. The kind that holds photos. I've seen it before, this wallet, or one like it, and it takes me a second to remember it's what I'd expected to find two years ago in Dad's wardrobe. I'd thought I might find it there, I wasn't looking for it here.

I hold the top of my backpack with my mouth, unzip it. Aunt Ruth was always giving out when I did that. When I get it open I shove the wallet in there and my hand feels something else, something unfamiliar. It's a Discman, Michael's Discman. I don't know what it's doing there, I didn't put it there, but I don't have time to figure it out, so I shove the wallet in and zip it back up again.

I'd love to say that I glanced back at her before I left, that I leaned over and kissed her head or even that I said goodbye, but I didn't do any of that and I want to tell you the truth, and the truth is that I slung my backpack over my shoulder and stepped back out into the corridor and hurried back to the lobby as fast as I could without running.

When I get there, Nurse Small is back on the other side of the reception desk. Now that we've got her talking, she doesn't seem to want to stop and she laughs a big laugh as she tells us about how Mr. Shapiro and Mr. Reilly always used to argue because Mr. Shapiro always wanted to watch *Jeopardy!* when Mr. Reilly wanted to watch the news and wasn't it the strangest thing, the two of them passing within two weeks of each other.

The strap of my backpack is burning a hole in my shoulder, as if she can somehow know what is inside, as if she might try and grab it from me. And maybe Sergei senses something, because he looks at his watch then and says something about how we're running late to meet his aunt and I nod and say we'd better go. But Nurse Small won't let us leave, goes into this whole thing asking us where we're meeting his aunt and starts to give us directions about the best way to get there. I think we'll never get to leave, but finally we're pushing through the revolving doors and onto the sidewalk and at last I can breathe again.

It's all I can do to stop myself breaking into a run, and I must be walking fast because Sergei's telling me to slow down and that she could be watching through the window.

At the end of the block, I wait for him. He's laughing, rubbing his hand over his hair so his curls stick up in all directions.

"Jesus, Sergei, I don't know where you get the nerve to do shit like that, I really don't."

"Me? My nerve? You were amazing, Irish bullhead—I mean Natalie Peterson!"

We're both cracking up. I don't know what's so funny really, but it's as if there's all this nervous energy in my body and I'll burst if it doesn't find a way out. I don't want to just stand there though, I need to put distance between us and the nursing home.

"C'mon, Serg, seriously, I need to get the hell away from here."

I'm leading the way, heading back the way we came, towards the subway. Sergei's beside me, until he's not, and when I glance back, he's stopped outside an Irish bar.

"What do you say to a celebratory drink?"

"It's not even two o'clock, Serg."

"It's five o'clock somewhere."

The bar looks posh, nicer than the places we usually go. "They probably won't serve us."

"They don't serve us, then we don't drink."

"Aren't you hungry, Serg? I'm hungry."

"So, you eat, I'll drink. Or we can do both."

I thought we were going back to Michael's. I'd been looking forward to it, having his apartment to ourselves, taking the packet of photos out of my backpack, lining them up next to each other on the floor.

"It looks pricey, Serg."

"Don't worry about it, my treat." He smiles. "Come on, we deserve a celebration."

We get seats at the bar and the waitress gives us a big menu. I've already made up my mind to get shepherd's pie before the barman puts down my Coke and Sergei's pint of Budweiser. Sergei's still deciding and I'm listening to the music, Van Morrison. Van Morrison makes me think about Dad. And thinking about Dad makes me think about the Hendrix CDs on my shelf back in Coral Springs, and that makes me think about Michael's Discman in my bag.

"Serg, did you put Michael's Discman in my bag?"

I ask the question in a really normal way. I have no idea, yet, where it will lead.

Sergei rubs his hand over his hair, looks at the menu. "What?"

"Michael's Discman. Did you put it in my backpack?"

He puts the menu down and takes a drink of his pint.

"Rhea, there's something I have to tell you."

Writing this, I'm remembering how my heart did that thing again, how it sped up in only a few seconds. Before Sergei can say what he has to tell me, the barman is back to take our order. Sergei smiles and his face is back to normal as he orders a burger, medium rare, Swiss cheese. The barman turns to me and I remember I want the shepherd's pie.

When he leaves, I'm about to ask Sergei what he was going to say, but I don't have to.

"I put the CD player in your bag. I . . . I wanted you to have it. A present."

A waitress passes by with two big plates of potato skins, crispy brown on the outside, melted cheddar, scallions. In the middle of the plates, there's sour cream dip. I should have ordered potato skins.

"What are you talking about?"

He rolls his neck, takes another drink of beer. He hasn't taken off Michael's jacket. "Don't freak out, Irish bullhead, but we're not going back to Michael's. He kicked us out."

Behind Sergei, there's a bald man at the bar eating French onion soup and reading a paper. I wonder, is he listening.

"Why? What did you do this time?"

I only mean to ask the first part of that question, the "why" part, but somehow the second part slips out. It's the hook that Sergei has been waiting for.

"What did I do? What did I do?" He looks around as if some-one else will answer. "He's the one with the problem, Rhea, he's the control freak."

I keep my face sympathetic, I try to. "So, you had a fight?"

"It wasn't just a fight, Irish bullhead. At first, he wouldn't let me into the apartment. When he finally did, he lost his shit. He told me not to come back. He called me a fucking rent boy, Rhea."

He says that really loud and the man with the soup looks over.

"When did this happen?"

"What? The other night."

"Which night?"

Sergei takes another drink. "I don't know, Wednesday, Thurs-day? Who can keep track."

Something is slowly starting to dawn on me. Sergei fixes the collar on Michael's jacket where it's sticking up.

"So how come we were there last night?"

He pulls something from his pocket and puts it on the bar. A set of keys.

"I knew he wouldn't be back last night. I heard him on the phone to his wife—it was one of the little brats' birthdays."

"You got a copy of his keys made?"

Sergei is grinning a weird grin. "Sure. Why not? What else would he expect from a fucking rent boy?"

The barman comes with our food, places it down. The shepherd's pie is in a bowl. Gravy drips down the side.

"What the fuck, Serg? You should have told me, I can't believe you didn't tell me. We shouldn't be eating here, blowing money on this—"

"Relax, Rhea, just eat it."

"How can I, Serg? This is pizza slices for three or four days for both of us, not to mention the price of the beer—"

He's started his burger already. "We're fine for cash, eat up."

"No we're not, I'm not. No one's giving me a job, Serg, I've tried everywhere and now if we don't have Michael's, if we've nowhere to even shower—"

"Rhea, we're okay for money, okay?"

"What does that mean? You've fifty dollars? A hundred? A hundred dollars barely lasts a week in this city, Serg."

He takes something from his back pocket, puts it on the bar between us. It is a clip, full of notes, a clip full of notes we've both seen before.

"You took his money?"

He takes another bite of burger, chews.

"You took his fucking money, Serg?"

"Keep your voice down, will you?" He snarls it, doesn't say it. His mouth is full. "Do you want the whole city to know?"

"There was over a thousand dollars there, Serg, you can't just take it."

He slams his burger down hard on his plate. The barman glances over.

"Why not? Why can't I? We need it, we need this money. What's he going to buy? More Ralph Lauren polo shirts? Another skateboard for his kids because the other one is an old model? More of those horrible pictures he had on his walls?"

"I like those pictures."

"It's not the point, Rhea, the pictures aren't the fucking point." He pushes his plate away and grabs his beer, spilling some. "He used me. He owes me. I deserve this money, we both do. We didn't trash the place, we left it nice, I didn't take anything else, I swear, just the money."

"And his clothes?" I say, gesturing at his jacket.

"One fucking jacket, a shirt, so what? Something for me, just like the CD player was a little something for you. I thought you'd like it, you're always going on about how much you miss your fucking music."

"I don't want it."

"So, fine, don't take it, give it to me. I'll take it."

He's calmed down then, is calming down, like he thinks the worst of the fight is over and maybe it is. He turns back to his burger and I pick up my fork, pierce the top of the shepherd's pie. Steam comes out. Lisa's mum made shepherd's pie a few times, in a big casserole dish. She'd cut squares of it, so it stood tall on a plate. It was nicer, somehow, than being in a bowl.

I don't know why but it's thinking about Lisa's mum that makes it sink in. Makes everything sink in.

"He could have come home last night and found us there. He could have called the police. Had us arrested."

"Rhea—" he says. "Come on."

"You said you'd made up with him. If the police had come, I'd have been arrested too, no one would have believed I didn't know."

He smiles his best Sergei smile, the one that had charmed Nurse Small and Michael and Nana Davis' doorman. And me. "I knew he wasn't coming back."

"You couldn't have known."

"I knew, Rhea. I knew we'd be okay. Do you think I'd have put you in any danger? We're a team, remember?"

A team, pitching our wits against the city, how long ago was that? Four weeks ago? Less? More? Being a part of a team means working together, being honest. Not lying to each other.

I put my fork down. "I want you to put the money back."

He laughs. Some bits of burger land on the bar. He wipes his mouth with the back of his hand.

"You know I'm not doing that."

"He won't be back until tomorrow. You have time to put it back and the Discman too. And then I want you to get rid of those keys."

He swigs the last of his beer back, signals the barman for another. "And if I don't?"

"Then that's it, I'm not on this team anymore."

He rolls his eyes. "Come on, don't be an Irish bullhead about this. I know you're mad at me but we both know you're not going to do that."

My heart is doing that crazy beating thing, my stump hurts. I feel sick, I don't even want the shepherd's pie. I push my stool back, stand up.

"Sit back down, eat your lunch. I'm sorry about last night, if you don't think I was a hundred percent honest with you."

"A hundred percent honest? Try zero percent honest."

I'm putting on my jacket then and he's laughing, but it's not his real laugh, I know him well enough to know that.

"Stop this, we both know you wouldn't last five minutes in this city without me."

I don't answer him, Mum. I don't say anything because I'm remembering that first time we met in the Y, when I stood up for him in a way he'd never stuck up for me. And I know that if I start to say anything, it won't just be about him, it'll be about every other person who'd never stood up for me since the beginning of time.

I reach down for my backpack. I pick it up, I don't grab it. I almost take out the Discman but what's the point? He's not going to give it back anyway. And I don't storm out, I take my time to put it on and then walk away from Sergei like I've always walked away from him, like I know I'll see him later. As I get closer to the door, my feet are going faster, they want to run, but I make them slow down to a normal walk, even when I hear him calling after me. The door is heavy but a man coming in holds it open for me and I thank him before I turn left, downtown. I keep walking, like I know where I'm going, but I don't know where I'm going. I keep walking, away from Sergei and my Coke still sweating on the counter and my shepherd's pie which is getting cold by now.

I keep walking, block after block, past Grand Central and Union Square and my backpack feels so heavy, heavier after each block, and I'm dying to sit down but there's nowhere to sit down so I keep walking, through SoHo and Chinatown, until I get here, to the water at the end of Manhattan, the end of the island. The end of the world.

It's nice here. It'd be nicer if it was a bit warmer. The wind off the water is cold and after being so hot on the walk I put everything back on again—my denim shirt and my Champion hoody and my jacket. And I like hearing the water lapping against the dock, like watching the green and orange ferry that goes to Staten Island and back and then over to Staten Island again.

I should be hungry, I haven't eaten today, but I feel kind of sick instead. Dizzy. I wish I'd had the shepherd's pie, or taken it with me, because I know without having to count it I have $74.15 in my pocket, which is less than fifty pizza slices or subway rides or two nights at the Y.

And I still don't know if I did the right thing or not. If it's bad news that I walked out of there and left him or if it's good news that I just don't see yet.

But I do know that I do okay on my own, that I know how to do it. And that being on my own is better than being with someone I can't trust, someone who steals, someone who lies to me. I might not know much, Mum, but I know that.

At least, I think I do.

Rhea

Dear Mum,

I'm still sitting here. I'm still sitting on this bench, next to the water. I'm freezing now. My hand is stiff and sore but I thought writing might help keep it warm. I don't know where to go next. I've been sitting here trying to figure it out, trying to come up with a list of things to do next in my head, but the only thing my head wants to do is to have imaginary conversations with Sergei.

What if he's sorry? What if he's changed his mind and taken the money back? People change their minds. They apologise. If I don't go to any of the places that I usually go, then he won't be able to apologise, will he? He'll never find me here. Laurie apologised. That was what changed things, I think, what started to change things. I'd been there seven months by then, it was winter time, not that you'd know it in Florida, but I remember it was November because the conversation over dinner started about Thanksgiving.

Aunt Ruth brings it up, how they need to get back to Cheryl about the plans for the day. Cooper doesn't look up from his food.

"I'll get back to her, Ruth."

"When, Coop? Thanksgiving is next week."

"Tonight, I'll call her and tell her it's not going to work out, we have plans."

Laurie is playing with her pasta while they are talking. It's fusilli, my favourite, and she's trying to twirl it, only you can't twirl fusilli so it keeps falling off her fork.

"Who's Cheryl?" I go.

I don't know why I ask, I don't think I care really, it's only something to say. I'm not expecting Aunt Ruth to say what she says next.

"Cheryl is Laurie's mom. She's an actress. She's in a show down in Miami."

"Cool!" I say it straight out, forget to pretend I'm not interested. I look at Laurie but she's still twirling. "Has she been in any films? Would I know her?" I'm asking Laurie but Aunt Ruth's the one who answers me.

"You might know her from this TV show she was in—"

Cooper bangs his hand down on the table, so the glasses rattle. "Jesus, Ruth, we don't need to go through Cheryl's resumé!"

Laurie pushes her plate away. "May I be excused?"

"Rhea's part of this family too," Aunt Ruth says, taking a mouthful of salad. "She has a right to know who we're talking about."

I'd wondered about Laurie's mum, why she'd never come to visit, why I'd never heard her on the phone. Somehow over the time I'd been there, I think I'd decided she must be dead too, but I'd never asked.

I've finished my pasta and there's no more left. Laurie looks like she's not going to finish hers but I need to wait until she leaves the table to take it.

Aunt Ruth takes a sip of her wine. "I know it's none of my business, but since she's only in Miami, maybe you should consider it, Coop—"

"Only in Miami? It's not the end of the block, Ruth. Do you want to drive down to Miami on Thanksgiving?"

"May I be excused?" Laurie says again.

"I'm only saying that, comparatively speaking, she's pretty close by—"

Cooper bangs the table a second time. "So we're supposed to be grateful that we don't have to travel out of state so she can get some annual holiday fix with her daughter? What about the rest of the year, Ruth?"

He's forgotten Laurie is there, that I am. When he stops shouting, there's only the sound of the fan swishing, and then he remembers.

"Sweetheart—" he goes, reaching out to her, but she's already pushing her chair back. It scrapes against the tiles.

"Dad, it's fine."

"I'm sorry, I didn't mean that the way it sounded."

"May I be excused?"

"Laurie, your dad didn't mean it like that," Aunt Ruth says. "He only meant—"

Laurie never hears what Cooper only meant because she leaves the kitchen then, slamming the door behind her. Cooper stands up too, like he's going to follow her, but instead he sits back down and turns to Aunt Ruth. "Now look what you've done."

The argument spins on, about whose fault it was, how Ruth should never have brought it up, how Cheryl is nothing but trouble. I hate arguments and I feel all jangly inside but I want to finish Laurie's pasta because I know they won't notice because of the fight.

After I'm finished, I excuse myself too and head towards my room. That's when I hear her crying.

I've never heard Laurie crying before, Mum, and I probably would hear her if she cried because we're in rooms next to each other. And it might sound really bad that I don't go in straightaway to see if she's okay, but we've perfected a rhythm of never having to speak at all by then. We ignore each other at soccer practice, on the bus to school; even at home both of us will only speak to Aunt Ruth or Cooper, never to each other. So I stand there, for ages, deciding what to do and while I'm deciding, the crying gets louder.

When I knock on the door, the crying stops and I wish I could pretend I hadn't knocked but it's too late.

"Laurie? It's me, Rhea."

I forget to say Rae, because I'm nervous. I hate that I made a mistake and I think about correcting myself, but that would be worse.

"What do you want?"

"Can I come in?"

There's a pause.

"Okay."

I've never been in her room before, only saw it on the fleeting tour of the house on my first day. She's sitting cross-legged on her bed, shredding tissue onto the yellow and pink duvet. When she looks up at me, you can tell that she's been crying.

"Are you okay?"

She sniffs. "I'm fine."

I stand there and when I look down I see that I'm cupping my stump, so I let it go.

"Okay," I go. "I just wanted to check."

I'm about to leave, have already turned around when she says my name. The new way. "Rae?"

I hear the tears in her voice and when I turn around they're spilling down her cheeks, faster than she can wipe them away with each hand. I close the door and sit down on the bed. There's a box of tissues next to a pink phone on the nightstand. I put it between us. After a minute, she takes one. "Thanks."

While she's blowing her nose, I take in the room. It's way bigger than mine and she has a mini stereo on her shelves, way better than the CD player and tape deck I brought from home. She has a TV too and, on the shelf above it, there's a photo in a frame of a woman with blonde hair and a movie-star smile. She has blue eyes, Laurie's eyes. She looks kind of familiar, only maybe I'm imagining that.

"Is that your mum?" I go.

She follows my eyes. Nods.

"I don't think Cooper meant what he said to come out the way it sounded."

She pulls her legs into her chest, hugs her arms around her knees. "Fuck it. It's not like I care. It's not like it's a newsflash that she's a selfish bitch. I should be used to it by now."

I don't know whether to agree or disagree, so I don't say anything.

"Listen, don't tell anyone at school who she is, will you? Okay? No one knows."

"No one? Not even Tanya?"

"No! Especially not Tanya. Or Becky or any of them. I'd enough of that at my last school—all the kids wanting autographs, asking me about her stupid show." She wipes a stray tear away with her hand. "She loves that shit, giving me photos for my friends. As if that makes up for everything."

I've never seen Laurie this angry before, never seen her care this much about anything.

"I won't tell anyone."

"Thanks." She stands and walks over to the window. "The last time she asked me if any of my friends wanted autographed photos, I told her that none of them have ever heard of her."

She laughs and I smile. I want to ask more about her mum, what's it like to have someone famous as a mother, but I think I already know the answer, so I ask something else instead.

"What age were you when your mum and dad split up?"

"Four." She twists the blinds open and closed again. "She left a week after my fourth birthday."

She should be in the photos of little Laurie, the baby ones, but she isn't.

"My mum died when I was three."

She leaves the blinds closed, turns around and pulls a strand of hair into her mouth, starts to suck it.

"How did she die?"

I take a breath before I say it. "She drowned." Laurie is still looking at me, wants me to say more, so I tell her the story the way Dad told me. "She went swimming in the sea every morning and that morning she got into trouble and there was no lifeguard on duty."

"Do you remember her?"

No one's ever asked me that before, I don't think they have. I close my eyes to remember.

"Sort of. Not so much actual memories of stuff that happened but more like a feeling, a feeling of before and after or something." She's looking at me, her blue eyes are, and suddenly I feel embarrassed. "That probably makes no sense."

Her head moves a fraction. "No, it does. I used to think I didn't remember Mum ever living with us at all, that my memories only started when we moved to Florida, but I don't know if that's true anymore."

"Where did you live before?"

"New York."

"Wow," I go. "You lucky thing. I'd love to live in New York."

She comes back over and sits on the end of the bed. "I think you're lucky, you know."

"Lucky? How come?"

She picks up the remote control, opens the back part where the battery goes in, and clicks it closed again.

"You're lucky yours is dead. At least you know she's gone, why she's not here. You don't have this crap every time she takes time out of her busy schedule to come see you."

Her voice is level, like there's not fifty thousand reasons why what she's saying is bullshit.

"That's total crap, Laurie."

"Why?" She looks up. "We're kind of in the same boat, right? But you get to make up the kind of mom you have, this mom who would have always been there for you and never let you down—"

"Laurie, it's totally different. You get to see your mum, get to know her. You know what I'd give to know mine?"

"That's what you think now, but what if you wouldn't? You might not even like her, you don't know what she was like—"

"I'm not listening to this crap." I'm standing up at that point and kind of shouting, but I don't care. "I came in here to see if you were okay, because I felt sorry for you because your mum seems like she's some selfish bitch—"

When she shouts back, her face is mean, the tears all gone now.

"How do you know yours wasn't a selfish bitch too? Just because she's dead doesn't mean she was perfect!"

I turn to leave, I come back, I want to punch her, hit her, hurt her—but I don't. I kick the bed instead. It hurts my foot. "Fuck you, Laurie!" I kick it harder. "Fuck you!" I half expect Aunt Ruth to come in, I nearly want her to, but she's too busy having her own fight with Cooper. They're in the living room by then, using the TV to try and drown out their voices but you can still hear them.

After the fight I put on *Are you Experienced?* really loud, but I put on my headphones so Aunt Ruth won't tell me to turn it down. I try and do my maths homework, but I can't concentrate. My eyes won't stay on the page, instead they keep going to your subway map on the wall, in between the two windows. And I go through the lines one by one, starting with the blue one, the AA, and I wish the folds hadn't made a tear in the paper, but it doesn't really matter because I still know all the stops off by heart, can still say them without looking.

And I've moved onto the RR next, and I'm at Borough Hall, then Hoyt Street and "Stone Free" is playing when I think I hear something and I turn the music down and I hear the knock on the door again. And when I open it, Laurie is there, sucking on a strand of her hair, looking at her feet, one on top of the other.

I take my headphones off and she looks up.

"I'm sorry, Rae, I'm sorry for what I said about your mom."

My foot still hurts from where I kicked the bed. I want to cup my stump, but I don't.

"That's bullshit, what you said about her. You'd no right."

"I know." She looks back down. "I know. I just felt so mad, you know, and I don't know why, but I wanted you to feel mad too."

It sounds real, what she says, not like lies. When she looks up, she smiles a little smile, holds out her hand.

"Truce?" she goes.

It's not just a truce for the fight but a truce for everything, I think it is. I take her hand.

"Truce."

For the second time, we stand like that, holding hands, but not. This time it's me that pulls away first.

I don't know why I wrote all that down, Mum, it's not like it matters. It's ancient history now, water under the bridge, like the water lapping here against the dock. Just because Laurie apologised and meant it once doesn't mean she ever will again. It doesn't mean Sergei will either.

It's late now and the sloshing sound of the water I liked earlier sounds different in the dark. It's cold, even with my jacket and my Champion hoody. I bet there's rats down here and I should probably move somewhere else, only I don't know where else to move to. And I like looking at the lights out there, the lights from the buildings opposite, white on the black water. But I don't know where those buildings are, whether they're in New Jersey or Brooklyn or even Staten Island, and out of everything I hate tonight, Mum, I hate that I don't know that.

I hate that there is no one I can ask.

Rhea

Dear Mum,

I made it! I made it through the night outside, all by myself! I didn't think I was going to sleep here, I hadn't planned it, I'd planned on getting up and finding a stick in the park and making it sharp and staying awake all night just in case, but I kept nodding off before I could do any of that. All night I kept nodding off and waking up, and nodding off and waking up, and the last time I woke up, it was morning.

And even though my neck and shoulder are killing me, I feel so fucking happy, so fucking proud of myself, because it turns out I don't need Sergei to survive in this city, no matter what he thinks.

I don't need anyone.

I have a plan this morning, Mum. Once I find somewhere to pee, I'm going to go to Duane Reade and I'm going to buy soap and shampoo and deodorant, and I'm going to go and wash up. Even though there's only a tiny bit of toothpaste left in the tube, I'm not going to buy any more because it's expensive, so I'll wait until I get a job. I'm going to look for a job today, that's the rest of the plan. I don't know why I've given up, this is New York, people are given a chance in New York, everyone is. I just haven't been looking for my chance hard enough, that's all. I got distracted by Sergei and by looking for you and finding Nana Davis and finding the photos and everything. I will look at the photos, I haven't forgotten about the photos, I plan on looking at them, but I want to be able to look at them properly and lay them out somewhere they won't get wet or blown away and there's things I need to do first, that's all. I'm going to be eighteen in eleven days and I have to prioritise, that's part of being an adult, isn't it?

So, this morning, my priorities are getting clean and getting a job. After I pee. And eat. I'm starving. I know a place on Eighth Avenue that does an egg and cheese on a roll with a coffee for only one dollar —the others all charge $1.25 or even $1.50—so I can walk there, unless I find somewhere as cheap along the way. And when I buy my soap and stuff, I'm going to go to a Starbucks and wash in there, because even though the bathrooms in Grand Central are good, you can't wash yourself properly and in Starbucks it's a private cubicle so I can stick my whole head in the sink and everything and even change my T-shirt.

It feels so much better to have a plan, you know? A game plan, I mean, to be in control of what I'm doing and not to have to rely on Sergei. I think it's best, what happened, you know? I think it's better. I'm better off on my own.

———————

Fuck it. Fuck it. Fuck it. Fuck it.

It's such bullshit, you know? I can't believe these people. They're so fucking obvious when they say no, the way they all look at where my arm should be, instead of my face. Even that kip of a diner with the "Help Wanted" sign in the window for a dishwasher said no. And every time someone else says no I can hear Aunt Ruth's voice in my head, during one of our arguments about the prosthetic, saying how the only people who go without them in this country are street people and I don't want everyone to think I'm one of them.

And now I am one of them and everyone knows it, and that's the real reason none of these people will even give me a chance when I say I'll work twice as hard as anyone else, work for free even, so they can see how quick I am at bussing tables and setting them up again or doing dishes or mopping floors or cleaning toilets or anything that will mean I'll be able to eat.

The absolute worst is that guy in the Irish pub, the one from Galway, who keeps me talking for twenty minutes, but when I ask about a job he just shakes his head and goes, "Ah no, love, we're grand at the moment."

Fuck him. Fuck them. Fuck this. Fuck you.

I'm sorry for all the cursing. I am. It's just, I don't know, this stuff is hard and the rain makes it so much harder. Earlier, I was thinking it must be miserable to be homeless in Ireland, with all the rain, but I never really saw too many homeless people at home, none in Rush anyway, maybe the odd person on O'Connell Street. New York rain is worse than Irish rain anyway, it's so heavy, you end up sloshing through water up to your shins when you cross the street. My Champion hoody is drenched, even through my jacket, and it feels like it'll never dry. I wish I had a raincoat with me, an umbrella. You see loads of people using black plastic bags to cover themselves and their trolleys, I even saw a guy with Duane Reade shopping bags tied around his feet. My Docs don't let in the rain much but even if they did, there's no way I'd do that, just like I wouldn't put a black plastic bag over myself because if you do that, everyone knows you're homeless.

I keep obsessing about how much money I have left, how many pizza slices it is, if I can afford to do laundry. The soap and stuff cost more than I thought—with tax it came to $7.11 for a bar of Irish Spring soap, a plastic soap container, and a roll-on deodorant. The cheapest shampoo was $2.99 and I decided that the soap was better because it can do both because I only have fuzz anyway. I took ages deciding between the bar soap and the liquid soap. Liquid soap was $1.99, which was cheaper than the bar soap and plastic container put together, and it'd be nicer for my head. But it was only fourteen fluid ounces and I think the most it would last is two weeks, whereas the bar soap will last longer and the plastic container is an investment because next time I'll only have to buy the bar soap which is 79 cents. Working it all out in my head makes me think about Cooper, because he was always going on about investments and financial planning—it was the only time he was really happy, I think, when he talked about money.

Apart from the time when he was planning our trip to Montana.

He drove Laurie mad then, going around the house all the time in his Stetson. She always walked out of the room when he came in wearing it, but I thought it was kind of funny. Other than Cooper, I was the only one who was excited that we were going to Montana— Aunt Ruth wanted to go to Paris and Laurie wanted to go to Hawaii. I wanted to go to New York but I didn't mind Montana either and, anyway, apart from the time I went to Sligo with Lisa's family when her brother got sick in the car, I'd never been on holiday. Dad always said with the shop it was impossible to get away.

For weeks, every night over dinner, Cooper talks about Montana and our forefathers on the frontiers and how it'll be great to get away from urban sprawl and back to nature. Aunt Ruth asks about the bears and whether there's a phone that works. Laurie mostly ignores him, but when she does say anything it's about learning to surf properly and that she can't do that in Montana.

By then, we don't hate each other anymore, Laurie and me. It's the middle part, in between not hating each other but not being friends yet either. At home, we talk sometimes, even laugh sometimes, but in school and at soccer, we ignore each other unless we're forced to talk. She's mad at me because I don't take her side about the Hawaii thing. She's convinced that Cooper's bringing us to some bumfuck town in the middle of nowhere to keep her away from boys, and I think maybe she's right.

To get to Montana we fly from Fort Lauderdale to Atlanta, Atlanta to Salt Lake City, and Salt Lake City to a town called Billings. Laurie says we could have flown to Hawaii in half the time and Aunt Ruth is scared on the last plane because it is so small. After all that flying, we're still not there and a man comes to collect us in a van to take us on a three-hour drive to the ranch. We stop at a Walmart in case we need anything because the closest store is ninety minutes away.

"Back to nature!" Cooper says, and heads towards the wine section.

Looking back, it's obvious that Laurie and me would be sharing a room, but I don't think either of us had thought about that, I know I hadn't. It's only when we're at the lodge and the lady opens the door to one room and hands the key to me and goes "that's for you girls" and heads to the end of the balcony to show Aunt Ruth and Cooper their room, that I realise. Inside the room, everything is made of logs—the wardrobe and the desk and even the two single beds—and when I turn to Laurie she's standing in the doorway sucking on a strand of her hair.

"There's no TV?" she goes. "Is he fucking kidding? What do people do around here without a TV?"

We find out that night over dinner that what people do is go horse riding, and there's this whole argument then about me not being covered by the ranch's insurance and that they should have known in advance that there was someone with a disability in our group. They say that word seven times—"disability"—Cooper says it three times and the ranch owner says it four. I try and tell them about the horses I rode before on the beach in Rush but no one listens. Dinner is homemade lasagne and salad and mashed garlic potatoes and you can go up for more and I go up three times while the conversation about insurance is going on. The lady tells me to save some room for their desserts, but she says it nicely, not in a mean way. Outside the window, you can see the tops of pine trees, all the way into the valley, and I listen to the ranch owner's wife at the next table telling an old couple about the bear cubs she saw earlier in the year.

The next morning, I get up at six a.m. when it's still really cold and there's pink in the sky over the mountain. There's only one horse in the paddock, a light brown one with a white stripe along her nose. She's friendly, she lets me pet her and stays near the fence so I can use it to climb up onto her back. I walk around the paddock on her a few times and that's what I'm doing when Bill, the wrangler, comes out of the stables and sees me. At first he looks mad, but then he smiles and calls the rest of the wranglers out to see. I've left my prosthetic in the room—I don't know how to do it with that, only the way I learned at home, slightly tilting over to one side, holding onto the mane with my hand—and they've probably never seen someone with only one arm riding a horse before because they all start to clap.

My horse's name is Heather and they say it's okay if I ride her, so long as Cooper signs a waiver and I use a saddle, stirrups, and reins. Laurie's horse is a girl too, called Snowdrop, and Cooper is on a big black horse called Jackson. Aunt Ruth had made this whole big deal about keeping me company and I don't think she's pleased that they'll let me ride after all, because even as Bill and Jamie are helping her onto a piebald called Apache she's still asking questions about insurance. She looks scared in the beginning, every time Apache moves, but they keep her up front, in between Bill and me, and she's getting the hang of it by the time we turn around to come home, so it's a pity that she drops out the next day to look after Cooper, who hurt his back.

I'm not going to go through every little detail about the holiday, Mum, even though I want to tell you about the bear-claw marks we find on the bark of the tree, and the picnic at the very top of the mountain the day we go hiking, and about the water of the Boulder River that's cold as liquid ice the morning I dip myself into it.

What I want to tell you about is the last night.

They always have a camp fire on the last night. You can probably picture it. You know in the country how it gets so dark that everything is just shades of black and lighter black? Well, it's like that—the lighter black is the sky and the darker black is the mountain and the trunks of the trees. You can only see parts of people's faces, lit up by the fire, the other parts are in shadow. Every time someone throws on wood and the flames jump up, you can see more people and the trees behind and sometimes there's sparks of fire in the air that float until they burn out. After the food, Bill takes out a harmonica and the singing starts and that's when Jamie comes over and hands a flask of something to Laurie.

Jamie's the youngest wrangler and he's kind of cute in his cowboy outfit, like a kid dressing up, except he's not dressing up because he's from Idaho and that's how they dress there. I knew from the beginning that he liked Laurie. She passes me the flask and I drink some and it's not as bad as I think it's going to be. It burns a bit but there's something sweet in there too—an orange taste. It's easy to drink in the dark and we pass it back and forth, smiling a bit at our secret, and every now and then Cooper tips his Stetson at us.

I don't know what time it is when the singing is over and we all walk back through the woods with only a few beams of torch lighting the way, but I remember me and Laurie bursting out laughing every time Aunt Ruth gets jumpy when she hears a noise in case it's a bear or a mountain lion. And back in the room, we're still laughing, but it's more awkward then, with the bright light and only the two of us, so we don't talk properly until it's dark again with me in my log bed next to the window and Laurie in hers next to the door.

"Oh my God, I can't wait for Dad to get rid of that hat," she goes. "He'll have to tomorrow, when we leave."

"I wouldn't bet on it."

"He's super embarrassing. I swear I wanted this mountain to open up and swallow me up when he started singing tonight."

"'Home, home on the range...'" I sing, making myself sound like Cooper.

"Stop it! Please! I'm sure Bill and Jamie think he's such an asshole."

"I doubt it."

"I'm sure they do. It's okay, by the way, I know you think he's an asshole too."

I don't know how to answer that, so I roll over. The curtains are open, like we agreed to leave them on the first night because the only thing out there is mountain and trees and stars. But tonight the stars are hiding behind the clouds.

From the bed across the room, Laurie starts to giggle.

"What's so funny?" I go. She tries to answer me but she's laughing too hard, really cracking up. Finally, she gets some words out. "I was just thinking of Dad shaking Jamie's hand, saying what an upright young man he is." She giggles again. "Not like the young people in the city who only care about going out and partying."

I start to laugh too, roll back to face her. "Imagine if he knew. What was in that flask anyway?"

"I don't know, but it was super strong," Laurie says. "I think he had a whole plan worked out to get me drunk. He asked me on the way back which room was ours."

"Did he?" I don't know why it shocks me so much to hear that, but it does. "Did you tell him?"

"No," Laurie goes, "I told him about Mike—that I have a boyfriend. Don't worry, we won't be getting any company."

There's silence for a second and I wonder if she'd have asked me first. What I would have done if Jamie did show up at the door.

"If it hadn't been for Mike, would you have? I mean, do you like him?"

I've never asked her anything like that before, we don't talk about that kind of stuff. She makes me wait before she answers.

"I don't know. Maybe," she says. "He's cute, don't you think?"

"I suppose."

"I mean, here, he's cute. If you took him home, like brought him to school, he'd just look weird."

"Yeah," I go. "Imagine him getting on the school bus in his cowboy outfit."

I think she's going to laugh again, but instead she says something else. "Maybe I should've said he could come over. Mike's not here. He'd never know. Anyway, I'd only make out with Jamie or whatever, I wouldn't do anything else."

I want to ask her about the "anything else." She's a year younger than me but I bet she's done more than I have.

"Mmmmm," I say instead.

There's silence for a bit then but I know she's not asleep yet, her breathing hasn't changed.

"So, have you slept with Mike?"

I launch the words out, like a missile into the dark. I don't know why I want to know, but I do. I'm glad that she can't see me. I hear her breathe in before she answers.

"No," she goes. "But I might, later in the summer. I've let him get to third base."

I don't know what these American bases mean, but I can probably work it out. I'm afraid she'll ask me something next but she keeps talking.

"Tanya let Chris Trifiro go all the way and she said it was overrated. That it hurt more than anything else."

"Yeah," I go. "I'd say it would."

I say that on purpose, to let her know I haven't done it without her having to ask, but she asks anyway.

"You've never done it with anyone?"

"No."

"No one back in Ireland?"

"No."

"Why not?"

I shrug, even though she can't see me. "I don't know, I think you've got to like someone a lot to do it, you know, love them a bit."

"Was there anyone you wanted to do it with in Ireland?"

"No."

"So, you've never loved anyone? Like, been in love, I mean?"

The question catches me off guard and I take too long to answer. Laurie hears the pause.

"There was someone! Who? Tell me!"

"There's no one."

"Rae, I can tell when you're lying. Come on, I was honest with you, it's not fair if you don't tell me."

I lie there, breathing.

"I thought we were starting to be friends, Rae, but we can't be friends if you don't trust me."

"I do trust you!" I don't know if I do or not but right then it seems like the right thing to say.

"Well, then? Who is he?"

"No one. There is no 'he,' Laurie, I'm telling you."

That's the end of it, I think it is, but I don't count on what she's going to say next.

"Is there a 'she'?"

In the dark, I'm wondering if I heard her right, if she really said what I think she did. I'm trying to figure out how to answer, but she speaks next.

"It is a girl, isn't it? I knew it! I don't care, it's no big deal, loads of people have girl crushes."

Girl crushes. I've never heard that before. I want to ask her how she knew, but saying that, saying anything, would let her know she's right.

"Come on, Rae, tell me something about her. What's her name?"

And I don't know if I want to tell her then, but it's more like I need to tell her. I need to tell someone.

"Nicole."

I can barely hear my voice over the bam bam of my heart.

"Nicole? Nicole what?"

"Gleeson."

"Nicole Gleeson."

Laurie says it slowly, like it's the name of a film star. I'm in Montana, thousands of miles away from Rush, but I'm on the 33 as well, with Nicole's leg pushed up against mine.

"What does she look like?" Laurie goes.

"It doesn't matter."

"Is she gorgeous? I bet she's gorgeous."

It feels weird, the question, and I don't know how to answer, so I don't.

"Is she dark? Like you?"

I'm about to tell Laurie that Nicole has blonde hair, but something stops me, makes me lie.

"Yeah, she's dark."

"Do you have a photo of her? Back at home? You can show me, if you want."

My school annual is under my bed with a class photo where Nicole is a blur of black and white, but the real photos are in my head.

"No," I go. "I don't have any."

She doesn't say anything after that and I don't either. I'm lying there thinking about Nicole. After ages, Laurie talks again.

"In case you're worried about me telling anyone you're a lesbian, I won't, okay?"

The matter-of-fact way she says it sends a jolt through me.

"Shut up, I'm not a lesbian!"

"Rae, you just told me—"

I can't let her finish her sentence, can't let her say that word again.

"Don't ever say that, Laurie, I'm serious."

"Okay," she goes. "Okay."

"You were the one who said loads of people had girl crushes, it doesn't make them all, all—lesbians."

I say it low, in case the family next door can hear through the log wall, in case Aunt Ruth and Cooper can, all the way from the end of the hallway.

"Whatever," Laurie goes. "Whatever, Rae. Whatever you say."

She doesn't say anything else about it, not that night, even though we both lie awake for what seems like hours, and she doesn't say anything in the morning when we're packing or on the journey back to Florida. And I wonder if maybe she forgot because of the drink Jamie gave us, the way Dad used to forget things sometimes.

And after ages of her not saying anything, weeks and then a month, I think that must be what happened, that she has forgotten, even though deep down I'm afraid she hasn't.

Deep down, I'm waiting for her to bring it up again.

Rhea

King Street, New York
2nd May 1999
2:33 a.m.

Dear Mum,

I've been doing this all wrong. I don't know why I didn't work it out before, that it's better to sleep during the day, that it's safer, way safer than doing it at night. The thing to do at night is keep moving, keep walking, look like you're going somewhere. So that's what I've been doing tonight, because I don't want to spend money on the subway and I'm a dumbass for not sleeping today.

It's not until Seventh turns into Varick that I realise I'm walking to Michael's apartment. I don't know why I am, it doesn't make sense. I don't go to Grand Central or Penn Station because I don't want to see Sergei, but I come here, to a place that reminds me of him.

So that's where I am now, sitting on my step across the street, like the night I waited for Sergei, only I'm not waiting for Sergei now. I'm only sitting here because I'm tired and I need a break from walking. The light in Michael's apartment is off, so he's probably asleep, which is a good thing because if he sees me, he could call the police because he probably thinks I stole his money. In the apartment next door, the light is still on and I wonder if that means the neighbours are fighting or fucking tonight.

Sex changes everything, doesn't it? Did you ever think it might be easier if there was no such thing as sex? If people were just friends and that was it? Like Sergei and Michael—if they hadn't been having sex, if they'd just been friends, I bet they'd never have fought. I bet we'd still be there.

Sex was what got me and Laurie grounded last summer, a few weeks after the Montana holiday. After we got back, Laurie started inviting me to parties with her and I'd been going. Cooper and Aunt Ruth thought we were going to the movies or to people's houses where their parents were supervising us. They were happy we were hanging out together, you could see it in the smiles they gave each other at the dinner table when we were telling them our weekend plans. They thought the smiles were secret, that we didn't notice, but I noticed and I bet Laurie did too.

I didn't enjoy the parties much. They were just kids getting drunk or stoned and falling in people's pools. They reminded me of the "Freers at Rhea's" the winter before Dad died when girls I was never even friendly with at school started to call in on Friday nights and pretend they wanted to hang around with me, but really it was because they knew I'd have a freer. The first weekend, it was Therese Roberts and Nikki Hartnett, and then Ronan Barry and John Duffy and Dominic Kelly called in with some cans. They came the weekend after too, and so did Tracey Dorgan and Alan Roche, and the next weekend Susan Mulligan called in and smiled and said "Hi, Rhea" as if she always called for me, and I let her in too. And even though Lisa said they were all only using me—even though I knew they were—it was kind of fun all the same. It wasn't anything to do with Nicole either—she was always at her dad's at weekends—it was just that I liked having the house full of people, playing Dad's Hendrix records for them and making batch toast for everyone.

It was fun, that's all. It's fun until the night I come in and I find Susan Mulligan and Therese Roberts in my room, and Susan Mulligan is ripping the fold in the subway map with her nail and Therese is on her hunkers, looking into the bedside locker where I keep your photos and the Carver book and saying something about you that's really horrible and that's not true. And that's when I kick her in the back, hard; I didn't know she was going to fall over, that she'd cut her face on the corner of the locker door. I didn't know she'd freak out when she saw the blood.

That's the last of the "Freer at Rhea's" weekends. Susan Mulligan's face is all mean as she walks out with her arm around Therese and she tells me I'll be sorry. At school she calls me Diarrhoea, which she hasn't done since about fifth class, but it sounds even more stupid now and she stops after a few days.

The parties me and Laurie go to are mostly in Shannon's house, because her father and mother are in Europe and Shannon's older brother is supposed to look after things but he's never there.

They're younger than me, most of the kids at the parties, because they're in Laurie's grade, and even though I recognise them from school, I don't know most of them. I make friends with Spencer at the first party, when he asks me to play euchre with him and I do. That's what we do all the time after that, me and Spencer, play euchre while he drinks neat vodka and I drink Coke. That night, we're playing by the pool and I'm winning for once. Nearly all the other kids are getting off with each other by then, on the loungers around the pool or upstairs. I don't want to get off with anyone and Spencer only wants to get off with Erica Simons, who's getting off with Jason Tomback. I'm keeping an eye on the time, because my job is to get Laurie from where she is upstairs with Mike when it's getting close to our curfew. I know she's using me, Mum, just like Susan Mulligan and Therese Roberts, but I'm kind of using her too. Glenda's away with her family for a whole month, and Cooper won't give me all the shifts I want in the restaurant, and playing euchre with Spencer is better than sitting at home with Aunt Ruth.

I never did find out how Cooper knew we were there, at Shannon's. It's before our curfew when he shows up—he should have still been at the restaurant—but he's in the kitchen, coming through the double doors onto the patio, waving my prosthetic in one hand.

He comes right over and I don't remember what I say, or if I say anything, but he's shouting about how much the prosthetic cost and that he didn't pay all that money so some dipshit could use it to fondle himself. Spencer is cracking up laughing but I can't look at him, because I'll start laughing too and that'll make it worse.

Cooper throws the prosthetic into my lap. "Put it on. We're going."

He's looking around the pool, his eyes squinting trying to make out who's who. I'm fiddling with the straps and they're even more awkward than usual.

"Where's Laurie?" he goes then, when he realises she's none of the people by the pool. "Where the fuck is Laurie?"

Shannon is coming over and he grabs her arm, spilling her drink. She giggles and gestures inside. "She's upstairs, Mr. Wilson. You want me to get her?"

I should have done something then, I should have acted quicker, but Cooper's already dropped Shannon's arm and pushed past her, through the double doors, back into the kitchen. I'm behind him and Spencer is behind me, all of us running around the kitchen counter, up the stairs. On the landing, the doors are open, all of them are, except for one at the end, and that's the one Cooper charges towards.

Me and Spencer get there in time to see what Cooper sees, Laurie with no top on, Mike grabbing a sheet from the bed to cover himself up as he runs to the corner. Cooper doesn't pause, if anything he speeds up as he strides into the room, his legs and his arms all one motion as he picks Mike up and holds him against the wall before punching him straight in the face, twice, three times.

Laurie's screaming and there's blood and then Mike's on the ground, his hands over his head, and Spencer is trying to grab Cooper's arms and someone on the landing is yelling about calling 911.

And then there's blood everywhere, on the sheet and the floor, and Cooper is throwing Laurie's shirt at her and Spencer's bent down over Mike and when I turn around, Shannon has a cordless phone in her hand and she's saying, "Hello, hello?" over and over, but I don't know if there's anyone at the other end.

Laurie cries the whole way home. Cooper doesn't say anything, only jerks the car around corners and stops too late at the stop signs. When we get to the house, Laurie jumps out before he's even turned the engine off and runs past Aunt Ruth, who's just opened the front door.

After that, there's no trips to the movies or the mall, no pocket money, no TV, no working in the restaurant, no leaving the house at all except when it's with one of them. Cooper even takes Laurie's phone from her room, as well as her TV. I don't have a TV so he takes my CDs and my CD player and my art stuff and my books. There's new rules in the house as well—no eating between meals for any reason and I have to wear the prosthetic all the time, except when I'm in the shower or in bed.

I didn't think it would be that bad, being bored, but it's really bad. The worst thing is my head, the way it keeps thinking of things I don't want to think about all the time, about Lisa and Rush and Dad and Nicole and even you sometimes. And sometimes I get this weird feeling, kind of like a stomach ache but not a stomach ache, in this place under my ribs which doesn't feel sore exactly, more like kind of empty, like a hole or something, and the only thing that will make it go away is sitting spinning in my desk chair and listing all the subway stops in my head, each line over and over, till I go back to the start again.

That's what I'm doing the night Laurie comes into my room after dinner. "I'm so fucking bored!" she goes, flopping down on the bed. "People can die from boredom, you know? I saw it on the Discovery channel once. I don't think I'm going to live long enough to go back to school."

"'Boring people get bored,'" I go. "My friend's mum used to always say that."

Laurie sighs. "So, I'm boring, then. So are you. All you ever do is spin in that stupid chair or do your PT exercises."

"You should tell your dad that. He'd be pleased to know I was putting effort into getting used to my prosthetic."

Laurie sits up, cross-legged, turns her feet so they are facing sole-up on her thighs. "I won't get a chance because he's never going to talk to me again. I swept up all the leaves on the patio tonight and he didn't even say thank you."

"Maybe he didn't notice."

"He was sitting right by the window, pretending to read the paper. He hates me. I don't care, I hate him too after what he did to Mike.

It's driving me crazy that I can't call him, see how he is. What if he's really badly hurt, Rae? What if he's brain damaged or something?"

"Laurie, we've had this conversation fifty times. When you managed to call Tanya that time she said she'd seen him at the beach. He wouldn't have been at the beach if he was brain damaged."

She pulls a stray hair from her ponytail, rolls her neck. "He must hate me so bad. As soon as I see him again, he's going to dump me."

"Want to play a game?" I suggest.

"A game?"

"You know—Monopoly? Or cards? Do you have Scrabble? I've never played Scrabble."

"They're kids' games." She makes a face, then smiles. "I know, how about Truth or Dare?"

I spin in my chair. "Now, that's a kids' game," I go. "Me and Lisa used to play it when we were twelve."

"Come on," she says, "one round. Three goes each, I'll go first. Truth or Dare?"

I spin so I'm facing her. "All right then, truth."

Laurie smiles, raises her eyebrows. "When did you first know you were a lesbian?" In the silence of my room, the word is like a bomb going off.

"Laurie, keep your voice down! They're only down the hall!"

"They're never going to hear us over the TV."

"I'm not a lesbian," I whisper. "You said you wouldn't say that again."

"Rae, you have to tell me the truth," Laurie goes. "It's Truth or Dare."

I swing a little on the chair, hold my prosthetic with my hand. I want to tell her the truth, but I'm not sure what it is. "I don't know."

She sucks her hair. "How can you not know?"

"Laurie, I liked one girl, once. Nothing ever happened, we never even kissed, so I don't know if I am. That's the truth." She's still sucking and I know she's about to ask another question, but I get in first. "My turn. Truth or Dare?"

"Truth."

I know what I'm going to ask, but I pretend to think about it. I keep my voice low so she'll answer me. "So, what was it like? Going all the way with Mike?"

She glances at the door, as if Cooper might come in at any minute, pulls her feet higher on her thighs, looks down at the bed, shrugs. "It was okay."

"Okay, that's all I get?"

Her eyes flick up to me, to the door, and back to the bed. "The first time, I thought it was just because it was sore, that it didn't work, and then after that, it was... I don't know... okay. Tanya was right, it's kind of overrated."

"Really?"

"Yeah." She smiles a proper smile. "Kind of like *The Big Lebowski*." We both laugh then because out of all the people we know who went to see *The Big Lebowski*, we're the only ones who didn't love it.

"Sex is like *The Big Lebowski*?" I go. "How disappointing."

"Maybe not all sex," Laurie goes, "maybe just sex with Mike. Anyway, my go. Truth or dare?"

I spin a full circle in the chair. There's nothing she can ask that's worse than what she did already. "Truth."

"Okay, so you say you don't know if you're a lesbian because you never even kissed this Nicole girl. So let me ask you, are there other girls you've wanted to kiss?"

There's triumph in her voice at how she's crafted the question. I answer too quickly. "No."

I don't look at her. We both hear the lie. Laurie slaps her hands on her thighs.

"Truth, Rae, come on! Who is she?"

My mind does this thing then, a thing I don't want it to do, more than anything I don't want it to do. It skips back to a few days before, by the pool, when she was wearing that silver bikini that Cooper hates her wearing. "There's no one."

"Rae, come on, I can tell when you're lying."

I don't know how she can tell, but she can. But she didn't know what I was thinking that day by the pool, because if she had she wouldn't have taken off her bikini top and started putting sun cream on her breasts, right there, right in front of me. Not that I looked, I made myself not look and I got up, really casually, and went to get a glass of water as if it had nothing to do with her at all.

Laurie's watching me, waiting for an answer. I need to give her something.

"Okay then," I go. "Yes." I look at her when I say it, hold her eyes with mine, those blue eyes I noticed that first day.

She's clapping her hands. "I knew it, I knew it! Who is she? Tell me!"

"That's another question." I hold my hand up. "My turn. Truth or dare?"

"Okay." She's shifted positions so her legs are hanging over the edge of the bed and she bounces up and down. "Truth. Ask me anything."

I want to ask her a million things but my mind goes blank. And then a question comes. "Why did you hate me so much when I first got here?"

She stops bouncing. "I didn't hate you—"

"Truth!"

She pulls her legs back up under her, studies her toes. On her middle one there's a toe ring like a mini belt and she twists it around. "I didn't hate you," she says again.

"Laurie…"

"No, wait." She looks up and I see her face is real, not pretending. "I know I was mean, but I didn't hate you. I was mad, I guess, with Dad for his whole fake happy family act. It was bad enough this shit about me having a 'new Mom' without having an 'Irish sister' as well."

She imitates Cooper perfectly, I can hear him saying it. "He really said that?"

"Yup," she nods. "I was fifteen, I didn't want a sister. I still don't."

"Me neither."

We smile. Laurie looks down at her toes again. "Plus there was something about you—you were so...I don't know, sure of yourself or something. Like you knew who you were. I don't know, maybe I was jealous or something." She takes the toe ring on and off, on and off.

"Me?" I go. "Sure of myself?"

She looks up, her hair half covering one eye. "You do your own thing, Rae, you're different. You don't care what anyone thinks."

I roll the chair a little closer to the bed so I can prop my feet up on it. The prosthetic is hurting me and I unstrap it, let it roll onto the floor. I rub my stump where it's been.

"That looks sore," Laurie goes.

"It is. They say you get used to it, but I don't think I ever will."

"What's it like?" she asks. "Only having one arm?"

"Is that your last question?"

"No!" She hits the bed. "That's not a real question! You know that's not a real question! The question I want to ask you is who this girl is you want to kiss?"

I smile. I have it figured out already, my plan. Checkmate. "Well, you can't ask me that because I don't choose 'truth,' I choose 'dare.'"

I lean back into the chair. I rub my stump again. There's only three questions, so she can't ask any more unless I agree to play again. And I'm never playing this game with her again.

She pulls her ponytail out from its scrunchie, flattening it between her hands. She's frowning, until she smiles a slow smile.

"Come on," I go, "you can't take a hundred thousand years. What's the dare?"

"I got it. I got one!"

"Okay then, what is it? Tell me, so I can get it over with."

There's something about the way she's smiling that's making my heart go fast and I'm afraid then it's going to be something really bad, maybe even worse than if I'd said 'truth.'"

"Okay." She smiles again. "You sure you're ready?"

"I'm ready."

She closes her eyes, straightens her spine, and puts her hands on her thighs.

"All right then, here it is. I dare you to kiss me."

I don't say anything. I sit there, frozen, for five seconds or five minutes or five hours. She opens her eyes. Smiles.

"Come on, Rae, don't be a coward. That's the dare—kiss me."

And then she closes her eyes again and puckers her lips a bit and I get up from the chair and sit next to her on the bed. And I lean over, really slowly, almost like I'm not moving at all, and then my lips are millimetres away from her lips and then they're on her lips and it's happening. Before I can think too much about it, we're kissing, me and Laurie are kissing.

And I don't know how long I have to kiss her for, for the dare, because she didn't say, but I don't stop and she doesn't either, and of all our kisses, that first one seems to go on and on forever. And sometimes it feels like it's still going on; if I close my eyes right now, I can still feel it—that kiss—still taste it. It might sound crazy, Mum, but if I close my eyes and picture that moment, it's as if I'm kissing her still.

Rhea

Central Park, New York
2nd May 1999
10:11 a.m.

Dear Mum,

Central Park is busy today, loads of tourists because of the sun. They never make it up this far though, to the reservoir, and it's nice and quiet here. Mostly, you don't see many tourists after you go past the lake. Most of them make it as far as the Bethesda Fountain or Strawberry Fields and think they've seen Central Park, which is like going to Florida and thinking you've seen America.

I've looked all over for your bench, checked hundreds of them between the 59th Street entrance and here, but I still can't find it. I'm not even sure if you have a bench here. Even as Dad was telling me, he said he might have been wrong, and Aunt Ruth never mentioned anything about a bench.

The night Dad tells me about the bench, Central Park is on the news. The funny thing is I don't even notice because I'm at the table, doing a still life of two empty bottles for my art homework. At first I don't know what Dad is talking about at all.

"There's a bench there somewhere with her name on it."

When I look up, there's New York on the screen, Central Park trees up to their waists in snow. A voice talking about a blizzard.

"Whose name?"

I ask even though I know he means you. I hope he does. He doesn't take his eyes off the telly.

"Your mother."

He has a can in his hand but it's only his third. He's not drunk yet.

"In Central Park? How come?"

He takes a sup from the can. "Her father. He put it there for her. You know, after."

128

After she died. After she drowned. I want to finish the sentence for him but then I know he won't say anything at all. I make my voice light.

"Whereabouts?"

He glances over, then back to the screen. Shrugs. "How should I know? It's the biggest park in the world, isn't it? Must be a fair rake of benches."

The news has moved on to the ad break. He tips his head back, empties his can. He's about to shake it and say he has time for just one more. After that, he'll leave the room and forget what we were talking about and I'll never find out. The trick is to pretend it's not important, that I don't really care. I keep my voice casual. "You never told me that before—I don't think you did."

He keeps looking at the telly. "Did I not?"

"No, I'd have remembered something like that. Definitely. You never said."

The ads are still on, he shakes his can, stands up. And that's when I blow it. "You should have told me, Dad."

He rolls his eyes. "Jesus, Rhea. I'm sorry I said anything."

"Why didn't you tell me before?"

"It's only a bloody bench! It's not like it's something important."

It comes on really quick, the anger, like it was there all along, just waiting. I'm standing up, balancing myself against the table with my hand.

"It's important to me! Do you ever think about what might be important to me?"

I'm shouting, but he doesn't shout back, only stands there holding his empty can. He looks tired.

"I shouldn't have said anything, it's only upsetting you."

"I'm not upset!" I shout louder, and I hate that I sound upset. "I just want to know, that's all!"

He looks back to the telly, there's a happy family getting into a new car. He shakes his can again. "I've told you everything I know, love. The mother told me that the father was going to put a bench there, but I don't even know if he ever did."

I stand there, looking at him, waiting for more. He checks his watch as if he has somewhere to be, as if people are waiting on him. "Just time for one more."

I don't know if I ever hated him as much as I do right then, watching his back as he walks into the kitchen, the sag in the arse of his jeans; the bald patch through his grey hair looks bigger than before. I circle my hand over the end of my stump. I don't get it—how he doesn't seem to care, how he never asks, how he never says anything. I know he loves you, like I do, it doesn't make any sense at all.

The bench I'm sitting on now is not your bench, the plaque says: "For Rosie, my one true love." I checked all the ones I passed by today on the way up here, all the ones without people sitting on them. Thinking about it, if there was a bench, it would probably be on the east side, over near 76th Street, near your old apartment, and I don't know why I'm only thinking about that now. *Dumbass.* That's what Laurie would say and then she'd laugh so it didn't sound mean. She's always telling me that I'm so busy looking at little things that I miss the big picture. I have a system, I'm trying to check the benches in order, but she wouldn't think that was important. She'd just start looking at benches near East 76th Street.

Maybe she's right. Maybe it's not important. Maybe I'll check over there later, after I sleep. I'm so tired, Mum. I keep dozing off, writing this letter. I need some proper sleep. Maybe I'll walk over there when I wake up and I'll let you know if I find your bench. Maybe I will.

———

It's his fault—that disgusting guy—it's his fault I forget about the best place to find your bench. When I wake up, it takes me a minute to notice him, sitting on the bench opposite mine. He's smiling, a weird smile I don't like. I notice that first and the fact that he's looking right into my eyes, before I notice his belt buckle and that his trousers are open. I don't need to tell you where his hand is.

Cooper said I was a pervert, but that guy is a pervert, people like him. Like the guy who stood outside our school and flashed through the railings—the nuns made us all stay in the gym hall until he was gone. If the word "pervert" exists for anyone, it should be for people like him.

I sit up, grab my backpack from where it was under my head. He's wearing a suit and a shirt and tie. I tell him that he's disgusting, a filthy perv, but his smile doesn't change and his hand only moves faster.

He's the reason I forget the whole thing about 76th Street and run to the nearest way out. It's not that I'm scared or anything, I just want to get out of the park, just get away. I don't think about where I'm going, I just keep walking west on 91st until I get to Amsterdam and I turn left, downtown. I'm only telling you all these details because I want you to be able to picture it—me starting to walk more slowly now, the backpack on my back, the sun in my eyes. That was when I first saw the poster taped to the lamppost, the poster with my face on it.

The photo is one that Laurie took, that summer we were grounded, one day by the pool. I'm sitting at the end of the sun lounger in my black jeans and my Docs and my Zeppelin T-shirt. My hair is pulled back, so even though it's long in the front you can see it's shaved underneath. My smile is a real smile. At the top it says "MISSING!" in red letters, all in capitals. I don't like the exclamation mark at the end, like it's a joke that someone is missing.

Underneath there are a few lines of words in black. Here's what they say:

Rhea (Rae) Farrell (Irish).
Age: 17.
5 feet, 3 inches, 164 pounds. Right arm missing from elbow.
Rhea has been missing since Sunday, March 12.
Last seen Broward Central Bus Terminal, Fort Lauderdale,
believed to be heading to New York City.
Loving family, very concerned. Reward offered.
Call Ruth: 407-555-0183.

I stand there reading and rereading. There are a gazillion questions in my brain: Has anyone called? How much is the reward? Is Aunt Ruth here, in New York, putting these posters up? Who'd seen me in Broward Central? Does Cooper know she's offering a reward? Does Laurie? "Loving family, very concerned." That's a joke. I want to cross that out. Cooper's voice is in my head: "We treated you like family." Fuck him. The number on the poster isn't their home number, though, it's Aunt Ruth's work cell phone. I bet he doesn't even know about these posters. I bet she didn't even tell him.

I can't believe she wrote that about my arm. As if it's not enough to see it in the stupid photo. I bet that's why she used that picture, it's probably one of the only ones without the prosthetic. I can't believe she put my weight. How did she even know my weight? Not that it's my weight anymore.

It's only when I see a Chinese lady looking at me looking at the poster that I realise how stupid I am to stand there staring at it. I want to tear it down, but she's still watching, so instead I walk down Amsterdam as if nothing is the matter. There's loads more lampposts, but not all of them have posters and I see four more between there and 59th Street and one lamppost with tape on where something had been ripped off. After 59th, Amsterdam becomes Tenth Avenue and there's only garages and storage units where no one's going to see any posters, so I turn back and walk up Broadway.

I've been walking for hours, Mum, back up Broadway and down the other side, but I haven't seen any more, even though I walked loads of Columbus too. Why are there only five? Why only on Amsterdam? I'm afraid to go further uptown, near Columbia, in case she put any there. But what am I going to do if I find them? I can't take them down, not during the day anyway. For the first time in ages, I wish Sergei was here—he'd know what to do. He'd make it a game, coming out at night to find the posters, he'd say we should wallpaper our apartment with them after we take them down. When we find an apartment.

I'm back in Central Park now, Mum, the touristy part. After

this, I'm going to go to the pizza place by Port Authority and if I run into Sergei, I'm going to tell him that he doesn't have to bring back the money. I still have the Discman, I could have brought it back. I'm no better than he is really. I'll say it doesn't matter, that we can be friends again. I'll forgive him. I might even tell him I'm sorry.

Can they arrest me, Mum? The police? Can they make me go back? I'm eighteen in ten days. Once I hold out till I'm eighteen, they can't make me go back, can they? Can they make me live with her until I'm twenty-one? I can't go back for three more years, for three more months, for three more weeks, for three more days, for three more minutes, even.

I'm all over the place, Mum. I'm here in Central Park but I'm back in Florida too and down in Port Authority making up with Sergei. I had this art teacher in Coral Springs called Miss Chen. She was way better than Ms. Ryan in Rush. Miss Chen used to say you couldn't do art if your body was in one place and your head was somewhere else, that you had to bring your head to the same place your feet were before you started.

She made us do this thing once, when we were drawing outside, to slow us down. We had to list five things we could see, five things we could hear, five things we could feel. And then we had to do four things we could see, hear, feel, and then three and then two and then one. We had to do it in our heads, not write it down, and we weren't allowed start drawing till we'd gone all the way through to number one. Right now, in Central Park, I can see the swings and slides. That's two things. Three—trees, four—the baseball field. Five—rocks coming out of grass. I can hear the sound of the swings swinging—they're creaking because they need oil—traffic, a helicopter. I can hear two little girls shrieking on the swings as their parents push them. Is that one or two things? The dad is pushing the bigger girl and the mum is pushing the smaller one. She wants to get off, the smaller one does, you can tell by the sounds she's making and because she keeps turning around, but the mum doesn't notice, keeps pushing her higher.

I feel my feet on the ground, my hand in my jacket pocket, the weight of the backpack on my back. I feel my breath, coming in and out. That little girl's shrieks are piercing, more like crying now, and I wish she'd stop even though I know it's not her fault, it's her stupid mother who keeps pushing her. I still wish she'd stop. It's hard to keep breathing with her crying like that.

I can't think of a fifth feeling thing. Feeling is always the hardest, seeing is the easiest. I cheat, make my hand a fist. Five—I feel myself making my hand a fist. The mother has stopped swinging the little girl, she's picked her up and is carrying her over to the benches. Their swing is still swinging, on its own. There's something I need to ask you. Do you remember the swings near the car park that faced the beach? Did you take me there? Lisa and I sometimes went there. I could be wrong but I think I remember being on those swings before then, way, way, way before then. I think I remember being there with you.

I wish I had a photo but that's stupid, because I haven't even looked at the photos I found in Nana Davis' room yet. If I had a photo though, I could trust the memory, but I can feel it, I think I can. Here's what I think I remember feeling:

1. Your hands on my back, my shoulder blades, your fingers touching me hard and then lighter and then not at all because there is only air behind my back.

2. My hands on the chain, rust coming away on my fingers.

3. The blue line of sea, above the brown line of sand and green line of grass and grey line of car park.

4. Going up, it goes: grey, green, brown, blue and coming down, it goes: blue, brown, green, grey.

5. My red sandals kicked out in front of me. The toe part is square and a bit scuffed.

6. Your voice and my voice laughing, together and far away, together and far away. Together.

That's it. That happened. I know it happened. I think it did. I feel like I can see you, standing behind me, pushing. You're wearing a denim skirt, a long one, and a jumper that's brown and white. You have red sandals on too—we both have red sandals—and your hair is longer than in the Columbia photo and it swings in front of your face with every push. I can't see if you're smiling, but I know you are.

I couldn't be on the swing and see you pushing me at the same time—I know that. I'm making that part up, I must be, but I don't think I'm making up the rest, the lines of colour and my sandals out in front of me and my hands around the chain. I can feel the rust, flaking away on my fingers, all ten of them.

Thousands of days after that happened, thousands of miles away from Rush, it feels like I still can.

Dear Mum,

Do you believe in God? Did you, I mean? I suppose you know for sure now.

There's a guy in Central Park who does. All day long, he's there, talking into a microphone about turning our lives over to God's will, that it's the only way to have the lives we want, the only way to be free.

I must have heard him repeat that fifty thousand times this afternoon. He was wrecking my head and I wanted to move, but every time I tried, I fell asleep. And then he was there in my dreams, the man talking about God and how I needed to ask Him for help. When I woke up properly, it felt like maybe it was a sign.

Dad didn't believe in signs. He didn't believe in God and we never went to mass, except when I made my Communion and my Confirmation. When I stayed at Lisa's on Saturday nights, I had to go with them on Sunday mornings, but, when we got older, Lisa stayed at our house on Saturdays so she wouldn't have to go either.

I still don't know what religion he was, the man with the microphone, even after hours of listening to him. Maybe it doesn't matter. Maybe religion and God are totally separate things anyway. When I got up to leave the park, he was talking about the power of prayer. According to him, we just needed to tell God what we wanted and have faith that He would provide.

I used to say my prayers every night and every morning. I don't know what age I was when I stopped, but I can remember what I prayed for. It sounds silly now, stupid, but I'll tell you anyway. I prayed for you to come back and for you and Dad to have another baby, so I'd have a little sister or brother. Thinking about it, I think that's when I stopped praying—when that didn't happen. I suppose you have to give God a chance and pray for something that's actually possible. Which is why I thought I'd give it another try.

Do you want to know what I prayed for today, Mum? I prayed for somewhere safe to sleep, somewhere to lie down and rest. That's it. That's all.

And when I leave the park, that's when I find this Y. I didn't even know there was one around here, I would've walked by without noticing, except someone comes down the steps with the Y logo on the back of their tracksuit top, right as I'm walking by.

And I nearly don't bother coming in because I'm thinking that they probably don't have rooms, because not all Ys have rooms, and that, even if they do, they'll be booked up because they always get booked up way in advance.

But I come in anyway. And they do have rooms. And the girl behind the desk smiles at me and, for a second, I think it's because she's seen the posters, but it's because someone just called and cancelled so they have one room available, just for tonight, and she says it must be my lucky day.

Sergei would say that I'm taking the easy way out, giving in, that it's stupid to spend nearly every last dollar I have on some room at the Y when there's rooms for free all over New York if you only know where to look. He'd say it was bullshit thinking that God had provided, that it was just a coincidence. But Sergei's not here and I've a good feeling, Mum, the first I've had in a long time and I don't care what anyone else thinks.

I don't have to check out till eleven a.m. tomorrow and that gives me eighteen hours here. Time to sleep and shower and get properly clean, so I can look for a job and leave my backpack here so no one will know I'm homeless. And I've time to look at Nana Davis' photos, to lay them all out on the floor so I can see each one properly, and I might do that first, before I do anything else.

———

Mum, I'm scared. I'm sick. I feel … I don't know how I feel. Angry. I feel fucking angry. *Dumbass, Rhea.*

Shut up, I'm not a dumbass.

Dumbass.

Shut up. Shut the fuck up. I'm so tired. I shouldn't be tired, I slept for almost twelve hours. What time is it? 4:35 a.m. What time was it when I started looking at the photos?

I can see them from here, sixteen photos, four rows of four. There's loads of us, just you and me, Dad isn't in any of them. Some of them are blurry but there's a really good one with me on your knee with your hands around my waist, and one where we're both making faces, sticking our tongues out. And there's some of Aunt Ruth, the two of us with her, on the beach in Rush, the wind blowing our hair, and then the same photo with you replaced by another woman, who looks a bit like you without your smile. Your handwriting on the back says the woman is Nana Davis. At first I think it's a mistake because there's no way the woman in the photo and the woman in the bed in Clover Hills can be the same person, but your handwriting on the back says she can.

I need Ziploc bags to put them in, the photos, to protect your writing. I don't have any Ziploc bags.

There's one photo of you on your own, standing in the kitchen, holding the red Nescafé mug and you're wearing a long denim skirt, a brown and white jumper, red sandals.

I threw that mug away, I'm sure I did, when we cleaned out the house. I didn't know. I would have kept it. How was I supposed to know? But I knew about your clothes. I remembered your clothes. I knew I remembered, that I didn't make it up.

How did I know?

I just knew.

———

138

It's 5:55 a.m. Have I been awake or asleep? I don't know. I don't know what's a memory and what's a dream. Laurie, kissing Laurie, her voice whispering that there's only ever been me, that's a memory, but Laurie turning into Nicole Gleeson is a dream. And then I'm driving. In real life I can't drive, but in the dream I can. There's no other cars on the road, only me, and when you walk out in front of me, I know I'm going to hit you, that I don't know how to stop, that I can't drive after all.

I never dream about you; I've always wanted to, but I never do. After that dream, there's a continuation dream. I'm still in the car and the doors are locked and I can't get out. I'm banging on the glass calling "Mum, Mum!" but even though you turn around and see me, you can't hear what I'm saying and you don't know who I am. You turn, really slowly, away from me, around a corner, out of sight.

There was a newspaper clipping in the photos. Your family like to do that. It's an obituary and I think it's going to be of your father, but it's not, it's of that man again, Cal Owens. I didn't read it all, only the beginning. He died the year after you did. Why did Nana Davis keep his obituary? Why would she have that and not her own husband's one? Was she having an affair with him? Is that why Aunt Ruth got all weird when I mentioned him? I bet that's why. I bet that's what the big lie is.

I dreamed about rats crawling under the bed, teeming rats. I fucking hate rats. It was only a dream, only a dream, only a dream. The rat in the front garden wasn't a dream the time Dad cleared out everything from the attic and the back bedroom and the presses in the dining room where Nana Farrell's stuff was and left it all in the corner of the garden—paint cans and a mattress and bike tires and old-fashioned ladies' shoes that he could have given to the charity shop. I'm at the beach with Lisa when he's doing it. When I come back, the speakers from the record player are up on the window sill, blaring "Voodoo Child," and the front door is open. When Dad comes out, his face is red and he's dragging a roll of carpet and he makes me take the other end, even though it's really heavy and filthy from being in the attic.

That night it rains and the next day I say he should get a skip like the Walshes up the road got but he says he has a friend in the Drop Inn with a van who's going to help him take it to the dump.

I don't know why I'm remembering that now, the pile of filthy stuff that smelled and got wet and never properly dried. Some mornings it would have other people's things in it, like a sewing machine, a broken deck chair. I hate it, every time I see it, from my window in the morning, having to pass it on the way to school, but if I say anything to Dad he only gets annoyed and says his friend is coming—but I know his friend isn't coming. And then, after forty-two days of it being there, I'm walking up the drive on my way home from school when I see the rat, pushing its way into the middle of the pile, under the mattress. And I run to Lisa's house and I hate that I'm crying, but I can't help it because I know there's a whole nest of rats in there, underneath everything, and I don't want to go home.

It's a Monday night, and they're supposed to be having liver, but that Monday Lisa's mum makes fish fingers and that's a nice coincidence because I love fish fingers. I stay overnight, even though I don't usually during the week. And someone calls the council to report the pile in the garden and they take it away the next day. When I come home everything is gone, except for one paint can lid that's mushed into the yellow grass. I'm glad it's gone, but I'm still scared about the rats. I know the council didn't take them too, that they must be living somewhere.

A different dream. I never remember my dreams but now I can't stop. I am teeming with dreams. There are missing posters all over Manhattan, blocking up every window of every building. "Missing!" written in red with a photo underneath. Except it's not my photo, Mum. It's yours.

9:42 a.m.

There are seventy-eight minutes to go until checkout and I haven't even showered yet. I haven't showered and I didn't look for jobs and now I only have $12.64 left. $12.64 between me and what? Starvation? Death?

Famines don't happen in New York, they happen in Africa where babies lie there in their mothers' arms with flies at the corner of their eyes, waiting to die, but maybe there's a famine here as well, a secret one at night that no one sees and maybe it's possible to starve here too, to die here too, right when other people are stuffing their fat faces all around you.

Fuck it. Fuck it. Fuck it. I can't believe I spent so much on this room. For what I paid for this room I could have had:

- 45 pizza slices

- 45 subway rides

- 15 trips to the laundromat

- 54 breakfasts of an egg and cheese on a roll and a coffee

- 9 trips to the cinema—you can sleep in the cinema you know, I never even thought about that, why didn't I think about sleeping in the cinema?

Dumbass.

And now the money's all gone and even if I live on the $1 breakfast special and two pizza slices a day, that's only enough for three more days, only until Saturday. Then that's it.

10:36 a.m.

Twenty-four minutes until checkout. I have to get up, have a shower, I'm not letting myself leave without a shower. Why am I so tired? I've had so much sleep and it's worse than if I'd never slept at all.

I want to leave the photos here, part of me does, but I'm not thinking straight. It would be fifty kinds of crazy to throw the photos away when I risked so much to get them, when more photos of you, of us together, is the only thing I've ever wanted.

If I still don't want them by the time it's my birthday, I'll get rid of them in Central Park. I'll dig a hole where I can bury them, or set them on fire or throw them into the lake, one by one. I'll stand on Bow Bridge and watch the water blur the colours of each photo together, watch the corners and the edges curl up, until they sink, down to the bottom, down to where the mud and the reeds are.

10:43 a.m.
Seventeen minutes. I'm getting up, I'm going. I need to say a prayer, like that man said, a morning prayer.

I don't know how to pray.

Write it down:

God. Help.

Mum, if for any reason God can't, will you?

Dear Mum,

It's been two days since I last wrote. But one day, two days... who cares really? I mean what's the point? I don't just mean the letters. What's the point of anything? Writing to you, looking for you?

You're dead.

Dead.

DEAD.

I know you're not reading these letters, that no one will. Yesterday, I decided not to write anymore, and now I'm writing again. I don't know why, except that I have paper and a pen and if there's no letter, then there's nothing. Really, nothing.

You know what I hate most out of everything that's happened in the past two days? That I found out the hour changed and I didn't know. On 4th April, the hour went forward—thirty-three days ago. Last night, this guy Jay told me about the hour, and I hate that for over a month, I've been totally out of sync with everyone else.

It was my own fault. I know it was stupid being in that part of Penn Station. I hate those back corridors, down near the tracks, but it was fucking raining and I didn't want to get soaked and if I stayed in the main part, someone might have seen me. Someone who wanted Aunt Ruth's reward.

So, that's the first stupid thing I did, heading down to that deserted corridor on my own. The second stupid thing was that I fell asleep. I wasn't planning to, I know it's dangerous. I was just so tired and I didn't even know I was asleep, until he's waking me up.

He's sitting right in front of me, too close, and his hand is tight on my elbow. He is a young black guy with a green and gold baseball cap with the letter "A" on it. He has a black tracksuit top on over a dirty white T-shirt. He's smiling, as if we are friends, and even though he's missing loads of teeth, he has a nice smile.

"Wakey wakey," he says.

His voice is friendly, like we know each other, and for a split second I wonder if we do.

"You've been sleeping a long time. Couple of hours. You don't usually sleep so long."

His fingers are gripping me, really hard, it's sore. His face is so close I can see white stuff at the corner of his mouth. But he's still smiling, so I make myself smile too.

"I don't normally come here, I missed my train. You must be thinking of someone else."

His eyes crinkle when he smiles wider. "I'm thinking of you."

My legs hurt from where they are scrunched up under me and I try and shift to one side so I can slide them out straight, but he's too close and he won't move.

"Thing is, I've seen you around. Been meaning to say hi."

His voice is deep, nearly like music. Every word, every pause, like it's timed. It's the kind of voice that slows you down, makes you feel sleepy, but I can't afford to feel sleepy, not now. I sit up straighter, push my bum into the tiles.

"Hey," he goes, "what's your favourite newspaper?"

"Newspaper?"

He loosens his grip on my elbow a little bit.

"Yeah, what do you like to read? You know, to keep up with things in the world?"

I say the first newspaper that comes to mind. "*The New York Times*."

He shakes his head and his hand tightens again, higher up this time, around my biceps. "*New York* fuckin' *Times*! No one reads *The New York Times* outside New York."

In Florida, Aunt Ruth got *The New York Times* delivered every Sunday and it was so thick there were always sections of the previous week's still around when the next Sunday came.

144

He's talking again, to himself as much as to me. "*The Wall Street Journal*, now that's a paper. *The Wall Street Journal* is read and respected all over the world."

The corridor is empty, not one other person in it. He could do anything to me here, no one would hear, no one would ever find me. His eyes are on mine, waiting for me to say something, to answer him.

"I'm not really into business stuff, finance and that."

He nods, keeps nodding. "I get you. Me, I'm a businessman."

"Really?"

My arm is hurting a lot, not only his grip but the angle he's holding it at. If I could get my legs out from under me, I could try and kick him in the balls, run for it. If I could get my legs out from under me, I might have a chance.

"They had this story last month, at the start of April—when the clocks changed. You know how much it costs this country every year? This daylight savings bullshit? Millions. That's what. Millions of dollars."

He makes his eyes bigger and that's when I notice how bloodshot they are.

"Wow," I go. "That's crazy."

"Crazy?" he goes, "it's fucking bullshit, that's what it is. It's fucked up."

He's silent then, for thirty seconds, or a minute, and he's looking at the wall behind my shoulder instead of at my face, and it's like he's forgotten I'm there. But then his eyes snap back to mine and his grip is tight again.

"How much rent you got for me?"

"What do you mean, rent?"

I know what he means. Sergei said it before, right at the beginning, that people had patches, territories we might not even be aware of. Fuck Sergei.

"Come on," he goes. His voice is gentle now, as if he's talking to a little kid even though he's probably not that much older than me. "Don't worry, show me what you got. I get some, you get some. That's how it works."

I have $6.83. That's all I have. $5 of it is in my sock.

"I don't have anything."

He pushes and twists my arm at the same time.

"Ow!"

"Come on now, we both know that's not true."

It hurts like a bitch, my elbow and my shoulder socket, all of it.

"Okay, so I have a couple of dollars. You'll have to let go of me, so I can get it."

He lets go, slowly, and I take the dollar bill from my back pocket, and eighty-three cents from my front one, put it in his cupped palms. He's not getting the $5 in my sock. "That's everything, that's all I have."

He puts it on the floor next to him and lets go of me to count it out, real slow. His fingers are long. Piano-playing fingers. He slides each coin along the tiles before he picks it up, stacks the dimes on top of the quarter, the pennies in a tower of their own. "That's it?"

"I told you, that's all I have."

He puts the dollar in his pocket, then the change. "That's a real shame."

"You can't take it, please! You can't leave me with nothing! What am I supposed to do with nothing?"

He takes off his cap, turns it in his hands. His hair is only bristles, shaved tighter than mine.

"Don't worry, I'll hook you up. Good money. You want to earn, right?"

I squirm to one side, wiggle my legs out a little.

"I don't beg, if that's what you mean."

He shakes his head, puts his cap back on. "No begging. Earning. Cute one like you—your accent, the he/she thing. People like that."

He's not holding on to me anymore, but my legs feel numb. Even if I managed to kick him, I don't know if they'd hold my weight when I stand up, if they'd be able to move fast enough to take me down the corridor.

He keeps talking, his voice slow, mesmerising. "You might not think it, but your arm—people are into that shit. People pay for that shit."

I cup my stump, I can't help it. "I'm not a prostitute. I'm getting a job. I'm not even homeless, I'm just in between places."

He laughs, tipping his head back. The laugh goes on for ages. When he stops, he wipes his mouth. "Honey, we're all just in between places."

There's a sound then, voices, two guys' voices. I can't see them but I can hear them, talking about the Knicks game. If I screamed, they'd hear me, they'd definitely hear me. I want to scream, but somehow I can't.

Their voices fade away and he keeps looking in the direction that they went, long after it is silent. When he turns to me again, his eyes are different, as if they are seeing me for the first time.

"What's your name?" he goes.

My brain can't think of another name. "Rhea."

"Rhea." He smiles. "That's cute. I'm Jay."

He holds out his hand and I take it. He lets go and reaches into his pocket, takes out the eighty-three cents. "Here," he goes. "When that runs out, come back and see me, okay?"

"Okay."

I take the change from him, hold it tight. I nearly thank him, but I don't.

"And don't be reading the *Times*. You pick up the *Journal*, remember?"

"Okay, I'll remember."

He gets up really slowly, he's almost graceful the way he does it, he doesn't have to push himself up with his hands or anything. I watch him as he walks away, towards where the voices were, and I notice he has a wonky foot, his left one. I'm watching how it moves, sloping out to one side and kind of dragging along the floor, when he turns around and tips his baseball cap at me and smiles.

That was last night—I think it was last night, not the night before—but it's hard to tell anymore. I'm not going to tell you how much of the $5.83 I have left. I haven't eaten since I've been down here on my bench by the water. It's kind of handy, not needing to eat, because I don't need to move, even to find a toilet, all I have to do is sit here and listen to the river lapping and watch the boats. In an hour or so, it'll get dark, the water will be black and in the blackness you wouldn't be able to see someone lowering themselves into the water, someone holding on to the bars of the railing, someone letting go.

It'd be cold, I know that. It would seep through my clothes, make them ice, make them heavy. Like a stone. "Stone Free." It's calm, though, flat, like in Rush. That day—you know the day I'm talking about—it was flat as a pancake, that's what they said. If someone who swims every day, someone who's such a good swimmer, can drown in calm water like that, it must be easier for someone who can't swim, someone who's never learned. It must be faster.

There's a payphone behind this bench. I can't see it because I'm looking at the water but I know it's there, five or six feet from where I'm sitting now. I could call Aunt Ruth's cell number, the one on the poster, I wouldn't have to talk to Cooper. I can imagine myself making the call, feel my neck holding the receiver, my finger punching the keys, hear the phone ringing, stretching out. You know how in films when someone is missing, the person answers the phone straightaway, all breathless and hopeful? I keep wondering if Aunt Ruth would answer like that.

This is how I imagine the call:

The phone would ring once, maybe twice, and then I'd hear Aunt Ruth at the other end.

Aunt Ruth: Hello?

Me: Breathing.

Aunt Ruth: Hello? Hello? Rhea? Is that you?

Me: Breathing.

Aunt Ruth: Rhea, please come home! I'm sorry, honey. You know I didn't mean it! I lied, what I said, I was only trying to hurt you—

And then I hang up.

I'm not going to call, though. No matter what happens, Mum, I'm not going to call. Even if Jay shows up at this bench, even if all the rats in New York come teeming out of the water.

The only possible reason in the world that I'd call would be if I was scared of dying. But people die, Mum. I mean you died, that's just what happens.

And I'm not scared of anything. I need to remember that, to keep remembering that, that I've never been scared of anything, of anything at all.

Rae

Dear Mum,

I went to Michael's to give him his Discman back. Everything bad that started to happen, happened since I took that Discman, as if taking it was bad karma or something, and the only way to undo it is by giving it back. That's what I tell myself the reason is, but on the way I think there might be another reason, like that I've no CDs or batteries. That maybe I'm going there to remember that only two weeks ago Sergei and I were in his apartment, eating dumplings and Pop-Tarts and watching a *Law & Order* marathon. I don't get time at all. Nothing interesting happens for months and months, sometimes even years, and then your whole world can change in only two weeks.

I don't expect to actually see him, he's upstate on the weekends, and I haven't figured out how to give him the Discman back, except maybe to wait until one of the neighbours is going in and ask them to leave it outside his door. That's what I'm thinking, but when I get there, there's a big people carrier outside his building, almost exactly like the car Cooper had except this one is black. The door of the building is propped open with a box and the lid doesn't shut properly and I can see there are CDs inside.

I have to be honest, Mum, I think about lifting the lid and taking one, which I know goes against the whole karma thing, but right then the idea of closing my eyes and listening to music, any music, is worth all the bad karma in the world. But before I have a chance, I hear voices coming down the stairs and that's when I hide in the doorway of the apartment building next door. Michael walks right past me, but he doesn't see me, and then a woman walks past, behind him. He's wearing a grey T-shirt with a line of sweat down the back and he's carrying a box. The woman is wearing a pink tracksuit and she's not carrying anything.

They put the box in the car and when they go back into the building, I run across the street, to where the lane is, so I can get a better view. It takes ages for them to come out again but when they do I get a proper look at the woman. She has sunglasses on, pink ones, and her blonde hair is in a ponytail, scraped back really tight so it pulls at the skin on the side of her face. It must be the woman from the photo, it has to be, but she doesn't look the same. She doesn't look the same at all.

They make twelve trips up and down to the car. Each time, Michael is carrying a big box that he loads into the boot and then when that's full he starts to load things into the back seat. The woman never carries anything except once when she carries a lamp. She could have just sat in the car and waited, but she follows him, a step behind his step, and it looks like she's talking all the time, even though he's not saying anything at all.

I don't know why watching them makes me sad, except that since that night at the Y, everything makes me sad. It's not like I even know Michael, not really, so it doesn't make sense why I don't want him to go. But I don't want him to go.

The last time they come out, he's carrying a backpack and a denim jacket, she has a white plastic bag. She says something and goes back into the building. I lean down and see her runners climbing the stairs. My brain is still deciding what to do when my feet decide first and run across the street. Michael is in the passenger seat with the window rolled down. At first he doesn't see me because he's looking in the mirror, doing something with his hair. I'm about to say his name when he glances over, sees me, does a double take. He jerks his head around to look over his shoulder, as if she's going to be right behind him, but she's not.

"Holy shit! What are you doing here? You got to get out of here."

"I came to give you this."

He looks confused at the Discman I'm holding up to the window.

He twists around in his seat to check the door of the apartment building, but she's still not coming.

"I shouldn't have taken it, I'm sorry. I haven't even used it, it still works."

"What the fuck? You scam me for over a thousand bucks and you come to bring this back?"

My stump hurts and I want to cup it but my hand still has the Discman.

"I didn't know about the money."

"Yeah, yeah, you probably put him up to it."

"I swear, I didn't know. He only told me after."

He's shaking his head, he doesn't believe me. He lowers his voice.

"You know what's fucked up? I can almost get the money thing, you know. I nearly can. But calling Melanie? What the fuck did you guys get out of that?"

"Melanie?"

"She's pregnant, you know. Did he tell you that? She could have lost the baby because of you."

His eyes are shiny and his hand is in a fist. I scrunch my toes up in my Docs. I hold out the Discman, but it's like he doesn't even see it. He glances over his shoulder again, his voice a whisper. "Where is he?"

"I don't know, I haven't seen him."

He looks at me then, his eyes properly look at me, take me in.

"You really haven't seen him?"

I shake my head.

"You have anyone else in the city you can go to? Any family?"

I bite down hard, clench. Inside my cheeks, I've all these sores, mouth ulcers, even though I keep brushing my teeth. Eating pizza hurts and so does eating bagels. He reaches into his pocket, takes out two twenties, holds them out the window in between his index and his middle fingers, like forty dollars is nothing at all.

"That's all I have on me, just take it."

I shake my head; that's not why I'm here. And then the fucking tears start leaking out, they're on my cheeks and I can't wipe them away without dropping the Discman and now he feels sorry for me, now he is pitying me.

"I don't want your charity."

"Fine," he says. "Give it to someone else who needs it."

He lets go of the notes and they flutter onto the road. One lands near my Doc, the other is next to the tyre.

"You have to go," he says. "Just take the fucking money and go."

I shove the Discman through the window at him, scrunch down and grab the notes. When I stand back up, he's looking at me differently, frowning this time.

"Hey," he goes, "did I see a poster with your face on it in the subway? Some girl missing from Florida. Is that you?"

My heart is kicking. I hoist my backpack higher on my back.

"Where?" I go. "Which subway station?"

We both hear it then, the noise, the sound of the apartment building door closing. There's panic in his face, but I know what to do. I cross the street, real slow, casual, like I was just walking by. I don't run. When I'm on the other side, I see the blonde woman. She hasn't even noticed me.

Melanie, her name is Melanie. Her hand is on her stomach, a little bump under her pink tracksuit top, a little bump that's a baby.

She gets into the car and as she puts on her seat belt, Michael glances over at me. She puts on the indicator, pulls away from the kerb, and they drive away.

I go to the diner, the diner where me and Sergei had breakfast that morning—not even three weeks ago. The hostess looks as if she mightn't seat me, then she does, at a table in the corner near the back. I'm looking for the waitress, the one who served us the day we had the row, but she's not there and that nearly makes the tears come again. I nearly order the pancakes, like Sergei had, but they're too expensive so I look through six pages of the menu before deciding on eggs and sausage because they come with hash browns and toast and coffee, and you get free refills on the coffee and at $4.75 before tax it's the best deal, plus it's soft so it won't hurt my mouth.

And now the food is all gone, like all food goes, and the thing about eating is as soon as I eat anything I always want more, like instead of making me full it just makes me more hungry. I want the curly fries, and the spaghetti and meatballs, and the waffles with cream and chocolate sauce. I want the loaded potato skins.

And I can't stop thinking about the look on Michael's face when he talked about Sergei calling his wife. Sergei must have been really mad to do that, or really hurt, but Michael was hurt too, I saw that, he let me see it. And in the movies there's always someone who hurts and someone who gets hurt, but maybe it's not always like that, maybe two people can hurt each other at the very same time?

Nicole Gleeson hurt me, Mum, but she didn't know she was doing it and maybe I hurt her a little bit too, by ignoring her after. With Laurie, it was different. She knew all along that I liked her and she hurt me anyway. You know what the funny thing was? In a way, I wasn't even surprised, like part of me knew she was going to do it, some part of me knew what was going to happen all along.

Rhea

West 46th Street, New York
11th May 1999
1:31 a.m.

Dear Mum,

Tonight, I did something different. I'm on 46th Street, just off Times Square. Usually I hate Times Square, but it's raining and I found a good spot, on a step under an awning, and I don't want to give it up. Nobody bothers me for ages, so I'm able to sleep on and off until, coming up to half ten, all these people start to arrive, one by one, to go in through the door behind me. It's a pain to have to keep getting up but I keep sitting back down on my step because it's the best spot. And one of those times, just as I'm about to sit back down, I see an old woman coming up the steps and something makes me stand back up and hold the door open for her.

"Thank you," she goes. When she pulls down her hood, I see she has really long, grey hair. "Are you here for the meeting?"

"The meeting?"

"It's a good one. I wouldn't come out on a night like tonight for any meeting."

She walks through the door and into a hallway, then she turns back to me. "Don't worry, you won't be the only new face. We get a lot of newcomers."

I'm still holding the door open and I don't know what makes me walk through it, what makes me follow her to the end of the hallway and up the stairs, except that maybe it seems like such a long time since anyone's invited me anywhere and it's nice to be somewhere dry and warm.

Halfway up the stairs, though, I start to get nervous in case it's a trap, some kind of cult, but there's a young guy behind me on the stairs and he looks okay and if I need to get out I know I could push past him easily. When we go into the room at the top, there's folding chairs

155

all laid out in a semicircle and two people behind a heavy table in the middle. The old lady hugs someone and they go and sit at the other side of the room. I take the seat closest to the door. And that's when I see the poster on the wall—the twelve steps of Alcoholics Anonymous.

I nearly laugh when I see that, because Alcoholics Anonymous is where Michael took Sergei one night, and Sergei said it was the lamest thing ever and the only good thing was that they had free coffee. This meeting doesn't have any coffee, I don't see any, but I'm glad Sergei told me about it, because he also said that you didn't have to say anything if you didn't want to, you could just listen. The man behind the table starts reading stuff from a folder, going on and on. It's warm and I know I'm never going to be able to stay awake. I'm taking off my Champion sweatshirt when he stops talking and introduces the girl next to him and everyone starts to clap.

She says her name is Tierney and that she's an alcoholic. I don't know why I'm calling her a girl because she's got to be in her thirties, but she seems like a kid in a way, especially when she laughs this really giggly laugh. She laughs a lot, right the way through, especially when she's telling us how she started to drink white wine because she thought if she drank it all there wouldn't be enough left for her Mom to get drunk. Everyone laughs at that part, only I don't, because I'm thinking it kind of makes sense and it reminds me of the time I poured Dad's Guinness down the drain. According to this girl, it didn't make sense though, because it didn't stop her mother drinking, the only thing it did was make her an alcoholic too.

I'm trying to get my head around all that and I almost miss the part where she says something about being a lesbian and I want her to back up and say that again, but she's moved on to talking about her work. I wonder if I'm imagining what she said, because she has long dark hair and she's wearing a skirt and red shoes with a little heel and she doesn't look like a lesbian any more than she looks like an alcoholic. And just when I think I must have heard her wrong, she starts talking about a date she was on earlier in the night with a

girl called Susan and that she was glad to have had an excuse to finish up, she was glad she was coming to the meeting.

She looks at the clock and says she'll leave it there and everyone
claps again. I hope there's going to be questions but there aren't, instead
it starts at the other side of the circle with each person taking turns to
talk about themselves and none of them are as interesting as Tierney.
Some people go on and on and others don't say much. Hardly anyone
talks about drink. The young guy from the stairs tells us all about his
dental work and how much it costs and the man next to him is from
Denver and he's in New York for a wedding and I feel sorry for him
that he has to spend part of his trip in a meeting like this. When it
comes to the old lady, she says her name is Winnie. She tells Tierney
that she reminds her of herself when she was younger, but I don't think
she means the gay part, because then she goes on about her pregnant
daughter and how she really wants to help her, but she has to respect her
daughter's wishes when she says she doesn't want her help.

It goes around the circle and then I'm going to be next. I'm not
going to say anything, I don't have to, Sergei said you don't have
to—but then the person next to me finishes and they all look at me.

I shrug. "I don't know what to say."

"What's your name?" the guy with the folder says.

I picture Aunt Ruth's posters, hiding, lying in wait all over the city.

"Lisa."

My voice sounds funny, not like my voice. I think maybe that's
why I want to talk to them, that maybe I want to say something
more than "I was wondering if you are hiring at the moment?"
Maybe I want to use my voice so I know I still have it.

The room has a rug in it, an attempt to make it homey, only it
doesn't work. The rug is purple and there's a red cross but it's kind of
off centre and that bothers me and that's what I start talking about,
the off-centre cross. And next thing I know, I'm talking and talking and talking, words spilling out of my mouth like I couldn't stop
them even if I wanted to.

I tell them about all the places I looked for a job today, how I went into every single shop, restaurant, deli, fast food joint along Broadway from 23rd all the way up to 50th and not one place said yes, or even maybe. I tell them about the two girls talking at the counter in the shoe shop who ignore me even though I'm standing right in front of them and they crack up laughing when I walk away and say something I can't hear but I know it's about me. I tell them about the guy in the diner who says that they don't let homeless people in, even before I get a chance to ask about a job. I keep looking down at the rug as I tell them everything, I don't look at any of their faces. And then I get to the part about the nice woman in the bakery, who isn't hiring either but she tells me that in a nice way, and gives me a bag of cookies that she says are broken and when I open them later, they're still warm and all in one piece and not broken at all.

It makes zero sense that I start to blubber about the nice bakery lady when I didn't cry about the two bitches in the shoe shop but that's what happens. And before I can stop myself, I blubber that I miss Laurie, that I wish she was here, that I wish I had her to share the cookies with.

It's awful then, only silence and the sound of my crying. I want to get up, to run down the stairs, to pick up one of the chairs and hit the girl who walks over to give me a tissue, but instead I take it and blow my nose. Someone says, "Keep coming back," and then it moves on to the lady next to me. And it's only then that I realise I forgot to pretend to be an alcoholic, and I hope they won't kick me out.

At half eleven, it ends and everyone holds hands in a circle, which is weird and like a cult and kind of awkward too, but the man to my right puts his hand on my shoulder and kind of squeezes it, which feels nice in a way. I'm getting ready to leave and when I look up the old lady is in front of me, the one called Winnie who was talking about her daughter being pregnant.

"It was nice to hear you, Lisa," she says.

For a second I forget my name is Lisa, then I remember.

"Okay," I go. "You too."

"A few of us go for fellowship," she says. "Would you like to come?"

"For what?"

She smiles, slides her glasses further up her nose.

"We go to the diner, for something to eat, coffee."

I swing my backpack over my shoulder. "No, thanks, I can't."

"They do the best burgers in Midtown." She raises an eyebrow. "My treat?"

"No, thank you. I have to be somewhere."

She looks at me, her eyes steady behind her glasses. We both know it's a lie. Right then, Tierney comes up behind her, puts her hands on both our shoulders.

"You coming to the diner, Winnie?"

"Sure am. I was just seeing if Lisa would come too."

Tierney turns to me. "Oh, hi. Nice to meet you. You'll come, right?"

I start to shake my head. "I was just saying I can't, I—"

"Oh come on, we don't bite. Get to know us, it'll be fun."

She giggles, like she did when she was speaking. She looks like someone who is fun. I look at Winnie and back to her. "Okay."

On the way to the diner, Tierney tells me that she's Irish too, that Tierney was her mum's maiden name and she wanted to keep it, even though it was a last name.

We're stopped at a light, waiting to cross.

"Did you get teased at school?" I ask.

She looks at me, makes a face. "Did I? You wouldn't believe it. Kids can be cruel."

"I believe it," I go. "I used to get hassled about my name too."

"Really?" I hear the surprise in her voice and realise my mistake before she says it. "Lisa's not a common name in Ireland?"

"I meant, for my last name," I go. "I got teased for my last name."

If she asks what my last name is, I'm going to pretend that it's Ass or Penis or something, but she doesn't ask. By then, we're at the diner and Winnie is in front, holding the door open for us. I'm scared they might say they don't want me in there, but walking in between Winnie and Tierney, no one says a thing and we all go to a big table at the back.

There's eight people altogether, two other women apart from the three of us and three men. I'm on the end, next to Tierney and opposite Winnie. Winnie's talking to the dental work guy next to her and Tierney's talking to the girl on her other side. I read the menu and pretend it doesn't matter.

I'm on the third page when Winnie leans across the table. "Don't forget to check out the burger section."

Michael's $40 is only $23.78 now.

"I'm not too hungry, I'm just going to get a bagel," I say, closing the menu.

"Suit yourself," Winnie goes. "But it's my treat, remember?"

Tierney's head is down, looking at the menu, and when she hears that, she turns to me. "Get a burger, I'm getting a burger. And curly fries."

Before I can decide properly the waitress is there and I order a burger because Winnie said twice she'll pay for it, and Tierney heard her too, so she can't back out.

When the waitress leaves, Tierney turns to me. "You sounded pretty cut up in there, about that girl. What's her name?"

"Laurie," I go. It feels like the first time I've said her name in years, so I say it again. "Her name is Laurie."

"Yeah, Laurie. Were you guys just friends or were you together?"

She says it real casual, just like that—"together"—and right then the waitress arrives with Cokes for me and Tierney and a cup of tea for Winnie. She spills some Coke and Tierney wipes it up and needs more napkins. With all the commotion, I don't want her to forget what we were talking about so as soon as the waitress is gone I answer her.

"I don't know if you'd say we were together, but—"

She nods, stirs her Coke with her straw.

"Let me guess—she blows hot and cold? One minute she's sure she's gay. But then it turns out she's just experimenting, having fun?"

160

She puts on this funny high voice then that makes her giggle, and I start to laugh too. "How did you know?"

She drinks some Coke. "God, that teen stage sucks. My first was exactly the same. Emily. At least now, horrible though the New York dating scene is, by my age most women accept the fact that they prefer to have sex with other women and not men."

She says that just as the waitress is coming over again—with the bread this time—and my face burns because I know she's heard, but it doesn't seem to bother her and Tierney moves the glasses to make room, as if she's talking about the weather.

I want to ask Tierney about Emily, to talk more about Laurie, but Tierney's talking to Winnie now, asking about her daughter's pregnancy. That conversation goes on for ages and I eat two rolls and a breadstick. When they bring out a plate of pickles and coleslaw, I take one of each, just like Tierney and Winnie do, but I eat mine straightaway instead of waiting for my burger. When my burger arrives it's giant, too big for the bun, and once I take a bite I am starving, hungrier than I've ever been before. I take another bite before I've properly finished chewing the first. Bite after bite. I eat my way through the burger as if I'm a machine, as if I'm in a race. As if finishing it quicker will make Tierney turn back to me and start to talk about sex again.

Eventually, the dental guy turns to Winnie, says something about pain meds he's on, and she sits back in her seat to talk to him. My plate is empty, clean, and I take another breadstick. Tierney pushes her half-finished burger out in front of her.

"I'm not even hungry for this," she goes. "I don't know about you but I can never eat when I'm upset."

"I don't have that problem," I go. "I wish I did."

We both laugh and she lifts up my plate and swaps it with hers. "Here, finish it if you want."

For a nano-second, I think about saying no but my hand decides for me and lifts it up to my mouth before I even say thank you.

Tierney flips her hair to one side and puts her chin on her hand and starts talking to me as if we'd never left off.

"The thing about Susan, the woman I was on the date with earlier," she says, "is that she's great on paper. Good job? Tick. Nice apartment? Tick. Right age? Tick. We like the same movies, the same restaurants, all of that."

I nod, chewing.

She shakes her head. "But there's just no—I hate to say it, there's just no spark, you know? I know I'm thirty-eight, but you need spark, right? You still need passion?"

I nod again. Answer her with my mouth full. "Yeah, you need spark."

"Right." She sucks up some more Coke. "I mean it's not that she's not attractive. She is. But when we kiss—I don't know—I don't really feel anything. It's like I'm going through the motions."

I swallow a bite that I haven't chewed properly and it hurts my throat as it goes down. "Laurie's an amazing kisser." I feel bold saying it, embarrassed but somehow proud too. I sneak a glance at Winnie across the table, but she's still speaking to dental guy.

Tierney giggles. "You know, I had such a hard time figuring out if I was gay or straight, all this angst. Then I kissed Emily and I just knew. Isn't it amazing, how different it feels?"

The burger is in my hand but I've nearly forgotten it. My face hurts from smiling. "Yes! Totally!" I go. "That's totally it."

She drains her Coke so it makes that sound at the bottom of the glass. "It's a simple fact—girls are better kissers. I bet a good kiss would turn a lot of girls."

I'm loving this conversation, and I want to tell her more about Laurie, to tell her everything, right from the start—how after the "Truth or Dare" kiss, we kissed again the next day and the day after and how we spent the whole time we were grounded lying on my bed or on hers, kissing each other and talking. It was so easy to talk, lying next to her, staring at the ceiling fan, and even when we weren't talking it was enough to lie there just touching, and even when we weren't touching sometimes breathing together was enough. I want to tell Tierney all that, I want to tell someone, but the waitress is clearing our plates and Tierney is pulling her wallet from her pocket.

"I've got to get going, early start tomorrow," she goes, throwing a ten and a five on the table. "That'll cover it."

She says goodbye to everyone, one by one. Winnie gets up to hug her, but I don't. She squeezes my shoulder as she passes by.

"Take it easy, Lisa," she says, still smiling. "I hope I'll see you around."

The tears are in my eyes again. That's the thing, Mum, the stupid thing about crying—after you do it once, it's like the tears are there all the time, the whole fucking time, just waiting for an opportunity to show again. *Dumbass.* That's what Laurie would say. I can hear her voice saying it. *You're such a dumbass, Rae. What did you think she was going to do, adopt you?*

The waitress is writing out bills for everyone, plopping them in front of us, but Winnie scoops up mine. There's still bread left in the basket but before I can take it, the bus boy clears it away.

"I can pay," I say to Winnie. "I have money."

My voice sounds angry but she doesn't seem to notice.

"It's my treat this time," she says, "maybe you'll treat me some other time."

As she's counting out the money, I notice her fingernails, all painted different colours—blue, green, sparkly purple, silver. It's kind of funny looking but kind of cool too, especially on an old lady and I want to tell her—I would have told her if I knew the tears wouldn't come again.

Out on the street it's stopped raining, but it seems colder now than earlier. The others say goodbye and then it's just Winnie and me in the light from the diner window.

"Thanks for the burger," I go. "You were right, it was good."

"You're welcome. Where are you going now?"

I jerk my head downtown, towards Michael's. "The Village. Me and a friend have a place there."

She smiles. "That sounds nice."

"Yeah," I go, "yeah, it is."

She points over her shoulder. "I live that way—Hell's Kitchen, right on Ninth Avenue. If you hadn't anywhere else to go, I was going to offer you my couch."

I answer her before I've even thought about it. "No, thanks. I'm grand."

"Okay." She nods. "I'd give you my number, but I don't have a phone. If you want to find me you could come back to the meeting."

I want to go now, am already edging away.

"Or on Wednesdays and Fridays I volunteer at a soup kitchen on the corner of 28th and Ninth."

"I don't need a soup kitchen."

She slides her glasses up her nose. "I only meant you could find me there. It's a nice place, good food. I eat there after I volunteer and I've eaten there other times too. People fall on hard times, there's no shame in it, you know."

We stand there for another few seconds and I say I've got to get going. I leave before she can give me a hug. I'm glad she told me where she lives so I can walk the other direction. And walking away, I have a feeling that she's watching me, so I don't look back. I cross the street, head towards the subway as if I really am going to Michael's and when I finally sneak a look behind me, she's not there, she's gone. Walking through the Times Square crowd, back to my step under the awning, with my belly full of burger and my head full of Laurie, I'm imagining what it would have been like if I'd said yes to Winnie's offer, what her apartment would be like and if her couch would be comfy and if I'd tell her today was my last day being seventeen.

But there's no point in writing about that, Mum, because I'm never going to see her again, her or Tierney. She must want something—even if I don't know what it is yet—maybe she even recognised me from the posters, maybe she wanted the reward.

Whatever it was, it doesn't matter, but I know she wanted something.

Everyone always does.

Rhea

Dear Mum,

Today's my birthday. You know this, of course, you're my mother. I hope you know.

Now that I'm an adult, there's all these things I can do today, that I couldn't do yesterday:

1. Have sex

2. Get a tattoo

3. Get married

4. Get divorced

5. Sue someone

6. Be sued

7. Buy a gun

8. Be incarcerated in prison

9. Go to a strip club

10. Sign a legal contract

11. Vote

I'm sure there's more but they're the ones I remember from when me and Laurie looked it up on the internet in the school library. One thing I can't do in this crazy country is drink yet. I could marry someone, buy a gun, shoot them, be incarcerated for it, sue my lawyer for not representing me properly, but I can't order a bottle of Bud Light.

Of these eleven things, ten are new and I don't really want to do any of them, at least not today. And the first thing, the thing I've already done, I don't want to do today either, I don't know if I ever want to do it again. Sex gets people into trouble, Mum, I told you that already. I know that, but the thing is, since talking to Tierney in the diner the other night, Laurie is all over my mind again, worse than before.

Like today, I'm walking up Sixth Avenue and I see this blonde girl from behind and I think it's her. She's wearing a white T-shirt and jeans and her hair is Laurie's length and it sways like Laurie's hair sways and I have this whole story made up in my head about how Laurie's here with Aunt Ruth, looking for me and putting up posters. I'm walking right behind the girl, really close, when she stops to look at something in a shop window and I nearly bump into her and she's not Laurie, she's nothing like Laurie at all. Last night, I rode the E train all night. It's funny because I never liked the E that much on your map, but it's the line I spend most time on now. If I had one wish to make, one birthday wish, it wouldn't be to see Laurie, it'd be to have my Discman and all my CDs, and out of all of the music I could play I'd play "Comfortably Numb" on repeat, over and over and over again, riding that train. But that's about Laurie too, that wish, because "Comfortably Numb" was what I was listening to the night she came into my room, the night of the day we'd had the big fight, the first fight we'd had in a long time.

I don't hear the door, because of the music, but I see the light change, her shape in the dark. I remember sitting up, pushing myself back against the pillows. "Laurie?"

I think I'm being quiet, but I'm not, because of the music, and I see her put her finger on her lips. She takes my headphones off, gently. Her hand on my face is cold.

"What are you doing here?"

"Move over."

She pushes me gently back in bed so I'm against the wall, she's on the edge. I'm wearing my Zeppelin T-shirt and knickers, no bottoms, and I can feel her leg against mine, skin against skin where her pyjama leg is riding up. I push back further into the wall.

"Laurie, what are you doing?"

She doesn't answer, just reaches over and kisses me. Her mouth is warm, familiar, exciting. I can taste cigarettes, a trace of beer from the party. That was what part of the fight was about, why I won't go to parties with her anymore, why I spend every Saturday night at Glenda's. It's been five weeks since I've kissed her, but kissing her again, it's like I'm missing it and enjoying it and hungry for it all at the same time. I pull away for a second and then we both close the gap and we kiss and kiss and kiss.

It's me who pulls away again.

"What?" she whispers.

I gesture towards the wall, make a face. "What do you think?"

"They're out cold," she goes. "They were loaded when they came in."

"Were they?"

"Yeah. I could hear him snoring when I was in the hall."

She moves in again and I move a little out of her way.

"What if they wake up?"

Her voice is impatient. "They won't."

The kiss begins where the other one ended and I am in it and not in it because my head is catching up with my body. I break away again.

"Rae, what's the problem? I'm telling you, they're sleeping! Nothing wakes Dad when he snores like that. Trust me."

My lip is a little wet where hers has been. Her hand is on my hip, the skin above my knickers, under my T-shirt. It's hard to speak.

"It's not that."

"What then?"

My arm is trapped under me and I shift a bit to free it.

"What, Rae?"

I don't know how to tell her. How I was getting to be okay about it, the fact that we'd stopped kissing, that signing up to art club on weekends and taking extra shifts at the restaurant and hanging out with Glenda kept me from thinking about it every second of every day, kept me from wondering how she could be dating Ryan Matthews after everything that happened between us. But if we did it again, if we did any more than kiss, I mightn't be able to forget. And I mightn't be able to stop.

"We've never done this, Laurie."

"We've kissed."

"Not like this."

Her fingers are on my stomach now, tracing a line of fire, everywhere is on fire.

"Don't you want to?" she goes.

My breath is hard, my headphones are choking me. "Comfortably Numb" is still playing, how can it be still playing? I rip the headphones off, throw them towards the end of the bed. "Do you?"

This is where she will say that she's doing it for me, to give me practice being with a girl, that it doesn't matter to her either way. For a minute, there is silence, her breath in the dark. I can see her eyes now, wide open.

"Yes."

"I don't mean just because you think I want to," I go. "I mean what do you want? Do you want to? For you?"

"Rae, come on. Please."

It's that that gets me, the "please," the way she says it. I'm not breathing then and neither is she but we must be breathing because we're kissing again and her hand is making a circle of flames and my hand is reaching out too, to feel the hem of her T-shirt.

What do you think would have happened, Mum, if I'd done something different? If I'd told her that I didn't want to, if I'd made her go back to her own room? Would I be having the perfect eighteenth birthday today? Waking up to one of Aunt Ruth's special breakfasts where she cooks the Irish sausages she makes Cooper source for me through the restaurant? Would we be going to Jaxson's later? Or to the Everglades again to see the crocodiles like we did last year on my birthday? Do you think Aunt Ruth's thinking about the day we could have had today?

Or Laurie? Do they all know what's in the envelope from Columbia? Would we be celebrating that as well, if I was still at home?

This is bullshit—BULLSHIT. Home? That's not home, it never was home. Here is my home, New York is my home now, this bench by the water is my home because at least here I can be me, I can be who I want, who I really am, without having to play "let's pretend" and be someone else. Isn't that what being an adult is supposed to be about, anyway? Isn't that the whole point?

Only a kid would be sitting here, imagining some perfect birthday that's never going to happen, that never would have been perfect anyway. An adult would get that maybe this is the perfect birthday, maybe in some way I don't get yet, this is the exact eighteenth birthday I'm supposed to have, even if it feels totally fucked up right now.

It's not like Laurie was ever any good at birthdays anyway—except her own—and my best birthday was years before I met her, the year I was thirteen.

My birthday was on a Thursday that year. Thursdays meant maths first thing, but it wasn't too bad because we had art after. When Dad comes into my room that morning I'm checking everything is in my geometry set, even though everything is always in my geometry set.

He holds his arms out, for a hug. "So it's official, I have a teenage daughter. Happy Birthday!"

His cardigan and shirt are the same as he was wearing last night and I wonder if he thinks I might not remember what he was wearing before he went out.

"Aren't you going to give your old dad a hug?"

I close the gap between us. "Thanks, Dad."

He smells like smoke, like the pub and something else that smells horrible but I hug him tighter so he won't know I've noticed. And I mean the hug, too, because I'm glad he remembered. I'd been dropping hints about runners I wanted for a couple of weeks. I wanted the runners but that wasn't the only reason for the hints—ever since he'd forgotten the year when I turned ten I've been scared that he'll forget again.

"I'm making a special birthday breakfast," he goes. "Hurry up, because we've got to get going soon."

I want to ask him what he means, but he's gone then and already bounding down the stairs. I check my geometry set again, zip up my bag. I haven't told him that Lisa's mum is making me a birthday dinner, that we're watching *Indecent Proposal* on video after, even though it's a school night, and I remember thinking then that I should tell him, in case he wants to do something.

The post comes just as I'm on the stairs and there's a yellow envelope on top of the bills. It has an American stamp, Aunt Ruth's scrunched-up writing. I put it in my school bag, in case Dad sees it. In the kitchen, Dad has our places set, two sausage sandwiches each. I can tell the white bread is fresh because it's taken on the shape of his fingers where he leaned down to cut it in half and the ketchup is starting to leak through.

He pours tea into the cups, sloshing some on the counter. I sit down and he plonks a mug in front of me, sits down opposite. There's no milk so he must have forgotten to pay the bill again but tea tastes the same with only water to cool it down anyway.

He takes a big bite from his sandwich. "Get that down you quick, we don't have much time."

The clock on the wall says it is twenty past eight.

"I've loads of time. I never leave till twenty to."

The sausage sandwich is nice, hot and greasy, ketchup sliding against butter against bread. I count my chews.

"No school today, we're going on a trip."

He's into the second sandwich already, even though I'm not even a quarter way through my first. I wait to swallow before I ask.

"What do you mean? It's Thursday, I have to go to school!"

"Or what? You think that old bitch MacNamara will call the guards on us?"

He jerks his head around, looking over each shoulder as if the police are about to arrive in.

I laugh. "No, but—"

"You won't miss anything in one day."

"I've got art."

"Sure, you're always drawing something, even da Vinci took the odd break."

Somehow he's finished his sandwiches already and he's up from his seat and brushing the crumbs into the sink. "Here!" He throws me a roll of kitchen paper that bounces off the edge of the table and onto the floor. "Wrap the rest of your breakfast up in that and take it with you so we can get on the road."

"Where are we going?" I go, reaching down to pick up the kitchen roll.

"I thought you'd never ask," he says, smiling before he disappears into the hall. "We're going out west."

Driving up main street, I see Angela Clancy and Sinead Hoey on their way to school and I wish I'd had a chance to tell Lisa, so she'd know why I wasn't calling. I hope she's not going to be late, waiting for me, that she's not worried. I want to ask Dad what time we'll be back, if I'll be back in time for her mum's dinner and *Indecent Proposal*, but asking him that would make it seem like I'd rather spend my birthday with Lisa instead of him.

His driving makes me scared, the way he keeps fiddling with the tape deck instead of looking at the road, but after a bit we hit traffic and he manages to get it working. "Beautiful Boy" fills the car and I like when he puts Lennon on but it's when he's singing the chorus that I remember about the shop.

"Is someone else opening up for you today, Dad?"

He lights his cigarette with the car lighter, so it makes a hiss. A little bit of ash flicks out and joins the rest of the ash that's like dust over everything, only thicker.

"What?"

"The shop—is someone else looking after it?"

He winds down the window to flick ash out, but it blows back inside. He laughs, looks at me. "Are you codding me? Do you think I'd let anyone else take charge? Place would probably be burned down when I got back."

"So, what? Is it closed, then?"

The car in front of us moves and he clamps his cigarette between his lips.

"Sure is. All the old biddies will have to wait till tomorrow for their housekeepers' cut and their chops and their feckin' sausages."

"Did you tell them?" I go. "Did you tell anyone?"

"Isn't that what the closed sign is for?" Dad goes. "Feck the lot of them! It's not every day your daughter turns thirteen."

Mrs. Lawrence always has a big order on a Thursday and Mrs. Gaffney does too. I imagine all his customers coming to the shop, one by one, and pushing their faces up against the glass, knocking for a while, before they go away again shaking their heads. I worry about that the whole way through town stuck in traffic and even the rest of the sausage sandwich doesn't make it go away. But after a while, we're on the motorway and Dad's changed the Lennon tape for his Hendrix one and he's doing his "Stone Free" dance as we're driving along really fast past bushes and fields and trees and cottages and pubs and I imagine Mrs. Lawrence and Lisa and maths class all being left behind, one by one on the road, and everything feels much better.

When we get to Athlone, Dad stops for petrol. I open Aunt Ruth's birthday card while he's inside paying. The card is yellow and pink and outside it says "Now you're a teenager" and the inside has a rhyme about being young and bright and on the cusp of life. Usually there's fifty dollars but this time there's a hundred, five twenties that all look brand new. I fold them up and put them in my sock.

"Lunch?" Dad says as he jumps back into the car.

"Is it not too early?"

"It's never too early for lunch, Rhea. Now that you're growing up you'll learn that adults lie to children all the time." He spins the steering wheel as we pull back onto the main road. "Truth is, it's never too early or late for anything—especially chips."

He drives into town and pulls over in front of a café, even though there's double yellow lines. It's nearly empty except for two old women having cups of tea and a man eating a burger. "Looks like what the doctor ordered," Dad says. "Cheeseburger and chips?"

"Maybe just chips."

He looks disappointed. "But it's your birthday! And you love cheeseburgers!"

I hesitate, smile. "Okay."

The woman behind the counter is friendlier than if it was a café in Dublin. She laughs when Dad searches his pockets for his wallet before he realises he's left it in the car and she doesn't seem to mind me taking the tray with drinks to the table while he runs out to get his money.

They give us a basket of white bread and I make a chip sandwich. Dad's finished before I even start eating it, his leg jerking up and down under the table.

"You can bring the burger in the car if you want," he goes. "I'll ask for something to wrap it up in."

"Are we late for something?"

"I just want to get on the road—make good time."

"It's not even a quarter past eleven. How much further?"

"All the way west, you'll see."

"But where?"

"It's a surprise. A birthday surprise."

In the car, I fall asleep, which I suppose makes sense because it's around the time I always fall asleep in school. Lisa gives out to me for that, says I shouldn't stay up so late watching telly, but it's not the telly that keeps me up, not really. I learned to fall asleep on my own, learned not to be freaked out by the weird noises the house makes, but since the time I found Dad at the bottom of the stairs one morning with the front door wide open, I try to wait up until he gets in. I don't tell Lisa that, and usually she prods me awake when any of the teachers are looking—except for the time she was doing sums at the board and Bean Uí Cheallaigh shouted, "Rhea Farrell!" really loud and when I woke up there was drool on my face and my copy.

This time when I wake up, we are off the main road and on a windy one with hedges close on both sides. The car is full of smoke and Dad's voice, singing along with Hendrix to "Foxy Lady." In the side panel on the door the cheeseburger is still there, squashed and cold. I take it out and begin to eat it.

"Are you going to tell me now where we're going?"

The window is open, blowing Dad's hair to the side so you can see the bald bits. He turns to me and smiles. The road goes uphill and around a bend at the same time. A white van lurches, really close, but it doesn't seem to faze him.

"Guess," he goes.

Outside the car, the fields are smaller than before, behind walls made of rocks. The colours are different from Dublin, from Rush. The green is greener, deeper, and there's loads of different blues in the sky.

"Connemara?"

I've never been to Connemara but I read somewhere that the landscape looks alive there and that's how it looks out the window with all the colours and everything moving—the hedges and the leaves and the grass all being blown by a wind coming off a sea we can't see yet.

"Close," he goes. "Guess again."

"Donegal?"

"No," he laughs. "Jesus, who's your geography teacher? You don't go through Athlone to get to Donegal!"

"Mrs. Dillon," I go. "We've been doing Europe, not Ireland."

He takes the last drag of his cigarette, lets the butt fly from his fingers and somehow the wind catches it so it bounces in front of the windscreen. And that's when I guess again.

"Are we going to the Cliffs of Moher?"

He doesn't answer straightaway but the look on his face tells me I'm right. He's calmer than he has been the whole way, even the car seems calmer, less jerky, the tyres more sure on the road. And I don't know why I guessed that, or how I knew, but I know then that this journey has something to do with you.

There's only one sign, hidden behind an overgrown hedge, but he doesn't seem to need signs, he knows exactly when to slow the car down, when to turn through the gap in the fence where there's a man in a wooden hut collecting the money. Dad pays him in coins and we drive across a bumpy field towards a low, white building and beyond that building is a strip of grass and then the sea, navy blue like my uniform, and a million white caps of wave.

A sudden gust of wind yanks the door back when Dad opens it.

"Jesus, it's freezing!" Dad shouts at me across the roof. "Did you bring a coat?"

The wind is whipping up my skirt and I wish he'd told me we were coming so I wasn't wearing my stupid school uniform, so I could have taken the hoody that Aunt Ruth sent over at Christmas.

"No."

"Shit! Here, let's have a look in the boot—see what's there."

I know there won't be anything of mine in the boot, and there isn't. All there is is Dad's old brown quilted jacket that he used to wear when we went for walks.

"Here, put this on."

"It's miles too big!"

"Put it on—I don't want you getting pneumonia, not on your birthday."

He holds it out and I put my arm in first, then my stump. Even on my arm the sleeve hangs seven miles long. The jacket itself is nearly as long as my skirt.

"I'm not wearing this."

"It's not a fashion parade, Rhea."

"I look stupid."

"You could never look stupid, you're much too lovely looking. Don't you know you're getting to be the spit of your mother?"

He's never said that before, anything like that, and I can't see his face because he's looking down, rolling the sleeve up over my stump. And after that he walks a bit ahead of me, over to the dirt path, where there's only a tiny fence between us and the cliff edge with the sea crashing against the rocks below.

He stops, looks out at the sea. "It'd take your breath away, wouldn't it?"

"Yeah," I go. "It's gorgeous."

It's a view but it's more than that—the wind, the salt in the air, the colours of the sky. It's a view but it's a feeling too.

He turns to look at me. "I knew you'd love it. When I woke up this morning, I wanted to give you something special ... something beautiful for your birthday ... " He stops, folds his arms. "Something you'd always remember."

His face is wet and I don't know if the tears are real ones or from the wind. It hits me then, there's no runners, no card. He'd forgotten again, he only remembered this morning.

"I'd love to have money to be able to buy you nice things, love, beautiful things. But this, this is something I can give you. This is something I can afford."

He holds his arms out, to the sea, to the cliffs, to the whole of the misty horizon as if it is mine now. And I know I shouldn't care about the runners, that this is more important. I tell myself that I'll grow out of runners, that by Christmas I'll want different ones, but this, this will always be here.

"Thanks, Dad, it's the best birthday present ever." I want to mean it.

He puts his arm around my shoulder and we stand like that, the two of us, with the wind blowing our hair, my skirt, the waves beating the rocks so far down below us we can hardly hear the crash.

His hand around my shoulder tightens.

"Your mother loved it here too. I took her here once. We hadn't planned it. We did the same as we did today—just took off one morning, drove and drove until we got here."

I time my breaths to the sea, in and out, and every time I breathe out, the waves hit the rocks. I want him to tell me more, I know there is more, but it's too easy to stop him, to break it without meaning to.

I ask the question on an out breath. "Was that before you were married?"

He shakes his head, stares at the sea. He's here but not here, he's seeing the sea but something else too, he's seeing you.

"After. She was expecting you at the time." He doesn't look at me. "She'd had a bad night—hormones and that, you know. I thought coming here might help lift her."

He swallows, his Adam's apple bobs above his shirt.

"Did it?"

The wind finds my uniform skirt and slaps it around my knees. I think he pulls me closer to him then, or maybe I just want him to.

"We parked where we parked, walked just where we're walking now. It was colder that day, an icy wind, no one in their right mind would come here on a day like that and I thought I'd made a mistake, because she was shivering so badly, but then she turned to me and she smiled, that smile. She'd such a gorgeous smile. And she thanked me. I remember that, she thanked me."

It's the most I've heard him say about you in years. I wait for more.

"I'll never forget what she said. 'Thank you, Dermot,' she said, 'thank you for showing me beauty today. For reminding me.'"

The tears are definitely real now, not from the wind. The one from his left eye rolls faster, over the redness of his cheek, reaching the grey-brown stubble, while the other tear is blown along the side of his nose. Maybe I should be crying too, but I'm not. Because even though I want to know, even though I'm always asking about you, right then in that one moment I want it to be just the two of us, not with you in between. And I want him to be happy again, without either of us making him sad.

He laughs then, a loud, sudden laugh. "I told her that if she needed to be reminded of beauty all she had to do was to look in the mirror, but she gave me a dig in the ribs and told me the reason she'd married an Irishman was so she wouldn't have to hear lines like that."

His face is crinkled, smiling, and I try to picture how he would have looked thirteen years ago, more. In my mind, I make his wrinkles go away, his hair grow back, thicker, make it all brown instead of faded and grey.

"Want to lie on our bellies and look over the edge?" he goes suddenly.

"What about the fence?"

"There's a gap up ahead, I can see it."

He lets go of me and the wind catches underneath his long jacket and my skirt, blowing them up and out in front of me. He's bounded ahead along the path, has found the space where the gap is.

"Come on, Rhea, don't stand around being Marilyn Monroe!"

I don't get it at first and then I do and I laugh and run after him. He's waiting for me at the gap and he's right, it is wide enough for us both to get to the edge. He gets down on his knees and then his tummy, pushing himself over the grass and bits of rock. I do the same, but the stupid jacket holds me back, getting caught underneath me. Near the edge the grass is thicker and I grab on to a bit of it to help pull me forward.

"Look it," he goes. "Long way down."

I shuffle forward over the last bit, right up to the edge. The grass is in my face, but I hold it down with my hand. At first my eyes look out, towards the outcrop of rock where the gulls are flying in a circle, but then I look down, all the way down the cliff face, over the lumps and bumps and seams of rock where the birds are nesting and down and down again to the swish of blue and white that's the sea below.

"I can't see the waves crashing properly," I say.

"It's because we're not far away enough to get perspective. We're almost on top of them here. Sometimes, you've to be far away to get a good view."

"Did she like the view?" I go. "Mum, I mean."

"Ah, yeah. She said she loved seeing the Atlantic from the other side. She said it was the most beautiful place she'd ever been."

"She said that?"

"She did. And she'd travelled, your mam had, all over the place. I never knew what she saw in a fella like me, years older than her who hadn't moved an inch from the place he was born and reared."

He laughs a bit, like it's a joke, but something in the way he says it makes me think that maybe it's not a joke, that maybe it's something he's been trying to figure out for a long time.

"When you were here with Mum, did you do this?"

He looks at me and I can tell he's really seeing me, not seeing some version of you.

"Were you listening to the story at all? She was pregnant with you, remember? Do you really think I'd have let her anywhere near the edge?" He laughs a proper laugh this time and I laugh too, because it was silly to ask that and because even though I wasn't the first one to come here with him, this was something we were doing together for the first time, something he'd never done with you. And he reaches out and puts his hand on my back and I can feel the warmth of it, the heaviness, seeping through the quilt of the jacket and through my school jumper and my shirt underneath it, all the way into my skin.

And it doesn't matter then that there's no runners, no card, that I'm in my school uniform and his big jacket. It doesn't even matter that I mightn't be home in time for Lisa's mum's dinner or the video. None of that matters, because we have this moment, me and Dad. And lying there with the wind in our faces, and his hand on my back, that's enough.

Rhea

Dear Mum,

I'm not dating these letters anymore. I know that you're supposed to, so the reader can place you in time or whatever, but no one is reading these anyway and, living like this, time doesn't make sense. It's not like when I was in Rush, or Florida, when you have a day, then sleep, then there's another day. Now, it's like one big long lump of time when I'm asleep, then awake, then asleep again, awake again, and not much of anything happens in between.

Because I'm not counting time anymore, I don't know how long I've been sitting here, looking at this fountain. It feels like a long time, it feels like I can't move from here. I know that's not true—I can move, I just don't want to. Moving will cost me something—money or energy and I don't have much of either. In my pocket, there is $4.36—not enough to even bother putting any in my sock. The rest of Michael's money is gone—it doesn't matter how I spent it, only that it's gone.

Last night, I found more of Aunt Ruth's posters, six of them, on lampposts along Broadway. It was late and quiet, as quiet as New York is ever quiet, and I took them down, all of them, and now they are in my backpack, squashed in next to the Carver book and these letters and the photos in the blue packet and everything is getting crumpled and damp and I think of everything I hate. I might hate that most of all, that there's nowhere to put anything.

The posters started at 86th Street, she's targeting uptown, towards Columbia, and maybe it's risky being here at this fountain, because it's near Columbia, but it's not part of it, so I think I'm safe.

After ages of looking at it, I can't decide if I like it or not—it's kind of ugly with a scary-looking moon and a giraffe and the devil but there's something I like about it too. And I'm sitting here, wondering if you liked it or not. I'd been thinking about that for a while, but when I walk around it there's the little plaque that says it's here since 1985 and after all that wondering I know you never even saw it—that you never will see it—and something about that makes me want to fucking cry again. Laurie would say that's dumb, getting sad over some fountain that I can't even decide if I like and she's right, it is dumb, but it makes me sad and who cares what Laurie thinks because sometimes I'm allowed to be sad, amn't I? People are allowed to be fucking sad. The plaque says that the pedestal is shaped like a double helix of DNA and I think my brain is on a go-slow because I hadn't even noticed that and I should have because we just finished doing DNA in biology. I liked learning about DNA, because they always use DNA to catch criminals in *Law & Order*. And DNA explains how things are carried through your genes; eye colour and hair and whether you can roll your tongue or have an ear for music. DNA is about family.

Around the side of the fountain, there's another plaque, one I wish I didn't see because it has the words of the song "Imagine" on it and "Imagine" makes me think about John Lennon and John Lennon makes me think about Dad. And right when I was trying not to think about Dad, these English guys are by the fountain taking pictures and they're talking about Spurs and that reminds me of Dad too, and right then, just as they are talking, the cathedral bells start, really loud, and you're not going to believe this but they are the same tune as our doorbell in Rush, only slower and louder.

Three Dad things, just like that. Bam—bam—bam. Memory bullets. Only they must have missed my heart, because I'm not the one who's dead.

Those cathedral bells are still going off. Four chimes down, then four back up, like walking down stairs and climbing them again. If everyone decided not to bother with time, we wouldn't need bells like that, or alarm clock buzzers or anything. The world would be quiet, no sound at all.

The chimes sound exactly the same as the night the doorbell rang when the guards were at the door.

The first time they ring, I'm asleep, but it wakes me and I'm not sure if I imagined it. My clock says 5:13 a.m. and it's nearly bright outside because it's the end of May. I don't know how I know that Dad's not home yet, but I know. The second time, I'm looking out my bedroom curtain and I see the police car, right outside the gate. The third ring is when I am getting dressed, the buttons on my Levi's take me longer but I want to be wearing them and my Hendrix T-shirt, I don't want to answer the door in my pyjamas. I don't have time for my Docs and the fourth ring is when I'm on the stairs and I must have been walking really slowly because I remember the carpet at the edge of each step being kind of burny against my foot. There are two of them, on the other side of the glass, in the porch. One has his face squished up close, his hands on either side, peering in, and he must see me because they don't ring the doorbell again.

The other thing we learned about DNA is that it can replicate itself. Each strand of it is like a blueprint, to make new cells, and that's what gives us new layers of skin when we peel in the sun and why our cuts heal and our hair grows. I bet it won't be long before scientists will be able to replicate people using DNA. It might take ten years, Mum, maybe twenty, but it won't be long before that happens. Sometimes I think it's scary and I hope it never happens and sometimes I wish it happened before so someone could have replicated you and you'd still be here instead of just in these letters that you never answer.

You never answer these fucking letters.

She's dead, dumbass.

They're nice, the guards, I feel sorry for them, especially the younger one who can't really look at me and just holds the back of his neck with one hand the whole time. The older one does all the talking. He sounds like something off RTÉ news. He says that there were no other cars involved, that Dad was fatally wounded and for a minute, I think that that means he's not dead, but he is dead. I offer them a cup of tea because that's what people on the telly do. They won't take it, and they ask how old I am and when I tell them I'm sixteen since last week, they say they've to stay with me until someone else can come and is there anyone I can ring. I hate ringing

Lisa's house in the middle of the night, but I ring anyway. It doesn't even cross my mind to ring Aunt Ruth.

If Lisa's mum had said I could stay, would I have? Would I have stayed with them, lived in their house instead of going to Florida? At school, the nuns were always saying "Tell the truth and shame the devil," and I'm trying, just sometimes I don't know. Part of me wanted to go and part of me wanted to stay, that's the truth, and Lisa's mum and dad weren't able to take me in anyway, even if I'd wanted them to. At least her mum told me out straight, didn't pretend, she looked me in the eyes and told me she thought the world of me and she'd love to be able to, but they just couldn't. She never lied, Lisa's mum, she always told the truth. Not like Aunt Ruth. Not like Laurie.

The night I found out what a liar Laurie is, I didn't even want her to come into my room, that's the truth. It was getting risky. Aunt Ruth knew something was going on. She was looking at us in a way she hadn't done before and she'd started asking me about boys all the time, boys in my class and in art club and some loser at Cooper's restaurant who apparently wanted to go on a date.

I keep telling Laurie to be careful but she doesn't want to hear it and that night she especially doesn't want to hear it because she's upset, crying when she comes into my room. She's talking too loud, all about my Columbia application, how she can't believe I'm going to leave her and go to New York.

I tell her to keep her voice down, that I mightn't get in anyway, but she says if I loved her I'd go to a community college in Florida and I wouldn't apply to Columbia at all. I try and explain to her, about Columbia, but she doesn't understand. I tell her she can apply too, that in a year we can be together in New York, but that only makes her cry harder.

"I can't be on my own, Rae. I'm not as strong as you."

I remember all our kisses, it feels like I do, but I especially remember those ones—the last ones. I kiss her cheeks and the side of her face that her tears have made wet. I kiss the line where her hair meets her forehead and I smooth it down under my hand. I kiss her mouth then, a soft kiss, and she pulls me kind of on top of her the way she always does and we are like that, kissing, when the door slams open, a crash against the wall.

I feel Cooper before I see him, his hand on my stump, grabbing it so hard I think he's going to rip it off. In one motion, he yanks me out of bed and onto the floor. My head hits the corner of the bedside locker on the way down.

Aunt Ruth is behind Cooper, screaming at him to stop. His face is closer, his anger, her face is over his shoulder, her hand at her mouth. When he hits me the pain in my jaw is an explosion. She pulls him off me, I don't know how she does, but she does and I roll away. Laurie is crying and Aunt Ruth is yelling at Cooper to calm down and he picks up my prosthetic from where it is on the desk and throws it at me, but he misses.

It happens really fast, Mum, all of that, in a nano-second. Aunt Ruth is pushing Cooper out of the room, towards the kitchen, and shouting back at me and Laurie to get dressed. Laurie runs into her room and I'm lying there on the floor and I'm not moving but it feels like the room is. When I get up, I think I'm going to be sick, but there's no time to be sick because in the kitchen Cooper's shouting at Laurie. My white T-shirt has blood on it and I want to find my Hendrix one but I don't know where it is. I want to wear my Docs, but there's a crash from the kitchen so I shove on tracksuit bottoms and run down the hall.

When I get to the kitchen, Laurie's already lied, Mum. She's already told them that I forced her, that she was scared of me, that's why she went along with it. The crash was the electric juicer. It's lying on the floor tiles, Cooper must have smashed it. He's pacing, listening to Laurie, and Aunt Ruth is begging him to calm down and he roars that he is calm.

I sit down in the chair nearest Laurie, but she doesn't look at me. Her knees are pulled up against her and she's sucking her hair and crying and saying she's sorry, that once we'd done it once, I made her do it over and over, and that I'd threatened to tell if she wouldn't. Her body is shaking and despite all the lies she's telling, part of me doesn't blame her for lying, part of me wants to get up and put my arms around her and tell her it's going to be okay.

Cooper walks around the table, towards me, face red. His hair isn't slicked back for once, but hanging down on either side of his face. When he shouts, his voice fills the whole room. "We take you into our home—we feed you, put clothes on your back, pay for school—"

Aunt Ruth is right behind him, trying to get between us.

"Cooper," she says, "take a breath, calm down."

He smashes his hand down on the table, right in front of where I'm sitting. "How am I expected to be calm when there's some pervert under our roof taking advantage of my daughter?"

"Cooper, please!" Aunt Ruth tries to grab his arm. "Don't use language like that—"

He swings around to her, jerks his arm out of her grip. "The hell I won't—I knew there was something wrong with her, I told you."

"Cooper, stop it. Please. Let her speak. We've only heard Laurie's side."

"What side? Laurie was fine before she came along. You heard what Laurie said, she was pressured into doing it by her!" He jabs a finger at me. "If it's not true, why isn't she denying it?" Aunt Ruth has somehow managed to get in front of Cooper. She's down on her hunkers, close to me, leaning against the table. Without makeup she looks way older.

"Rhea," she says. "Rhea, tell the truth, tell us what happened. Don't be afraid. It's important."

Her eyes are brown, like yours—mine are blue, like Dad's, because I have his DNA as well. My stump is throbbing, my face, my head. Cooper slams both hands down on the table.

"Say something, dammit!" he yells. "Fucking say something!"

Laurie cries harder.

"Coop, honey, please try and be calm." Aunt Ruth turns to him. "We can get through this, families get through things like this."

"Oh, really?" He stands straight and buries his hands in his armpits. "This isn't the fucking *Jerry Springer Show*, Ruth! This is my daughter we're talking about."

Behind both of them, Laurie's head is in her arms, her shoulders trembling. I can hear the words she's not saying, the words she said earlier. *I'm not as strong as you.* I can leave, I'm going to leave, go to Columbia, but Laurie has to stay. And that's what makes me say it.

"What Laurie said was the truth," I go. "It was all me."

I don't look at Aunt Ruth. I focus on the broken juicer lid under the chair, a spring from the mechanism is rolling across the tiles.

Cooper throws his arms in the air, like a victory. "Yes! Now, we're getting somewhere—now, Ruth, do you see? I mean it's hardly a surprise she has problems, with that drunk of a father and your fuck-up of a sister for a mother."

"Cooper!" Aunt Ruth's shout is louder than his right then. "I know you're upset but don't—"

"Don't what, Ruth?" He stands with his hands on his hips, almost as if he's enjoying himself now. "Don't tell the truth? Don't talk about what happened?"

"Cooper, stop." Aunt Ruth is back on her feet, her voice sounds like it's begging. "Please, just stop."

"We're supposed to pretend it didn't happen?"

"Cooper—" Aunt Ruth is grabbing his arm and he shakes her off again.

"We're supposed to pretend your sister didn't kill herself?"

There's silence then, as if what Cooper said has taken up all the oxygen, that there's no air for any more sound. Even Laurie's stopped crying. My chair scrapes when I push it back against the tiles and when I stand up, I stand up slowly. They're all looking at me, but Cooper's the one I look at when I say what I say next. He's the one I want to hear it.

"My mother didn't kill herself. You're full of shit."

I think he might start shouting again, but he doesn't say anything. I leave them there, the three of them and the broken juicer. When I go to my room and shut the door, I see the dent the handle made in the plaster when Cooper smashed it open. I get under the covers and the pillow still smells of Laurie and I let myself smell her but I don't cry.

And I'm not crying now, Mum, those blotches on the page are from the rain that's just started. It's coming down heavier and it looks like tears all over the page, but it's not my tears.

If they were my tears, they'd have my DNA in them, and they don't. They're only water. Only rain.

Rhea

Dear Mum,

I don't want to write anymore, I don't want to write this shit down. I thought when I moved inside here, to the cathedral, that it would break it, all this stuff in my head, but it's still there, going round and around and so I'm back to writing it all down because maybe if I write it in a letter, it will stop.

I wish I'd found this place before now. There's a desk at the front where they ask for money but you don't have to pay anything and there's loads of little side chapels off the main cathedral part and I have one all to myself. And there's a long bench with a blue velvet cushion and I've lined everything up along there—all the evidence, all the clues—the two photos of you from Dad and the ones from Nana Davis and the newspaper clippings of your dad and his boss and his boss's obituary and the Carver book. And that's everything—apart from the subway map on my wall in Coral Springs—that's all there is.

And looking at all the photos lined up, even though I love the ones of us together, the one of you in Columbia is still my favourite because looking at this photo I know, I can be fully and completely sure, that what Aunt Ruth said was a lie.

I know she's going to come into my room that night, that she's not just going to leave me alone. I've been listening to all the sounds in the house, Cooper slamming the front door, his car starting, the squeak Laurie's bed makes when she gets into it, the sound of her crying until she stops. Aunt Ruth's been in the kitchen the whole time and I bet she's cleaning up the juicer, throwing it away. I bet by tomorrow, there'll be a brand new one on the granite counter in its place.

I hear her footsteps in the hall, my door opening.

"Rae?" she whispers from the doorway, "Rae, are you awake?"

I'm not asleep but I pretend I am.

"Rae?" Closer now. "I know you're awake. I brought an ice pack, for your face."

She turns on my bedside lamp and she sees my eyes are open. "Can I sit here?"

She gestures at the bed but I don't scoot over to make room so she almost sits on my leg. Her eyes look tiny in her face and I'd forgotten that's how she looks when she's been crying, because I don't think I've seen her crying since the night of the Viscount biscuits back in Rush.

She reaches out to my face with the ice pack and it stings. I push my head back into the pillow.

"Sorry, I know it hurts, but this will bring the swelling down."

I let her hold the ice pack there, and, after a second, everything feels numb. She's wearing a hoody, one of Cooper's, it's much too big for her. I've never seen her in a hoody before.

"I'm so sorry Cooper acted the way he did. He was very upset—but that's no excuse. I want you to know that this isn't the end of it."

Now that my face is numb, I'm feeling the other pains, a throbbing in my stump, a deep ache in my back.

"It's been a long night, and I know we need to figure out this situation with you and Laurie. I don't believe it was all your fault, honey. We can talk more about it tomorrow."

I look at her. I'm too tired to argue. "Okay."

"And we need to talk about what Cooper said, about your mom."

The pain is back in my jaw, through the ice, pulsing with my heartbeat. I clench my toes, all ten together, hold them.

"She didn't kill herself."

"Rae—"

"She didn't."

Her hand stops moving. Nothing moves. Only that's not true because breath must have been moving in and out of us both, blood carrying oxygen around our bodies. But it feels like even that's stopped too.

"Honey," she goes, "please—"

"It was an accident. Dad told me all about it one Friday night, when we were eating raspberry ripple ice cream. He said that the sea was very dangerous, even if you were a good swimmer, and that's why he'd never let me learn to swim."

She's sucking in her lips, like she's holding her words back. I want to keep talking, because if I keep talking, she won't be able to say anything.

"He explained about currents and I got confused because I thought they were the same as currants in scones, but he told me these currents were different. And I even asked Lisa's mum about it, and she said currents could be dangerous, even for a good swimmer. She said Mum was in Heaven, with God. Looking down on me, keeping me safe."

My voice isn't my voice, it's some kid's voice. Aunt Ruth's lips have nearly disappeared and she's starting to cry.

I push her hand with the ice pack away. "Stop crying, there's no point in crying."

But she doesn't stop crying. Her tears make shiny tracks on her cheeks and drip off her chin and onto the duvet and make circles of dark green on lighter green. There are four dark circles, five, seven.

"Aunt Ruth, there's no need to cry."

She shakes her head, wipes her cheek with her hand. "This is hard, honey, very hard—but I have to be honest with you, you have to know the truth. Your mom, she was a strong swimmer, she went swimming every day."

I sit up in bed, as far away from her as I can. "I know, I know that—but you're not listening, there were currents. And Dad said she was tired, she hadn't slept."

She folds her arms across her chest, pulls the extra sweatshirt material around her. "Did your dad tell you about the sleeping pills?"

The way she says it, she knows he didn't tell me, that I've never heard anything about sleeping pills. I want to swing my legs out of bed, to get up, to get out of the room, but she's got me in a trap, the way she's sitting, I can't escape.

"They found the bottle on the beach, sweetheart, two days later, or the next day, I can't remember. Her name was on it, it was empty."

I know her faces, all of them—I think I do—but I haven't seen her eyes like this, the black circles so big they nearly take up all the brown.

"So what?" I go. "That doesn't mean anything."

She reaches out to touch me again, but I push back into the corner.

"The bottle was empty, it means she took them. She took them, honey, before she went swimming that day."

"No!"

I pull my legs up from under the covers, scramble up into a stand on the bed, towering over her.

"Honey, please."

I step around her, jump down onto the floor. "That doesn't mean anything. The bottle could have been empty already. You don't know she took them."

"Why would she have had them on the beach?"

"Maybe they were in her pocket. Maybe they'd been in the bin and they fell out when the binmen were collecting the rubbish and they ended up on the beach somehow."

"Rhea, come on, that's ridiculous—"

"No—it's not! There's a million reasons why the pill bottle could have been on the beach."

As I'm talking, I'm trying to get away from her, as far away as I can, but the room is too small and I hit into the desk and knock over the penholder so the pens and pencils scatter on the desk, roll onto the floor.

"Rhea, slow down—"

"They never found her body, so they couldn't do an autopsy. No one will ever know if she took the pills. There's no proof. There'll never be any proof."

I'm trying to pick up the pens but my hand is shaking and I let them drop, leave them there on the floor. She's crying again, I can't watch her crying. I turn my back to her, so I'm facing your subway map, on the wall.

"Rhea, I know this is hard. God knows, but you have to listen to me, the truth is the only way to heal."

The map is even more faded than it was in Rush. You can still see the crayon where I coloured in between the lines of the map when I was little and I hate that I did that, that I destroyed something you gave me.

"We have to talk about this, Rhea. You've got to trust me that I only want what's best for you."

I can see her reflection in the window, that she's standing up from the bed.

"Why do we need to talk about it now when you weren't bothered before?"

"It's not that I wasn't bothered, it wasn't like that."

I turn around, I want her to see my anger. "What was it like then? Tell me! Tell me why I should trust you when all you've ever done is let me down, lie to me."

She's crying more, I'm making her cry. Laurie will be able to hear all of this from her room, but I don't care.

"I've tried my best, Rhea, I really have. I've never lied to you, I've always been honest."

I make my voice high, mimic hers. "*You're welcome here, Rhea, I want you here. This is your home, we're family.*"

She's taking baby steps towards me, her hands outstretched. "I meant that, I meant that when I said it, I mean it now."

"Really? Is that why I heard you on the phone to Cooper one night in Rush, practically begging him to let me stay, telling him I'd end up in foster care if he didn't agree?"

She pulls down her fringe, folds her arms. "I was just explaining the situation, Rhea. You weren't meant to overhear that."

I make myself laugh, like I don't care. "I bet I wasn't. I should have stayed in Ireland, in foster care. It's got to be better than this."

She's shaking her head. "You don't mean that."

"Don't I?" I point at my face, the part where the pulse of pain is. "I bet this wouldn't happen in foster care."

That's when she sits down on my desk chair and covers her face with her hands, long fingers, nails shiny pink with a white rim that they call a French manicure. Her hair falls in front, like a curtain, still in shape even after everything that night and I'm remembering last week when she came home from her new hairdresser, how she admired it in the mirror in the hall and I'm wishing it was then, Mum, more than anything I'm wishing it was then.

When she takes her hands away, she looks at her fingernails, she doesn't look at me. "Your mom was an amazing woman, Rhea. She was beautiful and funny and smart. She was my big sister."

I'm not going to interrupt her, that's one of the decisions I make. The sooner she tells me whatever lie she's going to tell me, the sooner it'll be over. I turn back to the subway map, so I won't have to look at her.

"But she had—there was... a lot of darkness, Rhea. Stuff that happened in our family, stuff no one talked about."

Usually red was my favourite colour, but on the map, yellow was my favourite, because it was the RR line. R for Rhea and R for Ruth. I remembered telling her that, showing it to her, on the wall of my bedroom in Rush, saying we could share it.

"I thought they'd made a big mistake at first, that maybe she hadn't even gone swimming, that maybe she'd run off or something. But then they found her little pile of clothes, so neat, on the beach and that woman, walking her dog—Josephine Brady—she saw her, going in."

I turn around before I can stop myself. "Miss Brady? Who lives by the school?"

Aunt Ruth glances up at me. "I don't remember. She had a gorgeous Labrador puppy."

Miss Brady has an old Labrador on a red lead called Sandy, she gets a bone for him every Saturday, along with her leg of lamb. I think this, but I don't tell Aunt Ruth.

"There were so many people out looking for her, people in canoes and fishing boats as well as the coast guard. It felt like the whole of Dublin was looking for her. And when the police called around to your dad's house, we thought they'd found her, that they had news, but they'd only found the pill bottle."

I cup my stump. "That doesn't mean anything, it doesn't make it definite."

Aunt Ruth takes a breath, sighs. "There were other factors, Rhea, other things…"

I don't need to look at your map to see it in my head. I start with the A, at 207th Street, Dyckman Street next, then 190th.

"Without her body, nothing can ever be definite."

181st Street, 175th, 168th Street—Washington Heights.

I bend down, pick up the pens, this time my hand isn't shaking. I fix them in their holder, in front of Aunt Ruth. She stands up, pushes the chair back under the desk.

"It's been a big night, a lot to take in. I'm sure we could all use some sleep."

"Yeah," I go, "I'm knackered."

I walk past her, get into bed. I just want her to leave.

She stands over me, pulls the duvet up around my neck. "In a way, I'm glad things are out in the open; in a way, it's a relief."

She's so close the strings of the hoody dangle down into my face. She strokes my jaw, really gently, and kisses me on the forehead.

"You're probably exhausted," she says. "We'll talk about it tomorrow, properly. Just you and me. We'll go out, maybe to Jax-son's if you want? Talk about everything, okay?"

"Okay."

She turns off the lamp and walks to the doorway, and she's nearly gone when she stops, turns back. "Suicide is hard to accept, honey, no one wants to believe it. I didn't want to either."

She says that word like it's any other word, like "strawberry" or "theorem" or "spaghetti."

"Good night, Aunt Ruth," I go.

She closes the door then, and I'm remembering the first time I heard that word, I think it was the first time, in the sitting room in Rush, on *The Late Late Show*. And Dad, jumping up, switching the telly off so hard it nearly fell off its stand. *Bloody television's gone to the dogs.*

I lie awake, listening for ages to the silence of the house. There's no noise in the darkness, everything is silent, silence from Laurie's room, silence outside. I try and hear my heart but that's silent too and I can't hear my breath either and I wonder if I'm dead. And when I get up, I pack in silence, even the sound of my footsteps, past Laurie's bedroom, past Aunt Ruth's, they sound like nothing, they're only shapes made out of silence, barely any sound at all.

R

Dear Mum,

I didn't go there to see her—I'd forgotten what days she said she volunteered—I went there because I was hungry, because I don't care what Sergei said about soup kitchens being full of down-and-outs and drug addicts, I'm just hungry. This hunger is different than before, it's not only my body, it's my mind. I'm thinking about food all the time—like all the time—going through what I can eat next, where I will get it. Even when I've just eaten, I'm thinking about eating again, even as I'm eating sometimes, I'm not even tasting the food, I'm wondering when I'll have something to eat next.

It's not until I get there that I realise it's a church, she never said it was a church. There's a queue, all the way around the corner and onto 28th Street, and I watch it for a bit from the little park across the road before I join. There's a lot of men but some women too, girls, kids even. I imagine I might see Sergei, even though I know he'd starve to death before he'd admit defeat and come somewhere like this.

I'm waiting for the queue to die down but it doesn't die down, only gets longer, so, after ages, I take my place at the end, behind a tall white guy with wispy hair that goes down over the collar of his suit jacket. An old man joins the queue behind me with his cart, pushes it into my heels by mistake and apologises. I've seen him before, in Grand Central. He smiles, looks like he might want to talk, so I look the other way.

At the gate, we're handed a ticket and we have to wait until other people come out before we can go in. And standing there, waiting, I think about the poster with my face on it, about how this is just the kind of place Aunt Ruth might put up a poster like that.

People come out and it's our turn to go in, but my feet won't take me through the gate. I'm imagining it inside, a poster of me on a notice board, Aunt Ruth standing next to it. I'm holding up the queue and someone behind shouts out to move it. I don't know what to do, but I have to do something, I'm hungry and I have to eat and there's food in there, you can smell the food every time the door opens. I put my head down, follow the others towards the door where there's another guy collecting tickets. I'm getting close to him, I see his shoes, Caterpillar boots.

"Hey," he goes, when I hand him my ticket. "Is that what I think it is?"

I don't know what he means, but I'm ready to run.

"You think we allow Red Sox fans in here?"

When I look up he is smiling, he has nice eyes. He points to his baseball cap—a Yankee one like I used to have—and I realise that's what he's talking about, my cap. I try and smile back.

"Enjoy your lunch," he goes.

Inside there's another queue, this time in a tiny corridor. It's hot and we're closer to the smell of food. My mouth fills up with saliva and I don't know if that's because I'm hungry or if I'm going to be sick. A woman is coming the other way with a walkie-talkie. She says hello to people as she passes. She stops right at me and my heart starts beating, really fast.

"Excuse me," she goes.

"I have a ticket!"

She smiles. "I know, I just need to get into the office there."

She gestures at a door that I hadn't seen, next to where I'm standing.

"Sorry."

She jangles keys in the lock, turns back to me. "Is that a Scottish accent I hear?"

"Irish."

"Irish, yes, now I hear it," she says. The walkie-talkie crackles. "Enjoy your lunch—it's meatballs and spaghetti today, it's really good."

Ahead of me, people are starting to move, the man with the wispy hair is already a few tiles in front of me

"Thanks."

I don't know what I'm expecting, Mum, but after all the queues and corridors I was not expecting the space to open up as big as it did, for the whole inside of the church to be taken up with round tables and chairs like the parties that Cooper sometimes catered. There's people on one side, handing out trays of food and a drink, everyone smiling, everyone saying to enjoy our lunch. I've lost the wispy-haired man in front of me and I feel lonely all of a sudden, like I wanted to sit next to him. I don't know where to sit, so I walk over towards the huge organ, towards a table where there are two free seats. There's one other woman at the table, an old lady, eating slowly. She's wearing a cardigan, a nice watch. She's not someone I thought would eat somewhere like this. A young guy sits down in the other empty seat straightaway.

I barely even notice all the different things on the tray, just start eating it all, the meatballs and the spaghetti and broccoli and bread. I want to slow down, but I'm too hungry to eat slowly so I just keep eating and eating until it's gone. And it's only then I remember to check for any posters of me, but there aren't any—there aren't any posters of anyone.

The young guy next to me has already finished and is getting up to leave. He hasn't eaten his apple and he sees me looking at it. "You want it?"

"Okay, thanks."

It's on my way out that I see her, the woman from the meeting, at the table by the door in a white hat and apron, her grey hair tied back in a ponytail. I'm going to walk by, I'm pretending not to see her, but she sees me and starts waving.

"Lisa!" she calls, "Lisa!"

For a second, I forget that's my name and then I remember, smile. "Hi," I go.

"Hello," she says, "you remember me, don't you? Winnie? From the diner?"

"Yeah, I remember. Nice to see you."

"I haven't seen you," she says. "Are you still coming?"

"No," I go. "I kind of forgot."

That part is true, I had kind of forgotten, can't even remember how long it was since I was there.

"Do you want some bread to take with you? We got really nice stuff today."

The bread does look nice all laid out, Kaiser rolls and bagels and sourdough.

"I can take some of this?"

"Sure," she says, "whatever you want. You know you can go in for seconds too?"

I didn't know. "Can you?"

She smiles. "Sure, just join the end of the line outside, get another ticket."

Another meal would fill me up, another meal would last me until tomorrow, especially with the bread.

"And I can take the bread then, on my way out? Will you still have some, do you think?"

She slides her glasses up her nose. "I'll still have some, don't worry. If we're running low, I'll keep you some."

That's the mistake I make, Mum, going around a second time. If I'd left then and taken the bread and the apple, I'd have been okay. If I'd left then, I don't know where I'd be writing from now, maybe Battery Park or the new little playground I found near Varick with the benches where you can stretch out properly. But I didn't leave then, I joined the queue and took another ticket.

The second time, my table by the organ is full, so I sit at the one next to it, just me and all men, until two guys get up and a girl takes the place next to me. When she sits down, she takes time arranging herself, takes off her cap and her headphones. I watch her as I try to slow down my eating this time around.

"Hey," she says. "I'm Pat."

"Lisa."

She doesn't use the spoon, she picks up the broccoli, dangles it by the stalk into her mouth.

"Every damn day they have vegetables as part of the menu. I always eat it first, so I can get it out of the way, enjoy the rest."

I laugh. "You come here a lot?"

She nods. "Most days. It's a good place. Usually, I listen to my music if they don't have any playing, but you looked like you might want to chat."

"You're lucky," I go, nodding towards her Walkman. "I'd kill to have my music with me."

She puts the broccoli down, lifts her headphones from around her neck. "Here, listen to mine."

"No, it's okay, I don't want to use up your batteries—"

"They won't last forever, but you can listen to one song."

I take the headphones from her, put them on. They're the old-fashioned kind where the spongy bit sits on top of your ear. She reaches into her pocket, hits play, and I can hear the tape whirring, a bit of silence and then the twang of a guitar, real slow at first. I recognise the song even before Bono's voice starts, "Running to Stand Still," Lisa's favourite song from *The Joshua Tree*. Listening to the song it's as if I'm back in Lisa's house lying on the floor of the bedroom she shares with her sister. It's like I'm there but I'm in this church too, watching the people with empty trays and full trays all moving in time with Bono's voice. And just as he gets to my favourite part, the part about running through the streets, I see the woman with the walkie-talkie coming down the steps where the food line is, and she stops, right where the man is handing out drinks, and it looks like she's scanning the room for someone, she's definitely scanning the room for someone, and then I see the person behind her.

It's Aunt Ruth.

The music is still going, Bono's voice too loud now, and I rip the headphones from around my neck, shove them in a bundle at Pat.

In one movement, I twist around in my chair, slide under the table. I forget about my backpack and without my weight to balance the chair, it pulls it over with a crash.

200

Something kicks me in the back and I realise I was leaning into someone's legs, so I scrunch myself up, as small as I can. Hands are picking up my backpack, the chair. Pat's face appears in the space where I should be.

"What the fuck? You okay?"

"Did she see me? Is she coming over?"

"Who, Chrissie?" She says it loud, starts to look around.

"I don't know her name—the one with the walkie-talkie. Is she coming over?"

I wait for her to ask me why, but she doesn't.

"Sit tight," she goes. "Stay down."

A chair pushes back at the table and jeans and white runners are replaced by black trousers and black shoes. Pat takes my backpack and puts it under her chair and I hear a scraping noise on the table over my head and I know she's pushing my tray under hers.

Another pair of feet, legs are coming over to where my chair was. I hear Pat tell them the spot is taken. I hold my breath, the feet move away.

Pat's face is there again. "Chrissie's gone. She went outside with that other woman." I shuffle over to my empty chair. "They might wait at the gate though, until you come out. I've seen that before."

My heart is going too fast, my breath. "Is there another way out?"

"No. Best thing to do is hide out until they leave."

I knew this was a bad idea, coming in here, that it was a trap. "Where? Where is there to hide?"

"The bathroom is over there, by where you came in. Only place in the city where there's never a line for the women."

A young girl refilling the milk on the table sees me half sticking out from under the table. She looks scared, like she might call someone over, so I pull myself all the way out, sit on the chair.

I glance around but I can't see Chrissie, I can't see either of them. The door at the back of the church opens and closes as people leave. For a second I think I'm going to be sick.

"Here, swap." Pat is handing me her baseball cap. "If Chrissie's seen you already, it might throw her off."

Her baseball cap is purple, the inside has a line of sweat. She plucks mine from my head and it's stupid but, in the middle of everything else, I think about the day Laurie gave it to me and I nearly want to snatch it back. When I put Pat's on, it's big, falling down almost into my eyes, but I tip it up.

"Don't worry about your tray, I got it."

"Thanks, thank you so much."

I grab my backpack, take a breath, and start to walk towards the food line, where people are still streaming in, trays and trays still being handed out. A woman on a walker has someone carry her tray for her and I step around them both. Two of the volunteers are joking with a little boy, who is holding onto the handle of the buggy his mother is pushing. I put my head down. I am waiting for someone to stop me, for a hand to grab me, for someone to call out my name. There are steps up to the bathroom and I take each one without looking up. Outside the men's, someone is waiting. The women's is right next to me, I try the handle. Pat was right, it opens, I'm inside, I lock the door.

I take a deep breath, another one, like I haven't been breathing at all. I take off my backpack, lean against the door, and slide all the way down to the floor.

There's no window, no way out.

I don't know how long I'm sitting like that before the knocking starts. It stops and then I hold my breath and then it starts again. A voice comes through the door. "Hurry up in there, there's other people waiting. Other people need to go."

Maybe I should have said something back—that I'm sick or for them to go away—but I don't, I only sit there, gripping on to my backpack. The knocking stops and more time passes. If I'd still had my G-Shock, if I hadn't sold it, I'd know exactly how much time, but I don't have it and it could be minutes or hours or only seconds before I hear footsteps outside and the knocking starts again. This time, it is a different voice.

"Hello? Hello in there? Are you okay?"

I don't say anything.

"You need to open the door. There are other people waiting who need to use the bathroom."

I open my eyes. I recognise the voice, I think I do. It's Winnie. I'm almost sure it's her.

"If you don't open up I'm going to have to get someone to open it. We have a master key."

I push my ear up against the wood, to hear better. Outside, there is noise of people moving, other voices. The knock, when it comes again, is louder.

"Okay then, suit yourself, one of the guys will be coming back to open up."

"Wait!"

I push myself into a stand, grab the lock. It sticks a bit but then it moves and when I open the door, I hold it open a crack, to see if I'm right. On the other side of the door, I see grey hair, glasses. I'm right, it's her.

"Lisa?" She frowns and smiles at the same time. "What has you in there for so long, I was just about to get someone to—"

"Please, Winnie, you have to help me."

Behind her, the queue of people waiting for trays has stopped. One of the men is looking at me and I pull my cap down lower.

"What's happened? Are you sick?" Winnie's voice sounds concerned.

"I need to find a way out. Is there another way out of here?"

"Why? What's going on?"

A woman next to her grabs the door, pushes it properly open. "You coming out or what? You're not the only one who needs the bathroom you know!"

I step out of the bathroom so she can go in. I am totally exposed now.

"Winnie, you have to help me. People are here—looking for me. I can't go back. I can't go back."

Everyone in the queue can hear me, but I don't care.

"Who? Who's looking for you?"

"Please, Winnie. I thought it was safe here. You have to help me."

Winnie's eyes are on mine, as if she's trying to see into my head. She's on the cusp of helping me, I know she is.

"Please."

"Come on."

She doesn't wait to see if I'm following her, just starts walking back against the crowd of people flowing in. We pass by a man at the top of the queue and I hear his walkie-talkie crackling too and it sounds like Chrissie's voice and I know she's asking him about me. Winnie is leading me back the way I came in, right to where Chrissie's office was. And just when I think it's a trap, she keeps going, past the office and around the corner to a flight of stairs I hadn't seen.

"Careful going down here," she says.

For an old lady, she is very quick on the stairs and I am quick behind her. We are in a little kitchen where there are two women in white coats cutting up chickens, behind them there are basins and basins of it, still to go. Winnie nods at them and we hurry past, make a left around a corner, and another down a corridor that gets darker and darker until you can hardly see the light from the kitchen at all.

There's a door to the left and Winnie opens it. There's no light in here, but I can see bulky shapes in the dark, boxes.

"No one should come in here, but hide in the back just in case. Wait until I come and get you."

She doesn't wait for me to answer her, just closes the door and it is pitch black inside. I can hear her runners squeaking on the tiles as she goes back towards the kitchen and after all that, I nearly run after her. It feels like I can't breathe in the darkness, but I can breathe, there is air, there is enough air. I reach out and feel the shape of something in front of me, cardboard, then a gap, then splintery wood. I can smell apples, I focus on the apple smell. I remember what she said about getting to the back and I let my hand go that way first, leading me, then one foot, then the next. There's sounds in the room, a rummaging sound, something alive. My heart stops because I know it's a rat but I force a breath, force myself to move forward, to do what she said, to trust her.

Your subway map is what saves me, Mum, in that basement, waiting for Winnie. And even though it's pitch black, I close my eyes to picture it. I use my finger on the box in front of me to trace each line, each stop. I start on a really hard line, the pink one, the 7, and I hardly ever do that so I really have to concentrate on the stops and when I'm finished that I do the M and that's a funny one too because it starts and ends in Queens. And after those I do the J and then the GG and your line, the AA, and Dad's line, the D, but I don't do the RR. And every time I hear the rats, every time I think there's one of them at my foot, every time I forget to breathe, I scrunch my toes up inside my Docs and go back to the start of the line I'm on and I begin again.

And that's what I'm doing when finally there's a noise outside the door and it opens and I can see the insides of the room and Winnie, outside, peering in, her white apron and hat gone now. After the blackness of the room, the corridor feels light this time and the kitchen is so bright it's like my eyes are going to bleed. And when we get outside, my eyes are streaming and there's too much to see all at once, even though everyone is gone, and it's quiet now and the only evidence of all the people is one guy hosing down outside.

Winnie puts her hand on my shoulder, but lightly. "You okay?"

I nod, I don't know if I am or not, but I know I will be.

"Good, come on." She walks towards the gate, turns around when she sees I'm not behind her. "Are you coming?"

The guy is about to hose where I'm standing, I need to move. "Where?"

And she says it like it's so simple, as if there's no other possible answer.

"Home, with me."

Rhea

Dear Mum,

When I wake up, the clock on the mantelpiece says it's a quarter past ten and I'm confused, because it's bright still, but then I realise that it's a quarter past ten in the morning—that I'd slept all afternoon, all evening and all night.

Yesterday, the whole way up Ninth Avenue, I wasn't sure I was going to go with Winnie, I just kept saying I'd go another block and then another one and the only reason I went up the stairs to her apartment was because I really needed the loo by the time we got here and when I came out, she had the air conditioner on and the curtains pulled and it was nice and cool and shaded and she gave me a pillow and said that I might as well have a little rest before I get going again.

The apartment has no proper doors, I remember noticing that last night, only curtains to separate the main sections. This morning, the curtain into the bedroom section is open and the bed is made.

Upstairs someone is practising a violin and outside there's the hissing noise of a bus stopping. Inside the apartment it's quiet and I know already that I'm the only one here but I call out anyway.

"Winnie?"

When she doesn't answer I get up, fold the blankets into a square, and bring them both over to put on the bed and that's when I see the grey cat, curled up in a circle, fast asleep. It opens one of its eyes and stretches a paw out, so I can see its claws, but it doesn't move and I don't touch it. Next to the bed, there's a stack of books on her locker, lined up in size order with a notebook on the top. For a second I think about opening it, to see if she's written anything about me, but I walk away before I can.

The kitchen is a separate room, and I remember as I walk into it that that's where the bath is too, how she told me loads of the old tenement apartments in Hell's Kitchen were like that. There's a piece of wood on top of the bath to make it into a counter and she's left me a long note, next to a pair of khaki shorts and a blue and white stripy T-shirt. I pick them up and there is a pair of old lady knickers underneath. The note says I can have a bath, to use the clothes, that there's English muffins and cream cheese in the fridge that I can eat. I hate that it starts "Dear Lisa."

While the bath is filling, I look at the posters on her walls. They are on every wall, even the kitchen, and where there's a gap between posters there are post cards and photographs and sometimes ticket stubs as well. It should look messy, because there's no order, but it doesn't, it looks like there's an order only I can't see what it is yet.

It's ages since I've had a bath and even though the water is too hot, I take a deep breath and pull my whole head under, feel the water lift my hair from my skull. It's longer than I like and I wonder if Winnie would shave it for me, if she has a razor. I hold myself there for as long as I can before I burst back to the top and water gets on the floor, so I have to dry it off with the towel after I've dried myself. I'm not going to put her clothes on, except when I sniff the armpits of my T-shirts, they all smell bad and there's some weird black marks all down the back of my jeans, so I put on her clothes, all except the old lady knickers—I wear the cleanest dirty pair of mine.

Afterwards, I eat the muffin but it's small and I'm still hungry, but there's only one other one left and I don't want to finish it. I've just washed up and I'm thinking about what to do about my clothes, if maybe I could wash them in the sink, and that's when I hear the lock in the door behind me. Everything is all over the place—the Carver book and photos on the coffee table and my T-shirts all over the couch, and I try to clean it up a bit before she comes in, but it's too late.

"Hi there!"

Her voice sounds happy, light, but I don't turn around, focus on stuffing my clothes back in the bag.

"Sorry it's such a mess," I go, "I'm just tidying up."

She laughs. "Believe me, this isn't a mess. I've seen this place messy and you need to work a lot harder than that."

She sits down in the armchair by the window, kicks her sandals off and puts her feet on the table, so her toes curl over the edge. Her nails are painted silver but the polish is peeling. I can smell her feet.

"Thank you for the muffin," I go, "and the cream cheese."

"You're welcome, I hope you ate both muffins, they're very small."

"And for the lend of the clothes. I was going to put mine on but they're dirty, so—"

"We'll have to do laundry," she says. "There's a laundromat on the next block."

I hear it, the "we," but I pretend I don't. I push the Duane Reade bag of dirty clothes down further in my backpack.

"Are you feeling any better? I was worried, yesterday, when you slept so much. I called my friend Alistair, who's a doctor, and he said you probably just had chronic fatigue, to let you sleep."

"I feel fine," I go, "much better."

There are some things on the coffee table in between us and I wish I'd been smarter and packed them away first. Not your letters, Mum, they're safely in the front pocket of the backpack, but I left my sketch pad out and the packet of photos and the Carver book. When I turn around, that's what she has in her hand, and I can't believe she's just done that, reached over and picked up my book without even asking.

"Raymond Carver," she goes. "It's a long time since I read Carver. I prefer his poetry. You're a fan?"

"He's okay."

She turns the book over and I know your photo is going to fall out. I want to snatch the book back off her, but if I do that, she'll know it's important, so, instead, I roll up my Champion hoody. She pulls her glasses down from her hair and starts to read the back.

"He was one of us," she says, looking at me through her glasses.

"One of us?"

"You know, a friend of Bill's."

She slides her glasses up her nose; she's looking at me, waiting for me to say something.

"You're not an alcoholic, Lisa, are you?"

I want to tell her the truth. "No, sorry. I don't really like drinking, to tell you the truth."

I'm holding my breath, waiting for her response. She might be really mad, she might throw me out. That's what I'm thinking, in the pause between me saying it and her reacting. I'm not expecting her to tip her head back and let out a loud, long laugh.

Sometimes people laugh even when they're annoyed. Sometimes, Dad laughed and seconds later he could be shouting or even crying. You can't take it for granted that just because someone is laughing that they're happy.

"I'm sorry I lied, I had nowhere to go that night. It was raining. I thought there'd be coffee."

I'm trying to make an effort, to be honest, but it only makes her laugh more. She takes off her glasses, wipes her eyes.

"I'm sorry, it's just too funny. There are so many people in this city who need to get to a meeting and don't, it's just funny to think of someone being there who doesn't even like to drink. And as I remember it, I was the one who invited you in."

The cat has come in from the bedroom, is standing in front of Winnie, sniffing the air. "There you are, I was wondering where you were, Olivia. This is Lisa. Lisa, this is Olivia."

It's grating on me, the sound of the lie, every time she calls me Lisa, but I don't want to say anything, not yet, not this soon after apologising for the other one. I don't want her to think I'm a liar.

The cat ignores Winnie, so she goes back to the Carver book, opens it. She looks at the back again. "Columbia University Library? Are you a student there?"

"My mother was," I go. "I might be going in the autumn. I mean, I've applied."

I didn't think I was going to tell her that and as soon I do I wish that I hadn't.

"Good for you. When do you find out if you got in?"

Olivia jumps up on the couch, then walks onto Winnie's knee, standing so her tail is in her face. Winnie brushes it away.

"I don't know, I mean, they might have accepted me but I won't be able to go anyway, even if they did."

Her face scrunches up. "Why not?"

She's asking too many questions but it's my fault for bringing it up in the first place. "I've just missed a lot of school, that's all. Even if my GPA is okay, I've missed too much to graduate."

Olivia sits down, gets up, turns, sits down again. Winnie winces, but she doesn't make her move. I'm waiting for Winnie to say something about missing school, to talk about the importance of an education, but she doesn't say anything. Instead she puts the Carver book back on the coffee table and reaches over to touch the edge of my sketch pad.

"Can I take a look?"

"Sure."

Olivia jumps down from her knee when she leans forward. Winnie flicks through the pages slowly, sometimes turning one to the side and back the right way around again. She stops, looks up at me. "These are good."

"Thanks."

"I like this one here, of the tree. You capture such detail, the texture of the bark."

I don't need to look to know which one she means.

"You have talent, Lisa."

"Thanks."

"I'm sure being an artist you must spend so much time drawing the city—there's so much to be inspired by."

"I haven't drawn anything since I got here."

She looks at me, her glasses sliding down her nose. Sergei was always on about that, how I should use drawing to make money, go to Times Square with a sketchbook. He didn't get it when I said I hadn't been able to draw since I got here. Winnie doesn't say anything, just turns over the next page.

"I'm an artist too, I like charcoal mostly, sketching."

"I like sketching too and painting sometimes. I like oils, acrylics."

"Maybe we can find you some stuff at the league," she goes. "People are always leaving stuff behind." There it is again, the "we."

"What's the league?"

"The Art Students' League. I model there in return for some studio space."

"Model? As in nude modelling?" My tone is horrible and she hears it too. "I'm sorry, I—"

"It's okay," she says, flattening down her blouse. "People are sometimes surprised, but you don't have to have a young body to teach students how to draw."

Olivia is on the arm of the couch. She puts a paw on my bare leg, then another one. Her nails scratch a bit, but I don't mind.

"She likes you." Winnie smiles. "She's not normally that friendly."

"What's it like, modelling? Having everyone see you, like that?"

She tilts her head to one side, thinking before she answers. "It can be boring, definitely. But there's something freeing about having people see you, exactly as you are. Not having to hide anything."

She catches my eye and I look away because I think this is where she's going to bring it up, what happened in the soup kitchen yesterday, but she doesn't.

"I wouldn't have been able to do it when I was younger. I'd have been getting into the heads of everyone else, wondering what they thought of me, but now, at my age, I couldn't give a hoot."

Upstairs the violin music has started again and I feel myself stroking Olivia in time with it.

"Is that your neighbour playing?"

"Yes, that's Francis, he's a dear. Used to play at the Met. He minds Olivia whenever I'm away."

"Do you go away much?"

"Not too often. Only in the summers when I've worked at a camp or once when I went to see Melissa, my daughter. She lives in Connecticut."

The pregnant daughter from the meeting. Now that I told her I lied about being an alcoholic it feels like I should pretend not to remember.

Winnie reaches up to a shelf and takes down a photo in a glass frame. "There she is."

I think the photo is going to be of a woman, but it's of a little girl on a bike, with a big smile and two missing front teeth. The bike has a basket and it's full of sunflowers.

"That's a nice picture."

"I think so." She looks at it. "It was a rare vacation we took, out of the city to Long Island, with my brother. He took the photo, I didn't have a camera at the time."

She's tracing her fingers over the glass, and I feel my legs, jerky as if I'm impatient, even though we're not going anywhere.

I say what I say next before I know I am going to. "Do you want to see a photo of my mum?"

She puts the frame back down, smiles. "Sure."

Her eyes go to the packet on the table but the one I want to show her is in the Carver book. I open it to the right page, take out the Ziploc bag. I wish it had a frame too, but it doesn't so I hold it by the edge and place it on the table in front of Winnie. "That's my mum. When she was a student at Columbia."

She looks at the photo and then at me. "You look alike."

"We've different eyes."

"Different colour, yes, but you have the same kind of look too. The chin . . . " She touches her own. "You have the same chin."

I move closer to her, lean in to see the photo. Your chin is turned to the side and it's nice and slopey, nicer than mine.

"She looks happy, doesn't she?" I go. "In this photo, doesn't she look like she was happy?"

Winnie looks properly. Already I know she's the kind of person who wants to look before she answers. She's not just going to say it because I say it. Maybe that's why I ask her. Maybe that's why she's the first person I show the photo to since I showed it to Laurie.

"It's a special photo," she says. "It captures something about your mother, the essence of her."

I get up, move over to sit on the arm of her chair. Olivia rubs into my leg. "So you think she looks happy?"

"She does look happy, but she looks more than that. She looks very real, you know, very alive."

I'm studying the picture, looking into your face, your eyes, examining the line of your hair along your jaw to see what Winnie sees.

"She looks a lot like the woman at the soup kitchen yesterday who was looking for you. They could be sisters."

Dumbass. Laurie's voice is in my head before mine. What was I thinking, showing her the photo of you? Did I think she wouldn't see the resemblance? That she'd forget yesterday had happened?

I stand up quickly, nearly stepping on Olivia. I take the photo back from Winnie, put it back in the Ziploc bag, put the bag back inside the Carver book.

"Lisa?"

I pick up my backpack. I want to pack it properly, nicely, but there isn't time.

"Lisa, what's the matter?"

I shove my jeans in, my Hendrix T-shirt. "I thought I could trust you, that's what's the matter."

She watches me packing, not smiling, but not mean-looking either.

"You can, I just don't know if I can trust you. You lied to me about who you are. I know your name's not Lisa."

When she says that I stop packing, just for a second. She's known my name was Rhea all along, since yesterday. Of course she knew.

"So why'd you go along with it? Keep calling me Lisa, write that stupid note?"

She shrugs. "I was waiting to see when you'd tell me the truth."

My stuff is nearly all packed. I'm still wearing her clothes but I can go into the kitchen, take them off and be out of this apartment, back on Ninth Avenue, in five minutes, less.

"I had to lie, you wouldn't understand."

"Try me." Olivia is by my feet again, licking my big toe. Her tongue is rough and scratchy and kind of nice. Lisa had a cat but I never saw it lick anyone. "She seemed really upset, the woman who wanted to find you. Your aunt. She seemed concerned."

I stand there looking at Winnie, I don't sit down. "I'm not going back there—I don't care what anyone says. I'm not going back, you can't make me! No one can make me!"

Winnie stays sitting down, looking up at me. She doesn't interrupt me. She doesn't tell me to keep my voice down.

"You're right, I can't make you go anywhere or do anything, no one can. But if you're going to stay with me—that is, if you want to—you're going to have to tell me the truth."

We stay like that for ages, it feels like, me standing, her sitting, Olivia in between. She makes it sound really simple, and maybe it is simple. I think about what she said about your photo, the Columbia one. She'd understood that, without me having to tell her, so maybe, just maybe she'll understand this too.

So I sit down on her couch and put my toes around the edge of the coffee table, just like her toes.

"I don't know where to start," I go. "I don't know where the beginning is."

She slides her glasses up her nose.

"Start where you are, start at the end."

And I laugh, because it kind of makes sense, and she laughs too.

And that's where I start.

I start at the end.

Rhea

Dear Mum,

This is going to be the shortest letter ever because there's only another fifteen minutes until my clothes will be dry and then I've got to bring them home and collect the sandwiches Winnie made and our art stuff and meet her at the jewellery shop where she works. She'll be finished with her shift then and we're getting the subway to Brooklyn, the A train. I'm writing this from the coolest little garden in the world by the way, down the block from the Laundromat. You need a key to get in and Winnie has a key because she's a volunteer and I'm going to volunteer too, that's one of the things I've decided.

Today feels like a day for deciding things, it feels like the start of something. If I'd known it would feel like this, telling Winnie the truth, I wouldn't have taken so long to get the whole story out, I wouldn't have been so scared. Yesterday, sitting on her couch, it takes me ages to even get to the part about me and Laurie, and it's nearly dark when I tell her about us kissing during Truth or Dare. Her face doesn't change, even though she knows by then that Laurie is Cooper's daughter, and it doesn't even change when I tell her about us being in bed together. The only time in the whole story that her face changes is when I tell her about Cooper hitting me and the things he said. Her face gets really kind of hard then, like someone else's face, and she shakes her head over and over and says she's so sorry I'd had to go through that.

And the way she listens makes me want to tell her everything, Mum, and somehow we get onto this conversation about Dad, and I'm telling her about his music and how I'd read his mood by it, that usually Hendrix meant he was happy, unless he was listening to "Voodoo Child" because he only listened to "Voodoo Child" when he was angry about something. Lennon was his "loving music"—he always said that—and that could mean he was happy too, except for the times he was sad. She's interested in the times he was sad, asks a lot about that and I end up telling her about the times he cried in my room when he got home from the pub, talking about you or Nana Farrell—and just then Winnie jumps up and puts on her shoes. I haven't even gotten to the part where Dad found Nana Farrell on the floor and had to take her to the hospital but Winnie says she needs to run to the payphone because it's after nine and she always calls Melissa at nine. And I never get to tell her about that part because when she comes back, she heats up some beef stew she'd brought home from the soup kitchen and she sends me to the Chinese on Tenth Avenue for a pint of brown rice to go with it. On the way back, I'm thinking that I'm glad I stopped there because I might have ended up telling her too much, like about what Aunt Ruth said on my last night in Coral Springs.

And I'm glad I didn't tell her that, because I know that if I mentioned it, even if I told her it was a lie, it'd be in her head every time we talk about you, every time I showed her a photo, she'd be thinking about it, wondering. And I prefer the way it is now, like when she sees your Columbia photo and she says she sees your essence, and how alive you are, because that's the real you, Mum.

I can see it and Winnie can see it, and just because Aunt Ruth can't doesn't mean we have to listen to her pack of lies.

Rhea

Dear Mum,

Dumbass. Dumbass. Dumbass, dumbass, dumbass.

That's what Laurie would say, and she'd be right. I hate that she's right.

You're such a dumbass, Rae.

At first the afternoon started off nice, just like I thought it would, taking the A train under the water, getting out in Brooklyn. When we get out, it's like being in another country—the houses and the streets and the sky, nothing like Manhattan at all. Winnie knows her way to the promenade and across the other side of the water, the whole of New York is there, a giant blocky puzzle, like Lego, like you could reach out and pick it up. And as if that's not enough, there's the Brooklyn Bridge too, stretching out to reach it, and the Statue of Liberty, floating out in the haze. Winnie says you have to get out of Manhattan to see it properly and that reminds me of what Dad said at the Cliffs of Moher, about having to be far away to see the waves.

While we eat our sandwiches I'm making a photo of it all in my head, the way I always do before I draw anything—the greeny black of the Statue of Liberty, the shapes the buildings cut out of the blue sky. Winnie's talking about Brooklyn, the history and about famous people who live here, and even though I'm listening, I'm thinking about you at the same time, and I'm trying to understand how you could turn your back on all this. And I can't figure out how you could trade it in—the statue, the city, this whole beautiful city—for a nothing village in Dublin. How you could have left it all behind for Dad, for me.

After we eat, she holds out two pieces of charcoal in her palm and I choose the long skinny bit. And then I make the mistake.

"Did you ever come here to draw with Melissa?"

Winnie is adjusting her paper against the board, holding the charcoal between two fingers like a cigarette. I've done mine already but I'm waiting for her before I start.

"No."

"Did she not like drawing?"

The paper's not totally straight so Winnie unclips it, lines it up again.

"Not really. It's not really her thing."

When it's lined up perfectly, she sits next to me on the bench, starts to study the skyline.

"What is her thing?"

The wind has come up a little bit off the water and it ruffles our paper.

"To be honest, I'm not sure, Rhea. Farmers' markets, wheatgrass drinks. I'm sure she likes other things too, but that's as much as I know these days."

Her hand is over the paper and I know she wants to start, that I should stop asking questions, but somehow I can't seem to stop.

"Does she ever come to New York?"

"Not much."

"Does she not like it here?"

"I guess not."

"How can someone not love New York?"

Winnie hits her charcoal down against the page, hard so it leaves a mark.

"Probably because she doesn't want to take a trip down memory lane by coming back here. She has a lot of painful memories I guess, with a drunk as a mother when she was growing up."

I don't know if she's angry or sad because her voice and her face are switching between both.

"But that was years ago—isn't she thirty or something?"

She looks at me, right into my eyes. "These scars run deep, Rhea. I only got sober when Melissa was eighteen. I took her childhood away. If I could give it back to her, I would, but I never can."

There's more pain in her face than it feels I should be seeing, so I look down at the paper, shiny white, waiting for my first mark. I want to make her feel better, to make the day clean again, like the paper.

"She looked happy in the picture you showed me. I'm sure it wasn't that bad."

Winnie's hair blows across her face and she flicks it back behind her ears.

"I was an active alcoholic, Rhea. You know what that's like, growing up in a house like that."

It takes me a second to fully hear what she's said.

"What do you mean?"

She glances at me. "You know, the stories you told me about your dad."

At first I'm not angry, just shocked. I even laugh.

"What are you talking about? Dad wasn't an alcoholic—"

She bites her lip. "I'm sorry, I shouldn't have brought your dad into this. Come on, we should get started."

She straightens her board, lines it up against the skyline.

"He liked a drink in the pub, but everyone's dad did that. That was normal."

She draws really fast, her hand skimming over the page, making quick shapes. She smudges some of the charcoal, but she doesn't seem to care.

"Sure," she goes. "Forget it."

Her eyes flick from the skyline to the paper and back again. She doesn't look at me, and I look at the skyline and try to let its shape replace the things she'd said. But it doesn't work, because the shock turns into anger then, and I can't stop it, thinking back on all the things I'd told her and how she wasn't listening at all, only judging me.

I know then that I'm not going to be able to draw. Looking at the skyline, the gaps between the buildings turn into tiny streets. And I can picture the miniature yellow taxis, bumper to bumper on the miniature streets, tiny people teeming along the sidewalks. And it's too alive to draw, with all this life, all these people—miniature versions of Sergei and Michael and even Pat with her headphones and my Red Sox cap, living their teeny lives right in the middle of it all. I wanted to pick the city up and shake it until they all fall out—Pat and Sergei and Michael and even Aunt Ruth, a miniature Aunt Ruth, scurrying along putting up microscopic pictures of me.

Winnie's stopped drawing. She's looking at me. "I'm sorry, Rhea, talking like that about your father… It's none of my business."

The charcoal feels slippy in my hand. There's a mark on the white paper, kind of a circle, a smear, where I've been pushing it against the page.

"I didn't mean to upset you," she goes.

"I'm not upset."

She nods and starts drawing again, quick like before. She'll probably want to talk about it again when we get back to her apartment. And thinking about her apartment makes me worry about the fridge, how it was nearly empty except for the cream cheese and a jar of mixed garlic and some salad dressing and I hope she has a plan to get some food on the way home, because even though it's only half an hour since the sandwiches, I'm hungry again already.

"What do you think?"

Winnie holds up her picture to show me. It's smudgy and a bit of a mess. The windows of the buildings are all done in dashes or L shapes but what's strange is that even though it's not exactly how the buildings look, it looks real.

"It's good."

"You don't feel like drawing today?"

I shake my head, put my board down on the bench between us. She places hers down too, carefully, on top of mine.

"I was hoping you would. I was hoping you'd do something new so I could show my friend Jean."

"Who's Jean?"

She unwinds the pink and silver scarf from around her neck, holds one end in each hand. "She's someone I know from years back, from a rehab I was in. She's a counsellor and she runs a camp out in Long Island where we take kids from shelters for a few weeks every summer."

"You're going away?"

"I go every year."

"When?"

"Next week. Thursday."

Thursday is six days away, not even a whole week. I want to say that, but I don't say anything. I want to ask her why she didn't say anything before, but that's a dumbass thing to even think because she doesn't have to say anything, tell me anything. I'm just a dumbass for getting sucked in with all the "we's."

"Rhea, listen." She's pulling the scarf tight at each end. "I called Jean last night, told her about you, to see if I could persuade her to take on someone else to help me with the art classes. It's a lot for me now, all the kids."

She's smiling, holding the edges of her scarf, like this is great news. The wind has picked up a little and it's flapping her page. "I'm so excited, Rhea, because Jean said that we could sort something out. That if you can take on some of the other stuff—cleaning maybe, things like that—you can come out too."

Over the city there's grey clouds now, like smoke.

"We'll have to share a room, there are no extra ones, but that's fine with me."

"What if I don't want to?"

She looks confused. "Share a room?"

"What if I don't want to go? What if I want to stay here?"

She shakes her head. "You'll love it, Rhea. The money's not great but the food is always amazing and it's right on the beach, you can go swimming every day."

"I can't swim."

Her eyes glance towards my stump and back to my face. She thinks that's why I can't; even after everything I told her last night, she thinks that's why not.

"That's okay, maybe you'll learn. Say you'll come."

She moves closer to me on the bench, so her board falls onto the ground, banging off the concrete. She bends down to pick it up and she notices the daisy I've had in the lacehole of my Docs since the park. She points to it and smiles.

"So this woman—this Jean—she's just going to offer me a job, just like that? Without even meeting me?"

"She wouldn't be able to meet you anyway, she's out there already, getting the place set up. But once the background checks are okay—"

"Background checks?"

"You know, just the usual stuff. We're working with kids, they have to make sure—"

"No, no way. I'm not doing that."

I stand up and my charcoal falls on the ground.

"Rhea—"

"Aunt Ruth has probably been to the police. She must have. If they run a check, she'll probably find out. She'll probably find me."

Winnie's standing up too, reaching for my hand, but I fold my arm across me, put it in my armpit.

"Rhea, you're eighteen. She can't make you go back."

"No!" I stamp on the charcoal but it's too thin to break.

"Come on, don't mess this up. Even if it wasn't for the background check, I'd be suggesting you contact your aunt, let her know you're safe."

A drop of rain falls on Winnie's picture, then another one.

"Mess this up? I thought you got it, Winnie. I thought you understood."

"I do understand—but you're not listening to me, Rhea. You don't have to go back there. No one's going to make you go back. Just let her know you're okay, that's all."

There's more rain. The charcoal is starting to smudge. Winnie unclips her paper, rolls it up. I scrunch my toes tight inside my Docs. The daisy from earlier is turning to mush in the rain, it's already dead.

Winnie's got everything back in the bag, boards, paper, charcoal. She has her scarf over her head now. "Come on, we're getting soaked."

222

I hesitate, lean against the railing. As if I have another choice, as if there is somewhere else I can go.

"How do I know you're not going to call my aunt, tell her where I am?"

She rolls her eyes. "Come on, Rhea. You know I'm not going to do that. You're an adult. You're the one who gets to decide what happens next. Not me."

We don't talk anymore after that, just hurry back to the subway station, both of us trying to stay dry walking close to the buildings. And we don't talk on the train on the way home and I hate that things can change, from the way they were on the way here to being like this, with no warning at all.

She's out now, at an AA meeting and she's probably telling them all what an ungrateful bitch I am. And I thought about leaving while she's out—about taking my clothes off the shelf she made for me and packing them in my backpack again, but it's still raining and it's nice in here, listening to it on the window with the violin music upstairs and Olivia scrunched in next to me.

And I'm looking at your photo, the Columbia one, and I'm wondering what you'd do, what you'd want me to do. She hasn't said it, but I think she'll let me stay, till Thursday, if I want to. That's six days of food, six nights of sleep on this couch. Sometimes Dad would go on about principles, how they weren't worth sacrificing, and I don't know if I stay if I'm sacrificing mine because Winnie betrayed my trust by telling this Jean person about me. But I've nowhere else to go, no money even, not anymore. And it feels like I'm all out of options. That for six days of food and sleep, it might be worth the sacrifice, just this once.

Maybe, if I asked you, you might tell me that.

Rhea

Dear Mum,

I am copying out the letter I'm sending to Aunt Ruth because if she writes back I want to remember what I wrote. It's way harder writing to her than writing to you. I hope I'm doing the right thing, sending the letter, going with Winnie—I hope I'm not making a mistake.

As soon as I tell Winnie what I've decided she hugs me and then she runs out to phone Jean to start the background check. And I nearly change my mind then, after everything, I nearly take the red Converse she'd bought me and the shorts with all the pockets and the second-hand Walkman and put them all in my backpack and run, before I can think about it. But I don't run, I sit and stroke Olivia, and listen to her purring, and then Winnie's back, smiling, telling me everything we need to do next.

I didn't decide to go because she bought me that stuff, Mum, that wasn't it. It was all from the Salvation Army and it only came to six dollars. I decided to go because she's buying it for me anyway—the Converse and the shorts and the Walkman—whether I go with her or not. It's not a bribe and that's what makes me trust her.

The place we're going is called Turning Tides and I like the name and that it's on Long Island, in between a town called Amagansett and a town called Montauk. Winnie showed me where it is, on the map, and it's near where Aunt Ruth told me you used to spend your summers, where the ice cream place is, and that's another reason I decided to go, if you want to know the truth.

I don't think Aunt Ruth must have liked going there, because she was weird the time we talked about it in Jaxson's, but maybe that's because of Nana Davis having an affair with Granddad Davis' boss—at least I think they were. But I bet you liked it, Mum. Winnie told me about all the beaches on Long Island, some of the best in the country, she said. I bet you went swimming every day.

I'm not going to post the letter until Thursday morning, right before we leave. I know I don't need to worry about her finding me—the letter has the soup kitchen's return address on it because Chrissie is going to forward on anything that comes. And even if Aunt Ruth jumped on a plane straightaway, she wouldn't get here before we left no matter when I send it. But posting it on Thursday feels better all the same.

Making decisions is hard sometimes, isn't it? I wish I knew how to tell in advance if it was the right decision or a mistake, but they both feel the same, I think they do.

If you've figured it out up there, a way to tell the difference, do me a favour and let me know, will you?

It might be a handy thing to know.

R

Dear Aunt Ruth,

How are you? I am writing to you because I want to let you know that there is no need for you to worry about me. I am fine. I have a job in a summer camp so I'll have somewhere to live and I'll be earning money. It's not in New York, so don't bother looking for me there.

I would like to know if Columbia responded to my application. I don't expect you to pay my fees now, but I would still like to know if I was accepted.

You can write back and let me know using the address on the envelope and they will send the letter on to me. Please don't come to the soup kitchen again to try and find out where I am. They won't be able to tell you and by the time you get this, I won't even be in New York and no matter what happens, I'm not going back to Florida.

I'm sorry for everything that happened and for causing trouble for you and your family.

Yours sincerely,
Rhea Farrell

Dear Mum,

It's the first time I've had a chance to write to you and even now I should be in bed but I can't sleep. We have to start work at 8:00 a.m. here—not get up, start work—and after the kids come on Monday, we'll have to start at 7:30! It's like a prison camp here, Mum, there's so many rules.

I'm not even meant to be down here on my own, on the beach, after dark.

The best part so far was the train journey, with me and Winnie playing poker and the conductor walking through shouting out the name of each station. I'm winning—I would have won—if I hadn't got distracted when he calls out Bridgehampton and I lay down the wrong card. I want to play another game, but Winnie insists on packing the cards away to get ready to get off, even though we don't get to the Amagansett station for ages after.

Jean and David are waiting on the platform and it turns out Zac and Matt were on our train as well. Zac and Matt are twins who are a year younger than me but twice as tall. Both of them are starting at Brown University at the end of the summer and, so far, that's all they've talked about. Laurie would love them, especially Zac, because he plays football and you can tell he's the one who's the leader of the two of them, because he speaks first and laughs more and Matt looks smaller, the way he rounds his shoulders, even though they're the same height.

At first I don't know who she is, the woman who's hugging every-one—it takes me a minute to realise it's Jean. For some reason, I don't expect her to be black or to be wearing shorts and flip-flops and a neon pink T-shirt. She looks too young to be the boss, especially when she's wearing her Oakley sunglasses, which she is most of the time. When she hugs Winnie, they kind of rock back and forth, hugging for so long it's kind of embarrassing. I'm next and it's weird but it's like she somehow knows that I don't want to hug her because she only squeezes my shoulder and says that I'll be a great addition to the team.

David's the cook and the van driver and he has a long ponytail and a beard. He gives me a big handshake with his left hand and says he likes my Hendrix T-shirt. He's wearing a tie-dye one with someone called Jimmy Buffett on it and I pretend I've heard of him and I say I like his T-shirt too.

He drives really fast, David does, and we're all thrown around in the back when he takes the sharp turn off the road in through a tiny gateway. It's like a dirt track in Ireland—grass up the middle and trees and bushes scraping the sides of the van—but then it suddenly opens up and there's the house, with the sea, crystal blue, right behind it. This house is nothing like beach houses in Florida—it's old, white wood and four storeys and a big wooden deck that wraps all the way around.

Me and Winnie are staying on the top floor, in the attic room, up four flights of stairs with no air conditioner because apparently the window is too small for one. The only people who have their own rooms are Jean and Gemma, the other therapist who smiles a lot but hardly says a word. Zac and Matt are sharing, and Amanda is sharing with Erin, some kind of trainee therapist who's not here yet.

Amanda's the lifeguard, by the way, we meet her after Jean gives us the tour of the house. The pool is in the back, down the opposite set of steps than the sea, and when we get there it looks like it's empty until we see the bubbles and then Amanda bursts through the surface of the water, her cheeks puffed out.

"Talk about a dramatic entrance," Jean says, and everyone laughs. Jean laughs too, at her own joke, and her laugh is louder than everyone else's, loud and annoying.

"Sorry," Amanda goes, wiping her hair out of her eyes. "I was seeing how long I could sit on the bottom."

Jean laughs again and gets down on her hunkers next to where Amanda has propped herself up on the edge.

"This is Amanda, our trusty lifeguard who keeps all the kids safe in the water. Amanda, meet the troops—Zac, Matt, Winnie and Rhea."

We all say hi at the same time.

"Do you surf?" Zac goes. "I hear the surfing is awesome out here."

Amanda's wearing one of those lame necklaces with her name on it in loopy gold that's supposed to be handwriting and it glints in the sun.

"No," she goes, scrunching up her nose, "but I boogie board."

"Good enough," Zac goes. "David said he has a long board, I'll show you how."

Jean must have noticed the total flirting going on because she does this thing to bring the rest of us into the conversation.

"Maybe you can teach us all how to boogie board, Amanda," she goes. "I'd like to learn too."

"Sure, why not." She fiddles with her necklace, sliding it back and forth on its chain.

Winnie puts her hand on my shoulder and I think she's going to say something nice. "You can start with teaching Rhea how to swim. That can be your first challenge!"

She laughs, like it's a joke, and I can't believe she's said that in front of everyone, and I hate how they are all looking at me and at my stump and feeling sorry for me, like I'm some kind of victim.

"You can't swim, Rhea?" Jean goes.

"I hate the water, I've never wanted to learn."

She nods. I can't see her eyes behind her Oakleys. "I used to be scared of the water too, but I got over it, out here. No better place to learn."

I don't know if I already didn't like Jean or if that's when I decided fully.

"I didn't say I was scared," I go. "I just don't like it."

But she doesn't answer me because she's already leading the way back up to the house so she can take us down the other steps, to the beach. And I keep trying to catch Winnie's eye but she's not looking at me and I wish she wasn't Jean's friend because I want to say to her that Jean must be the biggest dumbass psychologist ever because she obviously doesn't listen.

That was yesterday. Today, I hate Jean more because of the way she sits up on the upper deck with Gemma, reading through folders, while Matt and Winnie and me are dragging all the furniture up from the basement and wiping it down and sweeping the deck. Zac's helping Amanda clean the pool, even though I think he should be helping us, and all you can hear is water splashing and their voices laughing—it sounds like there's not much cleaning going on, and I bet they are boyfriend/girlfriend already.

Matt offers to finish off the carrying part but I don't let him, even though my arm is killing me from all the lifting. And just when I think we're finished it turns out the basement needs to be cleaned out too, because it's the rec room where Winnie and me are going to be doing the art class, so we do that too.

After lunch, we have our meeting and just before it starts, Erin shows up, the trainee psychologist. And I wish that Laurie was here because she'd roll her eyes and laugh at how excited Erin gets when she hears my accent and how she goes around the table hugging everyone, just like Jean did. Laurie would hate Jean too, I know she would, and I know she'd think it was lame how the others all keep laughing at every one of her crappy jokes.

Jean hands out these sheets stapled together with each of our names at the top that have a printed schedule for each day with eight time slots. I scan the slots for my name, I'm in five of them, no, six. I count Winnie's—she's in four. Amanda's in five, the same as Matt and Zac. I'm doing more work than anyone else, but when I glance over at Winnie to see if she's noticed, if she'll say anything, she's writing down something Jean has just said. The talking goes on for ages—Jean first, then Gemma—about what it's like for these kids to be homeless and in shelters, as if they know anything about it. They take ages going through the activities. It takes longer because of all the questions—everyone has questions and after nearly every one Jean says "great question!" before she answers. I'm the only one who doesn't ask anything, just like I'm the only one not taking notes.

Jean is going on about something lame called "Be Myself Time" where kids sit around in the rec room and do anything they want. She's all animated explaining it, how the time is unstructured so the kids can pick up an instrument and play it or draw or read, whatever they feel like. She says it three times, "Be Myself Time," as if she's just come up with the name, as if it's the most amazing name in the world.

Matt is next to me and he's not writing anything down. I lean closer to him. "I think I'd prefer 'Be Someone Else Time.'" I whisper, but when he turns around his voice is too loud. "What?"

Jean stops talking and looks over and the silence is like school all over again. Across from me, Amanda's next to Zac. Now that her hair is dry I can see it's curly and blonde, even though it's tied back. She dips her chin down to her chest and I realise she's trying not to laugh.

"Did you have a question, Rhea?" Jean is smiling a pretend smile.

I look at my blank page and shake my head. "No."

Her eyes hold mine, they're big in her face, lots of white around her dark brown pupils.

"You're comfortable with your role? Helping out on the beach and in the kitchen and afternoons with Winnie in Arts and Crafts?"

"Yep."

They're all looking at me, everyone is, except Amanda, who's doodling on her page. Jean is still smiling, as if she is waiting for me to say something more.

"So, how do you feel about tomorrow?" she says. "Are you nervous? Excited?"

She hasn't asked anyone else a question like that, not even with all their questions, and I know it's a trick, that she's picking on me because I haven't asked her anything. And that's when I think of a question.

"Do you think it makes any difference?"

She puts her chin in her hand. "Makes any difference?"

"I mean, you've told us all about the lives that these kids have. Do you think a few weeks at the beach making sandcastles actually changes anything?"

She sits back, straight up in her chair.

"It's a lot more than building sandcastles, Rhea. I don't know if you followed the whole programme but there are many components—"

"Art, music, physical activity, nutrition, play, community." I list them off, exactly as she said them. "I know what they do, but I just wondered if it actually makes any kind of difference."

It's the first question that's not a "great" question, or even a "good" question. She looks down at her page and back to me.

"We give these kids a place to be children, Rhea, a place to heal. You'll see the difference for yourself." Her voice is annoyed, she's not able to hide it. "On the first day, they'll be shoving sandwiches in their pockets, hardly able to talk to us, and when they leave they'll be laughing and playing like children."

"Yeah, but what happens after? After they go back home?"

Winnie is looking at me now, frowning behind her glasses, and I know she wants me to shut up. In the beginning, I was asking to annoy Jean, but now I'm asking because I really want to know. Jean is pulling at the curl over her ear, where a little bit of grey is. She opens her mouth to answer, but Gemma gets there first.

"There's a lot of evidence to support the fact that helping children reclaim their childhoods can lead to a better ability to cope as adults." Her voice is so soft and I can hardly hear her over the noise of the air conditioner. "This programme is only five years old, though, so it's too early to track real outcomes."

"So you can't know for sure?" I go.

She shakes her head. "No, we can't."

Jean is the first one to get up from the table after that, and we have a break before dinner. When I go up to the room, Winnie's there changing her T-shirt and I'm glad we're sharing then, because we haven't had a chance to talk since the train.

"Well?" she goes. "What do you think so far?"

I lie down on the bed, even though I still have my Docs on.

"It's okay."

"Only okay?"

I know I should have pretended to like it, to like Jean, but Winnie's supposed to be my friend and I thought the whole point of having friends was to tell them the truth.

"I like the house, but it'd be nicer if we didn't have to share it with this bunch of whackjobs."

"Whackjobs? I haven't heard that in a while. Why are they whackjobs?"

I roll over onto my back, look at the ceiling.

"I don't know—they all are. Like, Erin. All she wants to talk about is some bumfuck part of Leitrim where her dad's from. I've never been to Leitrim. I'd rather kill myself than go to Leitrim."

Winnie laughs and that makes it okay to keep talking.

"And that other one, Gemma—what's up with her? She hardly said a word all day and now she's sitting on her own on the balcony upstairs with her eyes closed."

"I think she's meditating."

I can hear a smile in Winnie's voice, I think I can.

"And Jean, all that crap about healing these kids' emotional scars. That's total bullshit."

"You think so?"

"Yeah, I do."

I wait for her to say more but all I hear is the hiss of her perfume. When I look over, she's dabbing it behind her ears. She's wearing her white shirt, the one with the pink flowers on the collars.

"You're getting dressed up for dinner?"

"I'm going to a meeting after, in Bridgehampton."

"Again? You went last night."

She folds her T-shirt, doesn't answer me.

"David's going to drop me in."

"In New York you don't go to AA every night."

"Sometimes I do."

"Not when I was staying with you."

"No," she smiles, "not when you were staying with me."

She puts the T-shirt in the top drawer of the dresser, the drawer I said I didn't mind her having. Sometimes I hate these conversations, when Winnie just repeats everything I say.

"Is your meeting anywhere near the ice cream place? The Candy Kitchen?"

"I don't know—it's probably not too far. Why? Did you want to come with me?"

"No." I sit up on the bed. "No, I was just asking."

"Okay."

She slips her feet into her flip-flops. We have half an hour before dinner and I wonder is she going to walk on the beach and I'm thinking of asking her if she wants to do that, but then she says the most annoying thing ever.

"Just give the place a chance, Rhea. It's going to be okay. When I get scared, I'm judgemental too."

She leaves then, closing the door behind her, before I can say anything back, and that's what annoys me most of all, that I don't get to tell her that she obviously wasn't listening to me and that I'm not fucking scared.

It pisses me off, Mum, that she can be so wrong about me, and I should have said something to her but there was no time at dinner and later, after she came back from her meeting, she seemed really happy so I didn't want to then. But then I couldn't sleep, and lying in that hot-ass room with her snoring, it's all I can think about, and not even listening to David's Pink Floyd tape on my Walkman can stop it.

Because I'm not scared of Jean, Mum, or of this stupid place. And I'm not scared of the water. If I was scared I wouldn't be breaking the rules—I'd be in bed now, up in that stuffy attic, trying to sleep. If I was scared, I wouldn't be down here on the beach, by myself in the dark. I wouldn't be writing to you.

Rhea

Dear Mum,

I want to write a list of all the kids' names but I don't know what order to put them in and I can't remember all their names because some of them are names I've never heard before and I have to know how to spell something before I can remember it.

Out of thirty-six, only three are white, the others are mostly black and Hispanic. It might sound fifty kinds of crazy, but I can't understand half of what they're saying—even the ones who speak English—and they can't understand me either.

None of them are meant to be older than twelve but one of them claims he's thirteen—Marco, one of the white kids who wears a T-shirt with an Italian flag on it all the time. Erin makes him the captain of one of the volleyball teams which anyone with half an eye could see is a bad idea. Shirley is the captain of the other team and she gets to go first. She picks Amanda, straightaway, so I'm the only counsellor left, with all the other kids. Marco spends ages choosing, his arms folded.

"Come on," Erin goes after a while. "Pick someone!"

"Okay." He walks towards me and, at the last minute, whirls around to point at Isaac. "You!"

Isaac runs over and they high five. It was Shirley's turn again and her eyes hovered over me.

"Are we allowed to have two grown-ups on our team?"

She's asking the question to Erin, but before she can answer, Marco does.

"She's all yours. I don't want no handicapped bitch on my team."

I hate the way he looks at me when he says it, but I hate even more that I look away.

"Marco!" Erin goes. "Apologise, you can't call people names like that."

She doesn't know, Mum, that that's the worst thing to do, to make a big deal out of it, so I cut across her and laugh like what he said was a joke. "Fine by me. I'm going to enjoy kicking your skinny Italian ass!"

The kids laugh then and Shirley high fives me and they go on choosing until everyone is chosen and I pretend I don't see the pity in Amanda's face. And we do kick his ass, Mum. Even though it's only a kids' game, I run all over the beach like it's the Olympics or something and we beat them 21–7. I scored twelve of our points.

I'm wrecked now, Mum—it never stops here—volleyball, art, helping David make the rice for dinner and cleaning up after, although that was worth it because I got to sample his banana walnut muffins, straight from the oven. Tonight was movie night—*E. T.*— and I thought I was going to be able to watch it all, but even then they don't sit still. It was getting to the best part—the part where the plant comes back to life and then E.T. does—and then Natalie threw up all over her shoes and because I was sitting nearest I had to clean it up.

I'm not complaining, Mum, I'm not. It's just that

Dear Mum,

I fell asleep last night, right in the middle of writing that sentence. It's fifty kinds of crazy that I'm more tired now than when I was on the streets. When I say it to Winnie she says it's the sea air, but I think it's because Jean is working us like slaves and I have more work than anyone else.

Like this morning, I'm on breakfast, with Matt and Zac, even though I was on dinner last night. Breakfast is easier though because half of them are having "Be Myself Time" and eighteen kids between three of us isn't too bad—even though Zac doesn't do much and pretends he doesn't see the milk Luis spilled all over the table. I like him, Luis, but he's so scared all the time, you'd think I was going to hit him for knocking over a glass of milk. When I tell him it's okay and bring him another one, he starts crying and I pretend not to see the box of Cheerios he has shoved in his pocket in case it makes him cry more.

I don't know how to be with kids—what to do when they fight or cry or anything. It was Erin who stepped in when Maleika and Shirley were pulling each other's hair on the beach over whose turn it was to go on the Swingball and I don't know how she does it, because five minutes later, they were both jumping over the waves at the edge, each of them holding one of her hands.

They've all formed groups now, Mum, in only a couple of days— the girls in pairs mostly and the boys in mini gangs. The only one who always spends time on her own is Robin, a little black girl—one of the youngest. I tried to talk to her, but she won't speak to anyone, she didn't even say anything today when Isaac and Jeffrey kicked sand in her face on purpose, she didn't cry or anything.

Jean came to check up on me this afternoon. I'm down in the rec room, washing the trays and brushes after art, and when I turn around she's right behind me in a lime-green polo shirt. I'm holding four trays between my stump and my hand and I drop two of them on the tiles.

"Hi," she goes, bending down to help me pick them up. "Sorry, I didn't mean to give you a shock."

"You didn't," I go. "You're grand."

She hands me two of the trays and it's harder to carry them than if she'd just let me pick them up on my own.

"How are things going?"

"Fine."

I put the trays on the table and water drips on the floor.

"I just came down to see how you were finding things. If you're settling in okay. Some people find it a little intense at first."

She's holding her sunglasses between her fingers, swinging them back and forth.

"I like it," I go.

"Good." She swings her sunglasses, smiles. "You're not too busy? The schedule works okay?"

I have that feeling again, like on the train platform, as if she can see right into my head, that she knows I've been bitching about it, but I'm not going to give her the satisfaction of saying it's too much.

"I like to be busy."

She smiles too. "Then you're in the right place."

I think it's over and take the dirty brushes, lay them out one by one in the sink.

"Amanda mentioned that Marco said something nasty—on the beach?"

I don't look up or turn around, just line up the bristles so they all make one line of bristle. So that's why she's here, stupid Amanda and her interfering. I don't need her running to Jean any more than I need her pitying looks.

"It was nothing," I go. "No big deal."

"I can talk with him, explain that it's not okay to say what he said. He might not have met someone with a disability before."

She says it like it's any old word, like it applies to me. I want to tell her that I don't have a disability, that I can do anything she

238

can do, but instead I turn on the tap full force so the water almost drowns out what she says next.

"He might have questions about it, be curious."

She's a bigger dumbass than I thought, if she thinks that. Marco is the Susan Mulligan of the group—he's not curious, he's a bully. I don't tell her that, Mum, she's the psychologist after all, so instead I just watch the water making clouds in the sink, pink, green, blue, until everything is a muddy brown.

I don't know how long she stands there watching me, because I can't hear over the water, but when the sink is about to overflow, I turn off the tap and she's gone by then. All that's left is the sound of her flip-flops slapping against her feet as she climbs the stairs.

R

Dear Mum,

David goes to the farmers' market every Wednesday and today, when I'm helping him unload the corn and tomatoes and onions from the van, my heart nearly stops because I see all this post on the dashboard, next to a box of Marlboro Lights.

I'm looking at the envelopes, trying to see names on the top, when he comes around the side of the van and catches me.

"What are you looking at, nosy?"

"Nothing!" I turn around too fast, so I nearly drop the corn.

Walking into the house, my heart is beating really fast, Mum, as if one of those letters is definitely from Aunt Ruth, which is weird because, up until then, I'd kind of forgotten I even wrote to Aunt Ruth, as if my letter was something I sent into space, with no chance of her ever writing back at all. It takes ages to put everything away. When we do, David gives me a banana walnut muffin and I sit on the counter, watching him sort through the envelopes, laying them out on the table.

"Anything for me?"

I say it all casual, with my mouth full of muffin in case my voice sounds weird.

He stops and looks up. "Not so far. You expecting anything?"

"Uh huh." I shake my head, take another bite.

"A ConEd bill, circulars, the usual shit." He's eating a muffin too and there's a big crumb of it stuck in his beard. "But don't worry, I'll be back at the post office tomorrow. Jean's a stickler for checking the mail—has me down there every day."

"Why?"

David rolls his eyes but he smiles too. "You know what she's like, never gives up on these kids. In five years, I think I've picked up two letters, maybe three, for them, but she's always hoping that this year will be the year, that people will write."

I wish I didn't know that, Mum, about him going there every

day. Because now I know that every single day there's a chance *the soup kitchen could forward* a letter from Aunt Ruth, or maybe even from Laurie, and now that I know, my mind won't let me unknow it. And it's not like I want a letter from either of them—I didn't even write to Laurie. But if nothing shows up at all, I can't even tell myself that maybe it got lost with all the letters for the kids because there are no letters for the kids. And let's face it, not much can get lost in the middle of a few circulars and a ConEd bill.

Rhea

Dear Mum,

One of the things Jean is obsessed with, that she went on and on about that first day, is counting the kids. *Count the kids on the way to the beach, count the kids when you get back. Count kids at the start of art class, at the start of dinner, when they go to bed.* She says it fifty thousand times, over and over, as if we're going to forget.

Today someone forgot. It's Saturday—"Cowboy and Cowgirl" night—so we were having franks and beans around the campfire with stories after. Winnie and Amanda had been doing the nature walk so it was one of them who forgot, one of them who should have counted before they came back from the beach.

I'm helping David lay out the food and I'm not really paying too much attention at first until I hear Winnie's voice all out of breath, like she's been running.

"You must have missed one," she goes. "Count again."

Amanda walks down the line, tipping each of the kids on the shoulder, her voice and Winnie's voice counting out loud together. Marco pushes Luis out of the line and laughs but Amanda just walks past, counting. By the time she's at number twenty, I've counted ahead and I know they were right first time—that one kid is missing. By the time Amanda's at twenty-eight, I know the one missing is Robin.

I don't know who tells Jean what's happening, but she's there by the time they are counting a third time, her hand on Winnie's shoulder, scanning the line of kids. Matt and Zac come out with the soda coolers and she splits us all up into areas to search. Someone has to stay behind with the other kids to help David serve up the food and to make sure no one else gets lost. If anyone else was missing—even Genesis or Gabriel—I wouldn't mind staying behind, but it isn't any of them. It's Robin. And I want to find her.

I get to check the house—the rec room and the storage rooms behind it. Zac is checking the first floor and Matt's on the second.

Winnie and Amanda are searching outside and the beach. We have twenty minutes to find her, after that we call 911.

Did you ever just know something was going to happen, before it happens? Going down the stairs, I know I'm going to be the one who finds Robin. I don't know how I know, I just do.

The tables are all pushed up against the walls because last night was Friday and that's the night Erin does the dance party. If I was a kid who wanted to hide, I'd probably hide under a table. That's what I'm thinking when I get down on my knees, look under each one. And I think I'm wrong, that she's not there, and then I see her, under the very last table, scrunched up in the corner.

I don't stand up, instead I kind of slide over on my bum, my legs pulling me forward. She's not looking up and I can't make out what she's doing at first until I see a page, her hand moving, and I see that she's drawing.

"Hey, Robin."

She doesn't look up but the crayon stops for a split second before she starts colouring again, so I know she hears me.

"Are you okay? Everyone's looking for you—we were worried."

I'm about to tell her not to go anywhere, to wait right there while I go upstairs for Jean or Gemma, like we're supposed to, but something makes me crawl under the table next to her. She stops drawing, puts her hands over her eyes. After a second, she opens her fingers to peer out, sees that I'm still there, and snaps them shut again.

"It's nice under here," I go. "Do you like hiding out?"

I sit cross-legged, the same way she is. My head touches the underside of the table and I scrunch my neck down a little. Over our heads, I can hear footsteps, a voice—Zac or Matt's—calling Robin's name.

"What are you drawing?"

I reach out to touch her paper and she pulls it away. Her dark eyes take me in, everything about me—my face, my Hendrix T-shirt, my stump. Next to her on the floor, there's extra paper and crayons.

"Can I draw a picture too?"

She looks at me for a second, then she nods, pushes a piece of paper at me. I pick up a purple crayon and start to draw. And it's really weird, Mum, because, right then, it's like I forget about everything—about waiting for the letter from Aunt Ruth and about everyone searching the house and the beach and even about Robin sitting next to me. And halfway through I realise that it's the first time I've been able to draw since that night I left Florida, but I don't let myself think about it too much, just keep drawing, because if I think about it too much I might have to stop.

When I'm finished, Robin's still drawing, but she stops once she sees I have. She looks over at my page.

I hold it out, so she can see it. "That's my mom."

She leans closer but she doesn't touch it.

"I have a photo of her like that and I like to draw it. I don't need to look at the photo, though, I can see it in my head."

"My mom's in Heaven," she goes.

It's the first thing she says to me—the first thing I think I've heard her say to anyone.

"So is mine," I go. "My mom's in Heaven too."

She picks up a red crayon and goes back to her drawing. Her page is full of squares and circles and squiggles. She's colouring in a red part of one of the circles.

"Is that a bird?" I go. "Is it a robin? Like your name?"

"Robin is a thin girl's name."

At first, I think she doesn't understand that a robin is a bird, but when she starts to colour again I see the way her pudgy hand grabs the crayon, the dimples in her knuckles, and I know that what she's just said aren't her words.

"Who said that, Robin?"

She puts the red down, picks up my purple and starts to colour over her drawing, making circles of purple over and over on her page.

"Did someone tell you that, Robin?"

She moves her head a millimetre. A tiny fraction, a nod.

"Uncle Nat."

"My daddy always said not to mind people who called me names. He had a rhyme that said, 'Sticks and stones might break my bones but words can never harm me.'"

She starts to scribble harder, her crayon is going to rip through the paper.

"Uncle Nat says my mommy was stupid and fat too. But he doesn't say it in front of Nanny."

She says this like she's talking about something else, something she's seen on TV—maybe it is something she's seen on TV.

"What does your nanny say?"

Robin shrugs. "I don't know."

"Do you live with your nanny?"

The crayon picks up speed, making lines and zigzags so you can barely make out the shapes from the original picture.

"Nanny went to Heaven too."

I know I should be getting up, running upstairs to tell the others I've found her, that this is something Jean can talk to Robin about during "Be Myself Time." I know everything it says in the handbook but, right then, I don't care what it says in the handbook—Robin's not telling Jean this, she's telling me.

I'm thinking of what to ask Robin next when she turns to me. Her little face is serious.

"Is your arm in Heaven?"

I start to laugh, I can't help it, but I stop when I see that Robin's not laughing, that she looks scared.

"I'm sorry, I'm not laughing at you, it just sounded funny." I let myself hold my stump in my hand. "I don't know if arms go to Heaven."

"Where did it go?"

I take a breath, make myself smile. "When I was a little girl I had an accident. There was a machine in my daddy's shop and, because I wasn't careful, my arm got stuck in there."

I didn't think her eyes could get any bigger, but they're saucers now in her face. Now I have her full attention, whether I want it or not.

"In the machine?"

I nearly laugh again, but I hold it in. "I hurt it, really bad, and they had to take away the part that was hurt, so the rest of me would be okay."

Her eyes are on my stump now. She's turned a little bit towards me, the half-destroyed drawing forgotten on the floor.

"Does it hurt?"

I think about it. "Not usually. Sometimes."

"I fell and I cut my chin before and I got stitches."

She sticks her chin out, so I see the scar, a thin line, barely visible.

"Ouch," I go. "That sounds sore."

"Here," she goes. "Feel it."

I trace my finger gently along her chin. When I'm finished, I know she wants to touch my stump even before she reaches out her hand. I've never let anyone touch it before. I might have let Laurie if she'd asked, but she never did. I hold it out to her and she looks at it for a few seconds before she prods it with her index finger. She looks up at me. "Does that hurt?"

"No. It doesn't hurt when you touch it."

Slowly, she cups her hand around it, the way I was holding it. Her hand is much smaller than mine, so her palm just covers the end. It feels warm and kind of ticklish. I start to giggle and she does too and that's what we're doing when I hear footsteps.

"Rhea? Rhea? Are you down here?"

It's Winnie.

"Over here," I go, "in the corner."

I can tell already, by the way she doesn't answer me, that she's annoyed. I can see it in the way her feet move in her sandals as she walks across the room towards us, in the way she crouches down on her hunkers.

"They're sending a search party out for you, Robin," she says. "We were all worried."

Robin stops laughing. She lets go of my stump as if she's been caught—as if we both have—doing something bad.

"It's okay," I go. "You're not going to get in trouble. Sure she's not, Winnie?"

"No," Winnie says, "I just wanted to make sure you were up in time to get some franks and beans before they're all gone."

Robin shakes her head. "I'm not hungry."

"That's a shame," Winnie says, "because after that there's ice cream."

Robin starts to crawl out from under the table, leaving the drawing and the crayons on the floor. When Winnie puts her hand out to her, she doesn't take it and, instead, she looks back at me.

"You coming?" she goes.

"Rhea's going to tidy up your drawing stuff here," Winnie says. "We'll see her outside."

I don't know why Winnie's going to get to be the one to walk upstairs with Robin, to hold her little hand, when I was the one who'd found her, but I pretend it doesn't matter. And for the rest of the night I pretend I don't know she's annoyed with me, pretend everything's fine. But it's horrible, all that pretending and knowing we have to share a room together later.

She's in the bedroom already when I come up.

"Do you want the door open or closed?" I go.

It's not a stupid question because we've had the door both ways, but the way Winnie yanks her cardigan off and throws it on the bed you'd think it was. "Do what you want, Rhea."

I leave it open, sit down on the bed, and start to loosen the laces on my Converse.

"I mean, it's not as if you ever listen to anyone anyway."

I could ignore the first comment, pretend I thought she'd meant something else, but I can't ignore that one. I push my right Converse off with my left foot.

"What's that supposed to mean?"

"You know what it means. If you're going to do what you want all the time—never listen to anyone—what's the point in asking?"

Winnie takes off her glasses, steps out of her flip-flops. She has all her bottles of nail polish lined up on the window sill and she opens the green one.

"Winnie, that stinks, do you have to do that now?"

I think she's going to put it on anyway, ignore me, but she twists the polish closed, really fast, slams it back on the window ledge. "What would you have done tonight, if Jean had found you?"

"What do you mean?"

"Twenty minutes, Rhea. That's all we had before she was supposed to call 911. You were down there more than half an hour."

I rip the laces from my left Converse, kick it off. "It wasn't half an hour—"

"Jean was about to dial—she had the phone in her hand, and something told me just to double check, to take a look down there."

"I was on my way up."

She has her back to me, is halfway through unzipping her dress. "Did you even think how worried we might be? How worried I was? I thought she'd drowned or something—"

"I'd only just found her, Winnie, I swear—"

She spins back to look at me and her dress is half down, so I can see her slip. "Don't lie to me!"

"I'm not lying!"

"I saw your drawings—that one of your mother. You don't draw something like that in a few minutes."

"Winnie—"

"You're so self-centred, Rhea. You probably got lost in that drawing, didn't even think about me or anyone else."

I've never seen her like this, her face so red, her eyes. I stand up.

"Winnie, come on, that's not true."

"Oh yes, it is. The only person you ever consider, ever think about, is yourself." She's nodding. "Except for your mother, of course, but it might do you good to spend more time thinking about people who are living, instead of the ones who are already dead."

I hate her then, Mum, her face all red and mean looking, her bony shoulders and her stupid lacy slip and her smelly feet, and I wish I'd never shown her your photo, that she didn't know the picture was of you.

"Fuck you, Winnie!" I thrash my hand around and it knocks my bedside lamp off my locker and onto the floor. "Don't blame me just because you feel guilty! Don't blame me for Robin going missing! Don't blame me because you were probably so obsessed about getting to call Melissa that you forgot to count!"

I'm yelling and I want her to yell back, Mum, that's the whole point. Ever since we got here, ever since we left Hell's Kitchen, it's been weird and tense and horrible, and I want to just shout and shout until it goes away.

But she doesn't yell, she just pulls her dress back up and walks past me really slowly, out of the room and down the stairs, even though she's got no shoes on.

And she's still not back, Mum. And I don't know where she is and I keep listening, so I can turn out the light and pretend to be asleep, but the house is quiet and the only sound is the sea outside.

It's not fair. I didn't do anything. Since we came here, I can't do anything right—it's like she hates me. And I bet she wishes she hadn't asked Jean if I could come here.

I bet she wishes I never came at all.

Rhea

Dear Mum,

It came today, the letter. Actually, it came yesterday but David forgot to give it to me then so he gave it to me this morning, when I was sweeping the floor after breakfast, and I kept it in the side pocket of my shorts all day until tonight.

There's two envelopes, the outside one with Chrissie's writing in red sharpie and the inside with Aunt Ruth's. When I open the second envelope, money falls out, five $100 bills, so flat and crisp they're stuck together, so, at first, I think there are only three of them. Picking the money up off the floor, my brain remembers another time, one time or loads of times—American money falling out of birthday cards onto the hall carpet in Rush, picking up the notes from the hall carpet with the wine and pink swirls.

And it's really weird then, especially when I read it, to think those cards and this letter all came from Aunt Ruth, because reading this letter, she sounds like a different Aunt Ruth and not the same person at all.

R

Dear Rhea,

Thank you for writing to me and letting me know that you are safe. That's the most important thing. I've been very worried about you, I know you know that. Even before the sighting at the bus station, I knew that you would have gone to New York. I just knew.

It was terrible being there, seeing for myself how many kids there are on the streets. It's such a big city, I thought I'd never find you and I started to wonder if I was wrong, if you'd gone somewhere else. So when I got your letter, I was so happy just to know that you are safe and that you have friends and somewhere to live.

I'd love to see you or talk with you on the phone but you set a boundary in your letter and I want to respect that. If you change your mind and you want to reach out, please call me anytime—you can call collect, even in the middle of the night. It's okay if you don't know what to say or if you only have a few minutes to talk—it would mean a lot to me to hear your voice.

You asked about Columbia and I have good news! You were accepted—isn't that wonderful? I knew you would be, with your grades and all the effort you put into the application. Your mom and dad would both be so proud. I know I am. I've enclosed all the information they sent—I hope you don't mind that I opened it, but I knew we would need to respond and I did, I accepted on your behalf. You might be mad to hear that, you might not even want to go anymore, but I wanted you to be able to. I know how much you wanted it. You might think it's too late now, Rhea, but it's not. I spoke to the school, and with your GPA you only need to do a couple of extra credits to graduate. Of course school is out now, but I spoke to the principal and we came to an arrangement and they are happy to facilitate everything so you can graduate and go to Columbia in August. It would need to happen fast, but if you still want to, we can make it work.

I know we need to talk about what happened but it's hard in a letter. I want you to know that I know what happened with Laurie wasn't only your fault and that it wasn't fair that she blamed it all on you. I spoke to my therapist about it and she says it's quite common for friendships with girls to get out of hand, that a lot of teenagers go through phases like that.

I'm sorry Cooper lashed out and hurt you. He was very angry and upset, and we both know what his temper can be like. I'm not making excuses about his behavior, but he was in real shock that night and I think his temper shocked him too. I've talked to him about family therapy, with Laurie and with you, if you come back. Laurie is seeing a therapist too and I think it's a good thing. I think it's helping.

I'm sorry too for the way things came out about your mom. I should have talked to you about her a long time ago, but I didn't know what your dad had said and I guess I was just scared to bring it up. You don't know how many times I went over the conversation in my head—I even practiced with my therapist. I know it probably doesn't matter now, but I can't help wonder what it would have been like if I hadn't been so scared, if I'd told you before.

What happened to your mom has been hard to cope with. I'm not going to lie to you, it's been the hardest thing I've had to make peace with in my life. Some days, I still don't think I have or that I ever will. Other days, with God's help, I feel differently. I know you're searching for answers right now and that's natural, part of growing up. I'm sorry I didn't talk about her more when you were here. I don't know why I didn't—in some ways you remind me so much of her and I think maybe that scared me. It never seemed like the right time to bring it up—I always thought we'd have more time—the perfect moment to talk about it and start to heal together.

My therapist says there are no perfect moments, and I know she's right. She says there are only moments of vulnerability and courage and honesty and in each and every moment we need to choose, over and over, what kind of person we want to be.

I want to be a good aunt to you, Rhea. I want to be someone you can confide in and feel supported by. I want to be someone you can count on.

Please let me come and see you, please tell me where you are. I don't care where it is, I'll come anywhere.

I miss you so much since you've gone. I miss you as much as I missed your mom. You've lost a lot of people in your life, and so have I. We don't have to lose each other too.

Love always,
Aunt Ruth xoxo

Dear Mum,

I'm so tired all the time. Every hour here, every minute, is packed with something, from the second the kids get up until they go to bed. And when I go to bed, even though I'm so tired, it's fifty kinds of crazy that I can't sleep.

It's this shit with Winnie. We're talking again, but we're not talking properly and I hate that and I want it to stop but I don't know what to do about it.

This morning, it's five when I wake up and I lie there for a few minutes and then I get out of bed because with the heat and Winnie's snoring I know I'm not going to sleep again. And at least I get to shower before anyone else and go down to the beach without worrying about breaking more of Jean's stupid rules because it's already bright.

I walk past the part of the beach where we always play with the kids, keep walking. The sea is calm this morning, it's kind of pink, like the sky. I let the water wash around my feet and I'm glad then that I hadn't bothered with my Docs or my Converse. It's nice being able to feel each footstep, my heel and then my toes, heel again and toes again. The sand feels different from Rush, softer, kind of, but harder packed too. It's nice not to have to watch out for the wormy bits.

After ages of walking, I turn back and the sky is even nicer this way—stripes of orange and yellow and light blue as well as pink. And that's when I see Amanda, jogging towards me.

She waves a hand, starts to slow down. "Hey!"

"Hi. You don't need to stop—I mean, keep going if you want."

She stops anyway, wipes a curl from her face. "It's a nice excuse to take a break—it's so hot this morning."

She hits something on her watch so it beeps, and she leans forward to hold her knees. When she stands up, her curls have fallen in front of her face again and she fixes them back behind her ears. "Out for a morning walk?"

"Yeah."

"Best part of the day down here, before anyone else is up." When she smiles, it goes all the way to her eyes. Her eyes are blue but not piercing blue, like Laurie's, they're a lighter blue, kind of washed-out looking.

"Yeah."

We start walking then, slowly, in the same direction. I want to tell her that she can go on, but I've said that already. A line of seagulls are flying low over the water. I'm thinking about what she said to Jean about Marco and I'm trying to figure out how to bring it up without sounding like I cared about what he said. I want her to know that it hadn't any effect on me at all.

"I love being able to run barefoot," she goes. "It's totally the best thing about being here."

I look down and she wiggles her toes.

"Do you always run barefoot?"

"I'd never wear shoes if I could help it. I used to spend the summers with my grandma, down in South Carolina, when I was a kid. I'd kick my sandals off the first day I got there, wouldn't put them back on again until Daddy came to take me home."

That's the sound I've heard in her voice, a bit of a Southern accent that didn't make sense because I heard her telling David she was from Connecticut.

"Do you go running every morning?"

She pulls her curl back out of her face again. "I have been. I love it—the only thing that drives me crazy is the showers being such a clusterfuck by the time I get back, with all the kids."

I laugh, I can't help it. "Clusterfuck" is a Laurie word—it always made me laugh.

"What?"

I hear the smile in her voice and when I turn I see it, a smile and a tiny line of frown at the same time.

"That word—it's just . . . it sounds funny."

"Clusterfuck?"

She's fiddling with her necklace, the one with her name that she always wears.

"Yeah, we don't have that word in Ireland."

"What would you say, then?"

A seagull is in front of us on the beach, stone still. It doesn't move when we pass it, just stares at the sea. I try to remember what we would say in Ireland, I try to remember anything about Ireland, but it's like there's a big gap where all the memories should be.

"I don't know—probably that it's a mess or that it's crowded or something."

"Oh."

She sounds disappointed, and so am I—that I couldn't come up with something better, and suddenly, I think of a word. A Dad word. "Actually—some people might call it a schmozzle. We might say that."

"Schrm-uzzle? Is that Jewish?"

I glance over at her. "No! There's no Jewish people in Ireland."

"Really?" Her face is scrunched up, like she doesn't believe me.

"It's a Dublin word. We say it about the traffic or hurling, maybe. You know: *There's a schmozzle on the pitch.*"

"Hurling?" She dips her head and there's no sound, only a tiny squeak, and I realise that she's laughing, just like that day at the table with Jean. She catches her breath. "People hurl enough to have a word for it?"

It takes me a second to get it. "Not hurling, like hurl! Hurling, the sport."

I swing my arm to show her, but she's laughing again, doing that head dip thing and then I'm laughing too. I'm laughing at her laugh.

"Say it again," she goes.

"Schmozzle."

She repeats it but she says it wrong, like there's an "r" in it. Every time she says it, I repeat it the right way, and by the time we get to the bend in the beach where we can see the house she has it right, and it's kind of awkward then because there's nothing to laugh at anymore.

"You should run on," I go. "You don't want to be late for breakfast."

She checks her watch. "I guess, plus there's the schmozzle to contend with."

I smile. "That's right. The clusterfuck."

She makes the beeping sound with her watch again. "Okay, I'll see you at breakfast. Enjoy your walk."

She starts running then and even though it doesn't look like she's going that fast, in only a few seconds she has put a lot of distance between us. She stays close to the edge of the water where the sand is packed hard, and I can see when bits of it are flicked back into the air behind her, the splash when she lands too close to the water.

Watching her jog away like that, something weird happens, because for a second I feel really sad, like I miss her, even though we're not even friends, even though I'll see her in half an hour. And then I feel annoyed with her and annoyed at myself, for not saying anything about the Marco thing, but the truth is I didn't think about it once the whole time we were talking.

It's this Winnie shit that has me like this, Mum—feeling sad, missing people. Tonight, after dinner, I thought about saying something to her—not apologising or anything—but just talking to her totally normally, maybe even asking her if she wanted to see part of Aunt Ruth's letter, so I could tell her about Columbia. But when I came upstairs she was getting ready to go out again, to go to another stupid AA meeting and even though she was asking about my day and everything I knew she didn't really care, that she probably had to go and ring Melissa or something, so I just said my day had been fine and picked up my pad to write to you. And now she's gone, Mum, and I feel like I felt on the beach, like I might cry or something, like maybe I'm lonely or something. And that's fifty kinds of crazy because I never get lonely; I wasn't lonely on the street, when I was on my own, and if I was going to get lonely, I'd have got lonely then.

You can't feel lonely in a house full of people where you hardly get five minutes to yourself. It's impossible to get lonely somewhere like this. I know that, Mum. Everyone knows that.

Rhea

Dear Mum,

I hate Jean, you know that? I fucking hate her. She has it in for me—she's had it in for me since I got here. It's not my fault. Aunt Ruth would say I'm being paranoid, but ever since that first day, that first meeting, she hasn't liked me.

It's typical that she'd be the one who found us. I didn't see her in the dark, almost walked right into her coming up the beach path. Robin's really sleepy by then and she wants me to carry her again, but she's heavy and my arm is sore from carrying her earlier. She's only just started crying when we run into Jean, she's only just told me that she's scared of the dark.

It doesn't help that I scream; it's not that I'm scared, I get a shock, that's all—the way she's suddenly there, out of nowhere. It takes me a second to see who it is and once I know it's her, I feel sick, like I might throw up right there on the sand. I think she's going to interrogate me, start shouting, give me a lecture, but she doesn't do any of those things, just scoops Robin into her arms and hurries up the path with her. I follow them, into the house, up the stairs. On Robin's floor, Jean turns and tells me to go to bed and that we'll talk later.

That's all she says, but her eyes say more than that. All day, it's hanging over me, this talk, and I don't eat anything at breakfast or at lunch either. The first time in the whole day I've forgotten about it for a split second is when I'm on the deck with Zac and Amanda, and Zac is kidding around, imitating the way Erin looks at David and saying she totally has the hots for him.

Jean comes up from behind me and I see Zac's face change before I hear her voice. "Zac, the wind is coming up, can you go and tidy up the cones on the beach and wrap up the volleyball net?"

He jumps down from where he's sitting on the railing. "Sure, yeah. I'll do it now."

Amanda stands up too. "I'll go help. Unless you have something else for me to do, Jean?"

It's Amanda's break time, so she totally just wants to hang out with Zac. Jean ignores her and turns to me. She has her Oakleys on so I can't see her eyes and that makes it worse.

"Rhea, come upstairs with me, please."

I'm supposed to be doing Arts and Crafts with Winnie in a few minutes, but I don't say anything because I know she knows that too. And I bet she knows it's my favourite part of the day, that's what I'm thinking as I follow her up the stairs for the second time in twelve hours.

She stands by the door of her office, closes it after me. Even though there is no air conditioner it's fresh in the room because of the cross wind from the open windows and the fan. There's a desk with books and papers all over it, and the papers are flicking in the breeze.

"Sit down," she says.

There's three places to sit—a basket swing chair that hangs from its own frame in the corner, a long, low, battered black leather couch, and a brown corduroy chair opposite it. I'd love to sit in the basket chair, but instead I pick the couch. It's one of those weird ones, with the back too far back to be properly comfortable so I have to lean forward. I'm dying to pee.

She takes the corduroy armchair, puts her Oakleys on the glass coffee table between us. Her eyes look bigger than ever and I look down at my Docs.

"So, you know what this is about."

Behind her, there are shelves, packed tight with books but messy. They're not in the right order, tall skinny ones towering over short thick ones. There's even some lying flat on top of other books.

"What do you think you were doing, taking Robin down to the beach in the middle of the night?"

On top of the shelves, there's a photo, a black and white one of a black woman. She's wearing glasses and looking to the side, towards the edge of the photo frame. From her mouth, she's blowing a line of smoke, only I can't see a cigarette.

"Rhea—look at me. What the hell were you thinking? You

know the rules. What would make you take Robin out of bed, in the middle of the night, and bring her to the beach?"

Jean leans forward in her chair, puts her elbows on her knees. Sitting like this, you can see she's chubby, nearly fat. "This is a fire-able offence, Rhea. If you don't want that to happen, you'd better start telling me what's going on."

She has scars on her cheeks, faint but you can still see them, acne scars like David Flood back in Rush. They make her look young. I can't tell what age she is but I can tell she's getting madder by the way her jaw clenches. "Okay, have it your way. There's a train at five. David can drive you to the station—it gets into Penn just after eight." Her eyes hold my eyes. She said that on purpose, Penn Station, to make me picture it, those corridors, that night with Jay. She nods to herself, even though neither of us has said anything. "Okay then. I'll go tell David."

She stands up, heads towards the door. It's only when she has her back to me that I say anything.

"I couldn't sleep, that's all. I hadn't planned on getting Robin, but I heard her crying from the landing."

She turns around but she doesn't sit down, stands behind her chair. "First of all, you're not allowed on the beach by yourself after it gets dark. Second, you never, ever, take the kids anywhere on your own—anywhere—for any reason. Especially not at night, especially not the beach."

She counts her points on her fingers and she's on her third finger even though she's only made two points.

"Did you read the handbook? It says clearly that no counsellor is to remove a child from the house without authorisation. Do you remember how much I talked about that?"

She waves her arm in the direction of the desk, where there must be a copy of the handbook, under all her mess. Every question makes the white part of her eyes even bigger. She's firing me, she's decided already, it doesn't matter what I say.

"Do you know how many people drown on these beaches every summer, Rhea? Do you know how quickly it can happen?"

I don't know if she's expecting me to answer all her questions, but I don't say anything. In my head, I'm planning what to take, packing my backpack. I'll leave Winnie's Converse behind, to show I don't care, but I'm going to take the Walkman.

"Robin could have drowned, Rhea. Did you think about that? If you'd fallen asleep and she'd wandered into the sea. You can't swim. You wouldn't have been able to save her."

She walks around the chair, sits down again. Over her shoulder, there's a piece of bare wall, just the right size for your subway map, and I look at that instead of at her. I can picture the lines, don't need the paper they are printed on, can remember all the stops, the layout. I start with the A, at Inwood, 207th Street, and I'm at 59th Street, Columbus Circle, when Jean stops talking. I see her looking at my fingers, and that's when I notice they're moving against my thigh, drawing a line along the ridge of my shorts. I stop. She sits back in her chair, pulls her feet up underneath her. When she talks next, her voice is softer. "Rhea, where did you go just then?"

I put my arm across my chest, my hand under my stump. "What do you mean?"

"What's going on? Why were you up in the middle of the night?"

She's looking at me, like her eyes can see everything inside my head.

"If you're going to fire me, just get on with it. Just fucking fire me."

She looks at me but she doesn't say anything and I clench my toes inside my Docs. "Rhea, what are you scared of?"

It's a stupid dumbass question and I laugh, sit back on the stupid low-backed couch and cross my leg, so my Doc is on my knee.

"You think it's funny?"

"I'm not scared of you, if that's what you think. I'm not scared of you firing me and being back on the streets. I'll be okay, I was okay before."

An image comes into my mind, before I can push it away. The night I was peeing opposite Michael's apartment and that rat was there, the horrible rat that shuffled out from behind the bin and made me pee down my leg.

She keeps looking at me, like she can see the rat in my head too, like she can see Aunt Ruth's letter in my back pocket, the paper getting hot and damp in between the denim. It's like she knows, but she couldn't know, she's only pretending.

She threads her fingers through her toes. The soles of her feet are light underneath, like Robin's feet. Last night, we measured our feet up against each other, heel to heel on the beach.

"I don't want to fire you, Rhea, but the safety of every child depends on us all following the rules." Her voice has changed again, into her preachy one from the meeting. "Robin was in danger last night."

I slam my foot back down on the floor. "She was fine. I'd never let anything happen to her."

"I see that you care about her, but you can't make up your own rules. She's been through a lot, she needs consistency to feel safe."

Robin felt safe last night on the beach with me, I know she did. If I leave now, who's she going to show her drawings to? Who's going to make sure Marco or Isaac doesn't take her muffin from her at breakfast, like they had on that first day?

"I'm sorry, Jean." I say it low, don't look at her. She's watching me, waiting for more. She has all the power, she's always had all the power. "I know what I did was stupid. If you let me stay, I won't do it again. I swear."

She stays really still, watching me; the only thing that moves is the paper, blowing from the fan.

"You say that, but they're only words, Rhea. How do I know I can trust you?"

It's not enough, my apology, whatever I say to her will never be enough. I can stand up now and never have to see her again, never have to try and sleep in that stuffy room that smells of Winnie's feet. I feel my legs flexing, but then I think about Robin, can feel her leaning back into me, both of us looking up, counting the stars. I take a breath.

"I know I made a bad call. I won't do it again. I find it hard to sleep sometimes and I was just getting up to have a banana muffin,

I swear. And then when I heard her, I thought she might like some too. I planned to put her back in bed before I went down to the beach but she kept crying every time I tried to leave her. The only way she stopped was when I said she could come with me."

"She was crying when I found you."

"She'd only just started, I swear. She was fine up until then."

There is a plant on the third shelf, with green tendrils that go down low and out of sight. It's a fern, some kind of fern, but it reminds me of the spider plants Lisa's mum used to have all over the house that would grow as far as the floor and grow little spider plants.

"So what would you do differently, if it happened again?"

She's not going to send me home, maybe she's not. If I say what she wants to hear, parrot the handbook, word for word, maybe she'll let me stay.

"I'd check in to see if I could comfort her and get her back to sleep. If I couldn't, I'd wake Erin. Or if for some reason Erin wasn't there, I'd wake Gemma or you."

"Okay," she goes, nodding. "Okay." She stands up, walks around behind her seat. I stand up too. "But this is your last chance, Rhea. One more thing like this and you're out. Got it?"

"Yep. Definitely. Thank you, Jean."

She's in between me and the door. I look at the clock on the table, like I only just saw the time. "I should go and help Winnie with the end of Arts and Crafts. She'll be wondering where I am."

She steps out of the way and I walk past her. I think about saying sorry again, but that would be overkill. I have the door open onto the landing when she catches me. Her last sentence is like a line of tripwire. "You can tell Winnie you won't be helping her with Arts and Crafts anymore, from tomorrow."

When I turn around, she isn't looking at me. Instead, she's picked up a little jug and she's watering the fern.

"Why not?"

She walks over to another plant I hadn't seen, on the window ledge behind where I was sitting. She plucks off a leaf tinged with brown. "You can do the set-up and the clean-up, but in between you're going to spend some time up here with me."

Arts and Crafts is my favourite part of the whole day. She knows it is and this is how she's going to punish me.

"What about Winnie? She can't do it on her own."

She laughs, pulls off another dead leaf. "Winnie's been doing it on her own for years. She'll be fine."

I should have just said "okay, no problem" and walked out of there. I know I shouldn't ask her why she wants to see me, what she wants to talk about, but I do anyway. "Why?"

"Because I want to get to know you better. I want to make sure I know what's going on with you, so we can avoid anything else like this happening again."

"I already told you—"

"Rhea, you told me before that you understood the rules, you even signed a contract saying that you'd abide by the rules here, remember? I'm going out on a limb for you here and I need to keep an eye on things. I need to know that you won't let me down."

I should have let her fire me. I'd be packed by now, David would be driving me to the train. Maybe I could have taken Robin with me.

"Do I have a choice?"

She waits a moment before she answers. "We always have choices, Rhea. You can see me in the afternoons and stay here, or you can go home."

She says that on purpose, the word "home." She knows as well as I do that I don't have one. She might think she's the queen of manipulation, that she has it all figured out, but I can play at that game too.

I smile a big smile. "Okay then, I'll see you tomorrow."

I leave then and I run down the stairs and I don't give her a chance to answer me or say anything. And over dinner and afterwards, it's like I'm there and I'm not there, because some part of me is going over it all again, wondering if I did the right thing, as if I'm two people and one of me is already back in New York, switching subway lines, going one direction and then another, playing my game.

And when we're sitting down for the movie and Amanda's next to me, she makes a joke about "schmozzle" and she has to say it twice before I get it.

"Oh yeah," I go, and then I laugh, but any dumbass can tell it's a fake laugh.

"Is everything okay?"

When I turn around, she's frowning.

I nod, clear my throat. "Yeah, everything's fine. Why?"

She pulls her necklace back and forth. "I don't know. I guess you just seemed miles away, is all."

And right then, right when she says that, I wish I was.

R

Dear Mum,

There are loads of things I want to write to you about, but there's hardly any time to write here. The big thing I want to tell you is that me and Winnie have made up. We didn't make up in the way they do on television, with everyone sitting down and talking and listening to each other and hugging at the end, but I'd call it making up because we're talking again. Normal talking, not fake.

It happened last night, when I came into the bedroom after putting the kids to bed and she's there already, crying. I want to walk out, pretend I didn't see her, but it's too late because she looks around and sees me. She takes her glasses off, wipes her tears with her thumbs. I sit down on my bed, opposite her.

"Is everything okay?" I go.

It's a dumbass question, I know it is, but I don't know what else to say.

She nods her head. "It's fine, I'm fine, everything's fine."

"Okay." I smile but she can't see me because her eyes are closed.

"It's just that... Melissa's due today, that's all."

She opens her eyes and starts to cry again. There's tissues in a box on the window ledge and I hold them out for her and she takes one. I take a breath, ask her what I know I need to ask her. "Is everything okay with the baby?"

Winnie sniffs. "I don't know. When I called, there was no answer and she hasn't called back. I don't know what's going on."

Inside my Docs, I unclench my toes, even though I don't remember clenching them. "I'm sure she's grand, Winnie. I'm sure it'll all be grand."

I have no idea if she'll be grand or not, I don't know anything about Melissa or about childbirth and I'm not clairvoyant, but hearing me say that seems to make Winnie feel better and she smiles at me, her first proper smile in ages.

267

She nods again. "Thanks, Rhea, I'm sure she will be too. It's just very painful for me not to be able to be there, for her to be keeping me at arm's length. I just want to be with my daughter, that's all."

As she's talking, I take Aunt Ruth's letter from my pocket, smooth the envelope out on the bed. I'm getting ready to show it to her, part of it. I want her to see the bit about Columbia.

"But you wouldn't be able to anyway," I go. "Even if she wanted you to, so maybe it's just as well."

Winnie blows her nose. "If my daughter wanted me there, Rhea, if she called me, I'd be there, no matter what."

She keeps blowing for ages, doesn't notice me fold the letter back up, put it into my pocket again. And after that, she stops crying and she's asking me about my day and telling me she misses me in art class, but even though it sounds fine on the outside, inside it feels different and I'm all jangly, like I'm waiting for her to say something else. After we turn the lights out, I can't sleep, and all I can think about is what I'm going to do if Winnie leaves. All night, I'm lying there, thinking about that, and sometimes I feel like I'm going to cry and sometimes I feel like I'm going to jump out of bed and shake her awake and shout at her and maybe even hit her and sometimes I feel nothing at all.

I must have fallen asleep because when I wake up at 5:07 it's bright out already and I get dressed and go down onto the beach. The sea is different than the other morning—big rolls of wave instead of flat glassy water. The wind blows against the back of my head and my hair feels longer than I like it to feel and I wonder who's going to shave it for me if Winnie leaves.

I've just turned back towards the house when I see her shape, Amanda's shape, black against the sky behind, running towards me. Just because she stopped the other day doesn't mean I expect her to stop today. Just because we're both on the beach at the same time doesn't mean we have to walk together. It's not like I came down here to see her.

"Hey, Rhea!"

She beeps her watch, slows down, stops.

"You don't have to stop every time. I don't want to wreck your run."

"Running in this wind is a bitch. It's a nice excuse."

She is more out of breath today than she was the other day.

"Just make sure you don't hang on too long or you'll get caught in the schmozzle."

She smiles but she doesn't laugh, and I wish I'd never made the stupid joke because everyone knows that a joke can never be the same twice. I wish she'd run off then. If she's not going to laugh properly it'd be better if she just left me alone.

"Check out the kite surfers," she goes, tapping me on the arm. "Aren't they cool?"

I follow where she is pointing and I see the one with the purple parachute first, suspended between the sky and the wave below, before he disappears. My eyes adjust and there is another one too, a yellow one, and another one behind in black.

"Wow," I go. "Have you ever done that?"

"No." She shakes her head. "I can't even stand up on a long board for more than five seconds, despite Zac's best teaching." Bits of her curls are escaping in the wind and she holds them flat against her scalp. A wave comes close to my Docs and I walk around the other side of Amanda, to where the sand is dryer.

"How's that going anyway—you and Zac?"

"What?"

"You know." I raise my eyebrows. "Like, how's it going?"

She laughs, but it's not her squeaky one. "We're not together—Zac's not my boyfriend."

Her arm bumps into my stump by accident and I move further away, to where the sand is deeper.

"I know it's one of the rules, no couples. Don't worry, I won't say anything."

She stops walking, puts her hands in her back pockets. Underneath her running top, I can see the tan marks from her togs.

"Rhea, we're friends, is all." She looks down at her feet, wiggles her toes. When she looks back up, her face is redder than when she stopped running. "Zac's a nice guy, but he's not my type."

She's lying, Mum, loads of the signs are there—the fake laugh, not looking at me, the way she blushes. I know she's lying, that she doesn't trust me to tell me about Zac, but I don't know her well enough to say that.

"Okay." I shrug. "Whatever you say."

We both start to walk, but it's awkward, nothing like the other day and I wish she'd just run on again. I think she's getting ready to, but then she asks me a question. "How about you? Is there anyone you like here?"

I laugh. I can't help it. "Who, me? Here? No. Definitely not."

The sand slides under my Docs and I wish I hadn't worn them but it would take too long to take them off.

"You're... you're... a lesbian, right?"

At first I think I've heard her wrong, but when I look at her, she's looking at her feet again and I know I haven't.

"Who told you that?"

My heart is fast in my chest. I know who told her—Winnie. It had to be Winnie.

"No one. I mean, I just thought... " Her face is redder than red now, worse than before. "Oh, God. I'm sorry if I got it wrong."

She covers her mouth with her hand and for a second I toy with pretending I'm all upset but instead I shake my head, smile.

"No, it's okay. You're right."

"Thank God! I mean, I thought I'd really offended you then."

"No, I guess it doesn't take much to figure it out. Most people wouldn't ask, that's all. And it threw me when you asked if I liked anyone."

"Why?" She kicks at a shell, misses.

"Well, maybe because I'm the only lesbian here?"

"You don't know that for sure."

"Who else might be? Erin's got the hots for David, we all know that, and Winnie or Gemma aren't. Jean could be, I suppose, but if she is, believe me, I don't want to know."

She shakes her head. "I don't think Jean's gay."

"Well, there you go then. So I'm the only one."

She doesn't say anything for a second and it's kind of nice with just the sound of the sea, the wind. And then she goes and spoils it.

"You don't have to wear Docs and shave your head to be a lesbian, Rhea."

She sounds like Jean, the way she says that, like I'm some stupid dumbass child. I think about Tierney from the AA meeting and her red shoes.

"I know that, Amanda. I'm not stupid."

"Okay," she goes. "I know. I'm only saying, is all."

The awkwardness is back and she must feel it too because she checks her watch, beeps something. "I'd better get on, it's getting late."

She runs off before I can say anything else and I don't know why, but it's like she's mad at me. I can see it in the shape of her body, the way she tilts slightly from side to side as she bounces along the sand. And I don't want to watch her this time so I look out at the kite surfers instead.

She must be running faster than the other day, because by the time I look back, she's around the bend already. And it's confusing, Mum, because I thought we were at the start of becoming friends and now it's like we're fighting and I don't know why.

I wish things didn't change so fast, Mum, people I mean. I wish things stayed the same sometimes, even for a while, but they never do. Laurie, Sergei, Winnie, now Amanda, just when you think you know where you are with someone, it all turns upside down a second later and there's nothing you can ever do about it.

Not one single thing at all.

Rhea

Dear Mum,

Jean is out of her mind if she thinks I'm going to be able to do this every day all summer—sit and talk to her for an hour. A whole hour. You'd think it'd be easy just to talk about any old shit but she does this thing where she looks at me, like she can penetrate inside my head and excavate my fucking thoughts or something. I can't believe people pay money, hundreds of dollars, for this crap. Imagine if instead of everyone spending money on therapy, they gave their money to homeless people? They'd probably feel way better than they do talking about their problems for hours and there'd be no one sleeping in Penn Station. Unless the therapists all went broke and they ended up homeless. Which would be kind of ironic, if you think about it.

Today, I sit on the couch again, even though I want to sit in the hanging basket chair.

"You can sit in the swing chair if you want."

I haven't even looked at the chair—I hate how she knows what I was thinking.

"What?"

"The swing chair—sit in it if you want. The kids love it."

It's easy to see why. Apart from the fact that it swings, the seat part is shaped like a cave, a cave made of wicker. You could hide in that cave, burrow back into it. And right when you didn't want to answer her questions, you could swing it around the other way.

"No, I'm grand, thanks."

She's poured us both a glass of water, and she picks up hers, drinks some. "That expression has always confused me."

"Grand?"

"Yes—what does it mean, 'grand'? I don't think we use it the same way."

I shift on the couch.

"It's just another word for 'fine.'"

She smiles. "In therapy, we try and get to feelings. 'Fine' isn't a feeling. My supervisor taught me that if a client tells you they're fine, you ask them if they're fucked up, insecure, neurotic, and emotional."

She takes her Oakleys from where they're holding her hair back, puts them on the table next to the water. She thinks she's so cool wearing those and her Quiksilver T-shirt, just like she thinks she's cool using words like "fuck."

"Great, robust, adept, natural, dynamic," I say. "That's what I mean by 'grand.'"

She's wearing dangly shell earrings that match her bracelet. She pulls on her left one.

"It could also stand for: grieving, raw, anxious, numb, and depressed."

"Or grounded, real, assertive, nimble, and dexterous."

She's quicker this time. She must've been working it out in her head. "Not glib, reluctant, arrogant, narcissistic, and despairing?"

Before she's even finished I jump in. "Glad, resilient, adaptable, noble, and determined." I watch her watching me and I think she might go again, so I line up another one in my head: gracious, regal, appreciative, dashing. The N is hardest but then I think of nice, neat. This is fun. I can easily fill up an hour like this.

"You're a very smart girl, Rhea. You know that, don't you?"

I make a face.

"You don't think so?"

"At home, if you agreed with someone saying something like that, people would think you were a spa."

"A spa?"

"You know, an asshole. A dickhead."

She nods. "I get it. Where I'm from people don't toot their own horns too much either."

"Where are you from?"

It's the first question I've asked, and she doesn't like it. I can tell by the way she leans forward to take a drink of water before she answers. "New York. Harlem. It's the upper part of Manhattan."

"I know where it is. Harlem runs from 110th Street to 155th Street," I go. "The most famous street is 125th Street, where the Apollo Theatre is."

"You know a lot about Harlem."

"I know a lot about New York."

As soon as I say that, I wish I hadn't, because I think she's going to ask more about that but she's a dumbass because she doesn't notice and asks about Ireland instead.

"You said 'at home' earlier—you meant Ireland?"

"Yeah."

"Tell me a bit about Ireland—where you're from. Is it very different from the U.S.?"

I shrug. "No, not really. I mean it is in some ways, in other ways it's the same."

"Tell me some of the ways it's different."

I look at the clock on the wall, we're not even halfway through the time yet, but I can fill up the rest talking about America and Ireland. I take a breath, start talking as if it's a list.

"Americans wear the American flag on their clothes all the time; in Ireland you wouldn't be caught dead doing that unless it was the World Cup. The World Cup is football by the way, only you'd call it soccer."

She drinks a bit more of her water and puts it back on the table.

Every time she does, it makes rings on the glass. My glass stays where it is.

"America's got people of all different races, but in Ireland everyone's white, nearly everyone is. The only time you ever see people who aren't white are when you order Chinese or something. That's another difference—in Ireland the only takeout food is Chinese and pizza, and fish and chips, but here you can get Korean or Thai or Mexican or Indian. And when you get pizza in Ireland, you have to order a whole pizza, not a slice. And we call pizza a "pizza," not a "pie." And we say "take away" not "take out." Oh and the portions are way bigger here, which is why everyone is fatter."

She raises her eyebrows. "A lot of differences—you talked about food a lot."

"No, I didn't."

"Yes, you said that Ireland has no Mexican or Korean food, and that the portions are bigger here and about the pizza." She leans on her hand and tilts her head, keeping her eyes on me.

She's no idea what a cliché she is with her thoughtful expression and her bullshit questions, how easy it is to tell her everything and nothing at the same time. "Is food something you think about a lot?"

"No more than most people."

She lets the words hang there. We both know that there is no way I can know how often most people think about food.

"When we talked about Robin, you said you got up to get a muffin—"

"She was hungry!"

"—and now food comes up again."

"I thought we'd been through this stuff with Robin—why are you bringing it up now?"

"It just seemed interesting, this theme of food. It made me wonder if you always had enough to eat at home when you were a little girl."

Her voice is soft, silky. This is where she wants to lure me in, to make me lose my cool.

"Of course there was enough food—the Famine was nearly two hundred years ago."

"Did you always have your meals at the same time?"

It flashes into my head then, a picture of me standing on the chair taking the Jacob's cream crackers from the back of the cupboard, two triangles of cheese, a jar of jam.

I blow my breath like I used to do to get my fringe out of my eyes, even though I don't have a fringe anymore. "I can't remember."

I don't know when that was—I've never even liked jam—but I remember putting it under my bed, along with the crackers and the cheese, sliding over to the part where the dust was thickest against the wall. It was good to know it was there, just in case. In case of what?

"Did you ever get up in the night to eat? The way you and Robin got up to eat the muffins?"

I'm standing up before I know I'm going to stand. "You keep saying it's not about Robin, but you keep bringing her into it! It was only two stupid muffins!"

She stays sitting down, looking up at me.

"If you're going to fire me over it, I wish you'd just fire me."

"No one's getting fired. We're only talking." Her voice sounds softer than before. "Rhea, take a breath." She breathes in, really loud, and out again, Darth Vader breaths. "Sit down, Rhea. It's okay."

Standing, I see a stereo in the corner, an old one with a tape deck. In front of it, a tape is open, Pink Floyd's *The Wall*, the tape David had lent me before he took it back. More than anything, I want to listen to Hendrix—to "Stone Free"—but I don't want to ask her if she has it, I don't want to tell her about Hendrix, because telling her about Hendrix would mean talking about Dad.

"Rhea, sit down. Drink some water."

I look at her again. She hasn't moved. I sit, back on the couch where there's a dent from where I was sitting before. I reach out and drink some water.

"No one's getting fired, Rhea," Jean says again.

When I speak, my voice sounds small, tiny. "Then why do you keep going on about Robin, about the muffins?"

"Sometimes, we can end up identifying with the kids. I thought that maybe Robin reminded you of you, when you were a little girl."

Those words come out again—"little girl"—and it's like they're made of barbed wire or something, and I don't know that I'm holding my breath until I have to let it go. And that's when that feeling comes—the one at the top of my nose that happens right before the tears. I don't want to look at Jean, so I look at her bookshelf, just as messy as before, only someone has moved the photo of the black lady onto the shelf where one of the plants was. A tear slides from my left eye, all the way down my cheek. I don't touch it, don't wipe it. I don't know if she noticed it.

"My first year here, it happened to me. This little girl Chloe and I became really close and it was really triggering for me, because she used to cry for her mommy and daddy all the time." Jean picks up her water, drinks some, puts it down. Seven rings now on the glass table. "When I was five, my father shot and killed my mother. I was raised by my grandmother. He died in prison when I was eight."

I wish there was an air conditioner. My armpits are sweaty, even with the fan. Through the window I can hear the kids who aren't at Arts and Crafts playing by the pool—their voices laughing, squealing, a splash.

"I'd done a lot of work around that, in my own therapy. Thought I'd made peace with it, but this little girl... it all came back."

Amanda's voice is calling out, yelling at one of the kids to stop. It's probably Marco pushing someone in. I'm glad Robin's downstairs in Arts and Crafts with Winnie.

"That's shit, really shit." There's quiet between us, she's waiting for more. This is the part where I'm supposed to open up and cry on her shoulder and tell her some bullshit that she wants to hear. I take a breath and the feeling in my nose has gone. "My mum died too and I don't know what I'd have done without my dad. He was brilliant. The best dad in the world."

"The best dad in the world," she repeats.

"I mean, I can see how the kids here might remind you of growing up—but I grew up in a really normal house in a really normal town in Ireland by the sea. No one shot anyone, there were no guns—it wasn't like Harlem."

Her eyes flinch, just enough so I know I've hit the right spot.

"What does 'normal' mean to you, Rhea?"

"Normal—you know. Just normal. My dad had a butcher's shop. He worked hard, he was a good dad. Robin's mother was probably on drugs, that's what I think. No one took drugs where I come from. And Robin told me she hears gun shots at night. From my house, all you could hear was the fucking sea."

Jean nods slowly. "You don't like the sea?"

"What are you talking about? Of course I do! Who doesn't like the sea?"

"You said the 'fucking sea.' You sounded angry."

I'm about to say that I never said that, but then I remember I did say it.

Jean keeps her eyes on my eyes, like one of those games in the schoolyard where the first one to blink or look away loses. I'm not going to be the one to look away but neither is she. I think a whole thirty seconds might pass with us looking at each other like that before there's a knock on the door and we both look away at the same time.

Erin pushes it open slowly. "Sorry to interrupt," she says. She sounds breathless and I bet she ran up the stairs. "Winnie was wondering if you guys are nearly done? She needs Rhea's help to clean up after art."

A look of irritation passes over Jean's face but she hides it. I wonder if Winnie really needs me or if she knows I need to be rescued.

"Thanks, Erin, you can tell her we're almost done."

I want Erin to wait, but she's already disappearing out the door, down the stairs. She's left it open though, so Jean can't plan on saying much more, not when any of the kids could pass by any moment, not when I can hear Zac and Matt talking to each other on the landing.

I stand up from the couch. "Can I go?"

Jean nods, picks up both of our glasses, and wipes the ring marks with her hand so it makes it messier than before. I walk past her, don't wait for an answer.

"It sounds idyllic," she says to my back. "Growing up in a seaside village in Ireland."

"I didn't say it was idyllic, I said it was normal."

"Normal," she says, throwing the empty cups in the bin. "I get it. Dads out working, stay-at-home moms, 2.5 children?"

"Yeah," I nod, "something like that."

She nods too. "How many kids in your class at school?"

Behind me, I can hear Zac and Matt's voices getting louder as they come near the top of the stairs.

"I don't know—twenty-five? Thirty?"

"Thirty?"

"About that."

Zac and Matt are right outside the door. Zac's saying something about David and I want to hear what it is, but they're already going down the stairs.

"So, out of the thirty kids, how many had lost their mom?"

I should have been prepared for that, Mum, I should have known where she was going. Linda Dunne's father died in fourth class, he fell off a roof, but everyone had a mum.

"I don't know."

"You don't know?"

"It was years ago. I can't remember."

"Was it a special school, for kids with disabilities?"

"No! I told you, it was just a normal school—no one had any disabilities."

She puts her hands in her shorts pockets. "Except for you?"

I cup my stump, I can't help it. "I could do everything anyone else in my class could do."

She nods, so her earring bounces. "Were any of them gay?"

Her questions are coming too fast. She's a bitch, tricking me like this, right when it's supposed to be over.

"I thought we were finished."

"Did you know anyone in your town who was gay?"

Billy Tyrell. The name comes into my mind first and then I remember his face—smooth skin, like a little boy's face. His hair, wispy, soft looking, like a baby's. Dad's voice is in my head—*I wish that faggot would buy his meat from Byrne's instead of always coming in here.*

"No," I go. "Maybe. I don't know."

Jean walks over to the fan, shuts it off. You can hear the kids' voices downstairs clearer now, the sound of the house being filled up, plates being laid on the wooden table. She picks up the photo of the black woman from the shelf and starts to clean the dirt from the frame with the fingernail of her little finger.

"In a town that was so normal, it must have been hard for you, Rhea, being different."

I don't answer her, Mum, I don't have to. She already said it was over, so I walk out, onto the landing, take the stairs two at a time, all the way down to the rec room where Winnie's cleaning up the brushes and paint trays. She's chatting a mile a minute about the paintings they all did that are drying on the table and how it's so amazing to see them having fun and I'm listening... I'm trying to listen, but the whole time it's like Jean's voice is still there, underneath everything and I can't make it go away.

And it still won't go away, all those stupid things she said about being a little girl and being different and all that shit about food— all night they've been in my head. And that's why I'm sitting up now, Mum, writing it down, telling you. And I know it's fifty kinds of crazy but part of me thinks that if I tell you, then you'll remember the things she said and I won't have to.

I can just forget.

Rhea

Dear Rhea,

I hope you are doing well. I know I only sent my letter a few days ago, for all I know you may not have received it yet. I'm like a teenager on Valentine's Day, checking the mailbox as soon as I get in from work. I know you're probably busy but if you get a chance, drop me a line, or call me. I think I said in the last letter that you can call collect, but I wanted to make sure you had my cell phone number too, in case you were worried Cooper or Laurie might answer. It's 407-555-0183 and you know you can call anytime—anytime at all.

I keep thinking about all the times you asked me about your mom and I feel so guilty I didn't talk to you about her more. I don't know why I didn't—I guess I was trying to avoid my own pain and that wasn't fair to you. I see that now. Now that you're not here, I keep thinking of all these things I want to tell you, stories about us growing up. Some of the stories would make you laugh, Rhea, I know they would.

You're very like her, you know that? She was smart too, your mom. She was my big sister and she knew everything—there was nothing I could learn that she didn't already know. I was two grades behind her at Brearley and all the teachers expected me to be a straight A student like her. I tried really hard but I always got Bs, sometimes a B+. It didn't seem fair at all because she spent hardly any time on schoolwork. I don't know how, but she seemed to just know things. The only thing I was ever better at was piano, and I think she could have been better at that too if she'd had the patience for it. That was your mom all over—if she wasn't good at something straightaway, she'd give it up and move on to the next thing, something she could do better, that came easier.

At home, she was the one who always explained to me what was going on, she comforted me when our parents were fighting. I must have been about six and she must have been eight or so when she told me that Mommy was seeing an analyst. She said it just like that, "Mommy's seeing an analyst"—so matter of fact! She told me that was the real reason Wendy, our maid, was picking us up from school and so forth. I don't know how she knew that—maybe she overheard our parents talking—but I remember asking what an analyst was and she called me a baby for not knowing. Looking back, I bet she didn't know either—that was the hardest thing for Allison, to admit there could be something that she didn't know.

I don't know why I'm telling you all this now, or if you'll even read this letter, but it seems like it's important. I know what it's like to be kept in the dark about things, for people to keep secrets. At Daddy's funeral, I found out a big secret about his life, that he had a brother he'd never told us about. There were so many people there—his colleagues and clients and lots of people my mom and I didn't know. So when one of the men came up and started talking to me, I assumed he was one of those people. When he told me he was my Uncle Jacob, from California, I didn't believe him. Daddy always told us he was an only child, and, anyway, this man had an accent and Daddy never had an accent. He told me all this stuff that sounded crazy, that they grew up on Stanton Street on the Lower East Side and that their real name was David, not Davis, and that Daddy changed it after the war, when he changed Jeremiah to Jerry.

It wasn't until ages later, months after the funeral, that I started to remember things—like the time Daddy freaked out when me and my boyfriend got an apartment in the Lower East Side after we graduated college, when he said he'd pay for me to live anywhere else in the city. And then I remembered the lady who came to stay when I was very little, who wore black and had an accent and I was scared of her. It was your mom who figured it out—that she was our other grandmother and that there was no need to be scared at all.

I looked him up—Uncle Jacob—when I was in Sacramento at a conference, and he drove up from San Francisco so we could meet for lunch. He had a photograph of him and Daddy and their mother. It was black and white, could have been anyone I suppose, but by then he'd told me enough that I believed him. He told me more about their family than Daddy ever did, about their father who'd died in Russia before they came to New York and their baby sister who died a few months after they got here. He teared up when he told me that story, about their mother sending Daddy out to get the doctor, but the doctor wouldn't come because they didn't have enough money, and how Daddy went up and down every street looking for someone to help him, someone to come, but no one would. He dabbed his eyes with his napkin and said a lot of children died back then, so many children, and people didn't talk about it the way they do now. He told me her name was Ruth, the baby who died.

I'm telling you all this so you know more about your history, to show you that I understand what it's like to find out things like that, to find out people you love have lied to you.

Have you thought about what I said about school? I'm not sure how late they keep the places open for the fall, but if you still want to go, call me and we can start doing whatever needs to be done. Maybe there's even a private school in New York where you can make up the credits? Whatever it takes, I'll help you do what needs to be done.

I wanted you to know I've been thinking about that conversation we had on your last night. It's all I can think about at the moment and I'm working through it all in therapy too. It's really hard to try and figure it all out—what's fair, what you need to know, when I'm being overprotective. I have these letters that your mom sent me over the years, and I've been thinking about sending them to you because they might help you understand a bit more, get to know her in a way. But it seems like such a lot to lay on you, on top of everything else. My therapist said that you're an adult and that I need to be honest with you and let you make decisions for yourself. I know she's right. I know it's your life and that I can't live it for you, that I can't always protect you from the truth.

So if you'd like me to send you the letters from your mom, call me or write to me and I'll send them to you. I'll send you everything I have from her. I'll do whatever you want, whatever will help. Just let me know what it is.

I love you.

Aunt Ruth xox

Dear Mum,

I had my night planned out tonight, instead of waiting to see if Winnie would be around, because I'm getting the picture—she'd rather go to one of her AA meetings than be with me. I'd picked out my spot on the deck—the chair with the nice cushion, near the outside lamp—where I want to sit down and write to you, but when I come around the corner, Amanda's already there and she's writing too. I want to walk away, back quietly around the corner, but the deck creaks and she looks up.

"Hey," she goes.

"Hey. You look like you're busy."

She looks down at the notebook in her lap, closes it over. "Not really."

"You're a writer?"

She wrinkles her nose. "No. It's just a diary, that's all."

It's not too late to turn around, to find somewhere else. "I'll leave you to it."

"I haven't seen you on the beach all week."

"I've been sleeping better, getting up too late."

"I wanted to talk to you. Do you have a few minutes now?"

I could still go, say no, that I have to do something, I know I could but I hear myself saying "okay" instead. She clears her sweatshirt from the chair next to her, but I don't sit there, instead I pull myself up on the railing, tuck my feet under the middle bar for balance. There's two moths flying close to the lamp, bouncing off the glass.

"What did you want to talk about?"

I know she's going to tell me the truth about her and Zac.

"Sorry if I acted weird, you know, on the beach the other day?" The lamp lights up half her face, glints off her necklace. "Remember, when you brought up me and Zac?"

I nod.

"And remember I told you that he wasn't my type?"

"I remember."

She swings her necklace back and forth. "So when I said he wasn't my type, I meant something else."

I knew it. I raise my eyebrows. "That he actually is your type?"

"No." She shakes her head. From the road somewhere behind the trees, a trail of car light catches the edges of her hair, the frizz of curls that have escaped and frame her face. "I can see why you'd think that, but, no, he's really not."

Something about her voice makes me believe her. "What then?"

She looks over her shoulder, as if someone might appear from around the corner, then down at her feet. "He's not my type because guys aren't my type."

I shift on the railing. "What?"

When she looks at me, she looks like she might cry. "I don't like guys, Rhea. I think I'm a lesbian."

That's when I laugh, Mum. I laugh so hard I dislodge my foot and have to grab the railing to stop myself from falling off.

"What's so funny? What are you laughing at?"

I steady myself, take a breath, start to say something, but I laugh again. I don't know if I can explain to her what Tierney had said, how funny it is, how clichéd.

I shake my head. "You're not a lesbian, Amanda."

"What?"

I smile as I explain. "I know you probably think you are or you're curious about it or something. Maybe you're bored or you want some experience to tell your friends about back at school after the summer, I don't know…"

Amanda's looking at me, I can't read her expression. I wish I had Tierney's phone number and I'm thinking that Winnie might. I want to tell her about tonight, I want to tell her so she'll be proud of me for spotting it early this time.

"…and I'm flattered but I'm not interested, Amanda. Been there, done that, got the tattoo."

There's silence then for a second, the music from the movie downstairs, the beat of the sea.

Amanda tilts her head to one side. "You think I'm coming onto you?"

I put my hand in the pocket of my shorts, to feel Aunt Ruth's letters, to make sure they are there. "I don't know—"

"You do think that, don't you?" Amanda's standing up. "Get over yourself, Rhea."

I tuck my Docs tighter under the bar. She's bending down, gathering up her notepad, her sweatshirt. When she turns around, her face is totally out of the light, but I don't need to see her anger to know it's there.

"I thought of all people, you were someone I could talk to about this. I thought you were someone who would understand!"

She's convincing, I'll give her that, but Laurie was convincing too.

"Come on, there's no need for all the dramatics, I'm only saying—"

"Only saying what? That after less than a month you know me better than I know myself? That you know everything there is to know about being gay? Fuck you, Rhea!"

I hadn't pegged her for that type, Mum, the type to curse and storm off, but that's exactly what she does. When she's with anyone else, she's always laughing, smiling, even Winnie said she was easygoing, but she's not tonight. Tonight, she stomps off around the corner and I listen to her footsteps, heavy on the deck, the horrible squeak the screen door makes as it opens and then slams shut.

Jean's been on at David to put WD40 on that door but he hasn't. He said he asked Matt to do it but Matt said he must have asked Zac but either way no one has done it. And I think about doing it then, Mum, getting the WD40 from the shed in the back and putting it on so I can surprise David in the morning when he comes in early to bake, but then I remember it was Jean who wanted it in the beginning, that she'll be happy too, so I decide to leave it.

And instead I take the chair where Amanda was sitting, the one I'd planned to sit in, and I take out my paper and write this letter to you, the thing I'd wanted to do all along.

Rhea

Dear Mum,

I didn't hear anything in the night. I don't know how I didn't, but I only woke up when Winnie was zipping her bag. She's dressed. The room is still dark and it's hot. Always, this room is hot.

I sit up in bed. "What's going on? What's wrong?"

"Sorry I woke you," Winnie says. "I was trying to be quiet. I thought you were going to wake up earlier, when Jean came in with the phone, but you were out cold."

I am awake now, properly awake. The clock says 4:23 a.m. Winnie's bag is packed, I see that now. Jean was here with a phone. Phone calls in the night don't mean good things, nothing in the night ever means good things.

"What's wrong?" I go.

Winnie sits down on my bed, she's smiling. "Melissa had a baby! A boy!"

That's not what I was expecting her to say.

"She had a boy?"

"They're going to call him Darryl. She wants me to come and see him."

With each sentence her smile gets wider.

"Darryl?"

There was a film with a boy who was a robot called Darryl, but I don't say this to Winnie. She grabs my hand, holds it. "Isn't it the cutest name?"

She has her makeup on and her perfume.

"So, you're going? Leaving? Now?"

She squeezes my hand tighter, too hard, so my fingers are squashed too tightly together. "I can't believe it, that she wants me there. It's what I'd hoped for, prayed for, but I knew it had to be her decision."

"How are you going to get there in the middle of the night?"

She stands up, lets go of my hand and in the hot room it some-how feels cold.

"I hope I have everything," she goes. "I hope I remembered everything."

"What time is the train?"

She's going through the drawer of her bedside locker, pulling out tissues, a book.

"I'm not getting the train. There's a boat from Montauk to Block Island and from there I can get another boat to Connecticut. David's driving me and Dan's picking me up at the other end. Melissa's husband. I've never met him, Rhea. Can you believe that?"

She turns around and her eyes look different behind her glasses, bigger or something, or brighter, her whole face looks brighter, her skin. This must be what happiness looks like.

"But what about… here?" I nearly say "What about me?" but I stop myself just in time and she doesn't notice because she has her back to me again, unzipping her bag to stuff something inside, zipping it up again.

"Jean said not to worry about anything. She knows how big a deal this is for me."

"But what about Arts and Crafts?"

My voice sounds panicky and Winnie hears it too. She sits down on my bed again, puts her hand on my shoulder.

"Don't worry, you're not going to be thrown in the deep end to do it on your own. Jean's been talking to some lady in East Hampton, an art teacher. I think she wanted to line her up, just in case."

"Just in case?" So everyone knew this was coming, everyone except me. Winnie's hand kneads my shoulder.

"And I know it might be strange with me gone for a bit, but I'll be back soon. I know you have other friends here now—Amanda and Erin, not to mention all the time you're spending with Jean."

I flinch away from her, because she doesn't have a clue and I don't know how I ever thought she did. But just as I do, David is there, knocking on the door, and I don't think she notices because she kisses me on the cheek, holds my other one with her hand.

"Don't worry about a thing, Rhea. You'll be fine, you're doing fine. And I'll see you real soon."

And then she lets go of me and picks up her bag and when the door closes, it's only me in the hot room.

The clock says 4:47 a.m. now, twenty-four minutes after I woke up, and I wonder if I hadn't woken, would she have left without saying goodbye? And twenty-four minutes wasn't enough time to tell her about Columbia or what Aunt Ruth had said about your letters or what had happened with Amanda. It wasn't even enough time to ask what "real soon" meant.

And it seems like I'm making the same mistake, over and over, always thinking there'll be another time, a better time, enough time. But there's not, Mum, is there? No matter how long you have, it seems like you always want more, that there's never going to be enough.

R

Dear Mum,

I don't know why, but I don't feel like writing to you tonight. It doesn't make sense, because now I have the room to myself I can leave the light on as long as I want and write to you whenever I want, but it's like all I want is for Winnie to be in the other bed, even with her snoring, even with her smelly feet. She could have taken me with her, I was thinking that, I wouldn't have minded going. I'd never even have come here if I'd known she was going to leave a few weeks in. I wish she'd never asked me here or that I'd never gone to that AA meeting because if I hadn't gone there, I'd never have met her and I wouldn't give a shit about where she is tonight.

I pissed Jean off today by not showing up in her office. Part of me is doing it to piss her off, but the other part is doing it to help Hannah out, the new art teacher, even though Jean's already told me she doesn't need help. When I see Jean coming down the stairs, I know she's mad, but she pretends not to be in front of Hannah and the kids. And it's 4:19 by the time we're sitting down in her office and, even though she spent the whole walk up the stairs giving me a lecture on responsibility, it's worth it, to have only forty-one minutes to fill instead of sixty.

I'm on the couch, like always, even though it's uncomfortable. Maybe that's why I sit there because it's dangerous to get comfortable with someone like her.

"You never choose to sit in the swing chair," she goes.

"No."

She pours us water, spills a bit on her T-shirt, the neon pink one that she wore yesterday too. She sits down, crosses her legs under her. "We haven't talked about Winnie leaving."

The photo of the black woman has moved again. Now it's on the stereo on the bottom shelf. "Do you have any feelings about that?" She keeps her tone casual, as if we're talking about the weather.

"Not really."

"No feelings at all?"

I cross my legs, so my right Doc is on my left knee. I feel the holes with my fingers, twelve, always twelve.

"I don't know. I mean, yeah—I'm happy for her."

The house seems quiet today, no kids outside, only the sound of the fan. "Sometimes, when it's hard to identify a feeling, it's good to keep it simple. Do you remember the five we talked about?" Her shell bracelet slides down her wrist as she counts out each feeling on her fingers, "Glad, sad, mad, lonely, and scared."

I shake my head. "There are way more than five feelings. Everyone knows that."

Her face doesn't change, neither does her voice. "That's true. But most feelings can be traced back to one of those five. Disappointment, for example, is a version of sad. Irritation or resentment is a type of anger—feeling mad."

"So why is there only one good feeling and four shitty ones?"

She raises her eyebrows. "Why do you think, Rhea?"

"I don't know, Jean, I'm not the one who's a psychologist." My shoulders are sore from sitting up too straight and I lean back, stretch my feet out onto the glass coffee table. She looks at my Docs, but she doesn't say anything. "Is it supposed to mean that we feel good 20 percent of the time and the rest we feel like shit?"

"Is that how you feel?"

"Jesus." I tip my head back, so I can see the top of the blinds.

"How are you feeling now?"

The fan is whirling really fast, four blades that look like one blade, it's going so fast it looks like it might whirl right off the ceiling and decapitate us both.

"Mad." I don't need to look at her to know she's smiling that I've said one of the five.

"Who are you mad at?"

"You. With all these dumbass questions."

When I look up she's nodding, watching me. She's always watching me. "Are you mad with anyone besides me?"

The clock says 4:29, almost the exact same time Winnie left, forty-eight hours, no, sixty hours ago. I wonder if she'll be going to an AA meeting tonight in Connecticut or staying in with Melissa.

"Nope."

The bottom of her water drips on the arm of the chair, but she doesn't notice. "You've no feelings of anger towards Winnie because she left?"

She's doing it again, that mind-reading thing, and I sit up, put my Docs on the floor. I cover my face with my hand, not because I'm going to cry or anything, but because I want to make her stop. There's too much in my head—not her five stupid feelings, but thoughts, questions, so many questions. And they're whirling around, faster than the fan—when Winnie's coming back and whether I did the right thing writing to Aunt Ruth, telling her to send me your letters, if it was a dumbass move to tell her I didn't want to go to Columbia.

Even Amanda's there, whirling around too: whether I should say sorry or just leave it. Every single one of those questions is in my head every second now, spinning like a roulette wheel, a roundabout, like something that swirls in circles that won't stop, something that goes faster and faster and faster until it breaks or implodes or...

"Rhea? Are you okay."

"I'm fine." I say it through my hand. I say it again. "I'm fine." I'm not lying, I am fine. I was fine before I came in here and I'll be fine when I leave. I just don't know how to sit in front of her for another half an hour with all of that whirling around and not let her see any of it.

"What's going on for you right now, Rhea?"

I clench my toes, sit up, take a drink of water. "Why do we always talk such crap? Why don't we ever talk about the things I want to talk about?"

She's pulling on her hair, the grey bit of curl right above her ear. She's excited but she's pretending not to be. "What do you want to talk about?"

And that's when it comes into my head, just like that. Something I can talk about, something I can fill up the rest of the hour with and not leave any more room for her at all. "I want to talk about the New York subway." Before she can say anything, I launch right into it, everything I'd learned from the school encyclopaedia in Coral Springs, about how the subway started off as an elevated train line and the first underground one wasn't until 1904. I tell her about the three separate systems and how they all had their own maps and that even though they merged in the 1940s, it wasn't until 1958 that the first map came out that had all the lines on it. And it's easy then, once I'm into it, and part of me is enjoying telling her, and I don't stop so she can ask a question, I hardly stop at all and I talk and talk and talk and I wait until the clock gets to 5:02, and then I stop.

Jean doesn't say anything for a minute, just watches me. When she does talk, she smiles. "You know a lot about the transit system."

"Thanks."

"It's fascinating, all that history."

"Yeah, I think so."

I'm waiting for more, the trip wire, the grenade, but there's nothing, only Jean pushing herself into a stand, picking up the water cups.

"Can I go now? I need to help Hannah clean up."

"Sure. By all means."

She walks past me to throw out the cups, picks up her mini watering can to do the fern on the windowsill, plucks off the bits of brown leaf, just like I know she's going to.

"Okay then, see you at dinner."

I'm lingering by the door and I never linger by the door, especially now that I'm late, that Hannah will be waiting for me.

When Jean turns around her smile is a real one, I think it is, nothing hidden behind it.

"See you at dinner," she goes. "David's making mac and cheese."

"Great," I go, "that's my favourite."

And walking down the stairs, I'm thinking about her face when

I said that, the way she nodded, as if she already knew. And I didn't tell her that before, about mac and cheese being my favourite, I don't think I did, but maybe I'm imagining it, maybe she didn't know at all.

These are the things that drive me fifty kinds of crazy about Jean, Mum, because I can't tell what she'll think is important and what's not, and if any of it matters anyway. But no matter what I say to her, even if it's just about the subway, or about the mac and cheese, it feels better not to say anything. Safer, to say nothing at all.

Rhea

Dear Mum,

We had thunderstorms today so we couldn't take the kids down to the beach or the pool or anything. Some of them were scared and crying and everyone's saying that they hope the sun shines again tomorrow, but I hope we have another storm.

Here's a list of things I loved about the thunderstorm:

1. When I looked at the sea from my window this morning, I counted seven different shades of blue in it, not including the white waves and the grey of the sky.

2. David made brownies for everyone as well as extra banana walnut muffins.

3. We all got to take turns reading stories to the kids.

4. They played two movies today instead of one.

5. Hannah couldn't come because of the driveway being flooded, so I got to do Arts and Crafts by myself AND I didn't have to sit with Jean in her office. (That should really be two things.)

6. When Robin got scared of the thunder and lightning, she climbed onto my knee and she wouldn't let anyone else take her.

The rain stops during the second movie which is *Toy Story* and I'm enjoying it so I don't like when I see Jean in the doorway with Amanda, looking over at me. I pretend I don't notice them, but Jean starts waving at me and I know that if I don't she'll only come over and make a fuss in front of everyone. By then, Robin's sitting on the floor with Maleika and Angel and she doesn't even notice when I get up.

Jean reaches out to grab my shoulder as soon as I reach her, as if we're best buddies. "Rhea, can you help Amanda clean up the pool area?

Some stuff blew in with the wind earlier and it needs to be swept as well."

Anyone listening would think it's a question, but it's not a question. Amanda's looking at her feet in white and pink runners and I think it's the first time I've ever seen her in shoes. "What if Robin gets upset again?" I go.

"Something tells me she'll be okay." Jean nods into the rec room and I see what she sees, Robin laughing at a funny part, along with all the other kids. Even Marco's laughing. "It won't take long, you'll be back before the end."

Amanda walks on ahead of me and when she goes through the screen door, she doesn't hold it open for me. Outside, it's getting dark and the lights on the steps to the pool are already on.

"I hope Jean's right that this won't take long," I go. "I was enjoying that film."

Amanda's plait swishes. She doesn't turn around.

"Half the kids seemed to have seen it, but I never saw it before, did you?"

It's a direct question and I know she'll answer and she does. "Yeah, I saw it."

From behind, her legs look a funny shape, the way her calves run straight down into her runners, like she's no ankles at all.

"I liked that story you read today, by the way," I go. "What was it called again?"

I know what it was called, but, right then, it was like I wanted her to say something to me, anything. For things to be like they were the "schmozzle" day on the beach, before that stupid conversation on the deck.

"I only read a bit of it. The book is called *The Trumpet of the Swan*."

"Was that your favourite book as a kid?"

She glances around and I know I've guessed right. "Yeah, it was. My grandma gave it to me."

We're at the gate into the pool, she holds it open for me.

"The one in South Carolina?"

She fixes a curl behind her ear. "Yeah, that one."

In front of us, the whole pool area is a mess, with loungers blown over or turned on their sides, leaves stuck to the tiles and at the edges of the water. All the things that had blown in are clustered at one end, a plastic racquet, two of the noodles she uses to teach the kids swimming, a cone from the beach.

"Where do you want to start?" I go.

"Let's get these straightened first."

She walks over to the nearest lounger and I grab the other side and we lift it, walk it back in line with the others.

"What was your favourite book as a kid?"

I'm not expecting her to ask me that, to carry on the conversation. We put the lounger down.

"I don't know. I wasn't much of a reader."

Another strand of curl falls in front of her face when she leans down and she jerks it away. "That wasn't an option in our house. My dad dragged me and my brother to the library every week—we had to get at least two books out."

She's walking towards the next lounger when she says that, and I'm not expecting the memory to hit me then, of the library books on the hall table, the ones I took out with Lisa's mum, that I needed Dad to bring back. Every day he was meant to bring them back, but he kept on forgetting and saying we'd do it the next day, but he was always too busy the next day as well and then the books were later than the date stamped inside. I was afraid I was going to get in big trouble, maybe even get put in jail, so I hid them under my bed, pushed in as far as they'd go against the radiator. The next time Lisa's mum asked me to go to the library with them, I said I couldn't go.

I come up behind Amanda, grab the seat part of the lounger, start to drag it on my own. "My mum died, when I was three. And my dad wasn't much of a reader."

Amanda catches up, pushing, while I pull, so the lounger slides across the leaves. "Oh God, I'm sorry."

"That's okay." I pull harder. "My aunt used to send me books over—but she lived here and I didn't see her much, so they were always a bit too babyish, like she forgot what age I was."

The lounger is lined up, next to the first one. Amanda stands there with her hands on her hips, looking at what needs to be done. "You think you could do the loungers on your own and sweep up, while I do the pool?"

When she's not smiling, her cheeks look kind of saggy, like they're too big for her face.

"Yeah, sure. I'll try and manage on my own."

I cup my stump and she sees. I don't know why I say that, I never say things like that, and I could have done all the loungers on my own, every single one of them, before she'd even got started on the pool.

She bites her lip and she's probably blushing, only I can't see in the dark.

"Actually no, it's cool. We'll do these together, then the rest."

At the next lounger, she waits for me. When I take the top, she takes the bottom and we both pull. I don't know why I want to keep talking to her, but somehow, I can't seem to stop, like being with her is the exact opposite of being with Jean.

"I ended up living with that aunt—the one who sent me the books," I go. "I went to live with her after my dad died in a car accident a couple of years ago."

We slide the lounger into position and she straightens up, pulls on her necklace, swinging it, the way she always does. And I feel bad for her then, trying to stay annoyed with me and feeling sorry for me at the same time.

"Sounds like you've been through a lot, Rhea," she goes. "A whole lot."

That's all she says, no question for me to answer, so I just walk over to the next lounger. We get into a rhythm, like that, the two of us pulling and pushing and lining them up and it's nice with the fresh breeze after being in the house all day, the sound of the water lapping at the edge of the pool. When the last one's in place, we go to the shed, take out the brush for me and the net for cleaning the pool for her.

"It's probably going to take longer to clean out the pool than sweep, so when you're finished, just go back up."

"It's okay, if I'm finished first, I'll help you."

She shakes her head. "Don't worry, I won't tell Jean—you can catch the end of the movie."

I don't care about Jean and she knows that, she should know that. She's about to turn around, to start cleaning the pool, and it's going to be harder to call her back once she's turned away. I grab onto the brush handle, take a breath, and just say it.

"Listen, Amanda, I just wanted to apologise about the other night." I don't look at her, I look at the light on the water, the cones and the noodles and the leaves bobbing. "I was a dumbass, what I said. You know, about you not being gay."

I'd practised it in my head, figuring out what I'd have liked Aunt Ruth to say to me after her stupid letter about it probably only being a phase, and it sounded better there than it does out loud. She's looking at me, not smiling, not swinging her necklace, not doing anything.

"I mean, I believe you—that you are."

She puts her hand in her back pocket, makes a face. "You believe me?"

"I don't mean it like that, I just mean if you say you are, you are."

She looks at the pool, not at me, and I hate this bit, the part after you apologise where you don't know if things are okay or not yet.

"And it's none of my business anyway."

She looks back to me. Nods. "You're right, it's not."

She's still annoyed, it hasn't worked. I could tell her that she made it my business, ask her why she told me then. I nearly do, but then I swallow, say something else. "You just took me by surprise, that's all. I'd never have thought that, Amanda, ever. I had this whole thing in my head that you and Zac were like some perfect *Sweet Valley High* couple."

She laughs then, her real laugh. Head dip, silence, squeak.

"What's so funny?"

She looks up, shakes her head. "I don't know. The *Sweet Valley High* thing. I thought you weren't much of a reader."

"My friend Lisa read them. And they had pictures on the front."

She's smiling now, she looks so different when she smiles. "And I look like one of those lame-ass girls from the front of those books?"

I shrug. "You look more like them than I do."

She looks over at the pool and back to me, like she's figuring out what to say next. She sighs.

"What?"

"I guess it's not the first time I've heard that—the perfect couple thing—is all. I guess it won't be the last either."

She doesn't say it's okay, or that she's accepted my apology, but it feels okay then, different between us. And when I go over and start sweeping and she starts fishing into the pool for the leaves, it's not like we're ignoring each other, even though we're not talking, it just feels like we don't need to say anything else.

The sweeping takes way longer than I think, because the leaves are all slimy on the tiles and I want to get them all so none of the kids would slip on them, and Amanda's finished before I am.

"Here," she goes. "I got that."

She leans down to hold the dustpan and I want to tell her it's the last batch, that I can do it on my own, like all the others, but it's easier to sweep the leaves in with her holding it instead of the way I'd had it, up against the wall.

"Good job," she goes.

"Yeah, you too."

"It was kind of nice being out here too, almost worth missing the movie for."

"Yeah," I go, "it was."

We put everything away and she locks the gate behind us. I'm leading the way this time, up the steps. At the top, the house looks like a spaceship with all the lights on. Behind it, the clouds are still blowing fast.

"Hey," Amanda calls from behind, "I've been meaning to ask if you've heard from Winnie. How's her grandson?"

The path is wide enough now for us both to walk side by side and I slow down to let her catch up.

"I don't know, I haven't heard."

She picks at a leaf from one of the bushes. "She must be psyched her daughter asked her to come—she told me she thought her daughter wouldn't want her there. Sounded like she was worried about intruding."

"She was psyched all right. It only took her a second to decide to drop everything here and run out on all of us."

From the corner of my eye I see Amanda glance at me, but I keep looking at the house.

"You must miss her. You guys were close, weren't you?"

"Miss what? Her snoring? Her smelly feet?" I make a face. "No, I just think it's pretty shitty to run out on your responsibilities the way she did. She's the one who convinced me to come out here with her—I didn't even want to. And then, as soon as we're not getting on as well as before, she does a bunk."

"To be with her daughter, Rhea, who just had a baby."

"Convenient timing though? You know, that she could get as far away from me as possible when we were starting not to get on as well."

Amanda stops walking, but I keep going. Through the screen door I can see the swarm of kids coming up from the rec room, hear Matt calling out Marco's name.

"Rhea, you do know that's total bullshit, don't you?" Amanda's voice is loud. If anyone was out on the deck, they'd hear her, no problem. "Winnie was going to see her daughter, her grandson. You can make up whatever story you want, but you know and I know that her going had nothing to do with you."

I turn around to look at her. She's squinting into the light of the house.

"Whatever," I go, "it doesn't matter. She's gone now, so who cares?"

She has her arms wrapped around her, one under each armpit, her thumbs sticking up. She takes the steps slowly.

"She's coming back, though? Jean said she was only gone for a few weeks."

I don't want to get into this with her, with anyone. "Who knows? She said she was, but blood is thicker than water." It's cold then and I want to be inside, to see if there are any banana walnut muffins left or brownies or some of David's meatballs from earlier. Amanda's on the same step, too close now, and I stand back so she can go ahead.

"I guess it's up to you if you believe her or not. Might make it easier for you to be happy for her, though, if you took her at her word."

We've just made up and already we're fighting again—it feels like we are, only maybe it's not a fight, because Amanda's voice is soft, kind. I let her get two steps ahead of me before I start walking again too.

And watching her walk up the stairs onto the deck I'm thinking that it's not her fault that she doesn't get it, with her perfect family and their trips to the library and her golden granny in South Carolina. Sometimes I didn't even get it myself, why I'm so annoyed with Winnie, why her leaving hurts so fucking much.

I haven't told you that, Mum, but maybe you guessed. It does hurt. It's fifty kinds of crazy, but sometimes it feels like it hurts more than Laurie or than Sergei, or maybe it's just all of them are stuck on top of each other, hurt on top of hurt, so you can't tell which is which. Anyway, there's no point telling Amanda any of that—or Jean, especially not Jean. It's not like anyone can do anything about it and they'd only start to feel sorry for me and that would be even worse—that would be the worst thing of all.

Rhea

Dear Mum,

Something's happening. Changing. It's getting harder to write to you. It's getting harder to write to you and I don't know why. I didn't write yesterday, or the day before or the day before that either. It's because I'm busy, way busier than when I was on the streets; I know that's a lot of the reason, most of the reason. Being busy is like 80 percent of the reason, but it's not the full reason.

And it's not like there's nothing to write about, there's so much happening here all the time, there's always something to tell you, about the kids and the fight that Zac and Matt had on the landing and about David telling me really casually that he used to be homeless in Philadelphia and Erin showing me and Amanda how to do a yoga pose called "tree." But the 20 percent of the reason I'm not writing to you feels like I don't want to tell you this stuff, that I don't want you to know.

This is going to sound fifty kinds of crazy, but it feels like I'm angry with you or something. Which makes no sense because it's not like you can have done anything to make me angry with you, can you?

It might have something to do with the way I'm watching David, every day now, waiting to see if he has any post for me. Aunt Ruth is such a lazy ass, she clearly hasn't got her act together to go to the post office to send me your letters. Or else that stupid soup kitchen might have lost them. And I'm starting to wish I'd never asked her to send them, that I didn't know about them, because that would be better than all this waiting.

Today, I got really excited when David said he had mail for me, but when I see it, it's only a small green envelope and I knew it wasn't it. And I know I shouldn't have been disappointed that it was from Winnie, I know it was nice of her to send me the letter and the photo of her and the baby, but I couldn't help being disappointed because it wasn't what I wanted at all.

So that could be part of it and maybe the rest is because of Jean's nasty fucking trick today—the thing with the drawing.

The thing that annoys me most is that I thought it was going to be fun, a break from the stupid questions. The paper she gives me to draw on is really nice—proper thick paper—and the crayons are a new pack, not from the kids' supply downstairs, and she says she can get me paint, only I don't need paint.

I roll the paper out across the glass coffee table and sit cross-legged, and she sits on the floor too, across from me and down a bit.

"Try and draw how you're feeling this afternoon," she says. "What colours are your feelings? What shape? Do any images come to mind?"

I'm not even listening to her. I'm not going to draw my stupid feelings, I'm just going to draw. Drawing, I forget Jean is there, there's only me and the crayon and the paper and the colour, all there's ever been. The drawing is automatic, I don't have to think about it. The blue in my hand becomes waves, becomes the sea, I switch to red for the boat, purple for the two people in it. I pause for a second because I remember Jean but when I glance up she's doing her own drawing at the other end of the table, bent over concentrating, with one arm wrapped around it so I can't see it. I go back to my boat, let my hand choose the next colour, black.

I make the shape before I know what it is yet, something in the water, a triangle, a fin, a shark, two of them, three, next to the boat. I think I'm going to put the black down, only I don't. There are clouds to draw and lines, and now it is raining on the people in the boat. The waves get lined with bits of light black, grey, and then I grab the blue again to make blue-black waves that are big, bigger than the ones before, coming over the boat. The waves get so big and so dark on the paper you can't see the sharks any more but they're still there. I know they're still there.

I can't remember what else I draw before I end it, in the same way I always used to end it when I was a kid, circles and loops of black, round and around and around, on top of each other, next to each other until there aren't any circles anymore, just a big thick blotch of black crayon that comes away on the side of my hand, covering everything, hiding everything until there is nothing that anyone can make out in the picture anymore. Not even me.

When I stop, Jean is looking at me across the table. I cover my page before I know I'm going to and she looks down at the paper. And her eyes look from the drawing back to me, those big bulgy eyes, and it's like she can see through black crayon, just like she can see through my head.

"You scribbled over it."

I unfold my legs from under me, stretch them out underneath the table.

"What did you scribble out?"

That's a dumbass question because if I wanted her to see it, I probably wouldn't have scribbled over it.

"Nothing."

I look at her drawing, she's not covering it. There's a forest it looks like, two people, hand in hand, one big, one small, walking into it.

"Would you like to see my picture?"

"No."

I push myself back against the couch. She leans forward, close to my drawing but not touching it.

"You have a lot of black in yours—what does it represent?"

"Jesus!" I kick my heel off the floor. "It's only a drawing, Jean. It's not like it means anything."

Even as I say it, I know that's not true. It means something, I've always known that. I just don't know what.

She sits back, uncrosses and re-crosses her legs. "If you could find a word, just one word, to put on it—a title—what would it be?"

A word comes into my head really fast. "Lost"—that's the word. It's not a feeling, it is not one of her five, and I replace it with another word.

"Glad." I smile. I make myself look glad.

Her hair is getting long, the bits of grey are curling down over the top of her ears now and she pulls one down, lets it spring back up.

"Glad? Why glad?"

I look at the picture and back up at her. "There's a boat under there. I'm glad I wasn't on it."

"That sounds scary, being on that boat."

"I guess."

I think she's going to look at the drawing again, to see the boat, but her eyes stay on me. Dark brown eyes, different than your eyes, a different shape, too much white.

"What are you afraid of, Rhea?"

Rats. The answer is in my head and I feel my body tighten so I know it's the right one but I don't tell her, there's no point in telling her. Everyone's scared of rats.

"Here we go, I should have known it would come back to this."

"To what?"

"Being scared. You're always going on about being scared—right from when I first met you. You thought I was scared of the water, but I'm not."

"You're not scared of the water."

It's a statement, not a question. I think it's a statement. "No. I'm not scared of the water. I'm not scared of being in the fucking boat. I'm not scared of you or of being fired or going back on the streets. I'm not scared of anything."

"Okay. I get it. I hear you." She's nodding. "You don't do fear."

"That's right." I nod too, she's finally got it. "I don't do fear."

And we're out of time then, and I know she probably wants to keep the drawing so I take it with me, and after I've cleaned up after Arts and Crafts downstairs I rip it into tiny strips that I put in David's big stainless steel bin in the kitchen.

That's what happened today and I'm glad I'm writing it all down because I can see now that it's not you I'm mad at, it's her and her stupid tricks to try and get me to cry like some stupid baby. Just because she saw that stupid tear the first day she thinks she can do it again.

It would make no sense to be mad at you, it's not like anything's changed, it's not like anything between us can change. The reason you're gone doesn't even matter—whether you drowned or had cancer or got hit by a train or abducted by aliens or shot yourself in the head, the end result is just the same, the outcome, the consequences. You're dead. You weren't there, you're not here. The past is the past is the past is the past. It's over. I can't change it, no one can.

Jean would probably say it does matter. That's one of the most annoying things about her, that she'll hook on to anything you say and dissect it and peel it open until it becomes something else. Even that thing she said about fear—about me "not doing fear"—that's not what I said. I said I wasn't afraid and thinking about it now, "not doing fear" and "not being afraid"—they're different things, they're not the same thing at all.

Feelings, feelings, feelings, that's all Jean wants to talk about, she doesn't like it when I want to talk about facts, never asks me more about that. Sometimes I think being in Jean's office is the complete opposite of being anywhere else in the whole world. At school, the facts are what you need to pass exams, get into college, get a job. On TV—quiz shows, documentaries, even on *Law & Order*—it's all about facts, evidence, the facts are what gets the conviction and if there's not enough facts, the guy gets off.

Jean's full of it with all this feelings shit. Facts are more important, everyone knows that. Everyone knows that facts are what things all boil down to, that facts are what matter in the end.

Rhea

Dear Mum,

Amanda asks me to go to the beach with her after dinner. The movie tonight is *Free Willy* and I'd planned to watch it, but she's never asked me to do anything with her before, so I go, even though I'm not sure I want to.

The sand is wet, from the rain this afternoon.

"Want to sit there?" Amanda goes, pointing at the rocks.

"Do you want to go for a walk instead?"

She scrunches her nose. "We don't have too much time before it gets dark—we wouldn't get very far before we'd need to turn back, is all."

I don't care about that, but I know she does and I don't want to get her into trouble. "Okay, we can sit on the rocks."

We find a flat one, wide enough for both of us to sit on without touching. The sea is dark tonight, grey, not blue, with flecks of white for waves.

"I needed to get away from that house," Amanda goes. "Sometimes, being around those kids all the time is too much, they make me crazy."

"Me too. I thought I was going to strangle Maleika over dinner. The way she wouldn't stop snivelling about there being no cookies left."

Amanda rolls her eyes. "I know, thank God Erin gave her hers, otherwise she'd probably still be crying about it."

"She's really good with them," I go. "I don't know how she's so calm all the time."

"Well, she does smoke a joint in our room every night."

Amanda keeps her voice serious and, for a split second, she has me, until I see her head dip into her breathy laugh.

"Shut up!"

"I had you there."

"No you did not."

"For a second, I did. I had you for a second."

I sit back on the rock. It's hard to get comfortable. Amanda pulls her feet up, hooks her arms around her knees. "She was asking me the other night about boyfriends back home and stuff, and I nearly told her. But then I didn't because I didn't want to make her feel weird about sharing a room with me."

I dig my heels into the sand, make imprints with my Docs. "You could have just been really casual about it, said you had a girlfriend, to see what she'd say."

"I could, but that would be a lie, because I don't." She rests her chin on her knees. "Do you?"

I shake my head. "Not now. I did."

She sighs. "You're a step ahead of me. I've had drunken kisses and crushes—one huge crush on a girl called MacKenzie who I worked with in a record store. That's it."

I picture MacKenzie in my head. She has tattoos and a pierced tongue. People call her Mac.

"Were the drunken kisses with MacKenzie?"

"Mostly they were with my friend Ellen, from middle school, but, yeah, once with MacKenzie. We went to some party after work once at one of her friends' houses. We drank ouzo."

"Ouzo?"

She wrinkles her nose. "I know, gross. It was the only thing they had—I think the kid's parents had just come back from Greece. I don't remember too much after I drank it, except for this part where I was in the backyard by the garage and MacKenzie was kissing me, up against a wall."

"She was kissing you or you were kissing her?"

She smiles one of those smiles that changes her whole face. "We're both doing the kissing but I'm the one against the wall. I was so mad at myself after, because I was so wasted I could barely remember the details, after wanting it to happen for so long."

"Did it happen again?"

310

She shakes her head. "No."

"Did you ever talk about it afterwards?"

"Are you kidding? I don't know if she even remembered and I wasn't going to bring it up. We worked with each other for a few months after that, but she never asked me out with her friends again."

When she says that, I know MacKenzie did remember, and I think Amanda knows it too. There's silence between us then, only the sound of the waves. She's the one who breaks it. "Tell me about your girlfriend, I mean, your ex-girlfriend." It sounds weird, calling Laurie that. She was always Mike's girlfriend or Ryan's or Ben's, never mine.

"I don't know if she was technically my girlfriend," I go. "I mean we had this thing for nearly a year, but she was dating guys too. She always dated guys."

"How did you get together? Did you know her from school?"

I take a breath of the sea air, it feels fresh in my lungs.

"Laurie was my aunt's boyfriend's daughter. We lived in the same house."

Dad used to say this thing about people's eyes being out "on stalks," and when I turn to look at Amanda, that's what she looks like, her eyes big in her face. They change colour sometimes, I've noticed that, and today they look more grey than blue.

"Oh my God, are you serious?"

"Yep."

She starts to laugh, dipping her head down, breath and the squeak. The story is almost worth it, to hear that laugh again.

"Holy shit," she goes. "Did they find out?"

"Yep."

"Holy shit." She's still laughing and I am too and I think she's going to ask me about Cooper and Aunt Ruth finding out and I'm ready to tell her, only she asks me something else instead, something simple that I wasn't expecting.

"What was she like?"

It's getting colder now and the clouds are low against the horizon.

It's getting towards dark, time to go in. I can end the conversation here, but instead I push my feet harder into the sand and think of words to describe Laurie.

"Pretty. She was really pretty. And smart. She could be very funny sometimes too." I look down and I see I'm cupping my stump and I let go. "And she was manipulative and selfish and two-faced."

"Whoa," Amanda goes. "She was sounding perfect, up until that."

I laugh. "I only found all that out after—although maybe I didn't, maybe I knew all along. She was one of these cheerleader girls, all the guys loved her. She was used to all that, you know?"

"The attention?"

"Getting her own way."

The wind is getting stronger, blowing more of Amanda's curls out of her ponytail so they whip around her face. I have goose bumps on my legs, but neither of us move. I know what she's going to ask me next, before she asks.

"Did you love her?"

Of all the images in my mind of Laurie, the one that comes then is that first one, the time I saw her leaning at the front door, sucking the ends of her hair, one foot on top of the other. I want to be honest, I want to tell the truth.

"No. Maybe. I don't know. I thought I did, but it was all fucked up. The whole situation was fucked up."

I think that Amanda is going to push me on it, to say it has to be one answer and not the other, but she doesn't, she only listens.

"If I did love her, I don't love her now," I go. "I fucking hate her now."

Amanda has a look on her face that I haven't seen before, one I don't know yet.

"Well, they say that hate is the other side of love." She lets her feet slide down the rock, onto the sand, folds her arms across her body. "We should probably be getting back."

We don't say much on the way back up the beach path and I'm

thinking about Laurie, how weird it is that she's still sleeping in her white wooden bed and talking on the pink phone next to it and going to the mall. How it's fifty kinds of crazy that we can be so far apart and still breathing and existing and living. How you can go from being almost part of someone to just being nothing to each other at all.

Amanda's walking in front and I think about saying it to her, trying to explain what I mean, but it's not even making sense in my own head and I don't want to sound all show-offy about it, going on about Laurie when she's never even had a girlfriend.

We're almost back at the house when we see David coming down the steps.

"Hey, girls, enjoy your walk on the beach?" He checks his watch. "Good thing you're back before the witching hour."

"Shut up!" I turn to Amanda. "Don't worry, he's only messing, he's not going to say anything."

She smiles. "I know."

"Listen, Rhea, hold on a minute, will you?" David goes. "I have some mail for you. I meant to give it to you earlier, but I forgot. It's a big old parcel, had to wait in line to get it, took me forever."

Something happens then, to my heart and to my breath at the same time.

He smiles a cheeky smile through his beard. "What's up? You look like you've seen a ghost. Worried you can't keep up with all the fan mail?"

I clench my toes, unclench, smile. "I'm just shocked you bothered queuing, that's all—you're usually such a lazy bastard."

He winks. "Ah, you know, I thought there might be something valuable in it, but there isn't, I already checked."

"Yeah, yeah."

"Hold on, I'll just get it from the van. Be right back."

He jogs off, before I can tell him not to worry about it, that I'll get it tomorrow. Listening to his feet crunch over the gravel and around the corner, I remember Amanda is there, as if I'd somehow forgotten.

"You go on inside," I go. "I'll wait for him."

She has her hands in her back pockets. "It's okay, I don't mind."

"It's cold, plus it's dark now. No point in us both getting in shit with Jean if she comes out."

"She won't say anything, we're not on the beach."

"You know what she's like, no point in risking it. You go on, I'll be right behind you."

She looks down at her feet, then back to me. "Okay. See you inside."

And she's climbing the steps to the back deck when I see David coming over, walking now, not jogging. Behind him, the trees are almost fully black, and the only parts of him that I can see properly are the white of his smile and the large envelope he's holding out in front of him.

"Here you go," he says. "Don't be up all night reading whatever's in there. You're on early breakfast tomorrow, remember?"

"I know, I haven't forgotten."

It's lighter than it looks. It has the red sharpie writing again and $2.80 worth of postage—that's what I notice first.

Now the envelope is sitting on Winnie's bed and I don't know if I'll read it tonight or save it till tomorrow or Saturday when we're supposed to be going on the boat whale watching. I've been looking forward to whale watching, it's one of the reasons I wanted to see *Free Willy* tonight but maybe I'll fake that I'm sick, stay behind.

After all, I've been waiting ages for this package. It's nearly three weeks since I wrote to Aunt Ruth. So what's another two days, on top of three weeks? Nothing, nearly nothing. Two days is nothing at all, not when you've been waiting so long for something, not when you've been waiting your whole life.

Rhea

Dear Rhea,

Thank you so much for writing back to me. It didn't matter that it was short, just seeing your writing on the envelope made me so happy! I'm sorry I upset you with what I said about teenagers going through phases. Maybe you're right, maybe it's not a phase. I didn't mean to judge you or your feelings and I'm sorry if it felt like that. It's just been a lot for us all to take in—I'm sure you understand that. Sometimes things take time to adjust to.

You asked about Laurie and she's well. Yes, she's still in therapy —she goes once a week on Tuesdays over by the mall where she has a summer job at the Gap. She's happy because she gets a staff discount and her friend Cindy from school works there too. Do you know her? No, we're not going to Hawaii on vacation. We're not going away at all.

It's not too late to change your mind about Columbia, you know. You're right about the fall term but I spoke to them and they can hold your place until January. You could do your extra credits after the summer—here or in New York, wherever you want, I can sort it out for you. Just tell me what you want, Rhea, and I'll do my best to make it work.

I'm not surprised you want to see your mom's letters. I'm sending you everything she ever sent to me. I've put them in chronological order, so they will make more sense, although they are disjointed anyway because they span several years. I hope I'm doing the right thing sending them to you. I've thought long and hard about it and it's driving me crazy going over and over it in my head, but you're eighteen now and I know it's not up to me to shield you from anything. I know you deserve to know the truth.

I wish I could be there with you when you open them, so that we could read them together, but since I can't be, I hope that you get support from someone else, that maybe you read them with a friend, but my therapist says I have no control over any of that, and she's right.

Now you have everything I have, Rhea, everything from the past. There were photos I thought I had from a time we went over to visit you and your mom and I wanted to include them too but I can't find them. I don't know where they are. I want you to have everything, I don't want to hide anything anymore. There have been a lot of secrets in our family, Rhea, too many secrets, too much shame.

I showed your dad these letters once, the time I went to visit when you were six or seven—the summer before your accident. I brought them with me but he refused to read them. I left them on the kitchen table one night, in case he changed his mind, but the next morning they were all still piled up neatly, the way I'd left them, so I don't think he ever read them at all.

I love you, Rhea, you know that, don't you? I know you don't owe me anything, I know I have no right to ask you for anything after how I let Cooper treat you that night, but I'm going to ask you something anyway. When you read these letters, will you call me? Please? Just to let me know you're okay, that you're safe. It would mean so much.

Love always,
Aunt Ruth xoxo

Dear Mum,

I wanted to write to you one last time before I opened the letters. There are five of them, in order like Aunt Ruth said. The last one is the thickest and it has a whole line of Irish stamps across the top, the other ones have little groups of three or four. The first one has an American stamp and it's the only envelope that I can read the postmark on. It was sent in January 1979, two years and four months before I was born.

Your writing is the same as the writing on the Columbia photo (I knew that was your writing, I always knew!)—the slant is the same and the *t* and the *h* in "Ruth" are higher than the capital *R*, just like the *l* and the *b* are higher than the capital *C* in "Columbia."

The envelope paper is very thin, Mum, like tissue paper, and I love that I know you touched it, smoothed it, licked it. I run my hands over the envelopes, I smell them, I shake them to listen to what's inside. It sounds crazy, it is crazy, I'm just excited, Mum, that's all. It's like after all these letters, you're finally writing back.

Love,
Rhea

Dear Ruth,

I know you're mad at me, but hopefully you're not so mad that you won't open this letter. How's school? I hope you're doing well at school. It seemed like a nice place, that night I visited with Chuck. You seemed like you were getting on well there. I'd like to come and see you again sometime soon. What's the weather like there this time of year? Is it cold? I hope you're not too cold.

So, I guess I owe you an apology. I know everyone was mad that I missed Christmas and I know I made it worse by not telling anyone. I would have told you, I tried to, I called you at the dorm but you were already gone. I spoke to some girl—I don't remember her name. She said you'd already left for New York.

When I got back from California, Daddy had sent a letter to me. Can you believe that? He lives on the other side of the park and he sends me a letter. I read it, I knew I shouldn't but I did anyway. It was full of all this stuff about how he wasn't going to stand by and watch while I made a mess of my life and let things fall to pieces. He threatened me—can you believe that? He said that if I didn't get it together that was going to be that—he wasn't going to pay for school anymore and I'd be on my own! Just because I went on a road trip to San Francisco with my friends. That's making a mess of your life apparently, according to Daddy.

Part of me wants to drop out anyway. To say, fine, fuck it, I don't need your money, stop paying the damn tuition then if that's how you feel. But then, I like it here, you know? Even though it's only a fifteen-minute cab ride to their apartment, it feels like a whole other New York here, like a whole other city. Cathy, one of my friends, couldn't get campus housing and she's over on Amsterdam and there's an abandoned building on one side of her and a bunch of Hare Krishnas on the other. Daddy would have a shit fit if he knew I was walking around there and it is kind of scary, but it's an adventure too. Some girl from Israel got mugged in Morningside Park, but she was stupid because it says in the handbook to stay away from there. So don't worry, Ruth, I don't want you to get worried, I'm totally safe here. Columbia is like an island in the middle of everything, and apart from being on campus, I mostly only go as far as the diner and the West End anyway.

The West End is cool. I have to bring you there when you come. It's a bit like the bar you brought me to that night Chuck and I drove up to see you, but it's bigger. And dingier! That's where we were the night we decided to go to San Francisco—one minute we were there and the next we were in Frankie's car on a road trip!

The journey there was wild, all that driving. We hardly stopped, just kept going, taking turns driving through the day and night, stopping for gas and coffee and food at these ancient diners like some throwback from the 1950s. This one night, I was driving, and Chuck was in the front next to me, and I was chatting away about something and then I turned and saw that he was asleep and in the back, all the others were asleep too. And it was so weird then, because I was the only car on this road, stretching out for miles, there was only me and the dark and the stars, like I was the only person in the universe. And I had this feeling that the road was going to lift up—I could picture it happening, like a movie—and I was going to be able to steer us up right into the middle of all the stars. And no one would ever know where we'd gone but we'd be up there, lost in the stars but not lost at all.

I'm not sorry I missed Christmas. I couldn't have sat through it, a whole day of him being there, across the table, next to Daddy, clinking glasses of Dewar's. I think my ears would have bled to hear the sound of their goddam ice cubes rattling and the two of them talking about who bought what goddam piece of land and how much it was worth and how quickly they were going to be able to turn it over. I couldn't stand the idea of him asking me about my sociology class when all he cares about is money.

How was Mom? I called her after I got Daddy's letter when I

knew he'd be at work and Jacqueline answered and said that Mom was having a nap and she wasn't able to come to the phone. She said that the next day too and the day after, so I stopped calling. I might call her again or write to her. Who knows, maybe I'll go round there one day and burst into the room where she's lying in bed and make her talk to me. Only we both know you can't make Mom talk to you if she doesn't want to, can you?

So what else is new? Are you going home for Spring Break? What about the summer?

I'm thinking about going fruit picking in Florida this summer. Tawny's grandparents live there, they have some huge farm and they always need people to pick oranges and grapefruits. I like the idea, you know? Getting up with the sun, the earth under my feet, the sky blue and clean every day, the simplicity of it, just picking fruit over and over and over. Not having to think about anything or figure anything out, just letting my hands do the work for me. Chuck says fruit picking would bore him rigid. He wants to go to the Hamptons, he can't get why I don't want to go there, especially when we could stay in the Bridgehampton house, so I've stopped explaining it to him. I mean, really—how can he not get it? I think I'm going to have to break up with him, I don't think I can be with someone who can't even get that. Did you like him that night you met him? I know he was playing pool with Paul most of the time so you didn't get to talk to him much. He has nice eyes and a great smile and he cracks me up—that's what I like about him, but it's not enough, is it? Do you think it's enough? I liked Paul, you guys seem so happy together. He's totally your type—that cute and preppy thing. He reminded me of Jason Morton—and don't pretend you didn't like him, I always knew you did!

You know what it was I wanted to ask you—do you ever think about our grandmother? Not Nana Brooks, the other one, Daddy's mom. I've been thinking about her a lot lately—what kind of person pretends that their mom is dead, especially when she lives in the same city? Do you remember how scared we were when she came to stay? How we didn't even know who she was that first night? You were terrified when she took her teeth out! I never knew that Daddy spoke another language before I heard him yelling that night, the two of them at the top of the stairs shouting at each other. I didn't even know what language it was except it sounded like the way Mr. Stepanov talked to his son when they came to tune the piano. Do you remember that night? You were standing behind me in the doorway of the playroom—I remember that, because when Daddy saw us listening he yelled at us both in English to get into bed.

It probably seems weird, wondering about her now—our grandmother—but I kind of missed her after she left. It wasn't her fault that she scared us, with her teeth and her smell of smoke and her scary language. She did speak a bit of English—remember? She spoke a little bit. She showed me how to sew one day, remember those little round embroidery things she was always sewing? She threaded the needle for me and made me my own one, so I could follow her stitches back and forth and over and under. She went slow, so I could follow her, pointing if I made a mistake and smiling and saying "good girl" when I got it right and "little, little" when I got it wrong.

I was trying to remember why I ran into her room that morning and I think it was because of that—the sewing. I think I ran in to finish sewing one of those things, or maybe start a new one, and the bed was all made up and fresh and the window was open but you could still kind of smell her a little bit, if you breathed hard enough. Daddy was gone to work already and Mom said she'd had to go to the hospital because she was sick and when I asked her when she'd be better she said she didn't know. I waited up for Daddy that night, made myself sit by the door with the light coming in from the landing so I'd hear his key and even though I fell asleep, I woke up when I heard the front door opening and I ran to the top of the stairs and I asked him when she'd be back. He looked at me as if he didn't know who I was talking about at first and then he said he didn't know. It was Sunday at breakfast when he told us she'd died and I thought maybe I'd heard him wrong, because he didn't cry or anything, just kept reading his *New York Times* and then he asked Wendy to get him a glass of water and then he drank it all back and kept reading the paper.

You know what I've been wondering lately? When was her funeral? Did they even have one? Did Daddy go? I know I've asked you before and you said you don't remember any of this stuff, but I thought maybe Mom might have said something about it to you. Maybe she'd tell you if you asked. She'd never say anything to me.

Write me back, Ruth. I miss you, you know? Maybe you don't know, but I do. If you're there for Spring Break maybe I'll come up again? Or over, or wherever it is. I think that old joke about New Yorkers not knowing where anywhere else is is totally true. Chuck showed me this joke map in some magazine the other day, of the United States, and New York is huge and in the center, and all the other states are fucked up and tiny and weird shapes and some of them don't even have proper names and over West Virginia, which is only a tiny speck, there was a line that said: "Is there really a state called West Virginia?" You'd probably have to see it to find it funny but it cracked me up, it really did. I think you'd think it was funny too, if you saw it.

So let me know anyway, write me back. I hope school is good. I hope you're not too cold and you're not working too hard—there's plenty of time for that, you know, after. Enjoy school, Ruth, don't forget to enjoy it, will you?

Love,
Alli xx

P.S. They have this student exchange program here where I can go spend a semester in Europe!! I'm thinking about it... I'll let you know... you'd have to come visit!

P.P.S. Sorry about all the stuff I dumped on you that night Chuck and I drove up to visit. It was too heavy and you're right, it was mostly just the drink talking. Forget I ever said anything.

Dear Mum,

I can hear your voice! I know that might sound fifty kinds of crazy but I really can hear you, like you're talking to me! I want to say "it's wild" like you do, maybe I'll start saying that!

I love what you said about the stars, driving up into the universe. I can picture it too, the way you described it. I'd love to do a trip like that, drive across the country like that. Maybe I will, one day at the end of the summer.

I wonder if you made up with your dad. And what happened with Chuck? You were thinking about dropping out of Columbia even then, it sounds like, maybe it wasn't just because you had me at all.

Oh, and at first I was confused about who you meant at the table at Christmas but it was your dad's boss, I bet it was him, because you don't want to come out here either, to his house. And I bet I was right that he was having an affair with Nana Davis, I bet that's why you hated him.

Maybe you'll tell me in the next letter!!

Rhea

Dear Ruth,

Thanks for your letter! I loved getting it, it was such a surprise! I didn't know you had my address—I guess you got it from Mom because I gave it to her a while ago. She hasn't written yet, but, you know, she's not much of a letter writer, and I guess I'm not either. That's why I'm writing you today, because I know if I don't do it today, I might not ever do it!

You asked a lot of questions and I want to be sure to answer them all because I hate when I ask people questions and they don't answer them.

We've no phone, by the way, so I can't give you my number. I'm surprised Daddy didn't tell you that. It drives him crazy and he's always making snide remarks about Dublin being so backward. I like it though, talking to him from the phone booth by the harbor, especially when he starts on about Mom and how badly she's taking everything and how if I don't come home it might even kill her! He said that the other night— can you believe it? I bet you can. When he says things like that it's nice to be able to close the door of the phone booth and leave his words there, trapped inside the glass.

The place where I'm living is in Dublin but it's not the city exactly, it's sixteen miles outside, so it's kind of like living in Long Island or Jersey or something, but it's still Dublin. They call Dublin a city but it's not really. It's small, you know, the center of it is tiny, like a few streets and a river and that's it. Where we live is a village, smaller than Bridge-hampton. Dermot's store is part of this little strip of stores on the main drag and there's a market and a bar and a library and another bar and that's about it! In the summer, the market sells other stuff too—like beach chairs and towels and this soft whipped ice cream with a piece of chocolate in it that they call a "99." (I've no idea why it's called that by the way, but you have to have one when you come.)

It's wild being so close to the sea. I love it, it's my favorite thing about living here. I read your letter on the beach this morning—I swim there every day. The beach is really big and kind of stretched out, some days you have to walk miles to get to the water and other days it's right there. It's different from the beaches out in the Hamptons or anywhere else I've been. It's not the ocean though, it's the sea that separates Ireland from England, and Dermot says he's going to take me to the west coast someday soon so I can see the Atlantic from the other side!

There's no need to worry, by the way, the bombs and stuff you see on TV are all in the northern part, not where we are. It's not that far away, I guess, but it's so quiet here and really safe. It's like being in another world. I couldn't imagine a place more different from New York.

I'm sorry you're mad at me about the wedding, but there wasn't really time, everything just happened so fast! You know how people say you know when you meet the right person? From that first night I saw Dermot playing in the bar, I knew. I just knew, I can't explain it. I never used to believe in love at first sight until then, but there was something about him—I don't know, Ruth, it's like I was mesmerized by him or something. He has this kind of calm about him. He plays this kind of hand-held Irish drum—they call it a bowrawn—and his hand was moving so fast and he wasn't even looking at it and he was smiling and his eyes are gorgeous, and it was like his drum was the heartbeat of all the music, the heartbeat of the whole night, like it was kind of channeling into my heart or something, you know? And I just knew, then. Before we'd even spoken, I knew. Did you feel like that when you met Paul?

We look funny together—he makes me look tiny, he's so tall. When he puts his arm around me it feels so heavy on my shoulder. Once, when we were riding in a taxi cab, he cupped my waist with his arm and it felt like I was locked in so tight—like the way it feels on a roller coaster when they lock the safety bar. It felt so safe. He makes me feel safe.

You'd love him, you have to meet him. Mom and Daddy don't want to and that's fine. They can't see beyond his age but age is only a number, it's what's inside that counts. And no, he doesn't tour or anything—they play in bars in Dublin mainly, usually on the weekends. The rest of them play midweek too, but he doesn't anymore because he wants to come home after being in the store all day. You know that, don't you? He owns a store—a butchers. It used to be his father's. I offered to help him out in the store but he doesn't want me to. He's so sweet he says he just wants to take care of me and I shouldn't have to do anything, that especially since I'm "expecting" I should be a "lady of leisure"! He has all these cute expressions like that and it's so funny, all these other words he uses for regular stuff and a lot of the time we have to stop and figure out what we're talking about or we wouldn't know what each other was saying at all!

What else did you want to know? Oh, yes, the baby! You're going to be an aunt—Aunt Ruth! Wow, doesn't that sound stern or something? We have plenty of room in Dermot's house—it's where he grew up with his mom and dad but they're both dead now so it's all his. There are three bedrooms and we haven't cleared his mom's stuff out of her old room yet, so we're going to make the other one into a room for the baby. I want to say for "her"—I keep thinking it's a girl already, I have a feeling it is, but don't say it to Mom and Daddy though, just in case I'm wrong. I asked Daddy the other day if they might come over when the baby's born but he didn't answer, just went on about it being so busy at work. When I asked him why Mom wouldn't come over on her own, he wrapped up the conversation real fast.

Being pregnant is wild, this thing growing inside you so you can never forget it's there, but in a weird way I can't really get my head around the fact that it is a baby—an actual baby—that I have a human growing inside me, a human I'm going to have to push out of my body! It's wild, isn't it, the whole thing, when you think about it?

I just put my hand on my bump and I was hoping to feel it moving around so I could tell you it sends a kick to you but it's stubborn, like its Mom, and it stayed still. Maybe it's sleeping. I hope it's OK. I get worried sometimes. I hope I'm a good mother. I've been thinking about that a lot lately, thinking about Mom and it's weird I've been trying to remember things—like what she did with us growing up and this is going to sound crazy but I don't remember her doing anything with us at all, do you? I mean, I guess she must have done a lot of things with us, but I can't remember a single thing.

Instead of Mom, I remember Wendy. Remember how she used to let us hang out in the kitchen with her for hours and how it was always so warm there? She used to love jigsaws, remember? I'm sure they were in her way on that table, but I don't remember her ever making us move one of them. The first time I ever remember using the playroom was after she left and Jacqueline came and she put her foot down about having us hang out down in the kitchen where she was trying to work.

I want to be like Wendy was, with this baby. I'm going to be a fun mom. I'm going to play with her all the time and take her to the beach and make sandcastles and teach her how to draw and dance and sing. Or him. I don't know if it's my hormones or something but lately I've been missing Wendy, I know that sounds crazy but it's true. I don't think I even ever knew where she went when she left, or why we couldn't see her anymore.

The only time I ever saw her cry was that morning she was taking us to school and we passed by the apartment building on the corner of 77th, do you remember, the building just a block up from us? Wendy saw what was happening before we did and she was trying to get us across the street before we noticed, but I saw the cop cars and the whole block blocked off and the white sheet on the sidewalk that everyone gathered around. When I asked her what it was, she didn't answer and then you asked her why she was crying—I remember that, because I hadn't even noticed she was crying—and she dabbed at the corner of her eyes with her lacy hanky and said that we should say a prayer because some poor person had fallen from the window. Even though she told us not to look, I couldn't help it and I kept twisting my head to see while we were waiting for the lights to change. And that's when I heard the man with a microphone ask a woman pushing a baby carriage if she'd seen the jumper and she was crying too and she had her hand over her mouth so I couldn't hear her answer.

The whole way to school I thought about that and every time I got it, I'd kind of forget it, until I finally got it when Miss Everett was doing the spelling bee. A jumper was someone who jumped, not someone who fell. The person under the sheet jumped—they decided to do that, you could decide to do that. You could jump out of a window and then you'd be dead, the same way Mom's Aunt Mary died, except she died in the hospital, not jumping out a window. I don't know if you ever thought about it after that, but I did, all the time. Walking home after school, there was blue plastic over one of the windows, the third one down, second in from the corner, and that was where he'd done it. The next day, the plastic was gone, the window was glass, reflecting back the clouds just like all the other windows, but it wasn't just like all the other windows. I always looked up at it, the third one down, second one in, and I used to imagine it, the feeling just after the jump, so free, the wind lifting you, holding you, puffing out your sleeves, the legs of your trousers—you'd want to be wearing trousers.

In my imagination, it went slowly, like you'd be floating in the air, like music, lifting nearly, not falling at all until then the block of ground would rush up, quick, sweet, sudden, over.

I never knew what happened after that.

In my head, it was always a man who jumped that day, only years later I was walking by with Susan Sharp and she said her mother's tennis partner had killed herself jumping from that building, and I realized I'd been wrong all along.

I don't know why I'm writing to you about all this, what's making me tell you. Having this baby is making me remember all sorts of stuff and my emotions are all over the place but Dermot says that's normal. "Sure what other way would you be?" he says, exactly like that, and he cooks me dinner and plays his Jimi Hendrix records, or John Lennon for the baby, and that always makes things better.

Come see me, Ruth, won't you? Bring Paul, maybe after you guys graduate? When the baby is born, come and stay for a while. You'd love it here, we can go to the beach and go and see Dermot play and you can have your own room—the guest room—we'll definitely have cleared it of Dermot's mom's stuff by then.

I'm going to mail this now, I'm not even going to re-read it, I'm going to run straight to the post office and put a stamp on it because I want you to have it as soon as you can! I'm so glad you're doing so well at school, Ruthie, and that you and Paul are so happy together. I'm so happy things are working out for both of us—it was the best decision I ever made coming here. I have that feeling that things are working out exactly like they're supposed to, you know? I always knew things would work out, I knew they would. I always knew!

I miss you, Ruthieeee!

Love from
Allieeeee xxxx

Dear Mum,

You knew I was a girl! How did you know? There's no point in asking that—you just knew. I know what it's like when that happens, when you just know something. At the start of the letter I was beginning to wonder if you were going to say anything about me at all but then you do, you go on about me for ages!

You were seven months pregnant then. Wow. I wish I had a photo of that—I wish someone had remembered to take a picture of you being pregnant with me.

It's cool reading the stuff about Dad putting on John Lennon for me. I bet he was playing "Beautiful Boy," he always played that for me. I wonder, did that mean that he thought I was going to be a boy? Did you ever tell him you knew I was a girl?

The only part I don't like in the letter is when you talk about the beach. It's kind of creepy, that I can see what's going to happen to you on that beach and you can't yet. And it's fifty kinds of crazy that the thing you were most happy about, most excited over, is living by the sea and that's what kills you in the end.

Shit. Forget that. I don't want to talk like that, think like that. This is probably the reason Aunt Ruth didn't show me these before— she was probably worried I'd get all depressed or something, but I'm not, I swear I'm not. It's so cool to hear you, to listen to your voice, to see everything the way you see it—even the beach, even that.

I'm feeling one of Jean's five feelings, Mum—I'm feeling glad! I'm so glad Aunt Ruth sent the letters to me. I'm so glad I asked her. Even if the beach stuff is kind of weird to read it's only a small part and no matter what else you say about it, I know I'm not going to regret asking her to send them. I know I'm not going to regret it at all.

R xx

Dear Ruth,

I'm so sorry it's taken me so long to write back to you. I keep thinking of it, a million times a day I start a letter to you in my head, only by the time I get to sit down and have time to do it, it's like someone has sucked all the energy from my body and I can't remember a single thing I wanted to say.

Thank you for the baby blanket and the dress you sent for Rhea at Christmas. I know that's almost a year ago now and ridiculously late to thank you for it but she looked so cute in it, like a baby from a commercial. I should have taken her picture—Daddy sent over one of those new Kodak cameras but I haven't been able to find it, I don't know where it is. Dermot has this habit of putting things away in weird places, so I never know where anything is. It drives me crazy, the way he hides things from me like that.

He's out tonight—he's gone back to playing music twice a week, otherwise they were going to find someone else. He has to keep his slot. Tonight is one of those nights when I wish you were here, that we could sit down over coffee and have a chat. Not that they have decent coffee here—they only drink Sanka, and the whole country runs on tea. Even if I could only hear your voice that might be enough, but we still don't have a phone after a year on the waiting list and I've only just got Rhea down, so I don't want to wake her again to take her down to the phone booth.

I think that's what puts me off writing, how it makes me feel further away from you, not closer. I can't help but think that when you sit down to read this in a week, or ten days, or whenever, that these feelings will all be old by then, I'll be feeling something different completely. Sometimes, I think that as soon as words are on the paper, the moment has already changed, and when I think about that it feels like there's no point in writing at all.

I'm sorry, Ruthie, of course there's a point in writing, don't listen to me. I'm tired, that's all, so goddam tired. I've been tired a lot lately. I haven't been sleeping again. It's not the baby—she sleeps through the night now—it's just that those dreams are back, the ones I used to get. For a while, when I first got here, the sea air helped, just like I thought it would, that and Dermot's heaviness in the bed next to me, and I was able to sleep, really sleep. I even slept through his snoring and through Rhea's crying in the beginning. But lately, someone's stolen my sleep away.

Remember how I always used to have them when I was little? The dreams Wendy called "night terrors"? When I woke up crying and went into her room, she'd stroke my head and ask me to tell her about them and I couldn't describe them then and I can't describe them now. Sometimes I wonder if they're even dreams at all, or just feelings, shapes in the night, clammy dark shapes of fear shifting, layers of cold, that get too hot, wetness and scratchy dryness all at the same time. I can't describe them, all I know is that when I wake up I want to die.

The worst is when they happen when I'm awake and I'm not even sure if they're dreams at all. Like tonight, when I saw him—I was sure I saw him—at the back door, looking through the glass. I know it wasn't him, wasn't anyone, but I'd have sworn for a second I saw his horrible red face smiling through the top pane. I've asked Dermot to put a blind on that door so many times, I've asked him and asked him and asked him and he says he'll do it but he's lying. He says he'll do it but he doesn't care.

I'm sorry, Ruthie, I don't want to write to you about all this stuff. I haven't written to you in so long and I want to write things that will make you happy, make you smile. Make you want to come see us. I don't know what's gotten into me lately. Mom sent me over a newspaper clipping from *The New York Times* with him and Daddy in it, winning some award, and it started everything up again. He's in a wheelchair now, that bastard. He deserves it. The only reason he should be in the paper is because of all the things he did to me—he should be on the front fucking page.

I'm sorry, I don't want to write about him. I want to write to you about Rhea. I checked on her before I started this letter and she's asleep, lying on her tummy the way she's always slept since she was old enough to roll over. We've just moved her into a little bed in her own room, before that she was in a crib or sometimes in our bed. I know you're not supposed to do that with a new baby, but it's so hard not to when all you want to do is sleep—you'll see when you and Paul have yours. It's so nice too, the three of us curling up together. I thought she'd be scared of being all alone in her own room after all that, but it's only me who's scared.

She's so beautiful, Ruth. I can't describe how beautiful she is. How perfect—pure—that's the word, like nothing bad has happened to her yet. We had to get her baptized of course—those crazy Catholics wouldn't even let her into a school here if she wasn't baptized—so I went along with it, but really, how could anyone look at a little baby like that and believe she'd done anything wrong?

Sometimes, like tonight, I just stare at her, the way her hair is mussed up against the pillow and her arm sticking out over the blankets, the way it always pops out no matter how many times I tuck her in, those are the times I can feel my heart—really feel it, beating in my body, sending blood around my organs the way it's supposed to, those are the times I feel alive. I hope it wouldn't be hurtful if I told you that sometimes I feel that she's the only thing that connects me to this earth. I hope that doesn't sound bad, Ruth, but sometimes I have this feeling that if it wasn't for the weight of her in my arms, her little hand in my hand, that—I don't know—I'd float away or disappear or something. Does that make any sense at all?

I'm sorry, Ruthie, it's just those dreams, the dreams and the feeling in my body when I wake up—like my body's not even mine, like I'm not even there. Do you think I'd have always felt like this or do you think it's what he did to me? Annihilated. Is that a feeling? It feels like part of me was annihilated, that all of me was. That he crushed the germ of an essence that might have been who

I was meant to be. I wish I knew what age it was when it started—if I let myself remember, really let myself remember, I think I can remember something else, something before. A little girl who could sleep and didn't have nightmares. A little girl who didn't know the scratchy feel of hands too big for her body.

Stop. I have to stop now. I have to breathe.

Remember all those years ago at Brown, the night I drove up with Chuck and I told you? I was so relieved when you said that he'd never touched you, I was so happy—you don't know how happy I was. And it was only afterwards that I started thinking about the way you said that, that maybe you said it like you didn't believe me? Maybe that's not what you meant, maybe I'm wrong—I know I was drinking that night—but there was something about the way you were looking at me when I was talking, something about the way you were sitting back against the bench. And you kept asking me why I hadn't said anything at the time, why I hadn't told Daddy what was going on. And the other day, pushing Rhea in her stroller along the beach, the wheels got stuck in the sand, and it hit me that I did—I did tell Daddy.

It's not the first thing I've remembered since I've had Rhea—it's weird how suddenly all these memories are coming back and I don't know if half of them are real, but that one is real, I'm sure it is. We were in his study, me and Daddy, and it must have been night-time because the curtains were closed and he was in his chair, having his drink. I don't know how old I was, or what words I used, but I remember he got up and then back down again, onto his knees so he could hug me. And I remember the glass was still in his hand and I was afraid he was going to spill some on me and that I didn't like the way it smelled. With his other hand, he stroked my hair, I remember that, and he kept on saying "ssshhh" over and over just like he kept on saying that I shouldn't cry, which didn't make sense because he was the one who was crying, not me.

I don't know when Wendy walked in, but I remember her being there, holding my hand and saying I needed to go back to bed. And

Daddy was standing by then so it must have been after he did the other thing, when he held my face real tight, so close to his face I could smell his breath, and said that whatever happened I wasn't to say anything to Mom—that something like this would kill Mom.

You probably don't believe me, you probably think that I couldn't have forgotten something like that—if it had really happened I'd have remembered it earlier. But in a way I don't think I did forget, not really. Now that I remember, it's like what he said that night has been underneath every other thing he's ever said since, underneath every other reason I ever felt mad at him. Even tonight, on the phone, when he was trying to convince me to come home for the holidays, going on about Radio City and Santa Claus in Macy's and how much Rhea would enjoy it—I could hear what he was really saying underneath. He talked on and on, you know the way he does, and even if I wanted to say anything, there was no room to say it, so I just watched the sea through the phone booth glass, pounding on the harbor walls, and finally he said it, that if we came over it would make Mom happy and then he got upset because I said I couldn't remember anything that had ever made Mom happy.

You know what the kicker is though, Ruth? You know what's a real bitch? Despite everything, despite remembering that, I want to see Daddy—see both of them. I want to see New York decked out for the holidays—the tree at Rockefeller Center, the lights, all of it. I have this picture in my head of us going skating in Central Park—you and me and Rhea, maybe Paul too—and we're laughing, all of us, in the picture. Daddy and Mom aren't in it though and I just realized that Dermot's not in it either. It's probably because any time I bring up going back, he always has an excuse—that he can't leave the shop, or that he doesn't like flying or that I'd have more fun on my own. I could go on my own, I know I could, but if I went—if we went—I'm scared I might not want to come back.

I feel so terrible writing that, Ruth, and I don't want you to think badly of Dermot or that he's done anything wrong or that I don't love him, because I do. It's just sometimes, I don't think I understand him at all, how at forty-two years old he's never left Ireland—he's barely even left Rush—I can't understand how he doesn't want to. We're so different, it makes things hard between us sometimes. He says I'm impulsive and maybe I am, but he never wants to do anything. His shop, his music, me and Rhea—that's all he needs, we're enough for him, and I used to think it would be enough for me too, but now I'm scared because I don't think it is.

You know what he loves more than anything? Pushing the baby around the village in her stroller. The other men wouldn't be seen dead pushing a stroller, they'd never change a diaper, but he enjoys it. They're so backward here, none of the men can cook or anything, even Dermot can only really cook bacon and sausages. It's not that he's a chauvinist, he just never had to learn—his mother cooked all his meals for him and then when she died I came along. But he's not like the other men, he doesn't care who sees him with the stroller and he practically runs home from the shop every evening to see Rhea. He won't touch her until he's totally clean and he bounds up the stairs, two at a time, and I can hear him singing up there and he sudses up his arms and hands and scrubs under his nails. When I first met him, he smelled of cigarettes and Guinness but now he smells of soap.

I'm so lucky. I know how lucky I am. The women here tell me that all the time, how they wish their husbands were like mine. People have been telling me I'm lucky all my life and they can't all be wrong, can they? So, why don't I feel lucky? Why do I feel so mad all the time?

That's if I feel anything at all.

I had this thought lately, Ruth, a thought I can only tell you. I can barely say it in my head, never mind write it down, but I want to write it down because I want you to know—I want someone else to know. What if I was to leave, to go back to New York and leave the baby with him? I know, I know, it sounds awful, terrible, that only the worst kind of mother would even contemplate it, but just because you give birth doesn't make you a mother, you know that, Ruth, we both know that. And you know what I think? I think that having a Mom who was there but not there, having a Mom who looked at you and didn't see you, might be worse than not having a Mom at all.

No one would understand. No one would forgive me. Rhea never would and that would be the worst part. She wouldn't understand that I'd done it for her, that her dad could take better care of her than I ever could. That if she had to choose a life with me or with him that there's no question, no contest, that he'd beat me hands down.

He'd learn to cook, if I wasn't here, I know he would and he'd take such good care of her—she'd never need anything. I love her too but he loves her in a different way than me. The love he has for her is open, big, warm—she can be held in love like that. My love is brittle, something that lives in the dark. Something shrivelled, something afraid.

That night at Brown, I told you I was broken inside, remember? You told me I was fine, that everyone feels like that sometimes, and I believed you, I wanted to believe you. Only now I don't think I do, I don't think everyone feels this shattered, like a shell you walk on on the beach and you know there's no way it can be put back together again.

Outside, people don't know. They see that I smile and that my hair is brushed and that I can go grocery shopping and walk on the beach with my little girl and go swimming. But this baby, my daughter—she doesn't want my outsides, my outsides will not be enough for her. She wants what's inside, she deserves that much, and that's what scares me, Ruth, that maybe inside there's nothing.

Nothing at all.

I've written much too much, I've written so much and I've hardly told you anything. Dermot will be home soon and I want to make some tea for him, some toast with the strawberry jelly he likes. He says I don't have to wait up, that I should sleep, but I like to, I like to do that, to be a wife, a real one, not just pretend.

Maybe I won't send this letter. Maybe I'll rip it up and start another one in the morning. Maybe I'll call Daddy and say we'll come visit, maybe I'll make Dermot close the store, even for a few days, maybe someone could run it for him. We could stay in a hotel—Daddy would pay for that—we wouldn't even have to be anywhere near their apartment, we could stay in midtown, near everything. Maybe if Dermot came, if we were all there together, I'd remember I was someone's wife, someone's mother, and then maybe it would be OK.

I love you, Ruth, I know we don't really say that in our family, but I do. You're my sister and I love you. I always have. I hope you know.

Alli

Dear Mum,

This is the letter Aunt Ruth didn't want me to read, I know it is. She didn't want me to read what you said about going to New York and leaving me behind with Dad. She didn't want me to know you were thinking about that, that you could write that. But you said other things as well, about how you felt holding me and being connected and everything—you said those things too.

Everyone has bad days, Mum, everyone says things they don't mean. Like anytime I got mad at Aunt Ruth in Coral Springs, I'd shout at her that I was going back to Rush. I didn't mean it, I don't think I ever meant it, I think some part of me just wanted to hear myself say it.

Something horrible must have happened with that man. Something really scary. I think I know what it was, maybe I know. But if it is what I think it is, I don't know why your dad wouldn't have done anything after you told him, I'm not even sure from what you said in your letter if he believed you or not.

It's a bit confusing, Mum, all of it's a bit confusing. I probably need to read this one again, before I go on to the next one.

But I know one thing already for sure. I believe you that something bad happened.

I'd have believed you, if you'd told me.

Rhea

Dear Ruth,

Three days, four hours, and twenty-two minutes. That's how long it's been since you and Mom flew home. I'm so glad we went to wave you off, I'm glad Dermot talked me into it, that he reminded me that I'd still have to say goodbye anyway—it was just a question of where I'd have to say it.

Time is so weird, don't you think? When you were here, it felt like you were always here, like you and Mom were part of our lives. And even as we were at the airport saying goodbye and you were crying, some part of me still felt like you were only going to the store or something and that you'd be back in an hour. So, instead of feeling sad right then, I felt kind of relieved because I was getting an hour to myself and it's not until three hours have passed and then four and then five that it finally hit me you're not coming back at all.

But I don't want to sound sad, because we had fun, didn't we, Ruthie? I'm so happy that you and Dermot liked each other so much. He loved how you joked around with him about his bodhrán and even tried to play it, he got such a kick out of that and I know you did too. He's still talking about that night at the Meeting Place, how all the men had their eye on you and that you left just in time before he married you off. Reggie Burke has stopped by the last two nights and he never stops by like that. He says it's because he wants to talk to Dermot about what's happening with the band but he keeps asking me about you.

I know you and Paul are engaged now—how could I forget with that huge diamond!—and even though I'm delighted for you, part of me has this fantasy where you fall for one of Dermot's friends and move over here! Not Reggie—hell, no!—but maybe Dessie or Sean—I saw the way you looked at Sean. So, in this fantasy, you start dating Sean and you come back here every couple of months or something, and then you end up moving over here and you get married and you have a little girl too, and we all go swimming on the beach every morning together, have dinner every Sunday at one of our houses, and Dermot always gets us a good cut of meat!

What do you say, Ruthie? I know you liked it over here. I know you want to come back soon, you said you don't want to miss Rhea growing up. Maybe come back on your own next time, without Mom? And I'd tell Dermot to make sure Sean gets a haircut and a new sweater.

I'm joking of course, well, I guess I'm half joking. I know you and Paul are really settled in the city, especially now you have your high-powered job. I'm so proud of you—my little sister a hotshot executive—you know I am. I just enjoyed having you here, so much. I guess I hadn't realized that I was lonely. I thought I was happy here—I am happy here. But when you were here every morning when I woke up, I felt excited and I didn't know why, and then I'd remember.

Sorry again for that thing on your last day. I still feel bad. I know it was my fault that I was cranky with Mom, that I should have just let her sit there and watch TV like always, but it was such gorgeous weather out and I really wanted to walk Howth Head with you, so you could see how beautiful it is when it's not raining. I know she hadn't asked Dermot to take the morning off to drive us, and you hadn't either, but I just thought it would be such fun, you know. It didn't even bother me that she wasn't coming, to tell you the truth, but it just made me mad that you were going to stay with her. I didn't mean that thing I said, about you always choosing her over me, I know it was childish and that I'm not setting a very good example for Rhea when I act like that, but sometimes I can't help it.

Don't forget to send on all those photos you took of Rhea, will you? I left mine to be developed yesterday at Hickey's—they said it will take a week and I don't know if I can wait that long! I'm getting three sets—one for you and one for me and one for Mom. I don't know if she'll even want them but I know she'll be pissed if I don't get one for her. I like how I can say Hickey's now and you can picture where it is, that I don't have to describe it. I like not having to explain what a 99 is or a bodhrán or that it stays bright so much later or how the weather can change so much in one day. I like that you've held Rhea in your arms and heard the funny way she laughs and seen her do that jiggle dance she does when music is playing. You know, out of everything, I think that surprised me most, how she was so willing to go to you from the beginning, that it was like she already knew you. She's not always like that with people, sometimes in the village if someone tries to talk to her she can be shy and hide behind my legs, but from the start she went to you.

Do you miss her? I bet you do. I hope you mean it about coming back with Paul at Christmas—she'd love it, I know she would, and it's only four months away so I'm sure she'd still remember you. If I'd written to you yesterday, I could have told you that she missed you. How she went into your room, first thing in the morning, looking for you and how her little face was all twisted and confused when she saw the bed was empty. The first morning, she pointed to the bed and asked where you and Nana were and she cried when I told her, as if she'd only just remembered and you were leaving all over again. The second morning, she went into the room but she turned around when she saw the empty bed and she didn't ask and she didn't cry. This morning she went straight down to breakfast and asked when we were going to the beach. I'm sure she does still miss you, somewhere in her little head, but it just made me realize how quickly they get over things at that age, how much easier things are for kids. Which is good, I guess. That's why I wanted to get the photos though, to show her, because even though it's good she's not sad, I don't want her to forget too soon, you know?

I just checked through this letter and there's nothing in it to make you worry—I don't think there is. I'm sorry I got you so worried before, I didn't mean to. When I'm writing to you I just keep writing, let it all come out, like we're having a conversation, but I know that when you see something written down it can seem scarier and more serious than it does when we're having a chat. When you told me, that day on the beach, all the things that were in the other letter, I really don't remember writing them at all. I know I was having nightmares for a while after Rhea was born but I didn't think they'd gone on that long. Maybe you're right, maybe it was postpartum depression or something, but whatever it was, I'm glad it's passed now. And I appreciated you saying that I can always talk to you about anything and that you'd even pay for me to talk to a counsellor about it, but there's no need—from what Mom said, he's pretty much bed-ridden in that nursing home these days, so it sounds like he got what he deserved. There's no point raking it all up again.

I think it was something to do with having Rhea that made it all come up when it did, but it's gone now, honestly. I feel so much better—lighter, freer—and I know that other stuff is ancient history. I'm going to run to the post office now and mail this. I'll mail the photos as soon as I get them too. Write me back quick, won't you? And let me know as soon as you and Paul have set a date—I want to make sure Dermot has loads of notice so he has no excuse about not being able to close the shop! And thank you again for asking me to be your matron of honor. It means a lot, it really does. Maybe one day Dermot and I will get married again, so you can be there to see us this time.

Thank you again, Ruthie, for coming over to see me and spend time with us. You made me so happy—you make me so happy. And Rhea. And Dermot. I can't wait to see you, and we will see you very, very soon!

In case I never told you—you're the best sister in the world!! Ever!!!

Lots of love,
Alli xxxx

P.S. I'll call you next Saturday like we said. I hope it's still okay to call collect?

Dear Mum,

It's brilliant hearing you so happy again! I wish I remembered that, their visit, but even when I looked at the photos I couldn't remember it at all. It's fifty kinds of crazy that out of the three sets of photos you made, I ended up with your mum's ones! I knew I'd seen them before, I knew we must have had a set at home. I wonder what Dad ever did with them?

Aunt Ruth never mentioned anyone called Paul, I never heard of him. I wonder what happened. She's not divorced, I don't think she is, I'm sure someone would have told me that, so they must never have got married. If she'd married him then she'd never have been with Cooper and I'd never have met Laurie and, right at this second, I can't decide if that's a good thing or a bad thing. I've only one letter left, Mum, and I've decided I'm going to take it down onto the beach to read it, just like you did with Aunt Ruth's first letter. I know I can read them all again, of course I can, but I can only read it for the first time once!

I love you, Mum. You know that, don't you?

Rhea xxxx

Dear Ruth,

I'm sorry to ask you to do this but please—please just do this one last thing for me.

None of this is your fault, don't blame yourself, Ruthie, I couldn't take it if you blamed yourself.

Be there for Rhea for me, please. I know you will. Please give her this when the time is right. You'll know when, you always do.

I love you, Ruth.

Your sister,
Allison

Dear Rhea, baby Rhea,

I don't know how to start this letter. I've never been good at letters—
I've always preferred writing things that I know no one will read and I
know you'll read this someday years and years and years from now. Or
maybe I'll tear it up when I'm finished and you'll never read it at all.

I'm on the landing writing this, because you like to have the light
on in case you need to get up to pee in the night. And I don't want
to wake your father up by turning the light on in our bedroom, even
though I don't think anything would wake him up tonight—he's snoring so loud. It reminds me of the metronome Miss Hamilton used to
use in music class at Brearley. That's the school where I went as a little
girl and they taught piano there as well as normal lessons and I had to
learn to play when I was only a few years older than you are now. Your
Aunt Ruth started even younger than me—she was six, I think—and
I always wondered if that was why she was better than me or if she
would have been better than me anyway. When she played, the music
sounded like water, there were no corners. When I played, the music
was slow, clanking, it hardly sounded like music at all. My teacher said
I needed to be patient, that Ruth had to practice to make it sound the
way it sounded, but I knew that I could never make it sound like that.

One of the things that amazed me early on about you, Rhea,
was how you liked music, responded to it, right from the time you
were a baby. I remember your dad saying to me that he thought you
liked this John Lennon song, "Beautiful Boy," and you were only a
few months old. And I said to him that you weren't old enough yet
to recognize one song from another song, but when he put it on,
your little head started to bobble and you smiled and made that spit-
ting face you always do when you're happy. And it was amazing, but
it turned out that you did recognize it, that he was right.

I don't know why I'm writing to you about music, it's not what
I had in my head when I sat down, but sometimes it feels like my

hands take over and that's OK. Things are always better with music, you know? I want you to know that. Some days, when your dad comes in from work, I time it so his favorite Jimi Hendrix song, "Stone Free," is playing, the first beats of it, just as he opens the door. I have to watch him coming in the gate, and start the record just when he turns the corner to the porch. In the silence before the song, I can hear him take out his keys and unless he fumbles with them too long, the first note starts just as he opens the door and he smiles at us both, waiting for him. You get all giddy when he swings you up and starts to dance with you and he'll grab me with his other arm and it doesn't matter that he hasn't had time yet to wash up properly from the store because he's there, and you're there, and I'm there, and that's all there is—us and the music—and just for that few minutes, until the song ends and sometimes the album does, that's enough. What we have is enough.

On the good days, I feel that. On the good days I see you, the changes in your face, your eyes, your smile, and I can feel it grounding me, keeping me here, keeping everything here. That's why I called you Rhea, because my friend Denise in college told me the story of Rhea the Greek goddess who was married to a god who ate their children and Rhea protected them by making him swallow a rock. It might sound dumb to you, but I loved that story, the idea of you protecting, being protected, and there are days when I'm with you I feel like we're protecting each other. But then there are the other days, the days when—I don't know how to say it—it's not that it's not enough, this life, your dad, it's more like I'm not, like I'm not even there at all.

Yesterday was a day like that, yesterday morning—the mornings are always worse. We'd been out late on Saturday night—you'd even slept on the row of seats at the back of Ryan's and you'd barely woken up when your dad lifted you up to take you home. He let me sleep late, that's all it was. I know he was being kind, I told myself that, I know he didn't mean to leave me out. When I woke up the bed was empty, cold, he'd been up for ages. And coming down the stairs I could hear the two of you in the kitchen, your chatter and his voice, explaining something. He's always good at explaining things. The door was open a bit and neither of you heard me when I pushed it open more. The light was so beautiful—the way it fell across the table and caught a bit of your chair. And your dad looked so handsome in his white rib-knit pyjama shirt, the sun making the lines on his face deeper than usual. He'd made sausages and cut them up with soft pieces of white bread the way you like it, and the whole kitchen was a mess. You had your back to me but I could see your hand, holding the sandwich on your own, the way you've learned to do, could tell from the back of your head that you were smiling.

Can you see that scene, Rhea? You and your dad, me standing, frozen in the doorway? I can. I can see it more clearly than my feet on the patterned carpet in front of me. I want to go back to it and put me in it. I want to rewrite it, as if it's a play, and I want to make my character walk into the light and take a seat by the handsome man in the white rib-knit top. I'll hold his arm with my hand and he'll feed me a bite of sausage with the other. I want to let him push my hair behind my ear the way he likes to, and I want him to kiss me and for me to kiss him back, the way I always used to like kissing him back, and you might squeal the way you used to when we kissed. I want the scene to look like that, instead of the real one where I am already gone and all that's left of me is the sound of a door closing.

You're too young, Rhea, to understand any of this. I don't know what age you'll be when you read this but you'll always be too young to get it, even if you live to be a hundred. No one should have to get it, you know that? No one is ever old enough to get some things. And the more I write this letter, I'm not sure anymore why I'm writing it, if it's for you at all, or if it's for me, or if it's only by making these marks on the paper I can be sure I exist at all.

I love you, Rhea. Did I say that already? How could I have written this much and not said that? It's important that you know that. I want you to grow up knowing that. I want you to grow up here, in

348

this place that's safe, where the air is clean, and the only sounds you hear when you go to sleep at night are the sound of the sea and your dad's snoring. I want you to always have sweet sleep, dreams that make you smile, and wake up knowing that you are happy and loved and safe. I want you to have breakfast on Sunday mornings in a sunny kitchen with your dad while he plays you his Hendrix records and teaches you the words. And if I can't walk into that scene, if I can't be part of it, I want someone else to be part of it, someone who can be your mother even if she didn't give birth to you. Just because you give birth to a baby doesn't make you a mother—that's something you should know, Rhea, that's something I learned.

Your dad's stopped snoring. There's silence now in the house.

Maybe he's awake. Maybe he'll get up and find me here, writing this letter. But no, it was only a pause, the way he pauses sometimes and he's back to snoring again now and I feel like I might cry, even though I don't know why. I just thought that maybe somehow, knowing I was out here, knowing how I was feeling, might have been enough to wake him. I know it's stupid, but somehow I thought he might come out here and find me. And that this time he'd make me show him the letter and I'd give him the crumpled sheets and he'd read them and I wouldn't watch him reading, I'd only hold my knees and close my eyes and listen and when he was finished, he'd pick me up and carry me back to our bed and fold me up in his strong body and I'd tell him about all the things that happened and all the bad dreams and he'd tell me he believed me and that he loved me and that no one was going to hurt me again, not ever, not me or you either. That he'd protect us both from everything.

Only he's not coming. He's snoring louder than ever. And I feel so mad now, so mad at him, I want to run in and shake him and punch him awake, but I don't, not really, it's not his fault. Even if he was awake, he couldn't do what I want him to do. He can't protect me from what's already happened. He can't protect me from my memories, from the place the darkness is and the feelings that are still in my body, that live here, that'll never leave, like a country that was taken over, occupied, and even though the natives can take it back and build stronger borders, the land can never feel the way it did before the invasion, never, ever, again.

Your dad can't give back the things that were taken from me so long before I knew him, but he can protect you. He can look after you.

I am the link, don't you see that, Rhea? It's me. I am the one who is broken. Ruth says I kept her safe and I tried to, even when she got so mad because I wouldn't let her come upstairs and draw with us, but sometimes I wonder if I kept her safe at all. But I can keep you safe, my love, my darling, darling girl, my anchor, my heart, my breath, my blood, my veins, my cells, my body. I want to give you it all. I want to give you everything. Everything.

I want to give you freedom.

Don't ever believe anyone who tells you I didn't love you enough, because I love you more than anyone will ever know. My love for you goes deep, so deep, into that part of me, into the pain, into the part where I can never go again.

I've loved you, Rhea, and I will love you. Know that wherever I am, wherever I go, I'll love you more than any mother ever loved any daughter, that you'll always be part of me and that the best part of me will always be part of you and you'll carry me in your heart and together we'll make your life better, better than it could have been any other way.

I love you, my darling girl.

Mom xoxo

Jean thinks I should write to you again. She didn't say "should"—she made a "suggestion." According to her, a lot of people write letters to people who are dead or even to people who are alive that they're never going to send. People write so many of them, they even have a name— "DNS" letters, like DNA, except it stands for "Do Not Send." Jean says that some of her clients have sent their "DNS" letters by mistake, so the people end up reading stuff they were never meant to read.

This is not a problem I have.

She read everything, my letters, your letters. She found them all in my backpack in the dunes. She asked me before she read them and I said she could, I remember saying she could, but I think it was only because of that stuff the doctor gave me.

I wish I hadn't let her read them.

I wish I'd brought them into the sea with me, all of them.

I wish I'd let the water wash the words away.

Jean is coming to my room three times a day. I have to let her in, I've no choice. Maybe I do have a choice, but I let her in anyway. All she wants to talk about is your letters—how I felt after reading them, what was going through my mind that day on the beach.

I don't know how I felt then or what was in my mind—if anything was in my mind. When I tell her that, she crosses and uncrosses her legs, switches tack.

"How are you feeling now, Rhea? Mad, glad, sad, lonely, or scared?"

"Nothing. I'm not feeling anything."

She's silent for a minute and I think she's given up. "If you had to guess at a feeling, what would it be?"

I lie back on the floor, face the wall. "Tired."

"Tired?"

"I know it's not a feeling, but I'm just so fucking exhausted."

"You need to eat, Rhea. David will make you anything you want, you know that."

"I'm too tired to eat."

I'm not lying or being dramatic. I don't have the energy to bite or chew or swallow, it feels like the food would sit in my mouth and clog up my throat. My body feels like it did that night when the water filled up my clothes, turned them into weights.

Jean says I need to come outside, get some fresh air, another "suggestion." She waits for ages after she says that, only I don't turn around and I don't answer her so eventually she leaves. She might fire me if

I don't go outside, she might want me to go back to work, to see the kids, but I can't, I fucking can't and I don't care if she fires me.

I can't explain it to her, this tiredness, how anything is just too much, how even when I needed the loo I waited so long a little bit of pee came out before I was able to move.

So what if she fires me? So fucking what? What difference does it make?

No difference, that's what. No difference at all. Amanda tried to talk to me through the door today, but I just lay on the floor, breathing. I prefer the floor to the bed. I don't know how much she knows, how much Jean told her, how much she's told anyone. Amanda tells me she made me a mix tape, that she's going to leave it on the tray of food with a new packet of Walkman batteries and I know I should thank her but I don't want to thank her. I didn't ask her for food or her stupid tape. I didn't ask her to swim out and get me.

I wait for ages after I hear her feet on the stairs and the tray is on the floor, the tape next to a tuna salad sandwich and two banana walnut muffins and a bottle of water. I still don't think I'm hungry but when I pick up the muffin, I smell it and suddenly, I'm eating like a savage, like I've never seen food before. I don't even sit down before I smash it into my mouth, so crumbs go everywhere. And I've barely swallowed it before I start on the sandwich, so the taste in my mouth is a mix of sweet muffin and tuna and things that shouldn't go together.

After I eat, I lie back down on the floor again. I don't listen to the tape, I don't read the track list in Amanda's neat writing in black felt-tip pen. I'm remembering her face, above the waves, her hands under my head, my shoulders, and then the next memory on the beach, puking salt water and phlegm up all over her feet.

I didn't ask her to do that, any of that. I didn't want her to.

And I definitely don't have to thank her.

Jean has a new rule. It's a rule, not a suggestion. I have to shower and change my clothes and I have to come to her office to talk to her once a day.

"What happens if I don't want to do it?" I go.

She's sitting on Winnie's bed, her foot crossed over her knee. "It's for your own good, Rhea."

"What happens if I won't do it?"

She pulls her hair, above her ear, the grey part. "You'll feel better, trust me."

She's not answering me, she always answers me. I ask another way. "Do I have a choice?"

She looks out the window, back to me. "You always have a choice, Rhea. I hope you choose to stay."

I sit in the swing chair, far back in the basket part. You know what I keep thinking? Who else knew? Aunt Ruth and Cooper knew. Did Laurie? Dad must have known but if he knew then why didn't he tell me? He would have told me.

I can't see Jean but I can hear her. "Where are you, Rhea?" she goes.

"I'm here, I'm in the chair." Only I'm not in the chair, I'm back in Rush, going through lists of people I haven't thought about in years— Mrs. McLean from the shop, Ms. Bennett in school who was always extra nice to me, who once left a pound note in my copy when she handed it back to me. Did she know? Did she feel sorry for me?

Did Lisa? Her mum? Susan Mulligan? Nicole Gleeson?

Did Nicole fucking Gleeson know?

STOP. JUST FUCKING STOP IT.

Can you know something and not know it at the very same time?

Jean wants me to write to you and tell you what happened that day on the beach. She says if I can't tell you the feelings, I can describe what it felt like to walk into the water, to feel it lapping up over my Docs, my legs, up over my shorts.

Fuck that. Fuck her, with her suggestions. Fuck you and your letters. Why should I tell you anything more about me? I've told you everything, you know all there is, but I still don't know anything. I've more fucking questions now, more questions than answers.

What questions, Rhea?

Jean's not here, but that's her voice in my head, as if she is.

I want to make a list, you can't get lost in a list, but I don't know where the beginning is, what the first question is. Maybe I do know. Maybe this is the first question:

Did you always know? Did you always know you were going to do that?

You sounded happy, really happy, in the letter before, the August letter. Ten months. If even. When did you even write the last letter? How long before? What happened? What the fuck could have happened? Why didn't you write to Aunt Ruth again? Or talk to Dad? Talk to someone?

What did it feel like? The water, that day, swallowing those pills? Was it hard to push yourself out through the waves? The waves here would knock you down—they knocked me down, that was scary, I don't mind saying it. I was afraid of the way they pushed me over and twisted me under the water until I didn't know which way was up and which way was down. I wasn't expecting to find the air again, I didn't want to, but even though I didn't want to, even though my clothes were pulling me under, I tipped my head back, I opened my mouth and I breathed in air because I wanted to live.

I don't know why, but I wanted to live.

WHY DIDN'T YOU?

Why didn't you?

Today, Jean talked about secrets. She talked about her mother being a singer and that she only found out when she saw a record with her mother's picture on it in a second-hand store on Broadway. She bought the record and took it home and on the back it said that one of the songs was dedicated to her daughter, "Lady." I spin around while Jean is telling me this and it's nice, listening to her for once.

"I asked my grandmother who 'Lady' was, why she never told me I had a sister." I keep spinning.

"And she told me that my mother had named me Lady, after Billie Holiday, but that she decided to change my name to Jean after my mother died. My grandmother thought she was doing the right thing, that I'd have a better life with a name that meant 'God is gracious' rather than being named after a prostitute who died of a drug overdose."

The chair stops and I spin it back, the other way. I ask her about Billie Holiday dying from drugs and then we talk about Hendrix and I tell her about it being Dad's happy music and about Cash being his crying music, but that sometimes Lennon made him cry as well, even "Beautiful Boy" sometimes.

And she just listens, while I spin, she doesn't ask any questions and I tell her about the nights he came into my room crying and saying it's all his fault, how he never should have stopped playing music for you, how he loved playing you music.

Jean says it's good to talk about Dad's feelings, but she's wondering how I felt when all this was happening, what were my feelings?

360

I spin. I try and find them. I tell her it was my job to hold his hand and pat his hair, to memorise all the stops on the subway map hanging on the wall. To listen.

It wasn't my job to have feelings.

Jean's changed the rules again. If I'm going to sit in the swinging chair I have to help David in the kitchen for two hours and eat a meal that's not in my room. It doesn't have to be with the kids.

I nearly say no, but then I think about it and decide to eat breakfast with David, really early, so no one will be up and the muffins will still be hot.

I don't always hate her anymore but sometimes I do, like yesterday when she asked me what I would say to a friend whose mother had committed suicide. I hate that fucking word and I'm glad I'm in the swinging chair because if I'd been on the couch I'd have smashed my Doc through the glass table, I know I would. That's if I'd been bothered to put on my Docs.

"Stop saying that word."

"What word? Suicide?"

"Stop! Anyway, we don't know if that's what happened. We can't know for sure without a body."

"That's true. All we know for sure from the letters is that it appears she was suffering from depression, maybe some form of posttraumatic stress disorder."

I like when she uses words like that, proper words, medical words, words that make sense.

"What do you think he did to her?" I go. "Why do you think she had nightmares?"

I've been wanting to ask that for a while, and even though I think

I know the answer, I want to hear her say it. When she answers, her voice sounds the same as it always does. "I think he sexually abused her."

The chair keeps swinging. I look at her through the basket part. I know she can see me looking but I pretend she can't.

"Child sexual abuse leaves very deep scars on a person, Rhea, particularly if it was an ongoing situation, particularly if it was denied in the home, as it sounds like your mother's was." Her voice is still a normal voice. I want to hit her. I want to cry. I want her to hug me. I want to run. "She needed help and she didn't get it. I'm here to help you."

I used to tell her to fuck off when she said things like that, but now I'm too tired. Now when she asks about something I wrote to you in my letters I just answer her. Why not? It's all fucking stupid. The letters are nothing. Worthless, useless pieces of paper filled up with nothing.

They're nothing.

Nothing.

They're all I have.

Today, Jean takes out the paper and crayons, but I know better.

"I'm not drawing. I don't want to draw."

She's rolling out the paper on the table. "Oh really? I thought maybe you might miss it?"

It's like she knows that I'd thought about going down to the rec room to look for drawing stuff last night when I couldn't sleep, but she couldn't know. She leaves the paper on the table, sits back in her chair. "So if you don't want to draw, what do you want to do today?"

I spin away from her, shrug, even though she can't see me.

"Do you want to read me out what you wrote to your mom last night?"

"No."

"How about I read you the letter she wrote you?"

"Whatever, knock yourself out."

That was stupid, I know now that it was stupid, but I've read it so many times, your letter, I don't expect it to be different out loud, hearing it in her voice. And the whole way through I spin and spin and spin and I don't fucking cry and you know what part gets me? You know the stupid retarded part that gets me? The way you sign it off with "Mom."

I feel sick then, from the spinning, and I need to sit on the floor against the wall under the window. And I know already that I'm going to cry, but when it comes, it's not like normal crying, it's like it's coming from somewhere else, not only my eyes but my whole body. And it's not just the tears and the snot, it's the sounds as well, noises that sound like they are coming from someone else, only they're coming from me, from my stomach, deeper than my stomach, like they could be coming from my soul.

And I try and scrunch smaller, up against the wall, and Jean gets down on the floor too and I think she's going to try and hug me or touch me or something but she just sits cross-legged in front of me and leaves a box of tissues on the floor, between us. And every time I open my eyes, she's looking at me, not looking away, just looking at me and whispering that it's okay, I just need to let it out, let it out, let it out.

When I stop, the clock says 5:37 but it couldn't have gone on that long. I think it's going to be over then because it's dinner time and Jean never misses dinner time, but instead she calls downstairs and Gemma comes up with two glasses of milk and a plate with banana walnut muffins and David's brownies.

And when we're eating, Jean spills milk on her black T-shirt and then she makes a mess of muffin crumbs and she starts to laugh and I laugh too, proper ones, and it's weird how I can go from all that crying to laughing like that, at something that's not even really funny.

Jean says that if you don't let feelings out, they get stuck inside, frozen like glaciers. That what we're doing is melting the feelings so they can come out.

I tell her I hope that's all there is, that I hope there's not any more in there. She doesn't answer me but she puts her hand on my shoulder and when she smiles, it's a nice smile.

I listened to Amanda's mix tape tonight. You know what's fifty kinds of crazy? The first song on it is that song by 4 Non Blondes, "What's Up?"—the one I listened to seventeen times in a row in Coral Springs. And I don't get on to the next song, I don't care that I'm using up the batteries, I just rewind it and play it, again and again and again.

Jean would freak out about me going down to the beach at night, especially after everything, but I don't care, I really don't and I run down the steps of the house and onto the beach trail and the wind is hot in my face but the sand is cool and I'm singing the words out loud, shouting the words. And I turn the music up, so I can't hear myself anymore, but I know I must be screaming because my throat is sore—it's fucking sore—but I don't care, I stop, rewind, and play again.

After ages, I turn it down a bit and then a bit more and then more and the last time I play it I can hardly hear it.

I click "stop," pull my headphones off, and there it is, the sound of the sea. And I think about that line in your letter, the one that makes me laugh—that I'd only ever have to hear Dad's snoring and the sound of the sea.

Did you ever stop to think what I might think about when I hear the sound of the sea?

Today, Jean says this really dumbass thing about blame and things being people's fault. We were sitting cross-legged on the floor by the coffee table and colouring in and she says that some things aren't anyone's fault, that some things just happen.

Maybe some things do just happen but what you did, it didn't just happen. It was your fault, your fault, your fault, not Dad's, not anyone else's, only yours.

Even as I'm writing that I want to give you an excuse and I'm thinking about the dreams and what you said about that horrible bastard and his hands and his face at the window and I get to thinking that it's his fault. It's his fault, definitely, him and your dad's. Maybe your dad is worse, even, because he knew and he did nothing, fucking nothing at all. If he'd listened, believed you, he might have got you help, someone to talk to, and maybe you would have been okay.

But maybe if that had happened, then you wouldn't have come to Ireland and you wouldn't have met Dad and had me.

Sometimes I wish life was like maths, like algebra, where there's always a proper answer, a right one.

But what if there isn't an answer? What if someone did something to that man to make him do what he did to you? Or to your dad? How far back does the blame go? And what if it's a lot of people's fault, not just one person's? Does that mean it's no one's fault? Does it mean that these things just happen? Because if no one is to blame, then you can't control them, can you?

And if you can't control anything, isn't that the scariest thing of all?

Dear Mum,

That's force of habit, that's what that is, starting this letter like that. I'm not crossing it out, I hate crossing stuff out. Anyway, people write "dear" to strangers all the time—"Dear Sir" or "Dear Madam"—it's not like it means anything. It's not like it has to mean anything.

Jean's been on at me about it, why I don't address the letters to you the way I used to, it's another of her suggestions, just like she suggests that I start the letter with "I feel." But I don't know how I feel, and even if I did, that's not why I started this letter. I started this letter to tell you what happened today.

Robin hurt herself, that's what happened. I could tell you that, just that, but I want to tell you the proper story, how I'm on Winnie's bed listening to the mix tape and next thing Zac's hammering on the door and when I turn the music off I hear him saying that Robin fell by the pool, that she's hurt herself bad.

I run downstairs after him and it's only when I jump down the back steps that I realise I'm not wearing my Docs or even my Converse. The car park stones cut my feet, but I don't care, I run after Zac over to the car.

The back door is open and Jean is down on her hunkers, leaning in. There's a cluster of other kids around her and some of them are crying. Erin lifts up Maleika because she's crying louder than the others.

"Rhea's here," Zac goes, loud so they all turn around. "Rhea's here."

For a split second, it's really weird because I haven't seen them since what happened, but then Jean stands up so I can see Robin in the back seat and I forget about that. Her left hand is holding the top of her right arm. She's not crying.

"Rhea, you go round, get in the other side," Jean goes. "Robin, how are you feeling now, honey? Do you think you're going to be sick?"

The stones are sore but there's no time to get shoes. I slide in the back next to Robin.

"If you need to be sick, honey, you tell Rhea, okay? She'll tell Amanda to pull over."

I haven't even noticed Amanda in the front seat until Jean says that, even though she's looking back through the gap in the headrests. Her hair is wet and it's making little drips on her white shirt.

"Here's the insurance information," Jean says, handing her papers, "and the credit card in case there's a co-pay."

Amanda takes everything, puts it in the glove compartment.

Gemma appears behind Jean and gives her something that she hands across Robin to me. A plastic bag. "I hope you don't need it, but just in case she needs to be sick on the way."

Before I can respond, Jean closes the door and the car starts to reverse and it's only then it sinks in that she's not coming, that it's only me and Amanda. And that I don't have any shoes.

Beside me, Robin feels very small. We are close, our legs touching. Someone has draped a dry towel over her bathing suit and her pink hoody top around her shoulders.

"You okay?"

She nods but she doesn't look at me again, she doesn't smile.

"Would you like to hold on to me?"

She shakes her head. Amanda is driving carefully up the drive and even though she goes slow over the bumps I see Robin wince.

"Sorry," Amanda goes, after a bigger bump than the others. "This driveway—"

"What happened?" I go.

"She was running by the pool and she slipped. She fell down right on her arm. It was horrible, you could hear it when she smacked the tiles."

Robin doesn't say anything, just sits silently through this. When Amanda pulls onto the highway from the gate, I release my breath.

"How come Jean didn't come?" I call over the engine, which is louder now. "Or Erin?"

"Some big donor is coming to visit this afternoon so Jean and

Gemma have to be there. Erin's car is too small and she can't drive stick shift."

"She still could've come with you, though."

In the rear-view mirror, Amanda catches my eye. "Robin asked for you."

We don't talk much after that because it's too loud with the wind through the open windows, and even though I'm scared for Robin I'm enjoying being out of my room, out of the house. And it seems like the first time in ages I'm not thinking about your letters, not thinking about you, until we're going through Bridgehampton and we pass right by the Candy Kitchen. It looks cute, with its blue and white stripy awning, really old fashioned, and it's weird because one second I'm thinking I'd love to ask Amanda to stop on the way back, and the next I feel raging, so fucking mad at you, because after wanting to go so bad now I never want to go there at all.

There's traffic for a bit and then we pick up speed again, past shops and restaurants and houses and flat fields four times as big as fields in Ireland. And one of the shops has a statue of an Indian standing outside, waving his hand, and when I turn to point him out to Robin, I notice she's shivering, despite the heat. I roll up my window, reach over to touch her leg.

"We're nearly there," I go, for the hundredth time. "You're being such a brave girl. Hold on and the doctors are going to make you all better."

"Look," Amanda says from the front. "There's a sign, we're only five miles away." When we pull into the car park, Amanda drives right up to the entrance to let us out before she finds parking. At first, Robin won't move and when she finally slides across the seat, the hoody and towel fall off. I pick them up and try and put the hoody on her shoulders but it's hard without her help and it keeps slipping off. I wish I could pick her up and carry her, but instead I throw the towel over my shoulder and keep her hoody on with my hand.

At the reception desk, the woman gives me forms to fill out and it's only then I remember Amanda has all the insurance stuff, so we have to wait until she arrives, all out of breath and pushing her hair out of her face, before the woman will put anything about Robin in her computer.

There's only a couple of people ahead of us, but we're waiting forever and it's only when an old lady on a walker asks what's taking so long that we find out there's been a big car crash on Route 27. Hearing that makes me think about Dad, the ambulance rushing him into Beaumont that night, through the same glass doors where he'd carried me all those years before. But the policeman said he was dead when they got there, so maybe they hadn't brought him through those doors, maybe they'd taken him to some other part of the hospital. And suddenly, sitting with Amanda and Robin watching *Family Feud*, I need to know where they brought him, but there's no one to ask, and I get annoyed all over again with Lisa's mum for not letting me go and identify his body and insisting that Lisa's dad go instead.

At five o'clock, Amanda says she thinks we should call Jean, to give her an update, and when I come back from doing that, she and Robin are gone. It's worse, then, waiting on my own—freezing, with the air conditioning being so high. I want my Champion hoody and my Docs and I hate being there with no shoes on. I'm starving too, really hungry, but I don't have a single cent for the vending machine and I wish there wasn't one because it's harder to be hungry and see the chocolate and crisps behind the glass and not be able to have any. And it's fifty kinds of crazy but I start to get kind of panicky, as if Amanda and Robin might have left without me, as if we could somehow have missed each other, even though I know we can't have missed each other. Ten minutes pass and then fifteen and I'm just about to go and look for the car when they come out.

Robin runs straight over to me to show me her sling and the watermelon lollipop the doctor gave her, and after all her silence in the car, she won't stop talking now about the x-ray machine and the nurse. And when Amanda comes back from the phone and says that

Jean said we should go to McDonald's on the way home, I think Robin is going to explode from excitement, dancing between me and Amanda the whole way back to the car. It's only when she's eating that it hits her, the tiredness, and halfway through her burger she puts her head down on the table and me and Amanda almost have to carry her back to the car.

"She was really brave," Amanda goes, when we're back on the highway. "I was shocked when they said her arm was fractured in two places. With her being so quiet I thought it must only have been a sprain."

I glance at Robin, conked out in the back seat under the towel. I knew that because she wasn't crying it meant it would be worse than if she was bawling her head off. I don't know how I knew, but I did.

Trees are whizzing by the side of the highway, thin skinny trees close together, their trunks black in the orange light behind. Amanda squints into the sun, pulls down her visor. "When we were in with the doctor, she said this thing that shocked me. She asked him if he'd have to cut her arm off."

She laughs a bit as she says it, looks at me quickly. The highway turns and the sun is somehow behind us now, reflecting in the mirrors. Robin is still asleep, her little chest rising and falling under the towel.

"What did he say?"

"He said that of course he wouldn't have to do that. He asked her if that was something she'd seen on TV."

I hold my stump, I don't care if Amanda sees.

"She didn't answer him, but she must have said it because of you. Did she ever ask you about how you lost your arm?"

Amanda says it like that, comes straight out and asks, and I'm glad she doesn't leave the question hanging there, in both our heads but not said out loud.

"She asked me one time and I told her. She must have remembered."

Amanda switches lanes, passes out a pickup truck. "What did happen?"

The road seems narrower than before, darker. The car in front has a broken brake light.

"My dad was a butcher and I was playing with his meat mincer. My arm got stuck in it."

Amanda takes a deep breath. She holds her speed steady. "Oh God, Rhea. How old were you?"

"Seven. Old enough to know better."

A beat of silence passes and she fixes a curl behind her ear. "Come on—seven? Robin's age. That wasn't your fault."

"Well, it wasn't Dad's fault!" My words are sharp, loud in the car. The carpet is gritty under my feet and I wish I was wearing my Docs.

When she speaks, her voice is quiet. "Maybe it wasn't anyone's fault."

We don't talk for ages then and I think about turning the radio on but I don't. It's properly night now, the lights reflecting on the road signs. In the dark, in the car, it's kind of comforting, close. When I talk again, it's as if we are still having the conversation, instead of it being ten minutes since either of us said anything.

"You know, I've been thinking about it a lot lately, what happened. I don't know why, just been remembering it."

Amanda looks over at me to let me know she's heard me. I try and organise the words in my head so they'll make some kind of sense.

"Not the accident so much, but everything leading up to it. That day, just before it, and it's weird, like I knew something bad was going to happen, going near the machine."

I can feel the spongy car seat underneath me, but I can feel something else too, the scratchy wood of the counter where Dad cut the meat. Next to me, the machine was scary-looking, metal and dark bits. Even though it was clean, it was never clean.

"This is going to sound crazy but I think, in a way, some part of me wanted to have an accident—not what happened, but you know—something. I don't know … "

Maybe it's the glare of the lights that is making me a little dizzy.

Or maybe it's remembering Lisa in her white polo neck and her black dungarees telling me to get down, not to touch it, that it's dangerous. I take a breath.

"He used to be fun, all the time, my dad. That's how I remember it. We'd go for walks on Sundays and he'd play me his records." I think about telling her about writing to you, but I leave that bit out. "And then, I don't know, he was different. We never did anything, he hardly talked—it was like he didn't even see me. The only time I could get him to play Hendrix was when I was off sick from school with the mumps."

"You like Jimi Hendrix," Amanda goes. "I've noticed your T-shirt."

I smile in the dark. "It's twelve years old, that T-shirt. He bought it for me when I was six."

Amanda laughs. "When I was six my mother was buying me frilly dresses."

Through the back window, the sky is black. I'm halfway to telling Amanda what I want to say. I could stop now and make a joke, something about her in a frilly dress. Or I can say it—finally say it.

"I knew I shouldn't have been messing with the machine, that it was dangerous to take the safety guard off. I don't mean I wanted to lose my arm, or anything crazy, but maybe I wanted to be sick for a while." I pull my foot up on the seat, thread my fingers through my toes like Jean does. "So he'd be nice to me, play me music. So he'd notice me. I know that sounds crazy though, it doesn't make any sense." We pass by the Indian statue again, the one I'd pointed out to Robin. I can barely see him waving in the dark.

"What doesn't make sense about wanting your parents to notice you?" Amanda asks the question simply, like it's the easiest thing in the world to answer, to understand. "Everyone wants that. Whether that's by getting straight A's like me, or being the quarterback like Zac, or slashing your wrists like my friend Judy."

"You've a friend who slashed her wrists?"

The dashboard lights reflect on Amanda's face. "Yep. We'd been at the mall that day. I went home and did my math homework, she went home and slashed her wrists."

I don't know if it's okay to ask, but she brought it up. "Did she die?"

"No, they found her in time. I still felt really guilty though, like I should have known or something. Like I should have stopped her."

I want to tell her that it wasn't her fault, that she couldn't have stopped her, but what if she could have? So I say something else instead.

"Your way of getting noticed sounds better than mine or your friend's," I say. "Straight A's beat losing an arm or slashing your wrists."

In my head, it sounds funny, but out loud it just sounds stupid.

"I guess, but I don't know how well it works." Amanda's voice is different than before, harder. Her hands on the steering wheel look like they are gripping tighter. "Because everyone thinks you must be fine, because you're doing great at school; even when you try and tell them you're having a hard time about something, they don't even notice, they don't want to know."

"You mean about your friend—Judy?" It feels like the car is moving faster but the speed dial is still on fifty-five, the same as when we left the hospital.

"All of it. Grandma getting cancer, dying. Judy trying to commit suicide. Daddy moving up into the guest bedroom on the third floor. No one ever talked about any of it, like it wasn't happening."

"Your mum and dad never said anything about your granny dying?"

She laughs but it's not her real laugh. It's like someone else is in the car next to me now, someone else is driving. "Are you kidding me? Dad got busier 'working'—he was never home. Like we didn't all know he was banging his secretary."

"What about your mum?"

"Mom?" She raises an eyebrow. "Mom went shopping."

"Shopping?"

"Shopping." She nods. "My mother thinks the solution to any problem can be found at the mall."

I laugh.

"You think I'm joking, but I'm serious. The night I came out to her I was so upset, all the MacKenzie stuff was going on, she hadn't returned my calls or anything. So I went into Mom's bedroom and she was reading a magazine and I told her that I was in love with this girl and do you know what she said?"

I tighten my fingers around my toes. "What?"

"She said that there was a big sale on at Macy's and we should go and get some new clothes for me."

Amanda bows her chin to her chest and for a second I think she's going to cry, only then I hear the squeak that comes after it and I realise she's not crying, she's laughing, and that it's okay for me to laugh too.

"So did you go? Did you go shopping?"

She laughs more, catches her breath. "I'd love to say I didn't, but we did, the next day. I kept waiting for her to say something about MacKenzie, to bring it up, so I tried on all these hideous dresses and I even let her buy one for me, because I thought maybe if I wore one, maybe she'd say something, but she never said anything at all."

I'm not laughing anymore, not then, picturing Amanda, trailing after her mother around some department store. I want to tell her about me and Winnie buying clothes in the Salvation Army on Tenth Avenue and how it was the most fun I'd ever had shopping, but I don't want to make her feel bad.

"What about your dad. Did you tell him?"

"Mom must have, because he did what he always does to fix things, he sent me to see a shrink."

"Did it help?"

She tucks a curl behind her ear. "A bit, maybe. I only saw her like, six times. She said my parents hadn't got the capacity to deal with what was going on. That I'd feel better if I stopped expecting them to."

We're coming into Amagansett and Amanda slows down, changes lanes. I want this road, this drive to keep going, to stay in the warm darkness of the car with Robin in the back seat and the lights outside.

"What about you?" Amanda goes. "Did you ever get a chance to come out to your dad?"

"No." I could leave it there, I know I could, but it feels like there is more, that there can be more. "It's funny, I haven't thought as much about how he'd have taken it, but I've imagined telling my mum, what she would have said."

"You never really knew her, did you?" she goes.

I shake my head. "I was three when she died."

"How did she die? If you don't mind me asking."

The road sounds different now, under the tyres, than on the highway. I try and count the rotations, imagine the lines in the black rubber whirring along the tarmac. I want to say it out loud, I want to say it to her, to someone. "She committed suicide."

I say it, just like that. Just like it's nothing, maybe it is nothing. In the silence before she responds it's like my brain is doing a million things at the same time—I'm imagining the tyres, I'm looking at the trees, I'm thinking about the food back in the kitchen, what David might have made tonight—mac and cheese or roast chicken or meatballs—and whether he might have kept us some and I hope he has because even though it's not even an hour since we ate the McDonald's I'm starving again. And Amanda's looking at me, I can feel her looking but I don't have to look back.

"Oh, Rhea," she goes. "Fuck. I'm so sorry."

The tyres whirr. I nearly ask her why she's sorry, if she was the one who killed her, but I don't say anything.

"Fuck," she says. "I shouldn't have been so nosy…"

I shake my head. I want to tell her it's okay, that I didn't have to tell her, but I feel the pinpricks at the top of my nose that come before the tears, and I'm not going to let that happen, not here. Not in front of her.

I take a breath, hold it, let it go, the way Jean is always telling me to. There's something else I need to say.

"Thank you," I go, "for swimming out that day, to save me. I never said thank you."

A car drives towards us, the lights full on. Her necklace glints, yellow in the dark.

"You're welcome."

"I was in trouble—if you hadn't…"

I don't know how to end the sentence. I don't want her to end it for me and she doesn't.

"You're welcome," she says again.

I don't say anything after that. And she doesn't either. And as we drive I feel like I'm missing out on something and I'm not sure what it is, the chance to say more maybe, but I know if I say anything more, I can't be sure what's going to happen, I can't be sure it won't be like in Jean's office the other day. I'm still deciding when I see the "Turning Tides" sign, right before the gate, and she turns her indicator on.

She drives slowly over the dips and the bumps in the driveway and, in the back, Robin is still sleeping. The lights are lighting up the trees, the gravel car park, the house, and I know I need to say it before we stop, before the drive is over, or else I'll never say it at all.

"I never told anyone that before, about my mum."

My voice is quiet, nearly a whisper, and for a second I think she hasn't heard me, until she slows right down, so the car is nearly stopped, and she turns to look at me.

"Thank you," she goes. "Thank you for telling me."

And we look at each other for a second before she starts driving again and pulls into the car park, into the same space where we started from, and the journey ends like all journeys end and even though this one ends in the same place it started, in a way I can't explain, it feels like we are somewhere different.

Rhea

Dear Mum,

Three big things happened yesterday and I talked to Jean about two of them but not the third one.

The first is that I'm back at work, proper work, helping with breakfast and on the beach and Arts and Crafts and everything. And at first I don't like it, because everyone's being so fucking nice to me, Erin with her little smiles and asking if I'm okay, and David not slagging me about dropping the butter on the floor, when he'd always slag me about something like that. It's Marco who says it, the thing that everyone's afraid to say.

"Where have you been for the past few weeks? I heard you were hiding in your room."

David is coming out with a tray of bacon and Erin is behind him, with hash browns. I'm pouring orange juice from the pitcher, Jessica's, Curt's, Amy's. I don't spill any. "I was sick," I go.

"That's bullshit!" He has his arms folded across his Jets T-shirt. He nudges Isaac next to him. "She's lying—she wasn't sick. She nearly drowned and then she had a meltdown."

Behind him I see David's face, he's angry and about to say something.

"You're right," I go. "But I'm not lying—having a meltdown is like being sick."

I keep pouring. Terence's glass, Robin's. She's looking at me with big eyes and I smile at her.

"See," Marco goes, turning to Isaac again. "See, I told you."

But Isaac isn't listening, he's already picking up some of the bacon with his fingers, even though he's not supposed to, and Luis is behind him getting a plate. I move on to fill up Maleika's glass and that's it, everything's normal again and no one says anything else.

And the rest of the day is fine, better than fine. And playing football on the beach, chasing Matt along the sand to tackle him, I forget, totally forget, about everything else.

The second big thing that happens is that I speak to Winnie. She's called a few times, Jean's been telling me, and I know I should call her back, so when Jean comes in with the cordless phone from the hall after dinner I take it out on the deck and sit on the step and start to talk to her. And I think it's going to be awkward, after all this time and everything that's happened, but she asks me about it straightaway, like Marco did, only in a nicer way, and she listens while I tell her and she doesn't interrupt. It's different telling her than telling Amanda or Jean, I don't know why, but it is, maybe because she's seen your pictures. And when I finish talking, I hold the phone tight and close my eyes and her voice in my ear sounds really close, like she's sitting next to me.

"I'm sorry you had to go through all that, Rhea," she goes, "but at least you know the truth now. Truth is where healing begins."

That makes sense, when she says it, and I feel better, happy even, especially when she tells me she's coming back next week, when the second group of kids arrive. She asks if I'll mind sharing a room with her again and that's kind of a joke, because I have no choice, and anyway, I think she knows I miss her.

I'm excited after the phone call and that's why I start to tidy the room up, get it nice and neat again for Winnie. And I know, when I take my backpack off her bed, that I shouldn't take your letters out, that I shouldn't read them again, that I don't even need to because each fucking word is carved into my brain with a scalpel already, but my hands don't listen to my head and I open them and read them anyway.

Reading your letters, it's as if everything else goes away—chasing Matt on the beach, what Winnie said, all of it—and I know sleep won't ever come. So even though it's raining, even though the clock says 3:57 a.m., even though Jean would freak out and fire me on the spot, I decide to go to the beach. And that's what makes the third thing happen. I notice the line of light under the kitchen door and I nearly don't go in except I think it must be David making banana walnut muffins or brownies, only it's not David who's in there—it's Amanda.

She's at the cooker, stirring something, and she has her back to me. She's wearing sweat pants cut off into shorts and her hair is down. I've never seen her hair down before and it's way longer and way curlier than I'd thought it would be, almost as far as her waist. The air conditioner is on and she doesn't hear me and I wonder if I can go, step back into the hall and close the door without her hearing, but something makes her turn around.

She jerks a little against the cooker, so she nearly knocks over the pot.

"Holy shit, Rhea!" She has her hand clasped flat to her chest.

"Hey," I go.

"You scared the living crap out of me! How long were you standing there?"

"Sorry, I didn't mean to scare you. I'm on my way out, I'm just getting a jacket."

I hadn't thought of the jacket until just then, but I see them lined up on hooks by the table.

"You're going out in that? It's pouring."

"I'm Irish, we're waterproof."

Erin's jacket is nice but it would probably be too small for me so I grab the navy one behind it, Zac's or Matt's.

"I'm making hot chocolate, why don't you have some?"

"No, thanks, I just feel like a walk." That's not true, not exactly. The jacket is down to my knees and slips off my shoulders. I feel my breath, different, short as if I've been running up the stairs. Jean's obsessed with breath, she says it's a clue to your feelings. If she was here she'd say that breath like this might mean I'm scared, which doesn't make sense because even though I know it's okay to be scared sometimes, I'm definitely not scared of Amanda.

"Have some hot chocolate before you go then, I've made too much." She's already reaching up to take the mugs out. "My dad freaks out when I do this at home—put the A/C on to cool me down enough to enjoy hot chocolate, but it always helps me sleep."

The chocolate looks really thick and she fills up half the pink mug first, then half the green one, stirring it between each pour, then she goes back and tops each one up, so it stops about an inch below the rim.

"Perfect," she goes, putting the pot in the sink. "Which cup?"

"Either, I don't care."

The jacket slopes off my right shoulder. I want to roll up the sleeve over my stump but it's going to be too awkward with Amanda watching, so I let it hang down.

"Here." She puts the pink one down in front of me and the green one opposite. She slides onto the bench by the wall and I shrug the jacket off, onto the back of the chair, before sitting down across from her.

"Pink to make the boys wink," I go.

She looks out from under her curls.

"And the girls," she says, smiling.

The chocolate burns my mouth so I need to slow down, blow on it. Underneath her hoody she's wearing her necklace with her name on it.

"I've never seen you out of that necklace," I go. "You even wear it in bed?"

It comes out meaner than I think it will. She stirs her chocolate, drinks a little more.

"My grandma gave it to me." She fingers it. "I know it's kind of childish, but I like it. It makes me feel close to her."

"Oh," I go. "That's nice."

I think about Nana Davis, lying in her bed. If she'd given me something like that, maybe I'd wear it too, even if it was lame.

"It was good to see you enjoying being around the kids today," she goes.

She has a rim of brown over her top lip and I don't tell her but maybe she sees me looking because she licks it away and I look back down at my cup.

"Yeah," I go. "It was good."

That weird breath thing is there again and it's only then that I figure out what it means. That maybe it's there because of what I'd told her in the car, because we're both pretending that I never told her at all. And I know I have to be like Winnie, like Marco even, to just figure out a way to just say it, but it's her who speaks next. "Hey, you want to play Scrabble?"

My brain makes a picture in less than a nano-second, the box of Scrabble on the top shelf of the wardrobe in Dad's room, me standing on a chair to reach it, dust as thick as a carpet on the lid.

"I've never played," I go.

"You've never played Scrabble?" Her eyes are wide, saucers, not blue tonight but not grey either, a mixture, maybe, of both.

"Nope." I shake my head.

"I don't know if I've ever met anyone who never played. Dad used to make me and my brother play with him every night, before any TV."

"You must be brilliant, then."

She shakes her head. "No, that stopped by the time I was nine or ten, by then Dad was barely home."

The rain is getting heavier outside. There's still some hot chocolate left. I think of a way to say something about the other night, without having to say it. "I found this Scrabble game in my dad's room once and I was convinced it was my mum's. I left it out for him on the kitchen table but when I came down for my breakfast the next morning he'd thrown it in the bin."

She makes a face. "Why did he do that?"

I shrug. "I don't know."

"And you really never played, you're not kidding?"

"No."

"So, tonight will be your first time. Let me go find it."

She gets up and goes into the hall, where the games closet is, and I'm thinking about the bin in the kitchen in Rush, by the back door, the lid lifted half off because the Scrabble box didn't fit. He didn't just put the box in, otherwise I'd have taken it out—he emptied the bag of letters and when I look in a *Z* is inside half an egg shell, an *A* and a *U* on top of the mush of tea bags. Listening to Amanda rummaging through the games, I'm feeling angry, as angry as I was that morning in Rush, not just because he threw it away but because of the way he messed up all the letters, and that's when it hits me, eight or seven or nine years after that morning, that Dad throwing out the Scrabble must have had something to do with you.

"Found it," Amanda goes. "It was all the way in the back."

She's all business, unfolding the board, writing our names on a score sheet and for a second I want to get up, run out into the rain, and the next second I want to stay and it's driving me crazy, how my head is like a pinball machine and I'm hoping this isn't part of what Jean calls feeling your feelings.

Amanda shakes the bag of letters, holds it out towards me. "We each get seven letters but before we do, we'll each choose one letter. Closest to *A* starts."

I take a letter, it feels nice in my hand. Smooth. It's a *J*.

Amanda picks out an *N*. She smiles. "You go first—you can run your word any direction so long as it's over this square—it means you get double points."

I take my seven tiles and put them in the little holder. I like it already—the game—the feel of the letters, how everything has a number, the uniformity of the board. It's different now that we have something to focus on—easier—and my breath is normal again.

I lay my first word down. H-I-T-C-H.

"Great," she goes, "that's twenty-six points. Good start."

"Beginner's luck."

I pick five new letters from the bag. She takes ages on her first word, tucks her curls behind her ears as she concentrates and moves her tiles around. After a few seconds, a curl escapes. By the time she makes her move I've worked out four different words that I might be able to use, depending on what she does.

"H-U-R-L. Hurl." She lays it down. "It's a gross word, but didn't you say there's a sport called that in Ireland?"

"Yeah—the game is hurling. Well remembered!"

She smiles. "Who could forget a game called hurling? My letters suck tonight. I had three of the same vowel. Some people say you can swap them but I don't play like that, I like to play using the official rules."

She has two other *U*s, I know that, but I don't say it. I'm glad she likes the proper rules.

I lay down my word: F-A-S-T-E-R. "Nine points."

"Holy shit, Rhea. I haven't even had a chance to get my new letters yet!"

She's laughing and I am too and it's fun, this game. She takes her new letters and I take mine, only I don't turn them over, not yet. The clock over her head says it's 4:35. Only two hours and twenty-five minutes until wake-up call.

"Hey," I go. "How come you're up so late anyway? Won't you be going running in an hour or something?"

She looks up, her hands on either side of her hair, holding it back. "I haven't been going the last few mornings."

"Why not?"

She looks back at her letters. "I've been finding it hard to sleep, I don't know why. I've been lying awake until five most nights."

Her eyes go back to her letters. "P-R-U-N-E," she says, putting the letters down. "And I get the points for 'I-N' too. And N is on a double letter score. So that's... eleven."

She adds up the points.

"What's the score?"

"Thirty-five to you, twenty to me. Your beginner's luck is holding."

I'm about to turn over my letters but I want to say something about what she said, about not sleeping. I think about how Jean might ask her.

"You want to talk about it?"

My fingers flick the edge of my overturned tiles. I look from the tiles to Amanda and back to the tiles.

"I don't know. I mean I guess it's not such a big deal. I'm just feeling a bit bummed about the kids leaving on Saturday. I mean I know we have a whole second group coming, but it feels like it won't be the same."

"I know, it won't."

"And it reminds me we're halfway through the summer, more than halfway through. That in a another month or so, this will all be over."

She's fiddling with her necklace then, flicking it over and back against her skin. She lifts it up and puts it against her lip. I want to turn my tiles over but I don't.

"Can I ask you something, Rhea?"

The breath thing is happening again and I hold it for a second before I answer her. "Sure, what?"

"Would you be straight? You know, if you could choose?"

I don't know what I thought she was going to ask me, but something about the question is disappointing. I flick the tiles over, line them in the holder in order of value. "I don't think it's a choice—I don't think people choose to be gay or straight."

"I know, that's not what I mean." She's shaking her head. "I don't think people can choose either, but just say for some weird reason you could. Would you choose to be straight?"

She's looking at me differently now, like the answer really matters. It's ages since her last move and it's still my go but I don't know if we're playing anymore.

"No." My answer is definite. "I wouldn't. No way." She tucks a curl behind her ear and for once it stays. "Why, would you?"

She pushes her letters around, and if I looked I'd probably be able to see them. "I used to think I would. I used to pray to like boys, to be like everyone else. One night I remember I even got down on my knees and prayed that when I woke up I'd like Hank Zikorski."

After she says his name, she dips her head and laughs her breathy laugh. I wait for the squeak and when it comes, I laugh too.

"Hank Zikorski?"

"This guy in my class. He was really cute and we went to the movies a few times and all my friends were so jealous. We'd sit in the back row and hold hands and kiss, but I didn't feel anything at all, I just wanted to watch the movie. It was like my body was made of wood or something. You know what I mean?"

I nod. "I know what you mean."

"And when I kissed Ellen, that first time, even though it was only spin the bottle, it was so different, like my body came back or something. Like my head could lie to me and pretend I was straight but my body couldn't, my body told the truth."

I realise then that I don't want to talk about Amanda kissing Hank Zikorski or Ellen or anyone else, that what I want, more than anything, is for her to answer the question—her own question. "And now?"

"And now I think if I wasn't gay, I wouldn't be me. And I want to be me. I like me, being me."

My heart does a little swoopy lift then, and I let out my breath. "I like you being you too."

I think she's going to look away only she doesn't look away, she doesn't even blink, and it's me who looks away first at my letters lined up in my holder. I don't know how I didn't notice the word they make before.

I reach over and put them down in a line on the board, even though I'm not sure if we're still playing. I work backwards, putting down the S first, make "HURL" into "HURLS," and then I make the new word.

Amanda looks down at the word sitting between us. She smiles and spells it out.

"K-I-S-S. Nice. And you're on a double word score so that's sixteen, plus eight for HURLS. Twenty-four points."

I could say something to make it into a joke, to move her onto her next word, but I don't. I don't say anything, only look at her, and we sit looking at each other for seconds or minutes or an hour before I stand up and step over the jacket that's fallen off the back of my chair so it's in a pool on the floor, and she gets up too, and we meet at the end of the table.

And then we stand there for another fifty years, it feels like, and when I reach out and touch her cheek it's so smooth, smooth like Scrabble tiles. And when she smiles, her cheek moves under my hand and her eyes skim back to the board, to the word that's still there. K-I-S-S. And then she raises her eyebrow, just a little bit.

And then we do.

Rhea

Dear Mum,

I see them from the window of my room, which is weird, because I never look out that tiny window, but something makes me pay attention to the noise of the car driving in, something makes me watch it reverse into the only space left. There's a shine on the windscreen, reflecting the trees, so I can't see who's inside.

The driver door opens and the person who gets out is Aunt Ruth. She closes the door, looks up at the house, making a visor with her hands. In her white trousers and white top, she shimmers in the sun.

I am surprised and I am not surprised that she's here.

I'm not expecting the other door to open, the passenger one, and I don't notice it has until it closes. My eyes see her but my mind needs time to catch up. I hold on to the window ledge, keep looking to make sure it's her. And it is her. It's Laurie.

They stand still by the car, looking at the house just like I'm looking down. Aunt Ruth starts to walk first and she holds her arm out as if to put it around Laurie, but she walks past her and on ahead and then they're both out of sight.

My T-shirt has a stain on it, from breakfast, and I pull it off. I grab my Hendrix one from the drawer, sniff the armpits. It's not clean, but it doesn't matter. In the mirror, my hair is too long. It needs to be shaved again, Amanda was going to do it on Saturday, after the kids go—is going to do it on Saturday.

But it's not Saturday, it's only Wednesday and Laurie's here. Laurie is here.

"Rhea?"

The voice and the knock come at the same time. Matt's voice.

"Coming!"

I open the door and he's leaning against the wall, skinny and tall.

"You've got company," he goes. "Some lady and her daughter."

I run my hand down the front of my Hendrix T-shirt to smooth it.

"She's not her daughter."

I have Amanda's flip-flops on but I need my Docs, I need to be wearing my Docs. The room is a mess—I'm in the middle of tidying it for Winnie. I find one, circle the room with it in my hand looking for the other one.

"It's over there," he goes, pointing to the end of the bed.

I grab it from under a pile of clothes. "Thanks."

I shove my foot in, no time for socks, and the laces are undone. I pull at them, but they only come out more. "Fuck!"

When I look up Matt is watching me, and that makes it worse. "You don't need to wait, just tell them I'll be down in a minute."

"Okay." He's about to leave and then he stops. "Do you want some help?"

"No, I'm fine."

It's automatic, my response, but after he's left I know I don't have time, that my hand wouldn't be able to do them quickly enough, not with Laurie downstairs. He's still on the landing and I call him back.

"Matt? Yes, please, I could use your help, if you have a minute."

He's back then, smiling, and it's actually kind of nice, having him hold my foot as he does up the laces.

"Did you meet them when they came in?" I go. "What did they say when they asked for me? Did they say anything?"

He looks up, his forehead is peeling from sunburn. "I don't know, I wasn't talking to them."

He moves on to my right foot.

"How did you know they were here, then? How come you came to get me?"

I'm not sure if I'm imagining it or not, or if his face looks redder than a minute ago.

"Amanda asked me to. I guess she's the one who met them."

Amanda met Laurie. Amanda met Laurie and she didn't come up to tell me she was here. I'm not sure what that means, or if it even means anything, but there's no time to figure it out because Matt has finished my laces.

390

"Thanks a million, Matt." I jump off the bed and run past him, out the door and onto the landing. I'm at the top of the stairs when I see Jean running up, her Oakleys in her hand.

She's out of breath. "You heard?" she says. "Someone told you they're here?"

"Matt came to find me. Where are they?" We start to walk downstairs together.

"They're in my office. But you don't have to see them, you know, if you don't want to."

I didn't know that. "I know," I go.

"Do you want me to come in with you?"

My heart kicks and I realise then that I just assumed she'd come in with me, that I can't imagine being in that room without her, seeing them without her. "If you want to."

She raises her eyebrows. "You know that's not how it works. Do you want me to?"

We're on the second-floor landing by then, right outside her office. The door is closed.

Laurie is behind the door. Aunt Ruth is. Jean is the only one who knows everything, everything about them and about me, but even after everything I'd told her, she doesn't know anything at all. She doesn't know how Aunt Ruth's voice will sound or the look I know she's going to give me, and she doesn't know what it's like to look into Laurie's blue eyes, to feel the curve of her hips in my hands. "Yes," I go.

Sometimes things happen and you don't have time to prepare for them. You can be in a moment and then realise something big is happening, but this moment wasn't like that. This moment I have time to take it in.

I open the door slowly and Aunt Ruth is standing with her back to me, looking out the window at the beach. As the door opens, she turns around, almost in time with the swing of the door, it feels like. She's the same. I know these white linen trousers, the white shirt, the beads she wears over them. But her hair is different, longer, making wings where the layers are growing out. And her face, there's something different about her face. Like she's the same, but not the same.

"Rhea," she goes. "Rae."

In films people always run into each other's arms, but she doesn't run and I don't either. I stand there right where I am, and she walks over, really slowly around the coffee table. And when she holds out her arms to hug me, there's something else in the hug, a pause, like she's asking for my permission.

I nod.

Usually her hugs are quick, over as soon as they start, but this hug is different—tighter, longer. She feels bony under her white shirt. "Rae." She rubs my back in circles. "Rae."

That's when she starts to cry and I'm standing there, hugging, being hugged, and it's only then that I remember Laurie. I don't know where she is, or why she's not there, and then I see her climbing out of the swing chair, my chair. She walks into my line of vision, in front of the window where Aunt Ruth was standing a minute ago. Her vest top has red and blue stripes on it and it must be new, because I haven't seen it before and I wonder if she bought it with her staff discount at Gap. Her hair is down but she scoops it up with her hands, as if to make it into a ponytail, before she lets it fall again.

Aunt Ruth is crying harder, holding me too tight now, and all I can feel are her hands, her breath, her feelings. And in the silence, I can almost feel Jean behind me, her presence, and if she asked me now, right this second, how I'm feeling, I'd have to tell her that I don't feel anything at all.

Over Aunt Ruth's shoulder, I let my eyes see Laurie, take her in, even prettier than I remember, her legs tanned in her cut-off denim shorts, her eyes as blue as the sea outside the window. She looks just like that first time I saw her, only more grown up, not sucking her hair anymore. Her arms are folded and she unfolds one of them and waves, a soft, slow wave, one finger at a time like a ripple. And then she smiles.

Jean is watching, I know she's watching, that she sees the wave and the smile and the words that Laurie mouths at me: "I'm sorry."

There's no sound, only the shape of the words. And I don't know if she expects me to say them back—or if I even want to—so I don't do anything, only stand there and let Aunt Ruth cry and hold me, and I hold her back, with Laurie watching and Jean watching. And I try to remember to breathe.

R

Dear Mum,

I wanted to try one of Jean's suggestions, to start this letter with "I feel," only if I did that, the start of the letter would be "I feel weird"—and even I know that "weird" isn't a feeling.

Aunt Ruth wanted to go to a restaurant in East Hampton so we could talk, but I didn't want to go there with her so we decided to walk on the beach instead. And just as we're on the deck saying goodbye to Jean and Laurie, Jean calls after me and asks if I want her to come along too.

Aunt Ruth turns back to her, grips the banister. "Please, please give me this time with her alone."

Jean acts like Aunt Ruth hasn't said anything, keeps her eyes on me.

I nod. "It's okay. It'll be okay." I lead the way, down the steps and along the beach path, and when I look back to check Aunt Ruth is behind me, Jean is still on the deck, watching us, but Laurie must have gone inside. It's play time and the kids are on the beach, calling out to each other and laughing. When Robin sees me she shouts my name, starts to run over, and it's hard to have to wave and walk the opposite way. I hear Amanda calling her, telling her to come back to the others, that I can't play today. I can tell by the sound of Amanda's voice that she's looking over, and part of me wants to turn, to catch her eye and let her know everything's all right, but I don't know yet if everything is.

Aunt Ruth catches up with me and when I slow down, she slows down too so we're walking side by side.

"You look good," she goes. "I was so worried, I didn't know what to expect."

I've put on weight here with all those banana walnut muffins, but not as much as I lost. The words are in my mouth—about how homelessness is the best diet ever—but I don't say them, I don't say anything.

"It's so beautiful here, by the ocean. The children must love it."

I'm walking close to the water, daring the waves to lap up around the soles of my Docs, but they stop a few centimetres short every time.

"Jean was saying that a lot of them are from shelters. That's so sad but at least they can have a real childhood here, a real summer."

We're not here to talk about the kids, we both know that. I bury my hand in the pocket of my shorts.

"What did you want to talk about, Aunt Ruth? I don't have too much time. I'm supposed to be working."

I sound formal, wooden, and she changes her tone to match mine.

"Of course, I don't want to keep you from your job, Rae."

I crunch my toes inside my Docs. "Rhea, just call me Rhea."

"I thought maybe you'd changed it back, because of your letters, but I didn't want to assume. I always preferred Rhea."

Behind us, the sounds of the kids are further away, their shouts, laughing, fading away under the wash of the waves.

"I've something I need to ask you, Rhea."

I start to count my breath, time it to each step—heel, toe, heel, toe, inhale for four steps, hold for four...

"Did anything happen to you on the streets?"

I thought she was going to ask about you, I was sure. I exhale, four, five, six, seven, eight. "Lots of things happen on the streets, Aunt Ruth."

"But nothing really bad happened though, did it? Nothing that would... you know... leave lasting damage?"

She doesn't want to hear what happened on the streets, not really. I can tell by the way she asks the question that she doesn't really want to know. Up ahead, a man is fishing and we walk around him. When Dad was a boy, he got a fishhook caught in his cheek and years and years later he still had the scar, a tiny line of silver at the top of his stubble. Jean talks about emotional scars being like real ones, that you can clean them out, make them better, treat them until they heal.

"No," I go, "nothing like that."

"Thank God." The words come out in a sigh. "Oh, thank God."

We keep walking and I know I'm going too fast for her, that

it's easier for me in my Docs, but I don't slow down. We're walking towards the kite surfers and I want to stop and watch them, follow their movement, to just look and not have to speak at all.

"Rhea, I'm finding this hard—to know what to say. I don't know where to start with everything but I know I want to apologise for what Cooper did, what he said. I know it wasn't okay. It wasn't okay at all."

She's slowed down behind me, stopped. When I turn around to look at her, her hair is blowing into her face, her white shirt flapping around her. She's thinner, she's definitely thinner.

"I wouldn't blame you not wanting to come back home when he's there—not after everything. But we've decided to separate. That was one of the things I wanted to tell you."

She's lied to me before and I can't tell if she's lying now. "You wouldn't leave him just because of that night."

She fixes her fringe and it blows back the way it was. "It wasn't just that night. We're very different, we have different values. What he did that night just forced me to see it."

"So how come Laurie's here with you, then, if you're splitting up?" It's the question I've wanted to ask since we left Laurie behind, the only question in my head, and I'm glad, now, that I have a reason to ask it. A wave comes in and catches the heels of my Docs.

"As soon as I sent those letters, I knew I shouldn't have. I wanted to come and find you right away, make that soup kitchen tell me where you were. Cooper and I had huge fights about it. Huge."

When she talks about Cooper her face changes and I hope she won't cry again. "One night, Laurie heard us arguing and she barged in—said she was coming, that if we tried to stop her she'd run away too." The water is making a pool now around the edge of my foot, pulling at the sand underneath it. "I've never seen her so determined about anything. Even Cooper knew there was no point fighting her."

I feel a lift, somewhere in my body, my chest, maybe even my heart. Cooper fought Laurie over everything, but he knew there was no point fighting over this. Laurie was determined. Determined to come. Determined to see me. On the waves, the light is dancing.

"So much for confidentiality," I go. "That soup kitchen wasn't supposed to tell anyone where I was."

Aunt Ruth looks down at her feet and back up at me. "I wasn't exactly straight with them. In your first letter you mentioned a summer camp and in your second you said you were by the sea. I did some research and I found this place—because of the homeless thing I thought there might be a connection. When I went in to see the woman there, I pretended that you'd told me, that I already knew."

She looks sheepish as she tells me this and I imagine her at the soup kitchen, trying to make her elaborate lie sound casual. I laugh, and she laughs too.

"You'd get along well with my friend Sergei," I go. "He talked our way into your mother's nursing home."

She stops laughing mid-laugh. "You went to see Mom? Oh my God, I didn't even think to check there—had I even told you where she was?"

"No," I go. "I knew she was hidden away in a nursing home but I didn't know which one."

The wind catches her shirt and she smoothes it down. "She isn't hidden away. Clover Hills is one of the top senior facilities in the city."

"Call it what you want. All the fancy names in the world don't change the fact that you'd rather have her locked up there than come and live with you."

Her face changes; I know this face, her angry face. A couple are walking towards us from behind her, hand in hand, but she can't see them.

"Mom has severe dementia, she doesn't know who I am, where she is. I can't take care of her but I do make sure she gets the best care, that she—"

"The best care from the hired help."

She looks so mad then, Mum, with her hair blowing in her face and her hands clenched. For a second she looks like she might hit me and I hope she does.

"You can damn well stop it right there, Rhea! Don't talk crap about things you don't understand. I'll tell you about hired help—me and your mom were raised by hired help, we knew those maids better than our own mother. I thought you might have a pretty clear picture of that from her letters."

The couple are in line with us now and they walk by without looking over, pretend they can't hear. Aunt Ruth looks mortified and we stand there in silence until they've gone by. When they're at a safe distance, I answer her. "Okay, whatever."

"Look, I'm sorry. I shouldn't have brought your mom's letters up, not like that."

I turn my back on her, start walking again. If we are going to talk about the letters, I need to be able to walk, to count my footsteps, not to have to look at her.

"Rhea, hold on." She's behind me, walking next to me. "I know I shouldn't have sent them. As soon as I did, I couldn't get this image out of my head of you holed up somewhere, reading them all by yourself."

We're almost at the bend by then. Around the bend and on a bit, there's the dune, the one with the U-shape of grass around it. That's where I read your letter—the last one, the one you sent to me—and it's as if she knows, but she couldn't know.

"I'm glad you sent them," I say, fast. "You said it. I wanted to know the truth, and now I do."

The words sound logical, in the right order. They are what an adult would say. I am an adult now, not a kid anymore.

She sighs. "That's why I sent them—I knew you wanted to know the truth so badly, to find out more about her. But then, I realised they're not the only truth, not all of it anyway. You read those letters and you have a single view of your mom, you don't have any other memories to balance them with."

I think of the swing, feel hands on my back. "I have memories."

We're past the bend, in line with the dune, with the U-shape of grass. I look the other way, out at the sea, and it's just like any other part of the sea. Looking at it, you wouldn't know that someone had walked in there with all their clothes on, pushed through the small waves until they got bigger, until the big ones knocked them over, pulled them under. Looking at that part of the sea, you wouldn't know that if it hadn't been for a friend's help, that she would have drowned.

"I know you have memories, honey, but it's kind of like it's a scale. You need a ton of memories, a ton of good memories, to even start to balance what's in those letters."

I picture Dad's scale from the shop, electronic with meat-covered buttons and red digital numbers, but she means the other kind, the old-fashioned ones, like the Statue of Liberty. I picture it, the letters on one side, the Carver book on the other, the photos, the memory of the swing—if it even is a memory. The letters weigh more, they will always weigh more.

"Cooper said it was selfish, sending them—that I wanted someone else to carry the burden, and I started to wonder if he was right. I tried to show them to your dad once, years ago, but he refused to read them. Said he didn't want to invade her privacy."

Up ahead there are more surfers, normal ones, three guys sitting on boards, waiting for waves. I want to know if Laurie has learned to surf yet, but suddenly there is something else I need to know more.

"When?" I go. "When did you try to show them to Dad?"

"One summer I came to visit. You must have been six or seven."

"The summer before the accident?"

She frowns, brushes her fringe. "Yeah, I guess it was that summer."

The summer we stopped writing to you.

"He got mad at me, we had a fight, and he went out to the bar. I left the letters on the kitchen table for him, in case he might change his mind and read them. But in the morning they were exactly like I'd left them, so I took them back with me."

That's when it comes together, as easily as the wave lifts up two of the three surfers, carries them towards the shore.

No letters to you anymore, no Hendrix, no Sunday walks. Instead of the ocean, I'm seeing Dad sitting on my bed, tears rolling into his stubble talking about letters, saying he shouldn't have read them. I thought he meant my letters, the ones we put in the blue airmail envelope. Only he meant your letters, not the ones we wrote at all.

"He did," I go.

"What?"

"He read them."

She stops. "Really? How do you know?"

I have no proof, no evidence. I don't know for definite, but I am absolutely sure. "I just know."

The sun is high in the sky, the hottest part of the day. I've never walked this far on the beach before, not by myself or any of the times with Amanda.

"Want to head back?"

"Okay."

We turn around and the sun is in our eyes and I wish I had my sunglasses or my cap and a bottle of water. I wish we were back at the house, that this whole conversation was over, that I already knew the answers to everything, but the only way to know, to find out, is to ask.

"That man in the letters, the one my mum talks about. He was the one you told me about in Jaxson's that day, wasn't he? Your dad's boss?"

I know the answer, I think I do. When I look at her, she's hunched over, as if we're still walking into the wind, even though we're not anymore.

"Yes, Uncle Cal. He was more than Daddy's boss though—they had all this history. They were in the war together—he was always saying how he'd never have made it back alive if it hadn't been for Daddy, that Daddy was the son he never had."

I'm listening and not listening to her. We're in line with the dune again and I'm looking at the sand, trying to see if there's still a dent, an imprint of the place Amanda put me lying down, the place we were when Jean and David found us. I know it's stupid to think it'll still be there after more than three weeks, but I'm looking anyway.

"I don't know for sure, but I think he was the reason Daddy changed his name and everything; that's what Uncle Jacob said when we met in Sacramento that time, that it was after the war that Daddy cut off all ties with his family."

I have to say it. I have to say it out loud so I know we are talking about the same thing.

"He was a paedophile—your Uncle Cal—wasn't he? A child molester?"

"We didn't have those words then," Aunt Ruth goes, "not like now—but yes, yes he was."

The tide is coming in further and my feet are soaking, but I don't move to where the sand is drier. I don't want to ask the next question but I need to. "Did you know?"

"No." She shakes her head hard. "No! I had no idea. Even after she came to see me at Brown, when she first told me, I didn't know what to think. It seemed so incredible and she was drinking a lot at the time. Paul said he thought she was on drugs, that that could make you imagine that crazy things had happened." She glances at me. "I didn't tell her that, I didn't say much, but I think she knew."

Paul, I'd forgotten about Paul. The sun is beating down. Underneath my T-shirt I feel a line of sweat, running from my bra down my stomach and into my shorts. People always know when you don't believe them; you knew, you wrote it in your letter. I want to remind her about that, but I think she knows.

"What about your dad? Did you ever talk to him about it?"

"No, I never talked to Daddy."

"Never? Not even when you got her letters? Not even when she died?"

She stops walking, covers her mouth with her hand. She shakes her head, keeps shaking it. Her nails are bitten, not her usual French polish.

"That doesn't make sense! Why didn't you ask him why he didn't do anything? Why he didn't stop it?" I'm shouting then, but I don't care because there's only her and the seagulls to hear. "Why didn't you ask him why he didn't save her?"

She sinks down into the sand, right there, even though it's wet, even though she's wearing her white linen trousers.

"I don't know, I don't know." She's talking through her hand, breath and sobs as well as words. "He was drinking the night she told him, maybe he was drunk, maybe he forgot—"

"How could he forget something like that?"

"He was a good father, Rhea. He cared about us, he loved us—"

"How? By telling her to keep it a secret? By telling her not to tell your mother?"

Both her hands cover her whole face now and I have to bend down to hear what she's saying. "I don't know, Rhea, I don't know. Maybe he couldn't face it, maybe none of us could. I don't know."

Her shoulders are shaking. I've never seen Aunt Ruth cry like this before, seen anyone cry like this. And it's different than the nights Dad cried because she hasn't been in the pub and we're out in the open, where anyone could walk by. I sit down next to her but a bit back, where the sand is still dry.

"I'm sorry I shouted. I know it's not your fault."

I say that to make her feel better, but she only cries harder. A wave comes in, washing around her legs, her bum, and beyond her up to where I'm sitting. I feel it sucking the sand from under me, a pool of water sagging in my shorts.

"I should have believed her, I should have listened." She's crying and talking at the same time and I wish she'd stop—do one thing or another. "I should have listened to her, not Paul."

I'd wanted to ask about him, what happened, why they didn't get married, but maybe I don't need to.

"It was only in that last letter—the thing about the drawing—I remember that night, throwing a tantrum because she wouldn't let me go upstairs to draw with Uncle Cal." She's crying so much then I can barely make out the last part of what she says. "He never asked me again. He always took her."

She cries for ages without saying anything else, and I don't either.

Instead I make *Vs* in the sand with the heels of my Docs, deep ones that fill with sea water, until it swishes back out and steals some of the sand so I have to start making the *Vs* all over again.

When we stand up, Aunt Ruth's trousers are see-through, so I can see the flowery pattern of her knickers in the places sand isn't stuck to them.

"Look at me," she says, "I'm a mess." She tries to brush the sand away but it sticks to her hand. "I've never been such a mess."

"Don't worry, we can walk around the back way. Everyone is a mess around here."

You can see the house in the distance and we're walking slower than before, and I wonder if it's because it's hotter or because we're both heavy from the sea water or if it's something else. She doesn't say anything the whole way back and I'm glad, I don't know if I have room to listen to any more or get into some discussion about Columbia or Laurie or anything. It's easier just to walk and watch the kite surfers. And watching them, I'm thinking of the first time I saw them with Amanda, and how that was only five weeks ago and in five weeks so much has happened, so much of my life has happened, here on this beach.

"Where have all the children gone?" Aunt Ruth goes, when we get to the part of the beach with the volleyball nets.

"It's Arts and Crafts now, then dinner."

"What's the food like here?"

"It's good," I go. "David's a great chef."

"As good as Jaxson's?"

There's a smile in her voice and I look at her and smile too. "Not quite."

"After you left, I kept replaying that day in Jaxson's. How what you wanted to know was so simple and I couldn't even tell you. I'd grown used to never talking about her and that wasn't fair. So many secrets, all that shame. I can't go back and erase all that, but I can tell you more about your mom, Rhea. I can add more to the other side of the scale."

It makes sense what she's saying, reminds me of something Jean said before, about how the letters—the feelings in the letters—are only one part of you, not the whole you. I know that if she's going to tell me these things, I need to tell her something too and it needs to be before we are back at the house.

"Aunt Ruth, there's something I haven't told you. I lied to you."

On the sand in front of us, a big lump of seaweed has washed up and the seagulls peck at it. As we walk around them, I glance at her. Her arms are folded around her stomach, like she's bracing herself for the force of what I'm about to say. It's something I've been meaning to say for a long time, and the only way to say it is to say it fast and say it all.

"I lied to you about the safety guard. It was on."

"What?" I know from her face this wasn't what she'd been expecting.

"Dad put it on. He always put it on. I knew how to get it off, I'd watched him do it so many times. That night you asked me about it, I lied."

Her face is clearing, picking up the thread of a conversation that happened eleven years ago and thousands of miles from here.

"You lied?" She frowns when she says it. "Why? Why did you lie?"

My mouth is dry. "I don't know. I didn't mean to."

One step, two, three, exhale. A half-lie is still a lie. Say it fast and say it all.

"I was afraid. I was afraid that if I told you the truth, I'd get in trouble. That you'd leave. I wanted you to stay."

I can't look at her. I look at my feet, in deeper sand now, sand like the brown sugar David uses in his muffins.

"I think that I thought you might come and live with us. Or take me with you. That you might decide to take care of me."

It's out now, all of it, my words carried away by the breeze, into the sea. My feet keep walking, my breath keeps moving, in and out, in and out. I don't want her to touch me and she doesn't.

We are almost at the trail back to the house when she speaks.

"Thank you for telling me, Rhea."

"I'm sorry it took so long."

She stops and I do too. "That's okay. The truth is worth the wait."

Her face looks red and it could be from the sun or from crying, you can't tell. The Aunt Ruth in Coral Springs wouldn't have forgotten sunglasses or sun screen but this Aunt Ruth might, and somehow it feels like this is the version of her I know better than any other, the version that I have always known.

She reaches out to put her hand on my shoulder. It feels soft, solid.

"I understand," she says. "We all do things we don't mean when we're scared. I'm sorry I couldn't be there for you the way you wanted then. And that I wasn't there for you that night with Cooper, that I didn't stand up for you. But I can be there for you now, really there. If you want me to be. If you'll let me."

I don't know how long we stand like that. Her eyes are brown like your eyes, the ones in the Columbia photo, the same shape. I have Dad's eyes, I always wanted yours. Hers. We stand there so long, I forget that maybe there was a question in what she said, maybe she's waiting for me to answer her.

I nod. I smile a little smile and she does too. She doesn't hug me. I don't tell her I love her. She squeezes my shoulder and lets go, so she can walk ahead of me on the narrow path. I follow behind this time, and I notice that her trousers are already drying in the sun.

Maybe it doesn't sound like much, Mum, but it's enough.

For me, for today, it's enough.

Rhea

Dear Mum,

I told Jean that yesterday's letter was the last one I was writing to you, that I was never writing to you again. She says that saying "never" and "always" is something called "black and white thinking" and she asks me why I need to decide right now. And I guess she's right, I guess I don't need to decide. Which is why I'm writing to you again.

The other reason I'm writing, the real reason, is because I want to tell you about tonight, with Laurie. Because some day, maybe I'll want to remember everything exactly as it happened tonight, someday I might wish I'd written it down.

Laurie and Aunt Ruth drove back here this afternoon and Jean said it was okay for us to have a shorter session, so I had time to talk to Aunt Ruth before dinner.

We did a quicker walk on the beach this time and it was different than yesterday because we weren't talking about you or her or Cooper or even what to do about Columbia. We got into a conversation about music and how the two things she always wanted were a grand piano and a house by the beach with a room to put it in, and how she has neither. It sounds like it could have been a depressing conversation, but it wasn't because if she wanted, she could have both things, she just needs to decide if she wants to give them to herself.

She seems happier, Aunt Ruth. At dinner, she chats a lot to Erin about Ireland and to David about the garden. Laurie sits down at the other end of the table, in between Ezekiel and Brandy, but I don't see her talk to either of them. The only person I see her talk to is Zac, who watches her the whole time, and once I catch Amanda watching her too.

I'm helping clear the table when Laurie comes over. She picks up the empty bread basket, puts it on top of my pile of plates. "When you're done here, can we go somewhere? Talk?"

"Sure," I go, all casual, like talking is nothing. "What about Aunt Ruth, though?"

Laurie shrugs. "Can't she stay here with her new friends? Drink tea or something?"

"I suppose she could watch the movie—I think it's *The Lion King* tonight."

"Perfect." Laurie smiles. "I'll go tell her. Hurry up."

In the kitchen, David tells me I can leave the plates, but I clean all the bits of leftovers into the bin in the corner, help him stack them in the dishwasher one by one. After that, I sweep the floor, and I never sweep the floor, and that's when I know some part of me wants to delay the conversation with Laurie, that even though I've been dying for it, some part of me doesn't want to talk to her at all.

I find her in the hall, sitting in the chair by the door.

"Finally," she goes, pushing herself up. "So where are we going—the beach?"

"We're not allowed to go to the beach when it's dark."

"It's not even dark yet."

"It nearly is, we'd have to be back really soon."

She rolls her eyes. "Okay then, what about the pool? Are we allowed to go there?"

"Yeah, sure. We can go there."

Walking down the steps to the pool, the low lights are already on and I'm thinking of the last time I came down here in the dark, the night of the storm.

"So what do you do here at night?" Laurie says from behind me.

"Not much, hang out. Play games. Watch the movie with the kids."

"Ugh."

I can't see her, but I know she's making a face.

"You're not allowed to go into the Hamptons or something?"

"Most of us work in the evenings, help put the kids to bed."

"Sounds like a Nazi prison camp. Bet you can't wait to get out of here."

The little gate that should be closed is open and I'm not surprised when I see her, sitting at the end of one of the loungers, pulled up closer to the water than the rest. It's Amanda. I hold the gate for Laurie and I walk through after her. Amanda turns around, stands up, waves.

"Hey, Amanda!" I call her name way too loud, as if there are miles in between us, as if she hasn't already seen us.

"Hey."

We walk towards each other until we're standing there, the three of us in a semicircle between the gate and the pool. "Laurie, did you officially meet Amanda yet? She's our lifeguard. She's brilliant at teaching the kids to swim. She's going to teach me as well."

We've talked about that—Amanda teaching me how to swim— and up until then I hadn't fully decided if I want to or not, but right then I do. The light from the pool catches Amanda's necklace as she leans forward to shake Laurie's hand. "Hi."

"You obviously like a challenge, trying to get this one in the water." Laurie laughs, puts her hand on my bare shoulder. "I've been trying to get her to take lessons for years."

"Years" makes it sound way longer than it is. Her hand on my skin has a ripple effect through my whole body and into my breath. I think about the last time we touched.

Amanda fixes a curl behind her ear and it bounces out immediately. "Thanks for the warning. Good thing I'm pretty tenacious."

Laurie laughs again, like that's really funny, and Amanda does too, so I join in even though none of us are laughing our real laughs. And it goes on for ages, the fake laughter, like it's never going to end, like we've all forgotten what's even supposed to be funny.

Amanda's the one who breaks it. "I'll leave you guys to it." She puts her hands into her back pockets.

"You don't have to go."

It's a stupid thing to say and I pretend I don't notice Laurie staring at me.

"I'm beat," Amanda says. "Long day. I think I'll take a bath."

"At least there'll be no schmozzle in the bathroom."

I smile and she half-smiles back. Laurie holds the gate open for her and we both watch her slow walk up the steps towards the house, a shadow of dark between the lights.

Laurie turns to me and rolls her eyes. "Who takes a bath in ninety-degree heat?"

I don't answer her, instead I walk towards the sun loungers and sit on the one that Amanda had been sitting on. I think that Laurie is going to pull over another one and sit beside me, but instead she sits on mine, but to the side, so we're facing different directions. Her back is close to mine though and I can feel her heat, as if some outer force fields of our bodies are touching even though our skin is not.

"What's her deal?" she goes.

"What do you mean?"

"I don't know, she seemed kind of edgy or something. Was she homeless too?"

"Amanda? No! She lives in Connecticut with her family."

I sound impatient, defensive, but if Laurie hears it, she doesn't react.

"That makes sense. Her type wouldn't survive for five minutes on the streets."

I know that Laurie is waiting for me to ask what "type" Amanda is, and in some other version of this conversation I would have asked, and Laurie would have dissected Amanda and her family and made up clever things about them and we'd both have laughed. That's what we might have done another night, but not tonight.

"What did you want to talk to me about?" My voice sounds hard, harder than I thought it would. "I have to help get the kids to bed after the movie."

"It's only just started."

I shrug. I don't know how to say that just because the movie will be on for an hour and a half, that doesn't mean I want to spend it all with her.

"Okay then, let's get to it." She pulls her hair into a ponytail, lets it fall. "God, I've missed you, Rae. There are so many things I want to tell you—"

"Rhea," I go. "I'm back to Rhea."

"Really?" A look skims across her face. Disapproval, maybe? Disappointment? "I thought that was just for Ruth's benefit."

I don't react. "No—I prefer Rhea."

"Okay," she nods, "Rhea. I can get used to Rhea, I can tell Rhea how much I missed her."

I cross my right foot onto my left knee, feel the lace holes of my Docs, starting from the bottom, up to the top.

"Listen, I know you're mad at me. Don't say you're not—I can tell. I don't even blame you for being mad, I know I was an asshole."

I turn my head a little and she's looking at me. In the light from the pool, her eyes are shiny.

"Yeah," I go, "you were."

"I'm sorry. I was scared. I just... I didn't know what else to do. I panicked." Her first tear dislodges, slides down her cheek. I want to trace it with my finger, the way I always do. But she cried that night too, in the kitchen at Coral Springs. I picture it, I make myself picture it. Another tear follows the first. "I know it's not an excuse, being afraid, I know it doesn't make what I did go away."

I cup my stump. "No, it doesn't."

"You might not believe me, Rae—Rhea, but I knew you could handle it. You weren't scared of Dad or Ruth. You're never scared of anything."

Jean's voice comes into my head then. *You don't do fear.* We talked about it again this afternoon, about Columbia. How "not doing fear" is not the same as not being afraid.

"I get scared, Laurie."

She's shaking her head, sniffling. "Not like me. You don't go around worrying all the time about what everyone thinks of you—trying to be perfect for them all—the kids at school, Dad, even Mom. Not that she'd care."

She starts to cry properly and I grip my stump hard. It's not my job to comfort her, not anymore.

She reaches into her shorts pocket for a tissue, blows her nose. "The night of her show was horrible, Rhea. I wanted you there so bad, you were the one who was supposed to be with me. Backstage, she practically ignored us, like we were two fans or something."

I'd forgotten all about the show, hadn't even registered the date as it slipped by. After all the times I'd wanted to meet Laurie's mum, it seems weird that I hadn't thought about it at all.

"Did you go with Cooper?"

She brushes her tears away and her eyes close, just a little. I ask her again.

"Who'd you go with, Laurie?"

It's going to be Becky or Tanya. It's got to be them.

"I went with Ryan."

I breathe in slow and out even slower.

"I would rather have gone with you, Rae. I wanted to go with you."

Something has landed on the water of the pool, an insect, a mosquito maybe. There are little folds in the water where it is trying to get out.

"You're dating Ryan again?"

She reaches out again to touch my collarbone, traces her fingers up the soft skin of my neck.

"We're not dating, dating. I needed to keep Dad off my case. It's just a cover—"

"Does Ryan know it's a cover?"

Her fingers are up higher, on my cheek, her little finger grazes my lip.

"It doesn't mean anything, Rhea, none of them do compared to you. Compared to us."

She turns my face so it's closer to hers, half lit up from the pool light, half in shadow. It's a beautiful face, the slope of her nose, the shape of her cheek, her mouth, her chin. "I was so stupid, Rae. It's just like all those movies and songs... it wasn't until you were gone and I missed you so much that I figured out what it meant."

I almost correct her, tell her again to call me Rhea, but I don't, because I want to hear what she's going to say next.

"I love you, that's what I wanted to tell you. I'm in love with you."

Her fingers are still stroking my cheek and I feel my throat tighten. She loves me, Laurie loves me, Laurie's in love with me. So many times I've wanted her to say that, imagined her saying it, hoped she'd say it, dreamed she'd say it.

And now she's saying it, I want to talk about something else.

"Aunt Ruth said they're splitting up—her and Cooper."

If she's surprised that I'm asking this now, after what she just said, she doesn't let on. "They are."

"I'll believe it when I see it."

"No, seriously. He's looking at places closer to the restaurant. He even looked at one on Las Olas."

"Seriously?"

"Yep. And she's talking about moving up here, taking some transfer to her company's office in New York for a few months or something."

"Why?"

She shrugs. "I'm sure it's got something to do with you. She's been into the admissions office at Columbia so much, trying to figure out how to keep your place."

Laurie's too close and I push back a bit, feel the plastic edge of the seat bite into the backs of my knees.

"She never said anything to me. She hasn't even mentioned Columbia to me since she got here."

Laurie blows her hair out of her eyes. "I don't know. But I bet if you told her you'd come back to Florida, then she wouldn't leave. She'd stay in Coral Springs, I know she would."

"Why would I go back to Coral Springs?"

She leans in closer. "So we can be together, why else?"

That's when she kisses me, at the end of that sentence, before I know she's going to, before I've taken in what she's saying, what she's not saying. Her mouth is so familiar, I know her feel, her shape, my hand knows just where to touch her hair at the nape of her neck. My body likes this, loves this, and my legs turn towards her so our knees are touching. But my head is still whirring, there is something wrong—I'm just not sure what.

I pull away.

Laurie doesn't get it at first, comes in to kiss again.

"Laurie, stop."

"What?"

The same look is there, the one from earlier, only it's so fast this time I might have imagined it. "What is it, Rhea? What's going on?"

I take her hand off my shoulder, gently place it on her leg. I can't think with her touching me, I can't think and I need to think.

"This—it's not going to work. Cooper's not going to let you see me, let us be together."

She pulls her hair into a ponytail, holds it there for a second, lets it go.

"We won't be under the same roof anymore. What's he going to do—keep me under surveillance twenty-four hours a day?"

"So, you wouldn't tell him? You wouldn't tell him about us?"

She rolls her eyes. "'Course I'm not going to tell him, don't be a dumbass!"

"But he'll know, he'll find out—you know what he's like."

"I'll be eighteen in April, then I can do what I want. Plus, if we're both at school in New York, he won't be able to do anything about it."

She puts her hand on my knee, and I let her leave it there but I don't hold it. Inside my Docs I scrunch my toes.

"I don't know, Laurie. It feels like we can't just pick up where we left off."

"Why not? I said I'm sorry."

"Things have changed, though—"

Her fingers caress my knee. "What's changed? Did something happen on the streets?"

It irritates me, the way she asks that, the same way Aunt Ruth asked, as if that's the only thing that can happen. I pull my knee away.

"Yeah, a lot of fucking things happened. I was scared, hungry. People threatened me. I peed outside, in alleyways with rats, I lost my friend—"

She juts her chin out, the way she always does when she's angry.

"Don't blame me, Rhea. Don't blame me because you ran away—"

"What was I supposed to do?"

She shakes her head. "I don't even think you ran away because of what happened with us. I think it was because of what Dad said about your mom."

I'm about to deny it, but there's no point in denying it, not when it's true. I stand up, turn my back on her, walk away. Behind me, I hear her stand up too.

"I know about what happened to your mom. Ruth told me and I know you know."

I'm walking close to the edge of the pool, where the tile is dark blue. I put my heel down slowly, right in front of the toe of my other foot, pretend the line of tile is a tightrope.

"It was shitty the way you found out, what Dad said, but at least you know. At least you can deal with it."

She sounds so rational, as if it all makes sense, but nothing makes sense. I spin around fast, my Docs making a squeaking noise on the tiles. "You don't get it, Laurie. You don't just 'deal with it.' It changes everything, don't you see?"

She holds her hands out. "How? How does it change things between us?"

"You don't understand."

"So, try me. Explain."

I shouldn't have to explain, that's what I'm thinking, but maybe if I talked to Jean about it, maybe she'd say something different, maybe she'd say I should give her a chance. I take a deep breath.

"I don't know, it's just…" I run out of words, start again. "I mean, she drowned, I always knew that, but it's different knowing, you know, knowing that maybe she did it on purpose."

It's crept in, the "maybe." I don't know where it came from, but I let it stay.

Laurie's frowning again, the shadows and light on her face.

"But you were the one who always said it didn't matter how someone died? You said it didn't make any difference if someone was hit by a car or abducted by aliens or whatever, that the only thing that mattered was that they were gone. You were the one who said that, not me."

I did say that, I can hear my own voice saying it, meaning it.

"Just because I said it, Laurie, doesn't make it right—it doesn't make it true." My voice cracks then and I know I am going to cry and I've never cried in front of Laurie.

She takes a step closer to me, then another. Her eyes are as blue as the pool. "You're still mad at me, aren't you? You're still mad about what happened."

It's a declaration, it's a question. I can't answer her. I forgive her, I'm still mad at her—I'm mad at everyone. A tear comes.

"Having a mom doesn't make everything perfect, Rhea. Look at me—I'm a fuck-up."

"No, you're not."

"That night of her show, watching her on stage, it was horrible because I felt like I was so proud of her and mad with her and jealous of her all at the same time, like everything was like a ball of elastic bands in my stomach and I couldn't separate them all."

Jean and I have talked about this, how I don't know how to feel more than one feeling at the same time, so I know exactly what Laurie means.

"And all I wanted was for you to be there, sitting next to me, so we could hold hands in the dark."

Her hand slips into my hand, smooth, familiar. Our fingers interlace. Her fingers are longer than Amanda's fingers. I don't know what makes me say what I say next.

"Were there other times you thought about holding my hand?"

The question catches her in a way she didn't expect. "What?"

"You know, did you miss me at other times? Times when you were happy, I mean."

I love her frown, the way her face puckers into it, the little lines between her eyes.

"I told you—I missed you all the time. You don't believe me?"

"I'm not saying that. Just that some fun stuff must have happened too—Aunt Ruth told me you were working at the mall with Cindy. Maybe you guys cracked up over some joke, or maybe you saw a movie you wanted to tell me about or something."

Her frown is deeper, she doesn't get where I'm going with this at all and I'm not sure I do either.

"What the fuck, Rhea? You think because I went to see *The Matrix* and laughed with my friends that it means I don't care about you? Like I wasn't allowed to have any fun?"

I'd forgotten, until she says that, that I saw *The Matrix* too, or at least parts of it, before I fell asleep, which is why me and Sergei went in the first place. He liked it, I remember, but I didn't really. Somehow it made me think about Laurie, watching it, but everything made me think about her then.

"You've no idea what the last few months have been like for me. Dad ignoring me, him and Ruth fighting all the time. It took him weeks to even talk to me, to let me out of the house—"

I pull my hand away from hers. "Is that why you needed your cover story?"

"I knew it!" She points a finger at me. "You're mad about Ryan. You've always been so jealous, Rhea. I knew this is what this was about."

She's smiling a big smile, she's figured it out. She's on familiar territory, my jealousy about the guys she dates. We've been here, had this argument before, ten times, a hundred times. Except I'm not jealous tonight, not anymore.

She takes my hand again, in both of hers this time.

"Ryan doesn't mean anything, none of them do. You're the one I want to be with."

She moves closer, like she wants to kiss me again, and with the light of the pool I bet our silhouettes can be seen from the house, if someone was looking. I tip my head back, and above, the stars are so close and so bright I feel like I can reach out and run my hand through them. And I remember what you wrote in your letter, about the drive to San Francisco and driving up into the universe, and I think about saying this to Laurie, but that's when I know—she's not the one I want to say it to.

I shake my head. "I'm sorry, Laurie."

The pucker frown is back, she doesn't get it yet. I pull my hand out from hers, take a breath. "I don't think this is what I want."

She tilts her head to one side. The pool light is beautiful on her face. "But I love you. I told you that, Rhea. I'm not making it up."

"I'm sorry."

She says something else then, about me needing time after everything that's happened, how she can give me more time, but I've stopped listening. It's not that I'm not there, I'm more there than maybe I've been all night. I'm fully aware of my feet in my Docs, hot even at this time of night, the place where they tighten around my calf. Of the warm air around my body, coming into my mouth, my nose, and out again. Of my left hand, hanging down by my side, my stump, my missing arm, part of me, not part of me.

She's still talking when I interrupt her. "I'm sorry, Laurie, but I'm not in love with you."

She plucks a strand of hair, brings it to her face, sucks it. I love her hair, the feel of it in my hand. I'll never feel it again. Her face crumples.

"There's someone else, isn't there? I know there is."

The image that comes to my mind isn't a clear one, not the way I like things to be clear. It's not even all an image—there's sounds and texture in there too, warmth and coolness, a dark car, a Scrabble board, the sound of the waves, a kiss. I don't answer her, but she knows, I think she knows.

And standing there, by the pool, two feet and twenty thousand miles apart, there's more I want to say to her—that I don't know if what we had was love or something else, that I'll never forget her, that maybe she doesn't love me either. But I don't get a chance to say any of that, because she pushes through the gate and starts to run up the steps. And there's a moment then, with the gate swinging and her shadow, black against the darker shadow of the house, that I nearly call her back. And if Jean asked me the feeling right then, it's sadness, a wave of it, an ocean of it, and I don't know if it's my sadness or Laurie's or if that even matters, but it's nearly enough to make me call her name, call her back, to hold her and comfort her and let her kiss me again.

Nearly, but not quite.

Rhea

Dear Mum,

I was walking on the beach earlier and listening to the mix tape Amanda made me and writing this letter to you in my head at the same time. And I had all these things that sounded really great, these words that went in time with the music and the waves crashing, but now I'm sitting here to actually write them down, those words from the beach are all gone and there's only these ones and they're not the same at all.

Jean says it's one of the hardest things in the world to say what you really mean all the time, that it's even harder to write it down. She was talking about me writing to you, when she said that, but it made me think about your letters, to me and Aunt Ruth, and I wonder if they were 100 percent what you meant or 99 percent or only 75 percent, and I know that trying to apply maths to things like letters and feelings doesn't work, but sometimes I need to try something that doesn't work loads and loads and loads of times before I stop and try something else.

Until those other words come back, I'm going to tell you what's on the mix tape Amanda made me, the newest one. I like mix tapes because I like music and they're a list and you can't get lost in a list. Here's what's on the tape:

1. "My Oh My" by David Gray

2. "Seasons of Love" from the *Rent* soundtrack

3. "Stay" by Lisa Loeb

4. "Damn, I Wish I Was Your Lover" by Sophie B. Hawkins

5. "This Woman's Work" by Kate Bush

6. "Closer to Fine" by the Indigo Girls

7. "You Got the Love" by Candi Staton

8. "November Rain" by Guns N' Roses

9. "Babylon" by David Gray

The only songs I knew before were "November Rain" and the Sophie B. Hawkins one, but I didn't know she'd written it about a woman and it's cool, learning that, like there's a whole other layer of stuff underneath the song that I didn't know. I'd never heard of David Gray, even though he's English, so I should have heard of him, and his two songs are my favourites. I let myself rewind "My Oh My" seven times the other day so I'm glad it's at the beginning of the tape. Amanda says if she'd known that I always made myself listen to songs in order that she'd have put it on a few times in a row, that next time she's making me one, she'll do that.

I'm making her one too and it's taking me ages because I haven't got all my music here, and I want the songs to be right and in the right order. In the beginning, I was going to have Hendrix and Lennon and Cash on it, but they're Dad's music, not mine, not really, and I want to put on the songs I want, the ones I'd choose without having to worry about anybody else.

Jean's letting me use the stereo in her office to make the tape and last night she played me this record of her mum singing. It sounded so old, even the silent bit at the beginning sounded old, and listening to her mum's voice, I could picture the club in Harlem, smoke hanging in the air, her on stage, in a circle of white light. During the song, Jean closes her eyes, and when it's over she picks up the photo of the lady with the cigarette and points to it and says, "That's her, that's my mom," as if I didn't already know.

And that's when I decide to ask her what I've been meaning to ask her.

"You know what you said, about cleaning out the emotional scars? Do people always get better when they do that? Or do some things never go away?"

She puts her mum's photo back on the shelf, next to the fern. She won't lie to me, I know she won't.

"I think that people heal," she says, "I know that people heal."

"What's the difference between healing and getting better?"

She pulls at her curl, the one over her ear.

"I think that to heal, you have to be prepared to feel it all, good and bad. Some people don't want to heal, they just want to feel better."

I'm still not sure that I get the difference and I don't want to have to ask again—but I don't have to because she explains it more.

"Usually, with some kind of trauma, the bad feelings come up first and some people get scared and stop there, go back to doing what they were doing before, to numb out again. But if you stick out the bad feelings, you make room for the good ones too. You feel everything—that's healing."

I get what she means then, I think I do, because yesterday when we were washing down the deck, Erin puts her cheesy *Riverdance* CD on and Matt and Zac are egging me on to dance because they think that, because I'm Irish, I should be able to. At first, I concentrated really hard, trying to make myself remember Irish dancing from when we learned in school. I tried to follow the rhythm and the steps, but then Amanda joined in, and she just did any old dance and she looked so funny, with her hands on her waist and her curls jumping around her head and into her eyes. And that was when I let the music take my legs and my body, so I was doing this crazy dance too, that was nothing like the real *Riverdance* and nothing like Amanda's dance either. Matt was the next to join in and Zac was shaking his head, leaning against the railing, but Erin pulled him in too, so we were all dancing then, and laughing and dancing and laughing and dancing. And I was out of breath and it was too much to do both and I let my knees crumple and my body fall down and I lay there on the hot wood of the deck that was bouncing from everyone's pounding feet, and I let myself laugh and laugh and laugh.

I smile, remembering all that, but I still have something else I need to ask Jean.

"What if the bad feelings get too much?"

I want her to say they won't get too much, that they won't get as bad as that day on the beach but she can't say that because she can't know for sure and she won't say something if it's not true.

"The dark feelings can be intense, for sure, but you're learning tools—you don't have to stay in the dark places."

We've talked about this before, the dark places, the day that she said it was easier to increase the light rather than shrinking the darkness. I wrote that down, that day, in the new notepad I bought in East Hampton, so I won't forget. I can't forget.

"I feel scared sometimes—"

I stop. It's new, starting sentences like that and sometimes I can't do it, even with Jean. She waits, I think she knows what I am going to say, but she never guesses. She never fills in my words, always lets me find my own.

"My mum—she wasn't able to handle the dark places. What if... I can't either?"

I used to think she was really young, Jean, but up close you can see the little lines, little wrinkles, and I bet she's older than Aunt Ruth, probably even older than you would be now.

"You're not your mother, Rhea. Remember?"

"I'm not my mother."

We're covering old ground now, stuff we talked through all around going to Columbia, if it's still the right decision, if I'm making it for me or for you. If I'll be able to keep myself intact in a place I knew you'd been, where sometimes I get confused and think you still are.

"Your mother was an untreated victim of sexual abuse. People didn't know how to talk about things like that back then."

"I know," I go. "You told me all this."

Sometimes it annoys me when she repeats things, especially when it's something I already know, especially when it's something I should have gotten already.

"And being a victim of sexual abuse wasn't the only thing she was. She was a daughter, a mother, a wife, a friend."

I nod, I know this. If I know this, why do I need her to keep telling me?

"She had her own journey, Rhea, and you have yours."

Jean talks about journeys a lot and it reminds me of the subway, with all the different lines, different people all going different places, switching trains and running across platforms and down stairs and some of them are going the same way but nearly everyone is making the journey on their own. You know how sometimes you can be on a local subway train and the express one leaves the station at the exact same time as your train? And for a bit they're side by side and you can see into the carriage next to you, as clearly as if it was your carriage—the people and the ads and everything, so it feels like you're in there with them, like you're on the same train? Today, when Jean says that about you having your journey and me having mine, I think about those two trains, that no matter how well I think I can see into your carriage, it'll never be my carriage. We'll always be on different trains, Mum. They might run parallel for a bit but the express always pulls away in the end.

Shit. I'm crying. I didn't know I was going to. Since I've started crying it seems like I can never tell when it's going to happen again, there's always more there. It's stupid to cry because of the trains and I don't think it is because of the trains, not really. I think I'm crying because I think this is going to be my last letter and after all this time, all these letters, I still don't know how to say goodbye.

You want to hear something nuts, Mum? This is going to make me sound fifty kinds of crazy but there's still times, after everything, all my letters, all of yours, all these talks with Jean, that I can imagine you're not dead at all, that you swam somewhere else that morning, that one day the phone will ring and it will be you, living in London or France or Florida or Acapulco. And that's fifty thousand kinds of crazy because I know you are dead, I know it, I know it, I know it, but because you don't have a gravestone, like Dad does, with a start date and an end date and a dash in between, it's like I can still forget.

Aunt Ruth checked and there's no bench for you in Central Park, Mum. I don't know where Dad got that from or if he made it up, but he was wrong. At first I felt mad when I heard that, after all my looking, and then I felt better, that it meant I hadn't missed it. We're going to get one, Aunt Ruth looked into it and she promised we could and I trust her, I believe she'll keep this promise. She said to start thinking about what I'd like on the plaque but I told her I don't want it just to be from me, I want it to be something we do together.

I'll be able to visit the bench a lot, Mum, over the next few years, because I'm going to Columbia next year, in January, that's what I've decided. It means I have to go back to high school to get enough credits so I can graduate, but Aunt Ruth has found a school in New York that'll take me, so I don't have to go back to Florida. It's on the East Side, a private school, and Winnie says the East Side is really snobby so I hope it's not horrible but it'll only be for a few months. Aunt Ruth's new office is near there, and she says it makes sense to get an apartment near the school and her office and even though she's right, part of me wonders if that's the real reason, or if she wants to live near where she lived with you.

She won't be in New York all the time, Aunt Ruth, she has to work in Florida too and she was worried about me being lonely, but Winnie says she'll come up and see me on the bus and I can stay with her sometimes. When I talked to Jean about it, she said we can still meet if I want, in her office on Riverside and 90th Street, and even though I don't need to decide yet, I think I will. And I was thinking I might ask Winnie if I can volunteer with her sometimes in the soup kitchen, because I'd like to see Pat and thank her for helping me that day and give her some batteries for her Walkman and I'd like to see the man with the shopping cart who always smiled at me and the young guy who gave me his apple. I want to remember them, all of them, the people in Grand Central and Penn Station, even Jay with his wonky ankle, even him. And maybe one day when I'm volunteering, I'll look up and Sergei will be there and I'll give him double helpings on his tray.

The worst thing about the summer ending will be leaving Amanda, Mum. I keep thinking about that already even though it's still ages away. But Connecticut's only an hour from New York on the train, so we can see each other every weekend. She's told her mum and dad about me already and Aunt Ruth says she can stay in our apartment. She likes her, Mum, and I think you would too. It's different than with Laurie, slower in some ways and faster in others. I feel like I know her way better already than I ever knew Laurie at all. I love that people know about us, that we can sit on the beach and kiss, and writing about kissing her makes my lips tingle and I want to kiss her now! We're both going to come back and work here next summer and she's going to apply to colleges in New York so we can be together—that's one of the things we decided.

Jean says to take things slowly, that the only way the future happens is to stay in today, but I know she likes Amanda too, that she's happy for me, for us. It's really funny because I'd been afraid to say anything to her, because of the rule about couples, but apparently David and Jean have been a couple for nearly three years! Everyone knew, except me. I hadn't thought about it for a nano-second even though they were walking on the beach together the night Amanda swam out to pull me back in. It's just like Laurie used to say, that I notice the little things and I don't see the big ones—I can hear her voice calling me a dumbass, but when I talked to Amanda about it, she only smiled and said that people are different and that the world would be boring if we all saw things the same way.

Winnie came back yesterday, I forgot to tell you that. She has a photo in a frame by her bed now of her and Melissa and Darryl. And it's nice to have her back, sharing a room again, different than before. I wasn't expecting her to give me a present so I'm really surprised when she takes a book from her bag for me and when I unwrap it I see it's another Raymond Carver one, only it's poetry this time. The book is called *All of Us* and my favourite poem is called "Fear." I like it because it's a list and because it reminds me that everyone gets afraid, even Raymond Carver.

I'm coming towards the end of this letter, Mum, and I want to say something important. I want to tell you that even though I only found out what happened when I got your letters, I already knew, some part of me did. I can't explain it properly, make it make sense the way I want it to, but it's like reading the letters wasn't finding out something new, more like uncovering something already there, something maybe I'd hidden away. As if I could have known it and not known it at the very same time.

Does that make any sense at all?

Jean would ask if it makes sense to me.

The other thing I want you to know, Mum, is that I forgive you. Right now, I forgive you. At 11:12 p.m. on 27th July 1999, I forgive you. Maybe I won't tomorrow, maybe at 11:13 p.m. I'll feel like I felt yesterday afternoon when I got so mad in Jean's office that I wanted to kick my Doc through her glass table top, to rip the stupid swing chair from its frame, but right now isn't yesterday afternoon, and right now I forgive you.

I don't want you to think I'm forgetting about you, Mum, just because I'm not writing to you. I don't know if I can explain this right, but it feels like, before, I needed to write to you, to think about you, to feel you were there, but now I don't—not anymore. Does that make sense?

It makes sense to me.

And I keep thinking of the first time I saw Columbia, Mum, do you remember how I told you that I stood at the subway station and I watched all the students walking through the gate and I couldn't do anything, only stand there? In a few months, I'm going to be one of those students and I'll be walking through that gate, on my own, and up the steps into the library on my own, but I won't be fully on my own, you'll be with me too. You'll be there, all around me, in the redbrick paving under my Docs, in the light that hits the leaves of the trees, in the line of books on the library bookshelves, in the feel of the pen in my hand. You'll be in all those places, but when I choose my seat, I'll choose the one I want to sit in, and maybe it'll be where you sat or maybe it won't, but it doesn't matter because I'm choosing it for me. And even though you're in all those places, or maybe because you are, I won't have to look for you all the time, not anymore. And I don't understand how, but somehow in all of this, through all of this, it feels like I found you.

I read those last lines back and they reminded me of your letter— the ending of your letter. I've read that ending over and over, the part where you said you'd always be with me, even when I couldn't feel you. When I read that first I was so angry, Mum, that day on the beach, it sounded like such bullshit and I almost ripped it into tiny pieces, but I'm glad I shoved it in the backpack with the rest of the letters so I can read it again, and sometimes, now, when I read it, I think it's true.

I think you were always there, even when I couldn't feel you, even when I couldn't feel anything at all.

I'm crying again, Mum, I'm crying because I don't want this letter to end, because I want to keep writing and writing and writing. I'm crying because I don't know how many letters I have to write to say goodbye to you, I wish I knew. More than anything, I wish I knew.

I don't want to sign off leaving you to think I'm really sad, Mum, because I'm happy too and excited because tomorrow the new kids are coming. And it's scary too to have new kids, and I miss the old ones, I miss Maleika and Luis, I even miss Marco and I know that there's no way any of them will take Robin's place, because I miss her like crazy, but maybe that's okay, maybe they'll all have their own places.

And tomorrow night, it might be hard not to write to you about the new kids and if I want to, I might, I'm not going to say I definitely won't. Jean says I don't have to say definitely anything anymore.

But just in case I don't, in case this is the last letter, I want you to know that even when I don't write to you on paper, I'll be writing to you in my head. And that every hour of every day, every minute, every second, I'll be writing to you in my heart.

Love from your daughter,
Rhea x

Acknowledgements

My name is on the cover of this novel, but there are many people who supported and helped me along the way to publication.

Specifically, I'd like to extend my thanks to: Lisa Bezinover, Patrick Burhenne, Maura Cassidy, Paul Cassidy, Harold Dean James, Judy D'Mello, Christine Doran, Stan Erraught, Patricia Farnham, Bernie Furlong, Penny Goldenberg, Gerald Jonas, Penelope Karageorge, Rafiq Kathwari, Melissa Leong, Christine McKinney, Aisling O'Sullivan, Alexis Pace, Jennifer Paul, Rasha Refaie, Claire Rourke, Mindy Schneider, Jane Stark, and Jim Urbom.

Special thanks to three very fine writers who helped me enormously: Dominic Bennett, Eileen Kavanagh, and Annie Quintano. Thank you all for your insights, observations, and suggestions on an early draft and for providing these within such a short space of time.

Huge thank you to my wonderful agent Joy Tutela and to all at Flux, especially Brian Farrey-Latz and my eagle-eyed editor Sandy Sullivan.

And finally, thank you to Danielle Mazzeo—for proofreading, for brainstorming titles, for believing in me and in this book, and for always waiting to share dinner with me, no matter how late I came home from the library.

About the Author

Yvonne Cassidy (New York, NY) is an Irish author who has written three novels, including *How Many Letters Are In Goodbye?* When she's not writing, Yvonne works at Holy Apostles Soup Kitchen and uses her writing skills for fundraising and teaching creative writing.